# Out Of Time

*To Rosemary
Hope you enjoy the story
Pat Cox
2006*

## Patrick G. Cox

Bloomington, IN     Milton Keynes, UK
authorHOUSE®

*AuthorHouse™*
*1663 Liberty Drive, Suite 200*
*Bloomington, IN 47403*
*www.authorhouse.com*
*Phone: 1-800-839-8640*

*AuthorHouse™ UK Ltd.*
*500 Avebury Boulevard*
*Central Milton Keynes, MK9 2BE*
*www.authorhouse.co.uk*
*Phone: 08001974150*

*This book is a work of fiction. People, places, events, and situations are the product of the author's imagination. Any resemblance to actual persons, living or dead, or historical events, is purely coincidental.*

*© 2006 Patrick G. Cox. All rights reserved.*

*No part of this book may be reproduced, stored in a retrieval system, or transmitted by any means without the written permission of the author.*

*First published by AuthorHouse 10/20/2006*

*ISBN: 1-4259-5995-4 (sc)*

*Printed in the United States of America*
*Bloomington, Indiana*

*This book is printed on acid-free paper.*

# Prologue

# Out of time: Starliner *Artemis*: January 2204

The Chairman of the Board of Interplanetary Development Consortium was in an ebullient mood as he greeted the assembling chairmen and board members of the various companies in which the Consortium had a stake. IPD existed in two parts, the visible arm being the great freighters that shuttled between the earth and the growing number of colony worlds and the various mining and industrial operations on moons and asteroids dotted about the section of the galaxy the Consortium's ships could reach. The less visible part was the holding company that actually controlled, through various guises and false front corporations, almost two thirds of the world's major listed companies. This situation was the result of years of work on the part of several previous chairmen – in fact it was something the present chairman had been involved in from the start of his apprenticeship with the company some forty years earlier. The brainchild of a triumvirate of businessmen who saw in the inexorable rise of the bureaucracies that were slowly strangling the great democracies, an opportunity for the new aristocracy, the leaders of commerce and industry and their selected henchmen in the political classes, to seize control of government and direct the fate of nations for their advantage. The last hundred years had been spent in putting in place the people and the means by which this could be achieved and now they stood on the eve of obtaining that prize.

There was only one obstacle in the way of this ambition, a Fleet of starships established at almost the same time as the Consortium by visionary politicians who saw a need to have a powerful force of ships and men who could defend the earth and its multi-cultural peoples. A Fleet moreover, independent of political control, dedicated to the service of the ideals of the Alliance that created it. A Fleet composed of ships contributed by the various governments, and nominally manned and supported by them, but falling under the command of its own governing authority. Here the Consortium had not managed to penetrate, as it had hoped to do, into the command structure or the controlling authority. So they had changed their focus and, through the short-sightedness of the bureaucrats, obtained control of the support facilities instead. Thus, the Consortium now controlled the weapons development and repair company WeapTech, the repair docks and the building facilities in space within the solar system. As he rose to open the meeting, Ari Khamanei reflected with satisfaction that this had allowed him to build a fleet of his own at the expense of the Alliance Fleet and the bureaucrats and their political masters had even paid him to do it.

"Ladies and gentlemen, thank you for taking the time to attend our conference, I am sure you will all find it rewarding." he began, "I have excellent news to report to this assembly, the first we have held since the conference in 2199 in New Babylon. The work our founders began in 2089 is about to come to full fruition. Thanks to the enterprise of our many agents, we now have our people in key positions in all the ministries in the European Confederacy, and in the North American Union. In the Russian Federation we have key ministers as well as their bureaucrats and in the Southern European Union we have complete control of all ministries and the political parties. Only the defence forces controlled by the Fleet Authority remain outside of that control, but we now control their repair facilities, their weapons development and the ship building yards. We have also infiltrated their crews – as yet, not at command level, but our people are excellently placed to ensure that, when the time comes, the Fleet's ships will not be able to strike against us." Sure he now had their attention he continued as the huge screen behind him lit up and began to show pictures of huge new ships, bristling with weaponry, "I give you *our* fleet, ladies and gentlemen, every ship superior to its equivalent class in the Alliance Fleet, and now ready and manned by our own officers and ratings. Every ship that you see here has been built in our own facilities and at the expense of the Alliance, paid for by the gullible bureaucrats as we simply inflated costs once they had given us complete control of their own facilities." He paused as his audience laughed, and then added, "It was once said by a Russian Premier I believe, that the Communist philosophy would ultimately hang all the Capitalists – after the Capitalists had sold them the rope for the purpose. We, ladies and gentlemen, have turned that statement into a reality!" He smiled as they laughed at this, "I have called this conference to tell you that the time has come to start the hangings."

His speech continued for some time as he outlined the work and the achievements of the individuals and the companies under the consortium's umbrella. Included in this were advances in genetic engineering, xeno-biological advances which allowed them to control access to medicine, colonial development and, to an extent, energy sources and resources for the world's population. Exuding confidence, he outlined for them the next steps – steps which would take them to their ultimate goal of taking over the government of the Alliance nations, "First the Alliance," he told them, "then the rest of the world. And we are ready. Those first steps will be taken in a matter of months. Ladies and gentlemen, I give you control of the democratic world and the colonies they govern!"

※ ※ ※

## Bombay: 1804

HMS *Spartan*, seventy-four guns, HMS *Rajahstan*, forty guns, and HMS *Swallow*, twenty-two, weighed anchor and slowly made their way out of the roadstead to set a course south eastward towards the Cape of Good Hope, some seven thousand miles away. Homeward bound for the Spartan and her crew, she was turning homeward after a voyage begun in 1801 just after the Treaty of Amiens, and which had taken her to Port Jackson in New South Wales, the South Sea Islands and thence through the Coral Sea and into the Bay of Bengal. From there she had sailed to Trincomalee and onwards round into the Arabian Sea and Indian Ocean to Bombay.

Midshipman Heron stood with the large signal telescope resting in the crook of his elbow as his signal party folded and stowed the flags from the signal just hauled down. He watched as the sloop *Swallow* crowded on sail in order to beat her way to the station assigned to her as the eyes of the squadron in the van, ahead of the ponderous seventy-four. Astern, the sleek frigate *Rajahstan* settled into the larger ship's wake. Henry Nelson-Heron, or Harry, as his friends called him, had been twelve when he joined this ship after six months in HMS *Bellerophon*. Now, his fifteenth birthday recently behind him, he was already a seasoned sailor and trusted by his officers as a promising leader. He had enjoyed this voyage and felt very privileged to have been able to see and do so much, but now he was looking forward to seeing his home again, in the soft and cooler climate of County Down.

With luck, he reflected, they would be home in a little over four months.

# Chapter 1

# Departures and arrivals – Earth Date 2204

North European Confederation Starship *Vanguard* nestled against the docking port of Orbit 3, the North European geostationary transfer station. Against the bulk of the satellite, the ship's vast size was almost dwarfed by the station, yet; even so, she presented an impressive sight to anyone approaching with viewing screens set to wide angle. The ship's sleek lines were reminiscent of the greatest and most destructive ships of the Twentieth Century, the great nuclear powered submarines of the then super power fleets. The most obvious difference anyone familiar with those ships would have instantly spotted was the fact that she had four vast fins at the cardinal points around her hull rather than the single, often stumpy, feature of the submarines.

Presently she lay between the arms of two of the station's docking piers, each pier connected to airlocks in the lateral "fins" of the star ship's hull, and the ship was loading the final supplies and spares for her assignment. In the fins, crewmen swarmed about the ranks of interceptor strike craft and the larger, more graceful, atmospheric entry craft, referred to, in the time honoured traditions of a navy, as the ship's "boats". Each hangar was four full decks in height and each "fin" held two such hangars, the upper exclusively filled with strike craft, the lower containing a mix of escort fighter craft and the ship's 'boats', larger utility craft for troop transfer, shore leave duty and general shuttle work that required atmospheric penetration where there was no convenient station tethered to a planetary surface by means of the carbon fibre monofilament cables invented in the latter half of the Twenty-first Century - a major leap forward based on the carbon fibre nano-tubes invented in the closing years of the Twentieth Century, but not fully utilised until the beginning of the Twenty-second. Deeper inside the hull was equally busy with stores being secured, department heads overhauling their departmental inventories and running countless checks designed to ensure that the ship, when undocked and on passage, lacked absolutely nothing that she might need.

Even in this, the start of the second century of real space travel and the first of true deep space interstellar travel, once a ship left the environs of the home world, it was truly on its own. For that reason ships seldom travelled alone, and this voyage would be no exception. Almost eighteen thousand miles away, another pair of slightly smaller ships lay tethered for the moment to docking stations on Orbit Six, the Southern Australasian Orbital platform, completing their loading and final checks prior to undocking, yet, all knew, that once they entered the still incompletely understood realms of what had once been called "Hyperspace" they would effectively be isolated and have a limited ability to render assistance to each other until they could "drop out" and return to "normal" space. The level of importance of the mission was evidenced by the fact that these three powerful ships were to be joined by four more, smaller Star cruisers, a troopship and another of the same class as the *Vanguard*, a brand new ship named *Ramillies*, currently 'working up' for operational deployment. However, *Vanguard* and her consorts would arrive in the destination system, designated the Pangaea Alpha System, a week before the others. For this reason *Vanguard* carried two full Battalions of Marines and Mechanised Infantry – a total of four hundred men - with all their supporting equipment and the other ships carried similar landing forces in addition to their own Company strength Marine units.

Aboard the *Vanguard* her Captain listened as his Executive Officer, Commander Richard Grenville ran through the crew and station bills which made the great ship function. Not for the first time, Captain James O'Niall Heron reflected that he was fortunate to have secured such a meticulous officer as his second in command. From experience he knew that a less meticulous "Jimmy" could overlook some seemingly insignificant item which would jeopardise the entire ship. This would be all the more important as he, as senior Captain would be acting as Flag Officer for this expedition, and the Executive Commander would be effectively in command of the ship while he co-ordinated the Squadron assigned to him. The ships were about to depart on a voyage which would take them to a colony world where, if reports were accurate, the colonial government had been taken over in a *coup d'état* backed by a mysterious force of ships of unknown origin, but definitely commanded and manned by human crews. The Governor claimed that he had called on them for help as they were besieged by an intelligent alien threat and at the same time, by the refusal of the colonists to co-operate with the 'advisers' funded by a consortium of commercial interests. Thanks to increasingly blatant use of economic and political muscle, this commercial Consortium had succeeded in almost strangling the elected colonial government, a state of affairs backed up by some armed muscle brought in by the Governor to "protect Colonial assets", but in reality to keep him and his henchmen in power. The threat of the mysterious starships and their undoubted fire power also helped keep the populace in line!

Reports of seizure of assets by the Consortium's enforcers, of curtailment of hard won civil liberties and of mass forced removals of some of the colonists from farms, mines and positions in the administration had finally prompted the politicians on earth to investigate. Despite strenuous efforts to frustrate the investigation, a disturbing picture had emerged, one of rampant exploitation of the planetary resources, of asset stripping and of political corruption on grand scale. More recently, an attempt by the original colonists, still in a majority, although now excluded from power and virtually enslaved, dependent on the corporate appointees for food, supplies and essential resources, had led to a violent suppression of the protests and harassment of 'dissident' communities. There was growing evidence that several peaceful attempts at restoring their rights had resulted in reprisals and at least one instance of a civilian population being targeted and erased.

The Corporate interests had provided vast amounts of "evidence" to prove their innocence, blaming the colonists for the atrocities and the unrest, but then the Confederate Investigators had uncovered hard evidence of the real culprits – only to become the victims of a tragic 'accident' which destroyed their ship and much, but not all, of the evidence they had collected. Unbeknownst to his superiors or to most of his team, suspecting that there were double agents in both groups, the leader of the investigation had not only backed up key evidence but had ensured that the original material had been transported back to earth by alternative means.

The 'accident' had been the last straw for the Confederate Parliament, the blatant nature of the 'accident' – an unmanned freighter had been deliberately rammed into the investigators ship as she decelerated after exiting a Transit Point Gate - had finally tipped the waverers against the corporate lobby. A Fleet expedition had been authorised with a dual purpose; to restore order on the planet and to investigate and bring to justice those responsible for the exposed abuses and atrocities. That is what lay at the core of the Captain's orders, orders which made him a Captain and Commodore and gave him wide powers to take whatever action he considered appropriate to the situation. As usual the bureaucrats and politicians were demanding that the Fleet deal with an undefined problem, with incomplete information and with minimal resources. At least, he reflected with a slightly cynical smile, the politicians had learned that the commander in the field had to be allowed to make his decisions without their interference – a result no doubt, of an incident in the mid-twenty-first century when the military had refused, en masse, to obey a patently stupid order from the politicians. Their offer of allowing the politicians to replace the men being attacked in the frontline had been backed by a little more than irony. The message had sunk in – set the task and leave it to the professionals to carry it out. He listened as Commander Grenville summarised the logistical issues for the ship and her crew, satisfied that everything seemed to have been covered.

"There is one thing I feel I should raise with you sir," finished the Commander.

"Certainly Richard, what is the problem?"

"Not a problem, as such, sir, and we are not certain that it will affect us, but we are ordered to use NEG SHIO and there have been some strange reports from ships in and outbound through it recently."

"What sort of strange reports," frowned the Captain, suddenly alert, "I have heard that there was something going on there, but Gate Control insist there's nothing wrong with it!"

"They have been registering some sharp energy spikes as a ship passes the transition point of the Event Horizon in or outbound. Normally these would be read as possible initiation anomalies, but there have been some reports, 'officially' unconfirmed, that items have gone missing or been gained on the ships involved." He hesitated, "Fleet

Command are looking into it, but are pretty unforthcoming I have to say. I wondered if you would like to raise the matter with someone yourself sir, and see if they are prepared to throw more light on it?" he finished with a quizzical eyebrow.

"Number One, I suspect you have far better sources and know something more that you are not divulging at present!" smiled the Captain. "Would you advise me to apply to use the Lunar Orbit Gate until they can get to the bottom of this?"

"That is a possibility sir. The last inbound ship to use it lost a quantity of the ore they were carrying and gained a several tonnes of dead whale. I would not like to find we have lost anything vital on the way out!"

"Lost the ore?" the Captain frowned, "You mean there was a hull breach?"

"That's just it sir, no breach and no penetration of the hull – although their sensor arrays were damaged – just four hoppers of antimony ore vanished from the hold." He frowned and continued, "and they picked up a dead whale. Command has put a blanket news blackout on it," he added.

"Thank you Number One, I shall contact CinC and insist on more information – and a shift of gates!"

A communication link chirped on the Captain's arm and he touched the pad, saying, "Captain!"

"Sir!" responded a woman's voice that the Captain instantly recognised as that of Commander Petrocova, "I have the Admiral Somerville's Flag Lieutenant on his way to the boarding point. He says he has a signal from the Admiral for you."

"Have him brought to my quarters please Commander." He asked, "Who is the OoD?" Commenting to the waiting Executive Commander with a raised eyebrow, "It seems the Station Admiral is sending his doggie over to brief us on something – something he's not committing to normal signal traffic!"

"Lieutenant Pascoe, sir."

"Good, contact her and warn her that we may need to prepare to receive an Admiral shortly! I have a feeling about this little visit and the message our visitor is bringing!"

Commander Valerie Petrocova closed her comlink to the Officer of the Day, and surveyed her team gathered at their stations. She was a tall and striking woman with thick, straight brunette hair that she kept tightly braided in a single "tail". Efficient to the point of ruthlessness, she tempered this with a concern for "her people" that was almost as demanding as her exacting standards in running her department – the ship's weapons systems. She had taken the call from the Admiral's office as she was, at that moment, at her station in the ship's Command Centre – what would, in earlier ships have been referred to as the bridge or – in ships of the former Royal Navy – as the Compass Platform. From her station she could exercise complete control over the ship's impressive array of particle beam cannons, plasma projectors and a new and, as yet, untried projector weapon which had the power to vaporise quite large asteroids. In short the ship was more than capable of defending itself with its fixed and automatic tracking turret weapons mounted on the hull and fins. As a precaution the ship had a duplicate Command Centre further aft and this would be manned during "transition" and in any conflict by the deputy heads of all departments.

Valerie ran through her checks again, then, satisfied, gave a grudging smile to her small team of weapons specialists and nodded. "Well done Chief, it will do. Make sure that the second team submit their report to my terminal, I want to have a word with Lieutenant Williamson; his team is still a little slow to lock on to a target track! That will improve! Mid," she addressed the young Midshipman at the station immediately forward of hers, "That new primary weapon of ours is not one of your ancestor's puny battleship guns! I want it locked to a target and a firing solution at least fifteen seconds faster in future!" She grinned at his blush, and softened slightly, adding, "And we do have several advantages over those older ships. I will never understand how they could hit anything with such crude sighting and ranging equipment!"

※ ※ ※

In the vast hall of the ship's machinery spaces, Commander Mary Allison was trailed by a small group of Lieutenants and several Warrant Officers as she toured the spaces and control stations under her direction. At each of the three large "spheroid" fusion reactors she paused and ran through several checks with the Reactor Officer and his team, then moved on to the turbine rooms where the ship's huge demand for electrical power was met. Elsewhere in the hull there were three more such turbine rooms – all separated and contained in different compartments within the hull in an attempt to ensure that the ship's power could not be lost entirely. From there she moved to the environmental control room and satisfied herself that all of the vast ship's environmental machinery was functioning at peak efficiency, before moving to the propulsion space were she inspected the anti-matter containment field generators vital to controlling the violently reactive "dark matter" on which the ship's hugely powerful interstellar drive depended.

Thoroughly methodical and the epitome of an engineer, she was a terror to anyone who was sloppy or careless in their work, but, at a little over five feet, and very agile, she was highly respected by her teams who also appreciated her quirky sense of humour. As she was fond of saying, when it really came down to it, without her and her team to make sure the machinery actually worked when everyone else pressed the buttons – nothing would happen! Her favourite threat to those who teased her about her beloved machinery was to offer to let them experience a little zero-G in their normal stations – or worse – in the Wardroom. No one had so far dared to discover whether she would carry this out, but everyone knew that it was possible to do so from her Control Room and knew too what the result would be! She gave a frown as her comlink chirped, and answered it, pausing in her walk to do so.

"All HOD's to the Captain's Day Room in fifteen minutes," came the pipe from the Command Centre.

"On my way," she responded and snapped off the link impatiently. Turning to her second, Lieutenant-Commander Stuart Browne, she grimaced, "Carry on with the checks, there seems to be a flap on!"

\* \* \*

In the Control Centre Commander Ben Curran and his team of navigation officers and helmsmen checked through the latest data downloads on the quadrant the ship was destined to visit and in the flight control centre, his friend and drinking companion Commander Nicolas Gray briefed his Squadron and Flight Leaders, checking that all their strike and transport craft were fully operational, that their spares and repair kits were aboard and that the maintenance team leaders were satisfied. Like his fellow Commanders, he was a good leader who cared deeply for his men and their welfare. Known for his skill in handling the Confederation's small but powerfully armed and extremely manoeuvrable strike craft, he was just under six feet in height, athletic in build and possessed of a slightly cynical sense of humour. He broke off impatiently as his comlink chirped, "Gray!" he snapped as he keyed the message acceptance.

"All HOD's to the Captain's Day Room, sir!" came the voice of the Captain's Secretary.

"Very good, I'm on my way!"

Ben Curran and Nicolas Gray almost collided as they headed for the transport tube which would take them the three decks to the Captain's Day Room. "What's the flap Ben," asked Nicolas as they boarded the tube cabin.

"Beats me," came the reply, "I only know that our Admiral's Flag Bearer came aboard about half an hour ago."

"What, the illustrious Lieutenant Lovejoy himself? God, it must be important then!" Laughed Nicolas as the tube cabin stopped and they stepped out to join Valerie Petrocova and Mary Allison in the gangway.

As they turned to walk the short distance to where a Marine sentry guarded the entrance to the Captain's suite they were joined by several more of their fellow heads of department including the enigmatic Surgeon Commander Len Myers and the ship's Communication and Computer Commander Reinhard Diefenbach, an erect and sometimes frighteningly intimidating character whose expertise in his field was little short of genius.

* * *

The group found seats around the Captain's conference table joining "The Owner", the Executive Commander and the worried looking Flag Lieutenant. As soon as they were settled the Captain greeted them and got straight down to business. "As you know we are scheduled to undock in four hours and join our escorts over the Indian Ocean Equatorial Zone. Our orders are to make use of the recently completed Near Earth Hyper-jump Gate in geosynchronous orbit from there." He paused as they acknowledged this, and then continued, "You may also have heard that there have been a few problems with ship's entering and leaving through this gate recently. I have just had confirmation of this." He looked at the Flag Lieutenant and said, "Mr Lovejoy here has some details for us. Carry on Lieutenant!"

"Thank you sir," responded the young man, "we recently had a report that a ship leaving via this gate on a short hop to the Kuiper Belt mining station found itself with some extra cargo on board after what they described as some sort of anomaly during transit of the gate. They describe it as a huge energy burst just as they entered." He glanced at his notes, "Command have been monitoring the gate power flux ever since this event and we have noticed that there is a short duration surge in power in the gate as a ship transits the event horizon. It lasts for perhaps three milliseconds and does seem to be responsible for several instances of items, usually inanimate, being 'transported' on and off the ship."

"What do you mean 'transported'?" broke in Petrocova.

"And 'usually' inanimate?" chipped in the precise voice of the Surgeon Commander.

"Explain please Mr Lovejoy," nodded the Captain, "It will save time if you tell my officers what you have already told the Commander and me."

"Yes sir," the Lieutenant looked uncomfortable. Consulting his notes he continued, "The last ship to enter the system through this gate was the mining ship *Associate*, she 'lost' three containers full of ore rich in Antimony she also 'gained' some sea birds of a type thought to be extinct – they certainly are now! The ship which left just before her found itself carrying a part of a wooden ship having lost several containers of spares for mining equipment and the one before that found itself with a dead whale on board. Apparently they lost only some empty cargo containers." He hurried on before anyone could interrupt, "So far we know of no instance of a ship losing any member of its crew or being seriously damaged."

There was a general outburst of questions and comments which the Captain brought swiftly to silence by rapping sharply on the table, "Let's keep to one question at a time!" he ordered grimly, "Command assures me that no one has suffered hull damage although incoming and outgoing ships have been losing cargo while gaining something, in one case about a ton of frozen sea water. The Scientific Branch has had people working on this non-stop but doesn't seem to know what is causing it. More importantly perhaps, the items coming aboard seem to be from a different time period altogether!" He looked at the Lieutenant, who nodded and picked up the thread in obedience to the unspoken signal.

"Yes sir," he passed out a collection of photographs, "these pictures show some of the items, an early Nineteenth Century harpoon recovered from the dead whale, items taken from a ship of the late Eighteenth or early Nineteenth Century and a range of natural items which it is difficult to date."

"What did the whale die of?" came the laconic voice of the Surgeon, "I feel this might be significant!"

"Thank you 'Bones'," grinned the Captain, "I knew I could rely on you to ask the awkward question!"

"It apparently died of dehydration and asphyxiation sir," replied the lieutenant, "the hold of the ship it was found in was not part of the ship's atmospheric control system and is not kept fully under atmosphere unless being worked."

"So the harpoon was not the cause of death?"

"That is correct sir, although the harpoon was lodged in the whale's dorsal region it had not penetrated into any vital organ and was apparently an old wound."

"Well, that's extremely reassuring!" commented Commander Petrocova, "Anyone transported by this 'anomaly' has a fifty percent chance of survival – provided they land somewhere with an atmosphere! I feel this is significant!"

The table erupted in grim laughter which the Captain allowed to continue briefly before calling them back to the rest of the Lieutenant's briefing. From this they learned that there did seem to be some reciprocation, since everything coming aboard seemed to come from the planetary surface, the 'lost' items could be assumed to be forming some sort of 'exchange'. What was not known, since nothing 'lost' had so far been found, was precisely where or even when they might be returning to the surface. The lieutenant kept talking, answering their questions even as he passed out labelled packs, each containing a datachip. "The datachips contain everything we know to date. Science branch has managed to calculate the precise location in each ship where items are lost or gained – for *Vanguard* it is likely to be somewhere in the region of Frame

Two-Two-Three, probably between decks Two to Zero Two and within compartments Two-Two-Three Alpha Oscar Charlie or Two-Two-Four Alpha Oscar Charlie," he continued smoothly, using the system of identifying spaces with a ship first adopted in the days of steam and battleships. Since the advent of space travel the Fleet had adapted this so that the "Main" or "Weather" deck had become the central deck running from bow to stern and on which were located all the principal Control Centres. All decks numbered below this were in ascending order, the highest number being the lowest part of the ship. Above the 'Main' deck, identified on plans as Deck Zero, the numbers were prefixed with 'Zero' and ran again from Zero One to Zero 'x' with the highest number being to uppermost deck in the ship. Compartments within the decks were identified by reference to a Frame number, a Compartment, sub compartment and connecting compartment. Thus, a ship 'address' could be found fairly rapidly by reference to its Deck Number, Frame Number, Compartment Letter and so on.

There was a subdued muttering as the respective officers digested this. Then Nicolas Gray said sharply, "that places our 'arrival and departure' package right in the aft link companionway and transport haulway for the hangar decks and maintenance shop!"

"That's right, Commander," said the lieutenant, "and it will be vital that you have no personnel, strike fighters or equipment in that space during the transit of the gate."

There was an instant uproar as the assembled officers grasped the significance of what had been said. The Captain demanded their attention and then advised them that they would indeed be leaving through the gate – but with a science team aboard and a load of special tracer beacons in the space the lieutenant had just indicated. Despite the protests of the Strike Force Commander who knew full well that he had a very short time to relocate a lot of equipment and at least five strike craft and a transport "Barge" – one of the ship's very large atmospheric re-entry vehicles essential for planetary exploration.

The flow of discussion was suddenly interrupted by an exclamation in German from Reinhard Diefenbach which drew everyone's attention.

"Yes, Commander," asked the Captain, "You have noticed something significant?"

"I do not know, Captain," came the careful reply, "it may be. The gate is located precisely at the centre of the Indian Ocean Magnetic Anomaly!"

"Explain please?" said the Captain softly.

"There are eight such magnetic anomalies, four in each hemisphere. Perhaps the best known is the Bermuda Triangle – in these areas, the Earth's magnetic field is, ah, different to what it would be expected to be," replied the Commander thoughtfully.

"He's right sir," the Navigator, Ben Curran spoke up, "the anomalies are all roughly triangular areas where it is pretty well documented that some odd things happen." He looked at the VDU in front of him, and continued thoughtfully, "I wonder … the power output around the gate during a transit, coupled with a ship's own hyperdrive field …." He looked up suddenly frowning, "I think I need to run a few calculations on this sir!"

"Very well Pilot. Any more questions? No? Good, then I shall let you get on with your preparations. Commander Allison, the science team will need to link some of their equipment to your power grid, please arrange for them to have a liaison officer so that they don't short-circuit anything vital for us!"

"I will put Lieutenant Callaghan onto it sir, she's not one for letting anyone get out of hand," she grinned.

With a few more short instructions to various department heads, the Captain dismissed them to prepare for the departure, now bare hours away.

As they rose to go, the Captain asked the ship's CO of Marines, Colonel Mike Kernan and the Surgeon Commander, to stay. The Executive Commander joined the throng leaving and singled out Reinhard Diefenbach to accompany him to discuss linking the beacons to the ship's sensors and computer net. The others dispersed to their various departments singly and in pairs, all silently thoughtful and mentally compiling lists of tasks to be assigned or routines to be backed up and possibly even shut down to ensure that nothing vital could be damaged or lost. Nicolas Gray found himself in the midst of a complete maelstrom of Warrant Officers as he gave orders to clear the compartments identified by the scientists and fielded a range of grumbles, complaints and ideas for where the craft and equipment could be, should be or would be moved too. He fielded the complaints with cheerful firmness, knowing his team well and also knowing that the complaints usually meant only that they were already working out how to get their teams to achieve everything in the time available to them.

After the Colonel and the Doctor had departed, the Captain moved to his desk and began to run a series of checks on signal logs and standing orders until he found several which he tagged and placed in a download to his tablet. He had just finished when his Writer called on the link to tell him the Admiral was on the secure link and wished to speak to him. "Admiral Somerville, we have latest intel updates on the situation in the Pangaea system, but this problem with the gates seems to be adding a complication we don't need right now."

"James, this is a secure link so I will tell you openly that there are a number of problems we are trying to deal with here. The Gate provides us with an excuse to send a science team with you – they have a dual task, the gate and to look into certain other matters on Pangaea. Now I have to tell you, that you will be carrying the full authority of Flag Officer for this. For political reasons I can't send a Rear Admiral as would be normal for a force of this size, so I am sending you closed orders for yourself, your Exec and for Colonel Kernan. You will act on those as soon as you enter the Pangaea system and the ships joining you will have copies of these," the Admiral smiled, "I wish I was going with you, dealing with the politics is enough to send a man insane."

"Thanks for the opportunity sir," replied the Captain, "I take it the mystery forces we are hearing about have been identified?"

"They have, and there are some concerns there as well. We have a problem of loyalties in some places – and I would advise you to run some checks on all your personnel, particularly to watch your signal and comms systems for unauthorised use and access. We have done the best we can to make sure that the people on your ships are a hundred percent, but there may be a few rotten apples who have slipped through. Be vigilant!"

"Don't worry sir," grinned the Captain, "I have 'Fritz' Diefenbach looking after our systems, I'll make sure he runs checks on everybody else's as well – God help anyone who tries to slip something into his systems!"

They both laughed and the Admiral concluded the discussion,

saying, "Well good luck and good hunting James. You have the best ships I could get for you, better in fact than I'd thought we could pull together, and the best commanders as well. They're all of them sound and very capable. You'll have no trouble there. *Ramillies* is brand new so I can't tell yet how she will shake down, but Captain Bruce Wallace is experienced and I think you know him?" He caught the Captain's confirmatory nod, "There is something rather nasty going on inside Brussels and the Confederal government James, and the situation in Pangaea is connected to it. Deal with that for us and we will probably be able to see what needs to be done at this end to clean house. Use those ships well!"

Within the hour and just in time for the arrival of the new Science Officer and her team, the designated area had been cleared of everything movable or vital. Commander Gray and his team of officers, petty officers and 'ground' staff found themselves now helping as the scientific team began to fill the compartments they had just cleared with spherical tracker beacons, hyperspace signal transponders and a host of scientific gear that seemed to take up twice as much space as the equipment they had cleared! Nicolas commented on this to a tall and well built lady wearing a fairly ubiquitous coverall suit, "I hope somebody has told you scientific types that I'll need all this junk cleared from here as soon as you've finished! We need these maintenance and transfer bays for our strike and atmosphere craft you know!"

"Really?" came the somewhat amused reply, "I think that you must be assuming you will be able to simply send us back through the gate when we have finished then?"

"Not at all," he grinned back, "I know that may be tempting, but impractical. Thing is, where will all this go when we have finished – the ship's loaded to capacity as it is!"

"Perhaps then, it is your equipment which will have to be relocated?" She broke off to fire a string of instructions at several of her team who were positioning a bulky looking piece of equipment.

Nick let out a yell as one of the science team began to drill holes in the deck, "Hey! You can't do that! There are all sorts of services beneath that deck – if you cut them we'll have real problems!" He turned to the woman who was now giving him a steely look, "Look, if your people must secure this damned stuff to the deck, let my people do it! At least they know where the vital stuff is under the deck plates!"

"I think you will find we are aware of the problem, er, Commander!" She gave him a look that made him feel very small and as if he had just crawled out of something unpleasant, "I think my staff know what they are doing and the placing of this equipment must be exact!"

"Well, if you say so, but at least let some of my people assist, after all, they will have to repair all the damage when you've finished!"

"If you insist – by the way, I don't think we have been introduced, you must be Commander Gray, I was warned that you were very possessive about your hangars and connecting spaces," she paused, then extended a hand, "I am Silke Grüneland, Chief Scientist and in charge of this investigation."

"Pleased to meet you," replied the Commander, still conscious of "the look" he had received, "I'm Nick to most people except when it comes to running this area and my squadrons!" He gave her an appraising look and continued, "I was serious about the need to be able to clear this area back to its proper use as soon as possible, we need to be able to carry out essential repairs and maintenance and this is where it needs to be done."

"I appreciate your problem, believe me, we will do our best to clear it as soon as we have all the information we need to gather! Now Commander - or should I call you Nick? - we both have a lot to get done, do you want to instruct some of your people to assist me?"

"Make that Nick, and I'll get my people onto this immediately."

Both turned away to begin issuing instructions and orders and very quickly the work was being done efficiently and swiftly, a combination of science teams and deck staff securing and shifting the seemingly endless quantities of scientific equipment that needed to be installed. Nick saw the Science Officer joined by Lieutenant Callaghan and was satisfied he could leave the arrangements for power supply safely in her hands – and that she would also keep a close watch on where things were being attached. With both teams now working together the work proceeded swiftly until Nick's comlink chirped and when he accepted the caller, heard the voice of Mary Allison, "Nick, what the hell are you people hooking into the grid? The demand from your area is up to a hundred and ten percent of the design load for the usual supply for that zone!"

"Mary, it's probably this scientific kit, I see poor Karen Callaghan is doing her best to restrain the scientists. I'll see what I can do to help her! It's power hungry alright!"

"Bloody hell, you're not kidding buster, if they keep on drawing like this I'll have to shut the area down or run up some more generators and divert the power from elsewhere. What are they hooking up anyway? I was told it was only a small amount of kit and wouldn't exceed the normal parameters."

"OK, I'll talk to the Chief Scientist and see what she needs? Most of the stuff seems to be monitoring gear, but there are a couple of big pods which I am told are the probe units they hope to 'lose' – the rest of the kit is supposed to track it and figure out where it goes," Nick looked around at the clusters of scientists and the watching groups of uniformed technicians trying to see what was happening.

"Look – oh hell, the draw has just jumped another notch – get them to call me and tell me what they really need, OK?" she gave a short laugh, and added, "at this rate I won't be able to power up the hyperdrive so the whole deal will be useless anyway! I'll get onto Callaghan and see if she has been consulted on the power draw!"

Nick managed to attract the Science Officer's attention and explained the concerns expressed by Mary, then he asked, "Have you been issued with a comlink for the ship yet?" He looked around for Lieutenant Callaghan and saw that she was across the compartment apparently remonstrating with a group installing yet another piece of 'science junk' as his team called it.

"A comlink? *Nein*, I mean no. Is this important?"

"It will be once we get under way," nodded Nick a little grimly, "Right now it's an inconvenience. Engineering need to talk to you about the power you're drawing and the only way is to use a link." He paused then pressed the call button on his own link, "Patch me to Commander Diefenbach!"

"Diefenbach!"

"Fritz, we need comlinks down in Maintenance Hangar – Compartment Two-Two-Three Alpha Oscar Charlie – and we need them quickly, Engineering needs to talk to the Chief Scientist. Any chance you can get some down PDQ?"

"*Ja*, It is not a problem, I will have them to you in five minutes."

*Out Of Time*

"Thanks, Gray out!"

Turning to the waiting scientist he said, "You will have heard our Communications specialist. They're on their way, but the link will only work once it has been coded to your DNA and voice signature, that will take a couple of minutes. We will also need to get the principle people on your team fitted as well, but I guess that can wait for the moment!"

"Thank you, I think we have almost everything we need now connected to the grid as you call it. The power draw should drop off once everything is stabilised at the same frequency as the ship's power and all the power cells are fully charged." She shrugged and smiled, "I can understand the Engineer Commander's concern. I will contact her as soon as I have the means to do so!"

A bare few minutes later Commander Diefenbach appeared with one of his technicians in tow. Nick watched and listened as there followed an exchange in German, the Chief Scientist and the Comms Commander apparently hitting it off and enjoying a joke of their own. Then it was down to work and in a very few minutes after that, Dr Grüneland was speaking to Commander Allison in Engineering. Those standing nearby soon realised that there was a titanic battle of wills in progress, but, evidently the science team won – as evidenced by the appearance in the hangar of several personnel in uniforms with Engineering insignia very shortly thereafter, these joined Lieutenant Callaghan and very soon calm was restored.

※ ※ ※

With just under an hour to spare all Department's were once again assembled in the Captain's Dayroom, this time with Dr Grüneland and her assistant also present. One by one all departments reported that their preparations were complete, only Commander Allison was clearly concerned at the amounts of power still being used by the scientific equipment – but even she conceded that it was well within the capacity of her generators to provide it, "It's just that I don't like having to run all my generators to meet the demand – it means we have no reserve capacity, and" – she shot a dagger glance at Commander Gray who was grinning – "it wastes a lot of power!"

Captain Heron briefed the assembled team on the order of sailing and pointed out that the escort ships, *Bellerophon* of the North European Confederation and *Sydney* from the Australasian Union, would ride the *Vanguard's* wake through the gate – a tactic that mercantile ships had already discovered reduced the risk from the anomaly.

"I'm sure Dr Grüneland will not require you to remain at full output capacity for any longer than necessary, but I take your point Commander," the Captain smiled, then continued, "now we have the team aboard, and we have run a few more calculations on the data the Science Branch has been able to get from the previous flights. Commander Diefenbach has also alerted us to something that does not appear to have occurred to anyone when the gate was set up and we may have something as a result. Dr Grüneland," he added, "Perhaps you would tell us what your office thinks after their trial modelling exercise?"

"Thank you Captain, it is true that there does appear to be a connection between the Indian Ocean Anomaly and the Gate, but we do not, at this time, fully understand the mechanism. It seems that when the gate is actuated it creates a very strong – for want of a better word – 'backwash' in the Earth's magnetic field. This peaks as the ship entering or leaving the gate passes the event horizon and it appears to send a powerful energy beam of tachyon emissions in a very narrow band down to the surface. As you will know, research into the effects of tachyon emissions have recently shown that there is a potential for some very strange anomalies within a tachyon beam and we need to collect as much data on this phenomenon as possible. In theory it should do no more than cause a momentary disturbance in the atmosphere, but it seems to be doing something entirely unpredicted and we cannot as yet analyse exactly what is happening." She turned to the Engineer Commander and added, "One reason we have much more equipment with us than was originally planned, is that we hope, with equipment on the surface, to measure or detect exactly what happens on the sea level end of the burst."

"Thank you Doctor," said the Captain as she finished, "one thing I have just learned is that the surface teams have located something on the seabed which may be from one of the earlier incidents. I hope to hear some more soon after we have undocked." He looked round the table and thought for a moment that he was lucky to have such a collection of really competent and professional Heads of Department – especially in a command of this size, almost a mile in length and a half mile from

*Out Of Time*

'fin' tip to 'fin' tip carrying a crew of fully four thousand men and women. Just in the Engineering section alone the ship's power plant could provide electrical power for the entire continent of Australia and her engines combined the power of several supernova. With a smile he nodded and said, "Well the Commander tells me the undocking tugs are attached, and the loading docks are now sealed. We will undock in fifteen minutes, let's get to work!"

A watcher in space would have seen the vast ship, itself dwarfed by the Station to which it had been attached, eased gently away from the embrace of the docking arms, by a set of small tugs whose carefully scaled impulse generators created sufficient momentum to detach the vast ship from the gravitational attraction of the station, without disturbing the balance of the station's orbit. This use of tugs was something learned by near disastrous early attempts at docking interstellar ships to some of the original stations which had had seriously decayed orbits after being pulled or pushed by the momentum of a ship docking or undocking! The watcher would then have seen the great ship, at fifty miles from the station, swing round to face the direction of the gate through which she would have to pass at unimaginable velocity and gently begin to manoeuvre under her own ion engines even as her mighty hyperdrive pods began to light up with their power banked until released to accelerate and catapult the ship into that strange realm which, for want of any better description, writers had called "Hyperspace" ever since man first began to dream of travelling through the vast distances of space at speeds in excess of the speed of light. The watcher would have seen the vast ship joined by two similar ships shining as the dawn sun caught them as they moved from the night shadow of the blue green planet below and took station on the great ship's flanks.

Seemingly unmoving, the three ships crawled closer to the gate, which flared suddenly into life on command from the *Vanguard's* Control Centre, the great circular structure with its four cardinal projectors arcing brilliantly into life and the circle filled with blue-white light, streaked with yellow. *Vanguard* and her companions hung for a moment as if stationary, then the hyperdrive pods on all three burst into brilliant light and the ships lunged forward into the circle. As *Vanguard's* 'fins' vanished into the vortex, a purple flash illuminated the ship's after section and lanced directly towards the dawn lit ocean below, then the *Vanguard* and her consorts flashed from view as the gate's projectors winked out.

# Chapter 2

# Into battle: HMS Spartan 74 guns, Indian Ocean 1804

The ship rolled ponderously on the long Indian Ocean swell. Small unsecured possessions rattled gently as they slid or rolled with the motion within whatever confined them for the moment. The Gunroom was breathless in the warm heat of the equatorial trade winds as the ship rolled her way towards the Good Hope coast, still some two thousand miles distant – if the Master's calculations were accurate. They had slipped quietly past the hostile and garrisoned French colonial territories of Mauritius some twelve hours earlier, their accompanying Indian built frigate, HMS *Rajahstan* scouting to the North for the French ships known to be in these waters and the little sloop HMS *Swallow* sweeping ahead to seek any enemy ships making for the islands. Both had clear orders to close immediately with the heavy bulk of HMS *Spartan*, a seventy four gun ship of the line on sighting any enemy warship of superior force – and both kept within long masthead sight of the larger ship so as to make possible rapid communication with the senior ship.

Midshipman Harry Nelson-Heron, seated in *Spartan's* Gunroom, paused in his letter writing to day-dream for a moment. Closing his eyes he leaned back and tried to conjure up a picture of his distant home. The low stone house set in the rolling hillside of Scrabo, the view of Strangford Lough, just visible from his bedroom window at the Western end of the house and the new town of Newtownards clustered at the foot of the hill. The house had been in his family for generations and showed its age and its growth from farmhouse and hall to its present form of two wings and annexed stables and barns in the materials and building styles each new addition displayed. He had not been born there, unlike some of his older cousins, since his father had held a commission of Major in the Royal Regiment of Fusiliers whose barracks lay in Downpatrick some twelve miles to the South of Scrabo and South West of Strangford Lough. It was there that Harry had been brought into this world while his father was on garrison duty with his regiment in Gibraltar. Shortly after his birth, his uncle, his father's older brother, had died childless and the family farm and manor had passed to Harry's father. This had meant his father giving up his commission and returning home to set the family fortunes in some sort of order. They were not wealthy by the standards of London, but they were well provided for and had sufficient land and income to keep a good house and show traditional Irish hospitality to friend, visitor and family alike. As the tradition went, Harry, as the youngest child of three – his older sister Mabel, already destined for marriage to a neighbouring landowner and his brother James who would ultimately inherit the estate as the eldest boy – faced the usual choices of Army, Law or Church and had chosen, against all advice, to go to sea! Thus, at the tender age of twelve, his head stuffed with romantic notions and, his mother's and sister's tears moistening his collar, he had been consigned to the care of a distant relative in London and thence into the close knit and dangerous world of a Navy at war.

His first ship had been another ponderous "74", *HMS Bellerophon,* which he had joined on a cold blustery November day in 1801, her scars from the famous Battle of the Nile still visible three years after the event despite a year in dockyard hands. Many of her older hands still talked with awe of the moment when the huge French flagship, *L'Orient,* blew apart with the *"Billy Roughian"* still alongside! Then had come the Peace of Amiens and *Billy Roughian* had paid off and been laid up in ordinary. Harry had been lucky to be transferred, on the recommendation of *Bellerophon's* Captain, another Ulsterman, to *Spartan,* about to depart for the Indian Ocean and the prison colony in New South Wales. They had since seen the fabulous natural harbour of Port Jackson, the strange animals of the New South Wales coastal area, the Great Barrier Reef and finally the fabled Indian subcontinent and the approaches to the great trading ports of that land of extremes and wonders. Harry had written copious letters home to his father, mother and sister, letters illustrated with his drawings of the places he had seen and the strange and wonderful animals they had encountered. Then, all too soon, the Peace had been shattered. Napoleon had marched once more and *Spartan* had been ordered to protect the shipping plying the Indian Ocean for the Honourable East India Company. In this she was supported by the HEIC's own navy, the Bombay Marine, whose distinctive house flag of thirteen horizontal red alternating with white stripes and the Union Flag emblazoned in the Upper Quarter, was permitted to be worn only East of the Cape of Good Hope.

Now, having at last been relieved by a pair of "seventy-fours" and three frigates, *Spartan* was on her way home, deprived of the use of the base at Simon's Town by the short-sightedness of a Parliament obsessed with saving money, and the skill of the French and Dutch negotiators, she would need to avoid the Cape and it's sheltered bays and fresh supplies and make instead for the less hospitable St Helena island where they could replenish with some fresh food and take on water for the long haul home. But, between their present position and the island lay a prodigious amount of sea and several well equipped and well handled enemies!

He was jerked out of his reverie by a clatter of boots on the companionway ladder and the robust voice of the Gunroom bully, the twenty year old Eamon Barclay. "Heron!" he growled, "It's your turn to do rounds with the Fourth Lieutenant. Make it snappy or I'll put you on report!"

"I did the rounds yesterday, it's Dick Peterson's turn today!" replied Harry, deliberately not rising to the bait. Peterson was a favourite of the older Midshipman and frequently enjoyed his protection from the less enjoyable duties the Gunroom had to perform.

"It's your turn now! Do as you're told!" snapped the other.

"Very well, I'm on my way," replied Harry casually, "but the First Lieutenant has been asking why I am doing so many duties and others apparently so few." Having carefully locked away his letter and pens in his sea-chest, he picked up his jacket with its white collar patches and shrugged it on, then crammed his hat on his head and made to walk past the smouldering bulk of the senior.

The other stuck out an arm to stop him, gripping his shoulder hard, he lowered his face close to Harry's and growled, "Just because you are from the same County don't think you can get away with anything while I am watching you!"

Carefully removing the others hand, Harry looked him squarely in the eye and replied, "Indeed, I would not dream of it! My family have always stood for and by our own – and need hide behind no other!" He watched the flush spread up the others face and the anger blaze from his eye's then said softly, "And it would be most inconvenient for us both, I'm thinking, for me to have to report to the Fourth Lieutenant with broken knuckles or a black eye – especially as he awaits me!"

"Damn you Heron! I'll make you pay for that," the other began, his voice rising.

"Hold hard there, Eamon," came the polished accents of the second senior in the Gunroom, Tom Bowles. "Leave Harry alone, your Irish feuds can wait. Get going Harry," he said indicating the stairs as he turned to face the furious Barclay.

As Harry ran up the companionway he heard Bowles saying, "One of these days Eamon, you will push that fellow too far and he'll have you! Oh, he'll have you alright, I would wager a full pony on it!"

On deck Harry joined his friend Kit Tanner and the Fourth Lieutenant Matthew Beasley. "Good Lord, Harry," said the Fourth, "I wasn't expecting you tonight, what business detains Master Peterson this time!"

"Nothing I know of sir," grinned Harry, "Mr Barclay instructed me to replace him."

"I see," said the other with a long look, "Very well, let us proceed in peace, or pieces, as the Padre is so wont to say!"

Rounds took them around the upper deck, then down to the upper and lower gundecks to ensure that all off watch personnel were accounted for and that all guns, tables and accoutrements were properly stowed for the night. On this tour they were, as always, accompanied by the Master at Arms, the Boatswain and one of the other Warrant Officers. On this night all went smoothly and they emerged eventually on the Quarterdeck just as the fo'c's'le belfry struck seven bells. "Well gentlemen," said the Lieutenant, in dismissal, "Thank you for your company, you may away to your hammocks!"

"Thank you sir," said Harry, "But as I have the Middle Watch, I'll stay here if you have no objection sir?"

"None at all Harry," said the Lieutenant, surprised, "sleep earlier today did you?"

"No sir, I was busy with a letter and my journal when Mr Barclay called me."

"I see, well, make sure you do not sleep on watch my lad, or it really will be the worse for you!" he laughed as he turned away to attend to a question from the Third Lieutenant who had the Watch.

Harry spent a few minutes simply enjoying the coolness of the night breeze and the feel of the ship as it surged over the crests of the waves. Above him the rigging creaked and groaned and the wind caused the taut shrouds to hum in sympathy. Blocks rattled gently with the motion and the waves slapped sharply against the hull sending spray soaring over the beakhead and jib boom as the ship pitched forward across a wave. Looking aloft he could just make out the fighting tops against the stars and thought of his boyhood friend Ferghal O'Connor, now a youthful seaman aboard this very ship. Ferghal was the son of his father's Head Groom and had followed Harry to sea. Three years older than Harry, he always seemed to manage to be at Harry's side whenever there was a fight or danger and the bond between them was far more than master and servant or, indeed, officer and serving man. It had been remarked on in the Wardroom as well, and one or two of the ship's bullies had discovered the hardest way, that it did not pay to try to get at Harry by attacking Ferghal and vice versa.

A footfall and the feeling of a change in the breeze about his body, brought Harry back to the present and he turned to look at the stocky figure of the Third Lieutenant. "Good evening sir, I hope I may remain here until the Watch changes?"

"That you may, Mister Heron," the third replied, "I am glad of the chance to speak with you as it happens, it saves me having to send for you on the morrow."

"Sir?" wondered Harry, his mind quickly skimming recent events that might have given rise for a reprimand.

"You are presently in charge of the midship division of the battery on the lower gundeck are you not?"

"Yes sir, Numbers Eight to Sixteen. Mister Barclay has the after guns in that division and Mr Tanner the Forward part of the Battery with Mr Petersen."

"Precisely. I have it in mind, Mr Heron, to place Mr Barclay with

*Out Of Time*

the fo'c's'le battery of carronades and to bring Mr Petersen to the quarterdeck battery, but I do not have anyone to replace them under Mr Beasley in the Lower Battery. This would mean that you will have to take responsibility for both Midship and After divisions. Are you willing?" He paused, then added, "naturally, I will have to confirm this with Mr Bell and the Captain, but when I spoke to them earlier, it was agreed that this was a workable arrangement."

"I have no objection sir," said Harry, quietly thrilled to be entrusted with this extra responsibility.

"Very good, then I shall pass the word in the morning and we can make the arrangements once we are satisfied that the scheme is working properly!"

The Lieutenant appeared on the brink of saying something more, but a flash on the distant horizon drew their attention and a few minutes later there was a sound as of thunder in the air. From the masthead came a hail from the lookout, "Deck there! Gunfire on the Larboard beam!"

Instantly the Lieutenant turned to Harry, "Quick Mister Heron, inform the Captain!"

Harry turned and hurried to the companionway, descending swiftly to the deck below. Making his way along the passage to the door, he paused as the Marine sentry thumped the butt of his musket three times on the deck! Harry smiled at the sentry, a youth only a few years older than himself and also from Ireland and nodded, "Thank you Marine Dalziel!" He tapped at the door and heard the Captain's call of "Enter!"

"Ah, Mr Heron," smiled the Captain, "You find me sleepless. What is it?"

"Mr Rogers compliments sir, but we have heard gunfire to the South East!"

"Thank you Mr Heron, I shall come up. Inform the First Lieutenant!"

Shutting the door behind him, Harry hurried to the Wardroom companionway and sought out the First Lieutenant's small cabin. He tapped at the door and heard the Lieutenant call, "Come!"

He opened the door a fraction and said, "Captain's compliments Mr Bell, but we have heard gunfire to the South East and the Captain is asking for you!"

"Is he by God," retorted the Lieutenant, "Very good, lead the way; I shall be right behind you Mr Heron!"

Harry's re-emergence on deck coincided with yet more flashes on the distant horizon and a few seconds later by the accompanying rumble of artillery. He found himself standing close to the Captain and the gathered Lieutenants, all with night telescopes to their eyes. "What do you make of that Mr Bell, twenty-four pounders would you say?" asked the Captain.

"At least sir. A mix of sixteen's and twenty-four's perhaps?" replied Mr Bell.

"Just so! A ship, gentlemen, at least equal to ourselves then! But, the question is whose?" Captain Blackwood closed his glass with a snap and handed it to Harry, "I think we shall know at dawn! Hoist the signal for *Rajahstan* and *Swallow* to close on us if you please!" He gave a grim laugh, "If she is French, I'll wager she has consorts!"

"Shall I have the ship cleared for action sir?" asked the First Lieutenant, joining the group.

"Not yet I think Thomas, let the hands sleep a little longer and beat to quarters at eight bells of the Middle Watch. That should bring us a little closer to the action and it will be wanting but an hour before dawn I think," mused the Captain. He watched as a string of lanterns slowly mounted the weather rigging, two blue lights a single red and a further blue. He nodded in satisfaction, and then said, "Inform me the moment *Rajahstan* and *Swallow* acknowledge; then haul it down. We don't want to warn anyone else if we can help it!"

As they finished speaking, the belfry on the fo'c's'le struck the four double strokes of eight bells signalling the end of the Evening Watch and the start of the Middle Watch. Around the Captain and the First Lieutenant, the Watch changed quietly and efficiently, the lieutenants exchanging information as to course, speed, incidents in the log and the reported gunfire – which now seemed to have ceased. Harry joined the Lieutenants and listened as the course and heading were relayed from the Third Lieutenant to the Second who now had the Watch. They were joined too by Midshipman Tom Bowles, who, as the ship was short of a Fifth Lieutenant, due to the death of the original post holder of a fever, and none of the Midshipmen then being either suitable or old

*Out Of Time*

enough, was acting as the second officer on Watch, while Harry would be responsible for the lookouts and the signal party.

The First and the Captain having gone below again, Lieutenant Rae, the Second, gave Harry instructions to ensure that an extra sharp watch was kept on the horizon for any activity which would reveal the presence of an enemy. Harry conscientiously made a round of the lookouts with a Master's Mate and made sure that everyone knew where to watch and what to look out for. He returned to the Quarterdeck just as a hail from the Mizzen Topmast, where a signal lookout was perched, told them that the *Swallow* had acknowledged the signal. Harry checked and it was confirmed that *Rajahstan* was also flying an acknowledgement and he asked permission to haul the signal down and replace it with a light only their own ships would be able to see. This was confirmed and so the string of lights was replaced by a single blue light at the mizzen topsail yard where only the two consorts would be able to see it, both being upwind of *Spartan*, although *Swallow* lay well on her Starboard bow.

The Watch passed slowly, punctuated only by sporadic and increasingly infrequent, further gunfire, still on her Larboard bow. Fifteen minutes before eight bells and the end of the Watch, Harry was once more sent below to the Captain and the First Lieutenant, finding both in the Captain's great cabin pouring over a chart. He followed the routine of the Marine's stamped musket, knocked and entered the cabin, "Mr Rae's compliments sir, he wishes me to request your permission to beat to quarters shortly."

"Very well Mr Heron, we will be up directly!" responded the Captain grimly, "Has there been any further activity?"

"Not in the last half hour or so sir. *Rajahstan* and *Swallow* are still not in company sir."

"Thank you Mr Heron, we will have to make do. Now Thomas," he said to the First as the door closed behind the midshipman, "we shall see what Bonaparte has despatched to these waters since the peace collapsed!"

Harry had no sooner reported to the waiting Second than eight bells sounded sonorously from the fo'c's'le. The last stroke was still lying in the wind when the First Lieutenant appeared on deck and grasped a speaking trumpet to give the order, "Master at Arms, beat to quarters, clear the ship for action!" Instantly the staccato rattle of the drum began to sound – Harry guessed that the drummer, a boy a year younger than himself, must have been roused from his hammock in preparation. The response was swift, men burst from their hammocks and rolled and tied them, rushing to the upper deck, they stowed these in the hammock nettings that lined the bulwarks, then returned below to tear down the internal partitions and stow away the loose and unwanted gear in order to clear the gun decks and the guns for action.

Harry joined the throng and rushed to take his station at the rear of the Number Eight twenty-four pounder on the Larboard side of the Lower Gundeck. He watched critically as the gun's crews cast off the lashings on the guns and rigged the training and running out tackles, checked the recoil arrestors, quoins and priming locks. His eyes were drawn to where a diminutive boy known only as Danny, one of the ship's "Powder Monkeys" worked between the men with a bucket of sand, carefully spreading it on the deck on wide sweeps so as to ensure it was evenly spread. Harry knew that this could be vital once the decks became slippery with blood or water and even when not, ensured that the men would have the best possible grip as they strained to keep the guns firing. As he had been taught, he personally checked each gun captain had a new flint in his firing lock, and a smouldering slow match in the sand tub next to the gun. As yet they had not been given the order to run out, but this was not given until there was some certainty that the guns would be fired – the powder soon spoiled if subjected to dampness, as it would be if the guns were subjected to a lengthy exposure to the spray bursting across the ship's hull!

On deck, the dawn crept slowly over the sea. Spartan's topmasts blazed brilliant gold as the sun caught them and the golden light spread gently downwards, finding the topsail yards and then the taut topsails themselves. The ship was now quiet, every gun on the Larboard side ready and manned as the light slowly spread. The tension broke as there came a hail from aloft, "Deck there, sail fine on the Larboard bow! Two frigates, big ones; and a third ship dismasted sir!"

"Very good," roared the Captain, "Where away is the *Rajahstan* and the *Swallow*?"

"*Rajahstan* is hull down to windward on our Starboard Quarter sir, *Swallow* lies hull up abeam of us!"

"Very good Cromwell!" responded the Captain, his memory for the names of his crew as sharp as ever, to the waiting First Lieutenant he said, "Make to *Rajahstan* and *Swallow*, Enemy in sight, close on me!"

"Deck there," came a further hail from the lookout, "Them frigates are Frenchies sir! And they're making sail and altering course toward us!"

"Bold devils, they must be confident of their ability to behave so!" exclaimed the First Lieutenant. Turning to the Midshipman standing nearby, he said, "Quickly Mr Bowles, aloft with that telescope and tell me what you can of these French ships."

Some fifteen minutes later the Midshipman returned to the quarterdeck, face flushed with the exertion of having climbed to the lookout's position in the crosstrees at the head of the main topmast and then the exhilaration of a slide down the long backstays to return to the deck. "Sir!" he exclaimed as he gained the Captain's attention, "They're a pair of large frigates – at least forty-four's – and the lead ship is wearing a Commodores pennant!"

"Is he indeed!" replied the Captain, "Well, it would seem that the reports from the Bombay Marine have been accurate!" He paused for a moment thoughtfully, then continued, "Forty-fours you think?"

"Yes sir," replied Tom Bowles, "and very weatherly as well, sir, by the look of them!"

"Deck there!" came another hail from aloft, "The enemy has changed tack! They'm trying to cross our bows sir!"

"Are they by heaven!" frowned the Captain, "Bear up two points!" He ordered the helmsmen and watched as hands ran to adjust the sail trim as canvas boomed above them. The ship heeled deeper as the wind came more abeam, "We'll make them work for that privilege Mr Bell! Two to one, unless *Rajahstan* can close on us more rapidly! Her weight should be sufficient and *Swallow* can engage once we have their full attention!"

Slowly, painfully, the gap between the ships diminished until details of the leading ship could be made out as she lifted to the swell. Big and fast, the French ship displayed all the characteristics of that nation's ability to build beautiful and weatherly ships, something the Captain and First Lieutenant often debated. Just after six bells in the morning watch, a puff of smoke from the leading French ship's fo'c's'le showed that she had decided to test the range, the dull boom of the gun followed a few moments after the burst of spray about a quarter mile short of Spartan showed that neither side had the range to strike each other yet. More out of dignity than any expectation of success, the Captain ordered his own gunners to reply with the upper decks forward "Long Nines" – sixteen pounder guns with a nine foot barrel – and this they did, at an almost leisurely pace, each gun in the forward four gun division taking deliberate aim and waiting on the upward roll of the ship, to fire in turn.

While this was happening, orders were passed to the lower battery deck to ensure that all guns were loaded with double shot, something Harry checked personally in his division of the battery and which drew the remark from Ferghal as he passed that this meant they expected to be at very close range before firing. As he said this there was a heavy crash above them and the deck shuddered as a ball found its mark somewhere in the hull. A rush of feet on the deck above told its own story, but the word soon passed that the damage was minimal and no casualties had arisen. The waiting was always the worst thought Harry as he watched his friend and onetime playmate checking the rammer and sponge for his gun while the rest of the gun's crew made sure the training tackles, breech ropes and all their equipment was ready and to hand. The boy Danny walked carefully between him and the gun crew scattering sand on the deck, and Harry reflected that the crew would have a good grip of the deck as they worked around the gun.

"Mr Heron", the voice of the Fourth Lieutenant jerked him out of his thoughts, "A moment please, and you Mr Barclay!"

The two Midshipmen hurried to the foot of the companion ladder where the Lieutenant waited, "Mr Barclay, take charge of the Fo'c's'le carronades if you please. The Second Lieutenant will convey his desires for their handling to you. Mr Heron, we will be engaging on the Larboard battery, but the next division will also now fall to your care. Ensure that both batteries are ready in case the Captain sees an opportunity to affect a sudden change of plan!" He grinned at Harry and added, "And I suggest that you make sure the after division are well prepared! Mr Barclay is occasionally remiss in checking his captains!"

Harry hurried back to his station near Number Eight gun and then, having satisfied himself that his division were all ready he made a swift inspection of the division of guns recently assigned to his care. To his embarrassment he found himself being warmly welcomed by the crews who seemed altogether too eager to assure him that their guns were as ready as those of his own division of the battery. To make sure he was not being misinformed, he checked several with the Gun Captains and found that they were indeed ready. He passed on to the captains the news that they might be required to change batteries and must stand ready for a swift change of plan should the opportunity arise, then returned to his station where he found himself standing close to Ferghal and the boy, Danny, now clutching two large wooden cartridge cases. He noted with a grin that the urchin seemed to be trying hard not to be noticed and clutched two of the closed wooden cylinders that contained the prepared powder cartridges which would be required for reloading numbers Eight and Nine guns as soon as they fired as if his life depended on it. It would then be the boy's task to run to the magazine on the deck below and bring up two more and to keep on doing this until the engagement ceased. He grinned at the grubby face and said, "Here – Danny is it?" the urchin nodded, "Stand between me and Ferghal until we need you!"

Seconds later there was yet another crash above and shudder as the ship was struck by more than one heavy ball. This time cries for the loblolly boys told their own tale of injuries and perhaps dead on the deck above. A few minutes later they felt the ship plunge steeply as she bore up sharply – obviously the French were head-reaching on them thought Harry, and almost simultaneously they heard the sharp and distinctive bellow as the Larboard of 68 pounder carronade spat its vicious charge! Not for nothing were these guns called "smashers" by the British Tar and "the Devil gun" by the French!

"Open ports and run out!" roared the Fourth Lieutenant, in charge of the Gundeck. In response the crews sprang into life and as the ports swung upward, other hands hauled on the gun tackles and dragged the heavy guns into position, their muzzles protruding like teeth along the ships side. The French ships were now close to hand and their guns too were run out and ready. As Harry watched the leading ship fired a ragged broadside, all the shot seemingly aimed high. "Bastards are trying to dismast us sor," growled the gun captain as they saw this and Harry grinned at him in reply. At his feet the crouching Powder Monkey gave a small whimper and Harry heard Ferghal pat the child's shoulder and say something comforting as he watched the closing ships. Being the leeward side, spray burst upwards and inwards through the open ports and around the guns at regular intervals, but Harry could tell, by the way the deck was lying less steeply that sail was also being reduced aloft. The lieutenant's voice sounded above the sounds of the ship and of cannon fire from the approaching enemy, "As you bear – Fire!"

Harry held up a hand as he crouched to peer along the nearest gun. The French ship swam across the port as the deck plunged into a roll and he yelled, his voice cracking in the tension of the moment "On the up roll! Steady now!" the ship rolled again and the Frenchman, wreathed in smoke and now seemingly almost alongside, seemed to fill the port, "Fire!"

Along the line of guns all the gun captains peered along their guns, then stepped quickly clear of the line of recoil and as the ship rolled to windward tugged the lanyard attached to their firing locks. To Harry's right the gun captain jerked the lanyard and the gun roared, leaping backwards against its breech rope. Almost simultaneously there was another sound, high pitched and painful to the ear – then a sensation of falling, hearing the cries of Ferghal and a child and then blackness!

# Chapter 3

# Expect the unexpected: NECS Vanguard 2204

The *Vanguard* lurched as if some huge force had wrenched the hull in two directions as she crossed the gate's event horizon. In the Captain's Control Centre alarms sounded as several things happened at once.

※ ※ ※

Darkness gave way to light, a brief glimpse of a huge open space, of things falling about them – and then a sharp drop as Harry, Ferghal and the boy Danny dropped some fifteen feet to a hard deck and blackness engulfed Harry yet again!

※ ※ ※

The Captain called up the mimic readouts for the alarms on his personal display screen, noticing as he did so that he seemed to be struggling under increased gravitation. With an effort he overcame these and read the readouts grimly, noting that the operators at the various stations in the Centre were already dealing with their own sections. Swiftly the alarms began to fall silent and the readouts began to return to more normal levels. One caught his eye; it showed that there were now personnel in Compartment Two-Two-Three Alpha Oscar Charlie – and a quick glance at the visual scan link for the compartment showed three sprawled figures, one of them small and childlike, where one of the larger items of Dr Grüneland's equipment had been. Nearby lay a pile of shattered timbers and what looked like part of a cannon. He keyed his comlink, "Master at Arms, Security team and Damage Control Party to Two-Two-Three Alpha Oscar Charlie on the double. We may have casualties!" He heard the acknowledgement and then keyed his link again as the gravitational drag seemed to increase!

Aft of the Hangar decks and deep among the cavernous machinery spaces in the Engineering Control Centre, Commander Allison felt the shudder as the ship passed through the Event Horizon, then turned her attention to her read out screens and control desk. Alarms lit up on the Engineering Control boards as the generating turbines ran away, unloading power through any open circuit. At their consoles the Engineering staff worked frantically to uncouple, reroute or shut down some of the over supply to the various systems. Commander Allison watched grimly as slowly the alarms went silent, readouts returned to normal and she could feel confident that her team was once more in full control of their machinery. Although she was not given to swearing, she certainly felt like giving vent to her opinion as she saw where the power draw had suddenly been shut off! Her comlink bleeped.

"Allison", she snapped.

"Captain here, we seem to be a little heavy on gravity in the Control Centre, I'd appreciate it if you could drop it back to something like normal!"

"Yes sir," she replied, a wicked grin suddenly lighting up her face, "One moment please," she glanced across at the control station where three of her senior Technical Warrant Officers were engaged in what appeared to be a game of complicated chess on the panel before them, "Warrant Clarke, the Control Centre seems to be heavy on gravity, is there a problem?"

"We're trying to balance it out now Commander," came the reply, the Warrant Officer not even looking up from his task, "they have two point two-five G at the moment but it's coming down as fast as we can, there's worse in Decks Five and Six at Frames Ten to One Five Zero where we have four G at present."

"Very good, keep on it," replied the Commander, well aware of the tricky nature of what the three were doing, to the comlink she said, "We'll have your gravity level back to normal as soon as possible sir, should be down to one G in a couple of minutes. We do have some strange readouts from the hangar area, all the equipment that was coupled to our power supply seems to have gone off the board with the exception of some low power items still drawing in the peripheral areas to the target zone. I'd like to send a Tec Team to check the damage."

"Do that, the Science Team will be on its way as soon as we can get out of a seat easily here – and assuming the transport shuttles are working!"

"The transport shuttle systems are online sir – except through the area frames Triple Two to Double Two Four on decks Two to Zero Two. I will get a team over there to find out what the problem is and fix it."

"Do that." There was a pause, "And thank your team, the gravity seems to be getting back to something like normal here! Captain out!"

Mary Allison grinned at her panel, then said to the three Warrant Officers, "Well done Chief, the Captain's weight problem seems to be sorted out." She glanced at her panel and continued, "And the forward section seems to be getting back to normal as well. Good work!" Turning to her deputy, she gave him a string of names and then called another of her senior Warrant Officers over and repeated the names adding tasks to the list. The Warrant Officer grinned, nodded and began calling the team together while the officer downloaded data to a pair of portable diagnostic wands.

* * *

Senior Warrant Officer Eric "The Red" Suddaby, a squat and powerfully built man with a distinct "twang" in his voice which betrayed his home on the East Coast of England along the River Humber, closed his link and nodded to his team of ship's police "Right you lot, on the double, we seem to have some boarders in the hangar deck!" he nodded to the Royal Marine Colour Sergeant and added, "Jim, can you spare a couple of your Royals in case we have a fight on our hands?"

"Sure," Colour Sergeant James Nelson, known to his troops as Big J – though never to his face – nodded, "Marines Pollock and Knighton can hold your hands!" He keyed his comlink, "Pollock, Knighton, meet the Master at Arms at the access to Two-Two-Three Alpha Oscar Charlie!" He turned to the monitoring screens and keyed in a command at his keypad, instantly the screen showed the compartment and he studied the figures lying sprawled on the deck, then his eye took in the wreckage just beyond them, "I'll send down a stretcher party as well, looks like your boarders may need medics and not have much fight left!"

he said as the Master at Arms headed for the hatchway.

"Thanks, always good to know you care!" shot back the Warrant Officer to laughter from the rest of the crew present.

* * *

Doctor Silke Grüneland glared at her team, "What do you mean we have lost track of the probes? Impossible! With all the equipment we have on board?"

"Frau Doktor," said Dr Thomas Scheffer, the head of the tracking team responsible for the tracking equipment, "some of our tracking equipment seems to have been lost as well, and some tracked the probes for a matter of seconds – then lost contact. The power surge may have affected it, but the equipment is protected and reads a normal function!" his face a careful mask of seriousness belied by the laughter in his eyes as he saw her rise to his teasing use of her title.

"Thomas," said the Doctor coolly, "*Das ist höchst unwahrscheinlich*! Those probes are capable of withstanding atmospheric re-entry, the gravity in Jupiter's upper layers and the atmosphere on Venus! They simply are not functioning correctly! Find them, find the problem with our equipment. There is a rational explanation for this, you will all check and recheck everything until we find it!"

Doktor Scheffer, used to his boss, grinned, "*Jawohl Frau Doktor*!" He glared at his team from the full height of his six foot four inch frame – which, as an ex-rowing champion for his university was impressive – and said, "you heard the boss! What are you waiting for?"

* * *

Harry groaned as consciousness returned. His body seemed to be one huge ache, his head seemed to be spinning and he felt decidedly unwell. As he managed to get his eyes open against the hammering in his head, he registered that he was lying on someone's legs and that someone small was lying on him. Carefully he moved his arms and managed to ease himself free of the weight of the small Powder Monkey, noting that the boy seemed to be awake but frightened speechless. Ferghal, he noted was less fortunate, a slow trickle of blood ran from a cut on his head and one arm seemed to be bent at a strange angle. Harry eased himself upright and, somewhat unsteadily, looked around. He seemed to be in a vast chamber, man made by the fact that it showed many huge ribs of some strange material. The whole was tinted a pale grey, except for the deck on which they lay or stood which was a deep green with thick yellow markings inscribed upon it. Strange figures and numbers adorned the bulkheads above sealed openings or simply marking something indefinable. Pushing aside for the moment the strangeness of his surroundings, Harry knelt to see what he could do for Ferghal and satisfied himself that his boyhood friend was alive, the bleeding seemingly already slowing. The arm was another matter and he wondered how he could fix this, when the boy whimpered and clutched his arm!

"What is it – Danny?"

"The Frenchies sir! They've found us!" gasped the boy.

Harry looked around and saw the figures burst through an opening at the far end of the huge space. As they fanned out, he said firmly to the boy, "Take care of Ferghal! If it's a fight they're looking for, they've come to the right place!" He reached for his dirk, wishing he'd had the forethought to possess himself of a more workmanlike cutlass, still he reflected, the eighteen inches of his dirk's blade should give at least one of the approaching figures a nasty wound, particularly as they did not seem to be carrying any sort of weapon he could recognise. The uniforms they wore puzzled him as he could not recall ever having seen anything like this before. A short stocky man led the way, clad in a dark uniform obviously well tailored and with a short skirtless jacket ending in a stand up collar. The badges on his sleeve were apparently significant since none of the others questioned his authority as they fanned out. There were eight in all, four dressed in the same uniform as the stocky leader but with different insignia, two more in a similar uniform but wearing grey jackets and two on each side, dressed in a rather drab uniform which allowed them to blend with the background.

With a sinking heart he drew the blade and, advancing slightly, adopted a position his fencing instructor would have scorned as being neither "tierce" nor "guardant" but the best he could do with his short dirk as a weapon. The advancing figures stopped and the two in what appeared to him to be some sort of "motley" of dark and light tans and greys, dropped to one knee and pointed short stubby devices in his direction. The short stocky man slightly in the lead and at the centre of the group held up a hand saying sharply, "Steady! No firing unless he tries to shoot first!" Then he advanced a few steps, taking care to keep between the two men crouched and apparently ready to fire some sort of short musket at him.

Harry noted the accent; several of *Spartan's* crew came from the East Coast fishing fleets, but decided to be cautious. After all, it was not unknown for deserters to change sides as well. He tensed, waiting to see what the strangers would do next, wishing desperately that his head did not hurt so, and that his balance was a little surer. He watched as the figure in the vaguely naval uniform paused, and glanced left and right to check the positions of his two apparent guards. Harry decided to take the initiative, after all he reasoned, with these odds and Ferghal injured they stood little chance if the newcomers attacked – and he had not the vaguest idea of where they were anyway. He called, as commandingly as a fifteen year old voice would permit, "That, sir, is close enough until you make yourself and your intentions known!" He hesitated, and then continued, "I am armed and prepared to defend myself and my men!"

"So I see!" grinned the stocky man, "Very well, since you insist, I am Senior Warrant Officer Suddaby," he pronounced it as three syllables, "the Master at Arms of the Confederate Star Ship *Vanguard* and these," he indicated his companions with a wave of his arm, "are the ship's police and Royal Marines. And now, if you don't mind, I'd like to know who you are and what you are doing on this ship!"

Confused, Harry hesitated, then he said challengingly, "Why did you attack us if you are carrying Royal Marines? And they look like no Marines I have ever seen!"

"Us attack you?" the Warrant Officer looked taken aback by this, "we did no such thing! And I'd like to know who you are and how you got here!"

"I, sir, am Midshipman Harry Nelson-Heron of His Britannic Majesty's Ship *Spartan!* But, if you are not French, and this is not a French ship of the line, who are you?" Harry demanded, conscious of a dizziness that threatened to engulf him, and fighting desperately to stay in control of himself. Behind him he heard the boy whimper and Ferghal give a sharp and barely stifled cry of pain. He tried to seize the advantage again and remain at least in appearance in control, "I have a wounded man here; have you a surgeon or loblolly boy who can assist us to get him comfortable?"

*Out Of Time*

"A loblolly what?" demanded the Warrant Officer. "Never mind, yes, I have some medics here," he indicated two people in similar uniforms behind him, "Lower that blade of yours, or better still put it away, and I'll let them come to help you!"

Harry hesitated, then another stifled groan from Ferghal made up his mind for him, "Very well," he called, sheathing the dirk, "send your – medics? – and be sure that if they try anything untoward I shall not hesitate to deal sharply with them and you!"

The Master at Arms said softly over his shoulder, "MedTech de Vries, MedTech Thomas, go forward round to my left – slowly mind – and don't get between the Royals and that young fella! Go!" To Harry he called, "These two Med Techs will make their way over to you along a line on my left. The Royals have you in their sights and will shoot if you make any sudden moves Mister Midshipman, there'll be no attempts at hostage taking on my watch!"

Harry drew himself up to his full height, every bone in his body protesting as he did so, but he flushed with anger at the implied slur to his honour in the last words, "You have my word as an officer that your people are safe as long as they make no attempt on my people! And I take offence at your tone and your impugning of my honour sir!"

"Well, I'm sorry you feel offended, but until I know a hell of a lot more about who you are and where you dropped from, I'll take the precautions I think necessary to protect my people!" snapped Eric in response, a red flush creeping up his face at the youngster's tone!

The two Medics had reached the fallen Ferghal and Harry exclaimed in surprise when he realised that one of them was a woman, "Here, what trickery is this? You have a woman in uniform? In a fighting ship?"

"And why not? They have been serving in space and in all the services for centuries, why should they be different?" snapped Eric.

"But …" began Harry and stopped as his mind registered another strange expression, or had he misheard, "*Space?* You said for *centuries*? Why, what year is this?"

"Twenty-two zero four!" came the reply, "what else should it be?"

Harry felt his head reel as he heard this and staggered slightly, behind him he heard Ferghal sigh deeply and even the boy Danny had become quiet, he turned his head to see what was going on and noted that Ferghal's arm was no longer at a strange angle, in fact it was now encased in some sort of splint and Ferghal appeared to be no longer in pain. Danny seemed to be less frightened and quite enjoying the attention he was getting from the woman. Harry's head reeled again and he felt momentarily sick. He staggered again, and the man who had been attending Ferghal stood quickly and steadied him, saying, "Take it easy Mid, let us have a look at you too, you don't look too good yourself you know!"

"I'm sound my man," gritted Harry, "take care of Ferghal, I must see your Commander! We must be returned to our ship at once!"

"Easy youngster! All in good time!" the MedTech did his best to calm Harry, whose head was now spinning badly, "The Captain will certainly want to see you, but he won't thank us if we haven't made sure you aren't injured!"

Suddenly feeling very tired, weak and rather helpless, Harry surrendered, "Oh very well, if you must, but I must see the Captain as soon as possible!" He knew he was on the point of fainting and fought to stay conscious, desperately staving off the engulfing blackness that threatened to enclose him again.

"Don't you worry sir, you will see him soon enough I think," replied the medic and, as Harry seemed to fold at the knees and began to fall, caught him deftly and laid him gently on the deck. "Master, he's fainted, I think he may have some injuries we need to treat as soon as we can!"

The Master at Arms and the rest of the party hurried across, Eric keying his link and speaking rapidly, "MedCent, three casualties for transport for treatment, chop, chop! Compartment Two-Two-Three-Alpha-Oscar-Charlie! Security, stand down alert, I'm sending the Royals back, inform the Captain we have three casualties on the way to MedCent, one claims to be a Midshipman," he paused and continued half musingly, "of His Britannic Majesty's Ship *Spartan*!" adding under his breath, "This will be one for the grandchildren!"

In the Command Centre the Captain acknowledged the report and then opened a comlink channel to Flight Control Centre, "Wings, we seem to have some casualties from your hangar space. The Master at Arms is taking them to the Med Centre but he reports that they are apparently stowaways or boarders. Since it's your space they were in, I'd appreciate your going down to MedCent and taking a look at them."

*Out Of Time*

"Right away sir," replied Nick Gray, "We don't seem to have any damage to anything vital, but I have my team double checking all our systems anyway!"

"Good, I'll wait for your report! Out."

* * *

Nick hurried out of the Flight Control and made his way aft and down two decks to the Medical Centre, in fact a rather well equipped and staffed miniature hospital. He sought out Surgeon Commander Len Myers and was directed to an isolation suite where he found the ship's senior doctor studying readouts from the monitoring unit now scanning a youth whose pallor under his deep tan did not look healthy. Two Surgeon Lieutenants concentrated on further displays monitoring two more figures in adjoining med units to the first. All three were attended by some of his Surgeon Lieutenants and medical technicians in fully enclosed Isosuits and masks although only the smallest one seemed to be awake and talking. Nick looked again as the medic moved aside and let out an exclamation, "Bloody hell, that's just a kid! How the hell did he get aboard?"

"Are you asking me?" came the dry tones of the Surgeon Commander, "if so, a complete waste of time I assure you! I will tell you though, that none of them have seen a decent bath in weeks. They do seem to have washed at least some time in salt water and they aren't verminous, for which I suppose we can be thankful!"

"Sorry, Doc, rhetorical question!" grinned Nick, "Any ideas on who they might be?"

"A few; but none as urgent as trying to deal with a seriously broken and dislocated arm, a badly sprained ankle and mild concussion in the bigger one, severe concussion and possible internal damage in the other. The youngest is possibly the only one without injury – he seems to have landed on top of the other two," was the laconic reply. He broke off to dictate a string of instructions to the staff beside the sarcophagus like Medunits and the two Lieutenants nodded in agreement. "Right!" he gave Nick a wry smile, "I expect you will want to know who, what, why and how?"

"As ever Len, you are telepathic!" grinned Nick.

"Well, I have taken samples for DNA analysis and we are running

41

that now. So far no verified matches to any known Confederate crew or to any citizen database record for any of the Euro Con nations for the child and the older youth. Of course that doesn't mean they are not from a non-EC nation, but I'd say unlikely. Their injuries are consistent with a fall from about fifteen to twenty feet in height." He paused, and then continued, "The young man who says he is a Midshipman is different. We have an exact DNA match for him on almost every point – except it is impossible. From an injury point of view, he seems to have a lot of internal bruising, but no major damage to any organ, although he has taken a rather nasty knock on the head. Remarkable really, since they seem to have passed through solid metal to get into your hangar!"

"So we still have no idea where they are from?"

"None at all! The youngster says his name is Danny and he doesn't think he's got any other. By the way, he refers to the Midshipman as 'Mister' Heron and the other lad as Ferghal. He says he is a Powder Monkey and ship's boy, but he's no older than eleven at the most and probably nearer eight! Surely the last time any civilised nation sent children to sea must have been in the late nineteenth century?" said Len Myers speculatively.

"You're not suggesting that we've got time travellers here are you? That's not possible!" frowned Nick. He frowned, "and you say the Mid is called 'Heron'?"

"I'm merely repeating what the child has said, I will reserve judgement until I have more facts," retorted Len. He grinned mischievously, "And that is the name I have for him!"

"When can I talk to the Mid?" asked Nick, adding, "and you said there was something odd about his DNA?"

"Certainly not until we have him at least over the concussion. His DNA match is being rechecked but the computer has come up with an exact match for a large part of it. According to the computer he must be a very close relative of the Captain. I'll have to run a few more checks to make sure of the rest, but I rather think we have an interesting anomaly here!" grinned Len.

"The hell you say? The Mid's DNA matches the Owner's? Have you told *him* yet?" frowned Nick, "that's a bit more than an anomaly – especially as the Old Man is single and determined to stay so!"

"Well, with a match this close, he's either got a secret son, or a brother, but – keep that to yourself for now," grinned the Surgeon, "I'll let him know as soon as I have completed the checks. I want to tell him myself!" his grin widened, "and I want to see his reaction to the news – I think he thought he's the last of his family."

\* \* \*

In Engineering Control, Commander Mary Allison heaved a sigh of relief as all her readouts stabilised and the alarms ceased. She double checked the display and then said to her team, "Well done team! We don't seem to have any major problems as a result of our runaway." She smiled at them, then, issued a series of instructions to her staff to run diagnostic checks on all systems and functions in their control. With the prospect of two months in hyperspace, and possibly four or more if they had to find a repair base, they did not need any systems failing unexpectedly.

\* \* \*

In the Science Centre, now occupied by Silke Grüneland and her team, some answers were slowly emerging, but nothing they could do seemed to work when it came to finding contact with their probes. Silke looked up as the comlink attached to her wrist bleeped, keying the pad, she acknowledged the contact and listened as the Captain said, "Doctor Grüneland, I think we may have an answer to your inability to contact your probes. I shall link the information direct to your terminal – and you may like to accompany me to the sickbay. We have some extra passengers your team may find interesting!"

"Thank you Captain, when did this information arrive?" she turned her attention to the computer terminal at the workstation she had taken over, and gasped!

"The data file arrived just minutes before we jumped to hyperspace. According to the recovery team the object was recovered from the sea floor and appears to have been there for about four hundred years. There is a wreck nearby with debris that appears to be from a second one." She heard him give a short laugh, and he continued, "it seems we may have explained a four hundred year old mystery – and a family tragedy!"

"That is certainly one of our probes!" exclaimed Silke, signalling

Thomas Scheffer to her side and indicating the screen, "It appears to have been quite badly handled – certainly the gouge and crush marks indicate an impact of some sort. Ah, I see the remains, yes, that could be our second probe, but it appears to have exploded! That could only mean it had been penetrated and something caused it to decompress one or more of its pressurised systems!"

"So I understand," said the Captain. "Perhaps our new passengers can enlighten us? I will meet you in the Science Centre in five minutes and we can see what they look like."

As he left his Command Console he remarked to Commander Grenville, "This is going to complicate our mission! Better make sure we aren't compromised by this – it could get very ugly!"

❈ ❈ ❈

Calling Thomas Scheffer to her console, Dr Grüneland showed him the images. "I think we can stop looking, one of our probes has been recovered – but it has been submerged on the Indian Ocean floor for four hundred years according to this!"

"I guess that means we will not get the data we hoped for," grinned Thomas, "we had better hope for more luck with our other tasks!"

# Chapter 4

# Counting the cost: HMS Spartan 1804

A brilliant flash lit the Gundeck; Number Eight gun was enveloped in an incandescent flare as a vast shock flung the gun captain and several of his crew violently against the neighbouring guns or to the deck. A hole opened above the gunport and was instantly partly filled by the object that had made it, now jammed between the slewed gun and the deckhead and Number Seven gun on its forward side, but, in the heat of the moment, and with French shot striking the hull, few saw the object clearly or realised its significance. Fewer still saw the object which burst the timbers of the French ship and lodged obscenely partly inside and partly outside the hull destroying two gunports and part of the deck while blocking two more gunports fore and aft of the destroyed ones. Pandemonium reigned for several minutes as the crew of Number 8 gun attempted to free themselves from the wrecked gun carriage and to free their companions still trapped in the tangle of wreckage around it. Only one appeared to be injured, but immediately it was noticed that the Midshipman, powder monkey and one of their number were missing. Flames licked briefly around some tattered lines and then were extinguished when one of the men used a bucket of water kept ready for the purpose of wetting the gun sponge to extinguish them. It took a few moments for the stunned gunners to realise that they were staring at a strange object which seemed to be partly fused to the breech of the gun. The gun and its carriage, though still upright, were in fact unusable, the carriage slewed out of position and fouling Number 7 with the mysterious object jammed between the deck beams and deck head and the guns and wreckage below it. For the moment no one seemed to notice that the French ship had ceased fire – in fact had a gaping hole in her hull matched by a similar, though smaller hole in *Spartan's* planking

*Patrick G. Cox*

and through which protruded part of another of the strange devices.

After a brief moment of disorganisation, the combined efforts of Mr Beasley and Midshipman Tanner, the rapid servicing resumed its well drilled flow, pouring fire into the now crippled Frenchman. The remaining guns kept up their fire, their crews working like men possessed as they sponged, rammed home a new charge and wad, rammed home the ball, trailed onto the tackles and hauled the gun up to it's port, then a jerk of the lanyard, a roar and the gun recoiled back into the crowded deck. Smoke eddied and made eyes sting and throats to choke as the ships closed, the French ship's fire at first sporadic and disorganised, then slowly improving. The Fourth Lieutenant, Mr Beasley, worked his way forward, and called "Mr Heron! Mr Heron! Damme sir, show yourself!" A French ball smashed into the ship's side two guns forward of his position and a shower of splinters scythed across the deck. From the Starboard side, the few remaining men rushed to help the wounded and to fill places among the guns needing attention, while the Fourth, increasingly concerned, continued forward. Finding himself at the wrecked Number Eight gun, he asked one of the men working to clear away the wreckage and free the gun's captain, "Where is Mr Heron?" He paused to stare suspiciously at the metallic thing jammed between the disabled gun and the deckhead, demanding, "What the devil is that thing? Where has it come from? Some sort of damned infernal machine of the Frogs is it?"

"Dunno sir," was the frightened reply. "There were a big flash and Mr Heron, Ferghal and the powder monkey was clean gorn!"

"What mean you gone?" snapped the Lieutenant, pausing to shout, "Mr Tanner! Take charge of Mr Heron's guns! He seems to have been struck down!" Turning to the men again he asked, "What mean you, gone? Where is Wright?" He noted the bloodied figure lying next to the slewed gun carriage, "Ah, I see! Bates, you're the senior, get rid of this infernal thing, I'll send you some hands to help, and get Wright taken to the Surgeon!"

"It come through from behind us sor," came the reply. "Sumptin fierce it were, smashed into the breech and stuck right there! There's another gorn into they Frenchie! Summat big and nasty! Hit Joe in the kisser it did, he's out like a light sor! And Mr Heron were right there sor, him and Ferghal next him and the boy between them. They ain't here now, sor, is all we knows!"

"Thank you Bates, carry on with your work." He peered at the huge 'thing' and at the hole and noted that the splintered timbers all seemed to show something exiting rather than entering the hull. He had a momentary glimpse of the French ship which seemed to have another of the devices embedded in its hull blocking four gun ports, then smoke billowed around them once more and he hurried back to where he could see another gun with wounded round it. He ducked as another ball struck the hull forward and splinters again filled the air, then moved swiftly aft to where he could ensure his gun crews maintained their fire.

Summoning men from the few tending the guns on the disengaged side, he sent some to help clear the fallen Number Eight and several more to replace the fallen at the engaged guns. Then he sent a messenger to the quarterdeck to report the strange device and inform the Captain of his intentions to deal with it.

More crashes and screams from aft told the Lieutenant and his men that the second big French frigate had entered the fray, crossing their vulnerable stern to engage their Starboard side, or worse, to stand off and batter their nearly defenceless stern. Quickly the Fourth Lieutenant took stock and dispatched as many men as he could to the after part of the battery deck and the Starboard guns of the after division. Setting the men to work he set about trying to prepare them to give the Frenchman a warm reception as he came within the firing arc of these aftermost guns. He checked that they were trained round in their ports as far as possible, then that they were loaded with double shot and the biggest charge they dared to use. From the aftermost port he leaned out as far as he could and caught a brief glimpse of the Frenchman as she tacked heavily to cross her consorts stern and *Spartan's*. He quickly realised that she would be too far astern to effectively rake them, but could still do considerable damage with any hits she achieved. Drawing back he looked about him and spotted a scared looking urchin carrying his pair of powder cases, "Here boy," he called, "Run forward and tell Mr Tanner and Mr Petersen to be ready for an attack on our Starboard side. Can you do that?" The boy nodded and ran to do as he was bid, returning a few minutes later to tug the Lieutenant's coat tail and tell him in a frightened voice that Mr Tanner understood, but that Mr

Petersen was dead.

For a moment the Lieutenant didn't grasp the meaning of what the boy was saying, then it sank in and he nodded, "Thank you .." he paused, "What's your name child?" It suddenly seemed important to know this.

The boy looked surprised, and stammered, "Sean, sir."

"Well Sean," smiled the Lieutenant, "See to your duty. And well done." He peered through the port again, with Petersen dead and Heron missing it left just himself and Tanner to control all the guns on this deck. He sent a quick prayer to the Almighty to send some relief from their consorts as he knew they could not fight both batteries against two ships for long, already the 'Butcher's Bill' was higher than they could afford. He looked again, the second French ship was edging into position where she would soon be able to fire into their Starboard quarter – but, if he had his guns slewed far enough, she would also feel their teeth. He turned and walked along his gun captains and gave orders for them to ensure that once they had fired their first double-shotted loads into the newcomer, that they were to reload with Langridge shot – great weighted half balls joined by chain forged links and bars and intended to tear away rigging and masts – in the hope that they could cripple the second ship and reduce her fighting efficiency sufficiently to buy them a little time for their consorts to come up.

Another glance through the open port and he realised with a knotted stomach that the enemy ship was closing fast. He called to his gunners, "Starboard Battery, Stand ready! Gun Captains, as you bear, aim for his hull on this first shot! Make it tell!"

A chorus of agreement came back at him, even as the Larboard guns roared their defiance yet again and further crashes above them told a tale of increasing damage. He placed himself by the aftermost gun and joined the gun captain crouched to peer along the gun. The Frenchman's jib boom, dolphin striker and then his beakhead plunged into view, puffs of smoke showed as his foremost guns belched their first shots, then the gun captain jerked his lanyard and the gun lurched backwards against its breech rope. The smoke had hardly cleared when the next gun roared its spite, followed swiftly by another and then another. The 4th watched anxiously as the Frenchman slowly crept closer, feeling *Spartan's* hull shudder as the other ship's guns made themselves felt while his own seemed to be having little effect. Then his efforts were rewarded, a burst of splinters near one of the French ship's forward gunports was followed swiftly by two more such bursts around her bows.

He jumped aside as the aftermost gun ran up again and the Captain shouted, "We'm loaded with Langridge sor! See if'n we dassent knock her spars about and take some o' their speed off'n 'im!" He jerked the lanyard and Michael Beasley watched as the Frenchman's fore rigging suddenly seemed a little less taut. The next two guns fired almost simultaneously and he had the satisfaction of seeing the Frenchman's foretopgallant suddenly sag, then the yard seemed to fold on itself and he yelled, "Well done lads! Make them feel our shot!"

Almost as he said it, there was a huge explosion on the Larboard side of the ship – a flash that lit the gundeck through the open ports threw everything into stark relief. He rushed to the other side and peered through the nearest gunport to see the first Frenchman settling and rolling towards them, he sensed that the *Spartan's* helm was going hard over, and raced back to the Starboard side! He raised his whistle to his lips and blew long and hard! "Cease fire Larboard battery! Starboard battery ready! Fire as you bear! We will cross his bows! We'll rake him as we do it!"

The gun crews raced to obey even as the ship staggered and plunged as those on deck struggled to keep them clear of the capsizing enemy. Michael Beasley ducked to peer out of the nearest gunport. The other French ship seemed be in difficulties and he heaved a sigh of relief, shouting to his crews, "Standby! Wait until we have tacked, then give him everything we have!"

The ship plunged again and staggered, fighting to come about, the deck heeled steeply and some of the struggling gun crews lost their footing or slipped. A chorus of curses erupted as they fought to keep control of the cumbersome guns. The lieutenant threw his weight against the nearest gun as its reduced crew struggled to hold it. "Come on lads, we have him now!" he yelled as he did so. The ship heaved herself upright, leaned heavily again, then staggered round and heeled slowly to Starboard as she steadied on a new course. The lieutenant steadied himself and placed his whistle to his lips again, a glance through the gunport showed that the remaining French ship now lay almost abeam and bows on to their broadside, he blew his whistle, "Fire as you bear!"

On deck, Captain Blackwood watched the confusion on the remaining French ship's deck as his *Spartan* heeled to her new tack. Even as she did so he felt the shudder as the Starboard batteries began a rolling broadside and the bows of the Frenchman began to suffer the effect of the relentless and shattering fire of the combined batteries of sixteen and twenty four pounder guns. Moments later the Frenchman's bows began to swing to Larboard as her Captain made a desperate attempt to swing his ship away from the fearsome bombardment, and found himself attacked on his Starboard quarter by the newly arrived *Rajahstan,* even as *Spartan's* fire slackened as she drew ahead. He took swift stock of his ship and turned to the First, "Wear ship, Mr Bell, we will finish the business!"

Shouted orders brought the topmen and waisters rushing to the falls and sheets, the helm went over yet again and the great ship plunged round, this time in a jibe, as she turned her stern across the wind, to match course with the Frenchman now heavily engaged by the smaller *Rajahstan*. The Captain spared a moment to study the now capsized French ship and to ponder on the explosion that had so suddenly devastated her. He reflected that there was always the chance of a stray shot striking fire near exposed powder charges, but the explosion he had witnessed seemed almost to have been of an altogether larger quantity than a single charge.

At that moment a smoke blackened midshipman appeared in front of him and he acknowledged the youth's salute, "Yes, Mr Tanner?"

"Mr Beasley's compliments sir, but we have an infernal device of some kind lodged on the lower Gundeck and Mr Beasley asks for some more hands to free it so we can heave it overside ere it does to us what the one on the Frenchman did sir!"

"Does he by God!" exclaimed the Captain, "and he shall have them!" He turned to look for the First Lieutenant, and shouted above the din, "Mr Bell! Take charge here, I am going below to Mr Beasley to see the device he has there! I will require ten additional men to be sent there as soon as you can spare them!"

The First Lieutenant acknowledged the command and walked swiftly over to where the Captain stood, "I shall send them immediately sir, what device is this?"

"Evidently the same as the one which has done for our initial opponent! Come Mr Tanner, let us go to Mr Beasley and see this device!" over his shoulder he added to the First, "Mr Beasley is attempting to move it so it can be jettisoned. I wish to gauge what manner of thing it is before he does so!"

Captain Blackwood followed the youth below, noting the state of the upper battery as he did so, and mentally acknowledging that the casualty list would be a long one! Christopher Tanner led his Captain down to the Lower Battery deck and then forward to where his lieutenant stood watching as a team of men drawn from the now idle guns worked at freeing the jammed gun from beneath the large ovoid metallic device lodged above it. He acknowledged the lieutenant's salute, his eyes on the device. "What is it Mr Beasley? How came it here?"

"We do not know what it might be sir, but I observed another like it lodged in the French ship's side. I think it was that which exploded and sank her," replied the lieutenant, "Mr Tanner tells me that it seemed that one of our balls may have penetrated it as we closed with them for we fired just before the explosion. I did not observe it myself since I was directing the after division of the Starboard guns sir," he added.

"I see," came the reply, "Where is young Mister Heron? Are you and Mister Tanner alone here?"

"We are sir, Mister Petersen fell early in the engagement and Mister Heron and some others are missing. They disappeared at the moment that thing arrived and do not appear to be beneath the wreckage of either gun sir," replied Michael Beasley.

"Well, Mister Beasley, we cannot have that device remain where it is, especially as the remaining Frenchman must be dealt with! I shall send Mr Rogers to assist you and Mister Bell is sending another ten men to your aid. Have a care not to do anything which might cause it to explode, it would be very inconvenient!" the Captain smiled grimly, adding, "I think it will not pass easily through the ports or the opening I see it has started! Best heave it up on deck and we will cast it overside from there!"

"As you say sir!" came the reply, "We are almost able to remove the Number Eight gun. With it gone, we shall have some freedom to drag that device out and perhaps move it to the hatchway. It seems to be unconscionably heavy!"

The Captain returned swiftly to the Quarterdeck, pausing only to direct Lieutenant Rogers on the Upper Gundeck, to assist the Fourth on the lower, explaining the need to move the device carefully. On the quarterdeck he was able to take stock of the battle between *Rajahstan* and the remaining Frenchman and gave orders to close on the embattled pair as swiftly as possible, "I want that damned Johnny Frenchman to know he cannot expect to be allowed any further freedom in these seas Mr Bell. We shall board him as soon as we can get alongside! See to it please!"

The First called to the Master and immediately the course was adjusted as *Spartan* began to close the gap between her and the big French frigate, now hotly engaged by the smaller *Rajahstan* and the even smaller *Swallow*. On the lower gundeck the men worked like men possessed as they slowly and with great ingenuity, drew the damaged Number Eight gun from beneath the device, strops rigged earlier taking the weight of the object as they did so. Then, under the direction of Mr Beasley and supported by the Second Lieutenant, Mr Rogers, they began the delicate and extremely difficult task of moving the thing to a position from which it could be hauled up on deck and finally cast overboard. They had barely completed the first part of this task when orders were passed below to prepare to engage with the available guns as the ship closed in on her prey, so it was secured beneath the hatchway as the men ran to their guns and posts ready to commence firing.

On deck, Captain Blackwood used the signal telescope to observe the activity on the Frenchman's deck as his ship drew slowly closer and he noted with some satisfaction that the big frigate had been boarded by, it appeared, parties from both *Rajahstan* and *Swallow*. He closed the glass with a snap, and called, "Mr Bell, pass the word below, lower battery only to fire on the enemy. Upper battery to belay their guns and stand ready to support boarders!"

"Aye, aye sir!" responded the First, "here, you, Midshipman Horn, run below and pass the word for the upper battery to belay firing, then get to Mr Beasley and Mr Rogers on the lower tier and tell them to engage on my command!"

The youth had barely disappeared below when the Sailing Master called out, "She's struck by God!" He waved his hat in the air, "Damme! The fellow has struck!"

"Mr Bell! Pass the word to the gundecks, to secure the guns!" he

*Out Of Time*

smiled briefly then added, "We will heave too and send a boat with a party of our Marines to assist Captain Winstanley and Captain Bowen, I am sure they will have much need of it. I am going below to see to the removal of that infernal device and discover what has become of Mister Heron and the men with him!"

Calling to the second Lieutenant to accompany him, Captain Robert Blackwood made his way below. The scene on the gundeck was both familiar and surreal in the sense that the strange object was unlike anything he had seen before, and yet seemed almost benign as it squatted now in the space behind the freed guns. He examined it closely, noting the smooth metallic skin, unlike anything he had ever seen produced by any blacksmith, with strange stubby protuberances, some now irreparably bent or broken. It looked harmless enough, but, if those who claimed to have seen a similar device embedded in the now disappeared Frenchman's hull were to be believed, it was some sort of fiendish device of incomparable destruction. "Mr Rae," he commanded, "Have sketches made of this devilish thing, and of the position it was in. Then," he turned to the Fourth Lieutenant, "I desire you to heave it overside as soon as possible Mr Beasley! I want it not aboard my ship!"

"Yes sir!" replied the Lieutenant, "I shall see to it as soon as Mr Rae is satisfied with his sketches."

"Good! Now, explain to me please what you have discovered of Mr Heron's whereabouts."

"That is the damnedest thing sir! We can discover nothing of him or of the powder monkey and a seaman who where all stood close by him when that thing arrived, we know not from where!" Michael Beasley paused, then continued, "The Gun Captain had just stepped aside and fired his lock when he says there was a loud sound as of a thunderbolt and he and the others were thrown to the deck. They thought Mr Heron had been struck by it, but we have found no trace of blood or of their remains!"

"I see," said the Captain, his face stern, "Well Mr Beasley, I desire you and Mr Tanner to take statements from all present, both on this gun and any other who may have seen or heard something. I wish to assemble all the information you can find on it, their Lordships at the Admiralty will wish to have it in my report and there is almost certainly to be an enquiry into this! That Frenchman may well have been the source of this device, if so, he may have been the agent of his own destruction. We shall have to make a very close enquiry to discover which!"

# Chapter 5

# Stranger and still stranger: NECS Vanguard 2204

Doctor Silke Grüneland and Captain James O'Niall Heron studied the items on the table. A rather dangerous looking short sword with an eighteen inch long blade and a simple guard for the hand on the hilt sat exposed next to its scabbard, alongside this lay a utilitarian knife with a large heavy blade and something that looked like a knife without an edge. Several items of clothing were also laid out, all smelling slightly of unwashed human bodies, a scent totally unfamiliar in the Twenty-third Century – at least in the space faring nations! They stared at the worn and slightly stained uniform coat the Surgeon Commander held up to their inspection. It seemed very old fashioned, smelled vaguely of a sort of salty musk and seemed to have been made of very coarse fibre. They were sat in the Surgeon Commander's office, a larger than usual space which doubled as a conference room for the medical staff and could also be converted swiftly into a recovery and treatment room.

The garment was blue/black – except where it had faded or been bleached by the sun to a sort of blackish green – and trimmed with white edging to the open front, the cuffs and the stiff stand-up collar which also bore white patches with piping along the centre denoting rank, and gold, albeit very tarnished, buttons in a double row down the front and around the cuffs. It had seen a great deal of use and had been somewhat inexpertly patched at the elbows and on the skirt, but was obviously a jacket intended to show that the wearer held a rank in some fighting service. "The trousers the wearer of this jacket had on are here. Like this they appear to be made of a natural fibre and bleached but not dyed. The older youth was wearing these," he held up a pair of very coarse trousers made of some heavy material which showed several stains and much wear, "and a rather coarse shirt which we had to cut away as I didn't want to pull it over his head until I could be sure of his injuries. Their underclothes are rather simple and the cloth is not much better either! I have placed those in a separate container as they are somewhat," he grinned, "ripe! Clean underclothes obviously happened rarely, but it should provide plenty of interesting material for the labs!"

"I don't think I have ever seen cloth like that," mused the Captain, "but I have seen jackets like that one – or at least pictures of them!"

"The cloth is a natural fibre," said Doctor Grüneland, feeling the nap with her finger and thumb, "I would suspect it to be something called wool or perhaps what used to be called –" she paused to think carefully, "in English, 'Barathea'. My people could analyse it for you if you wish."

The Surgeon studied her for a moment, "No need, Doctor, my analysis equipment has already confirmed exactly what you said. It is wool, or at least the jacket is, as you said, it is a cloth type called Barathea – last made, according to our database, around one hundred years ago." He reached across and pulled out the shirt taken from the unconscious Midshipman, "this shirt is made of something called Indian Cotton, it was grown extensively and could be woven into a rather fine soft cloth which was quite expensive I believe. The other boy's shirt was made with coarser cotton and his trousers of a canvas material, both last produced at least a hundred years ago. The child is dressed in rags for the most part which appear to have been hand down clothes modified to fit him."

"Well, here we have a mystery then, because the style of that jacket, and certainly of the clothes that the others are wearing were worn by officers and men of the British Royal Navy no later than around eighteen-sixty – almost four hundred years ago!" exclaimed the Captain. He glanced at Doctor Grüneland, and asked, "Do you think it is possible we have triggered some sort of time warp which has snatched them from that period?"

"I do not say it is *unmöglich* – it is not previously recorded and should not be possible!" she grinned and added, "But, my predecessors in the Twenty-first Century would have described a *tachyon* as unlikely or impossible, yet we now know that they not only exist, but that hyperspace is their only natural environment." She grew serious for a moment, "If we have time travellers, you do realise that the scientific community will want to study them closely – perhaps even demanding our immediate return?"

"They might, but they won't get their wishes granted," replied the Captain with a tight smile, "Now Len, what else can you tell us about these boys?"

The Surgeon explained at some length the reasons for the boys being in an isolation lab, tended only by staff in isolation suits and the physical state of all three boys, their likely ages and the strange and rather quaint use of English they all shared. "The eldest is a strong youth of about eighteen years; he has a head injury and a badly broken right arm. Nothing we can't fix fairly easily. He also has a sprained ankle and some pretty severe bruises. It looks as if the others landed on top of him and that they all fell from about five to ten feet up in the air." He paused, and continued thoughtfully, "Almost as if they were taken from something about that height in exchange for the equipment we lost."

"There was nothing mounted at that height in the hangar deck, so that may simply be displacement due to motion," mused the Captain and Dr Grüneland nodded.

"The boy whose coat you have just examined is around fifteen years old and seems to be concussed, as if he struck his head on something, possibly when he fell or the youngest fell on top of him. That apart, he is healthy and although badly bruised seems to have few other injuries. We have checked for internal injury but they seem to have been lucky in that regard," continued the Surgeon, "and the youngest could be about eight or nine, certainly no older than eleven at most, although it is very difficult to tell since he seems to have been undernourished as an infant. He is otherwise fine, but terrified. We have had to sedate him so we can concentrate on getting the other two back into shape."

"Any idea who they are, or where they have come from Len?" asked the Captain.

"Well I have run a DNA check on all three and have some interesting results. They all fall into Haplotype R1b which means they are all North European in origin and have a mix of Celtic and Nordic antecedents with Germanic connections as well. They don't come up in any database held by any national resource since records began on European populations in 2057, but they do all have matches in their DNA to people alive today." he paused, adding mischievously, "one in particular has a very close relative aboard this ship!"

The Captain nodded, considering the implications carefully and missed the Surgeon's carefully suppressed grin, "Right, well, I suppose that could be expected if they are from a North European origin, but you say there is no record of them in the last hundred and fifty years?"

"None at all, apart from one very close match aboard this ship."

"Oh yes," the Captain paused, sensing the Surgeon's amusement, "out with it Len, who do you have in your sights?"

Dr Grüneland watched the interplay between the two men with interest; she could sense the Surgeon Commander's amusement was also tinged by a professional interest which had been stirred by something he had discovered. She interrupted, "This DNA match; is it based on Y-chromosome or Mitochondrial DNA?"

"On the Y matches," replied the Surgeon, "and the most interesting one of the three is the young man whose coat we are looking at. His DNA suggests that he is your brother or possibly your son, sir." He watched the Captain's face as he said it, and was satisfied by the flicker of surprise he saw register there.

"Well, Len, sorry to disappoint you, but I have neither!"

✳ ✳ ✳

While the Surgeon Commander, the Captain and the chief scientist were engaged in this a member of the MedCentre staff made an excuse to leave her station and went to one of the accommodation units used by the junior medical staff. Inside the small cabin, it was the work of a few moments to call up a screen, insert a small device not unlike a Twenty-first Century memory stick into a port, and a few minutes later to close this down, remove the device and exit the cabin. On earth, the message at first excited no real interest, until it reached a scientist whose role was to check incoming items of this nature and assess them for potential impact upon his company. One glance told him this could be what his employers had wanted for some time – and within the hour, certain bureaucrats and ministers were being approached to have the three boys arrested, impounded or in some way seized and handed over to the researchers employed by the commercial Foundation that made such generous contributions to their lifestyles.

※ ※ ※

In Engineering, Mary Allison went through her damage reports with her staff. "So we have one generator offline with a burned out winding and three consoles which have damaged relays to the main computer interface in our part of the ship. Then we have damage to the transport shuttle maglift system in the vicinity of the cross hangar at Frame Two-Two-Three and some AG units at below normal output in Decks Four and Five between Frames Five-Zero and Six-Two. All drive systems are operating at optimum. Have I missed anything?"

"Nothing Boss," grinned her second, Stuart Browne, "but I hear tell that the boys and girls in the forward compartments are nursing a few bruises from having the AG go off and then come back online at twice the usual level. Gravity bites I guess!"

"You know it," she laughed in reply, "Any lasting damage to anyone?"

"Nope, Lennie the Sawbones gave them all a clean bill after a check." He paused, "but I did hear he has three casualties in the iso-unit from the hangar deck."

"What? But that area was supposed to be cleared of all personnel!"

"It was, but we picked up some passengers in exchange for all that power grabbing junk apparently!" Stuart grinned at her surprise, "The Owner is in MedCent now according to his comlink so I guess the buzz must be on the nail!"

"Stuart, one day that ability of yours to get information that isn't general knowledge or is screwed down and labelled classified, will get you into hot water!" she grinned, "But it is useful to have your constant supply of juicy information up my sleeve – so don't get caught out!" Her comlink chirped, and she keyed the response, "Allison."

"Mary, I'd appreciate it if you could get one of your spanner wielding team over here, that little dose of heavy G you gave us a little while ago has warped some of my weapons control panels and we need to carry out a check to make sure nothing inside is likely to fail on us if we need to use the main weapons," came the dry voice of Valerie Petrocova. "We're still running diagnostics so we may have some more surprises!"

"Sorry about the heavy G Val," laughed Mary, "the result of losing some of the precious scientific stuff that was pulling all my spare power capacity." She nodded to Stuart Browne, and he eased himself out of his chair and called one of the Technical Ratings to him, "We'll get someone to you in the next couple of minutes."

To Lieutenant Commander Browne she said, "Right Stuart, break time is over, get along to the hangar deck and take Lieutenant Callaghan with you, better take a couple more of the Techrates as well and see what damage we have in the hangar. I just know the Flyboys will be screaming blue murder if any of the power outlets they like to plug their interceptors into aren't working!" She turned to one of her Warrant Officers, "Get over to Weapons, they need some help."

* * *

In Weapons Control Valerie Petrocova swore. To her Lieutenant Commander and second in command she said, "We've lost the power supply to the main weapon! Get the Tech Team onto it immediately; from what the Captain has told us, there is a good chance we could need it! I want it back online asap!"

"I'm on it!" responded the second, calling to one of the senior Warrant Officers and moving swiftly to get a team together.

Valerie made a report to the Command Centre, discussing the problem with the Exec, Richard Grenville, commenting "If we are to have another *'Revenge* in the Azores' situation to face we'd better have the weapons to do it!"

"I think I agree – my famous namesake notwithstanding!" retorted the Exec with a laugh, "I think I should avoid his, no doubt magnificent, example!"

# Chapter 6

# Where is Mr Midshipman Heron? HMS Spartan 1804

Robert Blackwood sat in the great cabin of his ship as the cabin slowly returned to its normal appearance. All through the ship the sound of hammers or mallets rang as the Carpenter and his mates set about making good the damage. Examination of the area around the point of impact by the strange device they had toiled to heave up on deck and then carefully hoisted overside (whereupon it had sunk like a stone once released), had revealed that the lower part of the mainmast was seriously split, apparently by the object as it had entered. Even now, he knew, the Carpenter was working to fit a truss about the damage in the hope that this would enable them to reach a place where the mast could be stripped, drawn and repaired or replaced.

Before retiring to his restored cabin he had visited the Orlop Deck where the surgeon had been having a busy time of it. Fortunately it seemed that they had suffered few deaths thus far, but several men were in serious case having had an arm or leg removed. Others were perhaps more seriously, if insidiously wounded by the terrible splinters which resulted from the shattering of the ship's structure under cannon fire. Splinter wounds almost invariably festered and even the most superficial could result in a painful and unpleasant death from gangrene if the victim was unfortunate. Thus far the butchers bill was ten killed and sixty wounded with three more missing. Among those killed were two of his midshipmen and a third, Midshipman Barclay, lay wounded with a leg removed. A fourth, Midshipman Heron, was missing, leaving the ship seriously short handed for officers as he had lost the fifth lieutenant to fever in the East Indies a year before and now the loss of four Midshipmen meant that his remaining officers would have additional duties to cover that would normally be assigned to the midshipmen.

*Out Of Time*

Abeam lay the captured French forty-four, a fine frigate named *Mistral* and to one side of his desk lay a transcript of a report from her surviving officers of their mission in the Indian Ocean. Her consort, *le Revolution*, also a forty-four gun frigate, had taken most of her crew with her in her death roll, although, as Captain Blackwood well knew, a wooden ship would take many months to sink entirely to the bottom. Her survivors had mainly been topmen, her Commander and the majority of his officers having gone down with their ship. The surviving officer, an arrogant young man from an émigré family who had been raised in England until his family returned after Napoleon Bonaparte had seized control of France, had clearly been under the impression that the device which had caused the destruction of his ship had come from *Spartan*. An impression reinforced by his arriving aboard just as the similar device on *Spartan* had been finally swayed up the companionway and dropped overside. Little information could be gained from him as he spat imprecations about the perfidy of the English and their devil weapons, but one item did strike through. No one had seen the device arrive; one minute it wasn't there, the next it was embedded in the ship's hull and two of their guns and a considerable portion of the hull and deck was not! Apparently none of their men had been injured or killed by it – until it suddenly exploded after attempts had begun to widen a split in the casing or its being struck by several of *Spartan's* shot in a broadside. Captain Blackwood mused deeply on this as he pondered his report and his journal.

Then there was the problem of his missing Midshipman, boy seaman and powder monkey. They had, seemingly, vanished into thin air! With a sigh, he reached into his desk for his personal journal, found his quill and inkpot, and thoughtfully re-cut the pen. His servant appeared with a glass of claret and carefully placed it within his reach even as he began to write. He wrote for several minutes then paused to think carefully, absent-mindedly sipping the wine, then resumed his writing. He glanced up as there was the sound of the familiar 'thump, thump' of a musket butt, the signal that one of his officers was about to knock, "Enter!" he called, laying aside the pen and closing the inkpot. "Ah, Mr Rae," he greeted as the second lieutenant opened the door, "Come in and take a chair sir! Some claret perhaps?"

"Thank you sir," responded the second, "I have the statements from all those on the lower Gundeck for you, and my sketches of the device."

"Good, good, I will study them directly. Have you any answers to the question of what manner of thing it was, or, more important, from whence it came?" he nodded as the servant placed a glass in front of the lieutenant and made to refill his own, "Perhaps you can tell me in summary what the men saw?" He accepted the roll of drawings from the lieutenant and stretched them out to study them.

"Aye sir, the men say there was a very bright flash and the thing was lodged between the deckhead and the Number Eight gun, half obstructing Number Seven. The deck beams and planking are certainly strangely reduced at that point, almost as if some device had sawn or adzed them away. Part of Number Eight gun is missing as well sir," said the lieutenant.

"As I can see from your excellent drawings Mr Rae! Is anything else adrift?"

"Yes sir, the ramrod, sponge and wad hook are there, but one of the training spikes is gone as is the flexible rammer and the rack is gone as well. So are the powder cases the boy was holding and a few other fittings beside. The damage to the mainmast appears to be related to it as well sir, the iron bands have been partly destroyed and the mast has a section missing, yet no trace of splinters or of the debris one would expect from a strike from by a ball."

"Any sign of what became of the three missing men?"

"None sir. No blood, and no trace of their fate." He paused to take a drink from his glass, and added reflectively, "it is almost as if they were entirely replaced by the thing that struck us."

The Marine sentry's musket thumped twice outside the door, and simultaneously a heavy knock fell upon it. In answer to the Captain's summons, the tall broad figure of the first lieutenant entered.

"Ah, Thomas!" greeted the Captain, "Mr Rae tells me that the damage from the device is unusual and that there is no trace whatever to give a clue to the fate of Mr Heron and the two who were with him. Have you any word from our prisoners and the survivors of *le Revolution* that would give us a better lead?" He grimaced, "Lieutenant Renault seemed to think it was yet another of perfidious Albion's dastardly devices and apparently knew very little about it!"

"Do we know anything more sir?" smiled Thomas Bell, "I'd wager my share of the prize money that we don't!"

"Very true Thomas, and I fear you would ruin me if I accepted! Mr Rae here has made some excellent sketches of the damnable thing, but nothing tells us what it was or from whence it came!"

"Well, I have with me the notes taken from the interviews with the survivors. None seem to have much idea as to whence it came, except that they all think we fired it from some hidden gun. They all describe a brilliant flash of light at the moment it arrived, saying that it seemed somehow to just arrive – one minute not there, the next there!"

"Exactly as our own people describe the arrival of our device!" the Captain exclaimed, "I wonder if they are in some way linked?"

The discussion now turned to the damage and how it could be repaired. The mast was of particular concern as the Captain learned that a survey of the damage had revealed that the pressure of the reduced sail they were carrying to remain hove too, was even now threatening the weakened mast. Mr Bell assured him that the Carpenter and his mates were already at work to try and build a 'splint' to support it until such time as it could be drawn from the hull and rebuilt. Already the shot holes sustained during the battle had been plugged - the Carpenter and his mates kept a regular stock of such plugs to ensure they could stop such damage speedily – and the chain pumps were now reducing the water in the hold very rapidly.

"Ideally, of course, sir, we should put in to Simon's Bay and carry out repairs, but it is now in Dutch hands again, and I fear we would receive a rather warm welcome should we show our faces there!" remarked the First.

"Indeed Thomas, so what alternatives have we on this?"

"There are several bays along the coast which we have reason to believe are not guarded or garrisoned. If we could find a suitable place, such as the anchorage at Algoa Bay – sadly, guarded by a fort we built for just that purpose – we might be able to lower the topmasts and careen the ship to draw the mast, but the Sailing Master tells me that even that bay is very exposed at this season. Sailing north would give us access to shelter among the island groups, but I believe we would not find suitable timber there!"

"What a damnable situation! You confirm my thoughts Thomas; it seems we have no choice but to attempt to reach St Helena, a damnably long way to sail under reduced canvas – especially around the Cape!"

"If I may sir," offered Mr Rae, "There is the Portuguese colony at Delagoa Bay – we may find the resources that we need there, and it lies very close to our present latitude and thus should be relatively easy sailing to reach."

"Well done Mr Rae, I think you may have hit the very thing we need! A chart Thomas, we need a chart – and Mr Wentworth the Master!"

❉ ❉ ❉

Some six hours later, and with a freshening wind from the North-North West, *Spartan* was once more underway with canvas reduced to ease the pressure and strain upon her mainmast. The sloop *Swallow* maintained a scouting watch ahead of the wounded seventy-four and her consort HMS *Rajahstan*, towing a disabled Indiaman named *Minerva*, while the captured French forty-four, *Mistral*, lay to leeward of the *Spartan*, her prize crew enhanced by a large Marine contingent. The French officers and all of their Warrant Officers had been taken from the ship and distributed among the three British ones to reduce the likelihood of an attempt to recapture her – something Captain Blackwood was determined to prevent. The voyage would be a slow one he knew, and there was also a degree of uncertainty as to their reception even though he knew that General Wellesley was doing well in defending Portugal itself from the French occupiers of neighbouring Spain. Still, the small colony would have the facilities he desperately needed if his ship was to be fit to make the voyage round the Cape and through the Atlantic. At least he had a fair wind he reflected as he sipped a glass of claret. He looked at the patterns on the dancing wake beneath his windows made golden by the setting sun and wondered at the fate of the young Midshipman so strangely lost. The boy had been full of promise he reflected and would be a sad loss to both the ship and his family. He thought of his report, the draft written and now locked away in his desk, and reflected that there was not much more he could say or do. The ship had been searched "from truck to keelson", as the saying was, and no trace could be found of young Heron or the young seaman, O'Connor, nor yet of the powder monkey known as Daniel Gunn – a euphemism

*Out Of Time*

which indicated he was the son of a seaman and a bumboat woman – and his report contained all the details together with the drawings of the device they had extricated and thrown overside.

His interviews with their French captives had thrown even less light on the devices – or what had caused the one embedded in the *le Revolution* to explode the way it did. The one they had manhandled overboard had resisted all attempts to pierce it or to dismember it, thus, he could only conclude that it must have been some internal mechanism which had caused it to explode and he had to admit that it was certainly the most violent explosion he could recall. His thoughts were interrupted by the familiar "tap-tap" of the sentry's musket. "Come" he called as a firm knock sounded on the door. He looked towards the door, suddenly conscious of the fact that his servant must, at some time, have lit the lamps in his cabin, "Ah, Thomas, what new problem have we developed?"

"None that I know of sir," smiled the first lieutenant, "but I thought I should remind you of our invitation to dine in the Wardroom tomorrow with our French guests?"

"Of course Thomas, and how is *Capitaine* de Villiers accepting our hospitality?"

"He is expressing his satisfaction with our arrangements sir, in fact he admitted that he would have wished to do the same to us had the position been reversed."

"I make no doubt of that!" returned the Captain wryly. He thought for a moment, then continued, "I have been thinking Thomas. I must write, of course, to the parents of our Midshipmen lost in the engagement. Two are relatively easy to do, but I know the Heron family – or at least Master Heron's uncle in the City – and I really have a difficulty in how to phrase the events that have led to his demise!" He took another sip of wine and continued, "we seem to have no evidence at all of his death, nor yet of the manner of his leaving us! Is it possible that he could have boarded the Frenchman and been lost when she blew up and sank? Could he have been the architect of that event?"

"Most unlikely sir if I may say so. The captain of Number Eight gun is most insistent that young Heron was stood with O'Connor and the powder monkey next the breech of the gun between Numbers Seven and Eight. The captain of Number Seven confirms this, even saying that

Harry had told the boy to stand betwixt him and O'Connor while they waited the signal to fire!" replied Thomas Bell. "All our witnesses speak of the same thing – a great flash of light and suddenly that device was there and the trio were not!"

"That, Thomas, is what troubles me most!" said the Captain heavily.

# Chapter 7

# Discovering the new realities: Vanguard 2204

Harry struggled to clear the disorienting confusion from his mind. His head seemed filled with a foggy haze which prevented him from seeing properly or moving. Gradually his senses cleared and he realised with shock, then fright and finally outrage that he could not move because he was encased in some sort of metallic – at least that is what he thought it must be – sarcophagus, with only his head protruding, and that supported and restricted in movement by some sort of helmet which seemed to be attached to the device enclosing the rest of him. The lighting in the chamber seemed to be very dim, but Harry was blessed with excellent night vision - a handy attribute when keeping a night watch at sea – and could make out the fact that the walls seemed to be lined with materials similar to that which formed the device enclosing him. Strange equipment, the like of which he had never seen before, seemed to be placed or attached to the walls and to the device in which he lay. Moving his head as far as the helmet would allow, he was able to determine that there were at least two more of the devices in which he was imprisoned in the chamber and these appeared to be occupied as well – the nearest holding Ferghal, whose profile he could just discern on the edge of his field of vision, allowing him to guess that Danny must be in the third.

His anger at this treatment boiled up and he began to struggle to try and lift the upper part of the device in order to escape. Nothing seemed to be prepared to give, no matter how hard he struggled and the confines of the device were so limited that he hardly had any purchase at all. After a very few minutes he was forced to give up frustrated, angry and flushed with exertion. It was then that he noticed that lights had begun to flash on several of the devices mounted on the walls and that somewhere else and insistent buzzing sound was just audible. He had barely noted this when a door slid open with a soft hiss, at least, he assumed it was a door since it was like no other he had ever seen, and two strangely dressed figures hurried into the chamber! From what little he was able to see in the dim light they looked barely human, apparently glowing softly as the light caught them, and his childhood in Ireland came rushing back! The Banshee – a spectre that folklore says perches on the roof of the house of a person about to die and wails frighteningly – sprang instantly into his mind! He put an almost superhuman effort into bursting out of his prison and yelled in fright, "Begone you fiends! You shall have none of us! In the name of God, begone!"

The figures checked in their stride, and one said, at least, it appeared to Harry that the figure spoke, but he could see neither mouth nor any other orifice through which it could speak, "Easy now! Easy, you're safe! The treatment unit is just to accelerate your recovery!"

"Let me out of here!" shouted Harry, struggling in the confinement of the unit, "I know nothing of this thing! If you mean to torture us, you will learn nothing from us!"

Another figure entered the chamber, this one at least, as far as Harry could see, was human, a tall slim and rather aquiline featured man with piercing eyes and wearing the dark blue uniform he had seen before. Joining the two strange figures, he addressed them, saying, "Wait in the monitoring station. Oh, and you can shed the suits, they aren't carrying anything infectious!" He turned to Harry, "Now then young man, calm down please! You are not in any danger and you and your friends are simply receiving treatment for the scrapes and bruises you got arriving aboard!"

"M'suie!" protested Harry in appalling French, "This is outrageous, we are prisoners of war and I am an officer! Why are we confined?"

"I'm sorry lad," frowned the Surgeon Commander, "I do not understand the language you are speaking, in fact I think it has defeated even our supposedly 'universal' translators! Would you mind speaking English?"

"Sir," gritted Harry, his face flushed, "If you are French, I must protest! Why are we confined in this manner? And what have you done to us?"

"Me? French?" Len laughed, "God forbid! My God, that's rich!

French? No lad, you are in the Medical Facility aboard NECS *Vanguard*. You and your companions took a few knocks when you came aboard, a feat of quite some magnitude I have to say, and we have placed you in our isolation chamber and into treatment units which help your body regenerate the damaged tissue."

"But ...," began Harry, confused, "if you are not French, then who are you? And what is this that you speak of? Regenerate tissue? What is this?" He had a sudden terrible thought, "Ferghal! You have not taken his arm? You must not! It was a clean break with no wound, it can be set, if done with care!"

"What?" Len looked puzzled for a moment, "Take his arm? Why the devil would we want to do that?" He studied Harry for a long moment, then said slowly, "Ah, I begin to understand! This could be difficult to explain, but I had better try. Your friend is going to be OK; we have set his fracture and reset his dislocated shoulder, in another few hours he'll be fully recovered. You young man, had a nasty crack on the head and suffered a concussion – you do know what concussion is?" He saw the blank look, and nodded, "let me explain it this way, have you ever seen a man who has been hit on the head by something heavy?"

"Yes," replied Harry carefully, "Tom Carrol, the Foretopman, was struck by a loose block and laid out. When he came to he knew not where he was and then was ill for three days."

"That would be right, a very severe case of concussion," said Len, continuing, "that is similar to what happened to you. Do you remember what happened when you came aboard?"

Harry thought hard, "A little," he said finally, "we fell into a large hall or chamber and I struck my head as I landed on Ferghal – and Danny came down on top of me. When I awoke there was a party of men – except one was a woman ...." His voice trailed off, "We parleyed and I allowed them to send forward some ..," he searched for the word, "medics to see to Ferghal. One of them was impertinent and suggested he should see to me as well - and then I fainted I think!"

"You did," nodded Len, "and you were then brought here where we can treat your injuries. How do you feel now?"

"Rested, I thank you," replied Harry suspiciously.

"Hmmm! Well you were just about healed until you set about trying to break your way out of the unit, now you have given yourself," he consulted an illuminated panel out of Harry's vision, "mild muscle strain in your lower back, shoulders and abdomen. Does anything feel as if it's stretched or pulled?"

Harry looked surprised, "Indeed! My stomach muscles feel a little like a cramp and my shoulders as well."

"OK, we'll soon have that fixed," grinned Len, apparently pressing a number of points on the panel, "now, just take it easy will you young man, no one here is going to kill, hurt or otherwise do you any harm. As soon as we are sure that you are fully recovered, we will let you out of the treatment unit and see about how we sort this out from there." He broke off as a loud wail from the unit on the far side of the unit occupied by Ferghal penetrated his eardrums, wincing, he said, "It sounds as if the youngest member of your party is awake! I'll have to leave you now to report to the Captain," he turned to the woman Medical Technician who entered at the run, "MedTec de Vries, can you deal with the youngster please! Before he does himself or my ears any further injury! If possible!" He waited until the wails had subsided a bit then asked, "Before I go young man, what is your name and rank?"

"Harry Nelson-Heron, Midshipman, sir, of His Britannic Majesty's Ship *Spartan*."

"Well, Mid, I am Surgeon Commander Len Myers, of the Starship *Vanguard*," He grinned, "Heron did you say? Well I'll be damned! Now, relax and rest, my staff will take good care of you all."

✳ ✳ ✳

Three decks down and almost five hundred metres forward of the sickbay, Silke Grüneland addressed several members of her team. "We may have a project to get started on in advance of the original purpose for your accompanying this trip," she said to the four people present. "Doctor Williams, your socio-history team and Doctor Maartens your xeno-biology team may have an opportunity to commence work immediately." Both men expressed interest and surprise, as she continued, "Our probes, intended to track the extent of the gate anomaly have been recovered – but without any really usable information gained. One survived, but on the seafloor of the Indian Ocean! We may have lost the probes, but in exchange we have gathered a number of artefacts, including," she paused, "three youths who appear to come from the distant past."

The buzz of interest from the others was immediate and Doctor Williams spoke up, "Doctor Grüneland, if they are, this presents us with a truly remarkable opportunity to learn first hand about the period they come from! We must begin interviewing and observing them immediately!"

"Please call me Silke, it is much less formal!" smiled Dr Grüneland, "and, yes, I agree, but they are presently being treated for minor injuries in the Medical Centre and we cannot do anything until they are declared healed and safe from any infection we may carry – or they could give us."

"Rhys," began the other, continuing, "I understand that Silke, but what an opportunity to study the impact of sudden exposure to our period on people from the past! How soon are we able to have access – oh, and my colleague, Doctor Bischof is a psychologist, he will need to be included in the team to study them!"

"Certainly," Silke smiled, "but we must also remember that they are not zoological specimens, this will need to be handled very carefully. One more thing, the Captain requires that there is to be no communication of their presence to anyone. He has already communicated with his *Admiralstab* and they have ordered that there is to be no word of this until they authorise it. Please assemble your staff and I will brief them in an hour in this room." Turning to the xeno-biologist, she said, "Frederik, you will be wondering what you have to do with apparently human subjects?"

Doctor Maartens smiled, "Silke, knowing you and your sense of humour, no, I am sure you will surprise me!"

"Spoilsport," she laughed, "The Surgeon Commander asked if we could assist his staff in the Med Centre with this. These boys are carrying antigens to bacteria and virus that we have not seen for at least two centuries. He suggests that some of these could be useful to us should we encounter anything similar on some of the worlds we will be visiting."

"I will have my team in this Med Centre in five minutes!" he exclaimed rising to his feet, "I was right, you have surprised me!"

"It will take you at least ten minutes to get there!" she laughed, "even if you all run all the way! Surgeon Commander Myers is a very shrewd Doctor and I suspect knows a great deal more about these things than he tells us. I am sure you will find it interesting!" Turning to the remaining pair, she smiled and said, "Your tasks will be to document everything, especially the wreckage that you will find in the hangar bay. I want it recorded, analysed and preserved, the Captain has given orders that it is not to be moved until we are finished, so get to work please. Since it may give us some indication of what is happening when that gate is used – and where our probes have gone – I want a very thorough examination please."

* * *

The excitement of the scientists aboard *Vanguard* was matched by the interest of a team currently seated in a board room in a building in a remote mountain sanatorium in the east of the European Confederation. The Chairman had just outlined almost exactly the same sentiments as the scientists, but with one important difference, "Gentlemen, we have an opportunity to acquire the DNA of some pre-nuclear humans. I do not need to tell you the value to our organisation of being able to use this for our genetic engineering and reconstruction programmes! In addition, we have the opportunity to use these boys in some of our alien/human genetic experiments. I have been in contact with the Ministry and I have every confidence they can get the ship recalled – if not, it is destined for Pangaea and we have people there who can secure them for us!" He smiled at the other members, in rather the same way that a snake surveys potential meals, and finished, "And the Chairman of our major backers informs me that the moment is rapidly approaching for their taking full control of the Fleet and its resources. I expect that we will have these boys in our hands very swiftly."

* * *

Deep inside the hull, Nick Gray and his second in command of the strike squadrons, Lieutenant-Commander Karl Pedersen, surveyed the wreckage that had replaced the missing pods. Several things stood out, among them a simple wooden lever, about five feet in length with a shaped end, obviously used to apply leverage to something, two closed wooden cylinders with rope handles and several pieces of crudely (to their eyes) worked iron and some heavy pieces of timber. A little further away lay a pile of broken timbers, all somehow joined by pieces of beams and some heavy pulleys with lines still attached. Poking from beneath the timbers was the unmistakeable black muzzle of a large calibre cannon and another was just discernable deeper beneath the wreckage.

"I'm not sure I like the look of those!" exclaimed Nick, "I hope to hell they aren't what I think they are – and if they are – I hope like hell they aren't loaded!"

Lieutenant Commander Pedersen crouched to study the object, "Bad news Boss," he said in his slightly accented English, "they are cannon – but the only way we can find out if they are loaded is to push something into it to see how far it goes," he grinned and added, "and I don't volunteer!"

"Great! Thanks for the sharp appraisal of the situation! I knew I could rely on the ship's only Viking to be so eager to solve the problem for me!" laughed Nick and the other grinned broadly.

"I might be the Viking, but we were always the winners because we always made sure it was someone else doing the dying for us! We weren't stupid you know!" laughed his companion.

"True!" grinned Nick, "what do you make of those wooden cylinders, they look like some sort of buckets, but why the lids?"

"Never seen anything like them before," answered the other, "should we take a look or let the scientists do the dangerous bit?"

"Better leave it to the scientists!" grinned Nick, "it might be vital to their investigation or something, but I think I'll make sure I'm here when they open them!"

※ ※ ※

Len Myers entered the Captain's anteroom and acknowledged the greeting of the Captain's Clerk. "Good evening Adriana, an eventful day!"

"It certainly has been sir; go straight in the Captain's waiting for you!"

Len thanked the writer and stepped forward as the door hissed silently open, to find the Captain seated in an easy chair studying his tablet. He looked up and smiled, "Ah, Len, what have you got on our new passengers?"

"Some interesting responses to being confined in the medunit for a start," grinned Len, "a name for our young officer and some interesting bio-data on them."

"You mean they're non-human?"

"No, they're human all right, but carrying antigens to bacteria and viral diseases that we have not seen in Europe since the Twenty-first Century!" responded the Doctor accepting the offer of a seat indicated by the Captain.

"Ah! Anything that could prove dangerous to us?"

"Not any more, but more importantly we can use these antibodies to manufacture vaccines for all our people which will increase the protection we have against similar bio-agents we might encounter elsewhere." He laughed, "you should have warned me the science team included a xeno-biologist and socio-psychologist on their team – my staff are having to hold them back, they're that keen to get their hands on the boys DNA, tissue and blood samples and into their heads!"

"Well, I hope they remember the youngsters aren't lab rats or something!" smiled the Captain, then he recalled, "You said you had a name?"

"Yes, I do. The young Midshipman says he is Harry Nelson-Heron," he said carefully, watching the Captain's face.

"Harry Nelson-Heron?" responded the Captain in surprise. "Are you sure?"

"As I'm sitting here!" said Len, noting with interest the Captain's response, "Have you heard of him before?"

"Heard of him?" said the Captain absently, "Yes, you could say that. There is a plaque in an old church near where my family had an estate until the mid-twentieth century with that name on it. It says that he was lost at sea in a battle with French ships in eighteen-O-four. I think the name of the ship concerned was *Spartan*, but I may be wrong." He paused thoughtfully, then said slowly, "there was another name on the plaque, that of a seaman and sometime stable hand on the estate, it will come to me eventually, but it was very Irish, Fergie – no, Ferghal, that was it! Ferghal something!" He glared at the grinning Surgeon, "Len, if this is one of your wind-ups I'll have you .." he searched for a suitable term "… keelhauled!"

"No wind up, I promise you," laughed the other, "that is his name, but I think we should search the historical archives to see if we can verify it. God knows, we may need to prove his existence if the bureaucrats get hold of him!"

"Good thinking! But I think I had better see him as soon as possible." He touched his link and when the writer responded, said, "Come in please Adriana, I need you to do some searching in archives for me!"

Ten minutes later the writer returned with a tablet which she handed to the Captain, "You were right sir; his details are in the old Royal Navy archive. Warranted a Midshipman first to *HMS Bellerophon seventy-four,*" she grinned, adding, "Probably not our *Bellerophon* either!" then continued, "Transferred by request of his Captain to HMS *Spartan* for a commission in the Great South Sea and the Indies. Lost in battle with two French ships, *le Revolution forty-four* and *Mistral forty-four*, presumed killed at his post on the lower battery. Also lost or killed at the same time and in the same position were one Ferghal O'Connor and a monkey of some sort named Daniel Gunn." She looked up puzzled, "What would a monkey be doing at a gun in a battle?"

"Monkey?" queried the Captain, "What is the full entry for this?"

"It says in the record that Daniel Gunn was a Powder Monkey," she said looking puzzled, and blushed as the Captain and then Len burst into laughter!

"A Powder Monkey! That is the child you have in MedCent Len," laughed the Captain, to his Secretary he explained, "A Powder Monkey is a child whose job on the ship in battle was to bring powder charges from the magazine to the guns. There would have been several of them onboard a warship of the type that account describes. What is the date on it?"

"It says here eighteen zero four sir," she replied surprised into checking it again, "They used children to carry explosive to the guns in a battle?" She asked in an appalled tone.

"They did, the children were 'volunteered' by a parent, 'uncle' or 'aunt' and were usually illegitimate kids from prostitutes, girls who had no husbands, young widows or impoverished families who couldn't support them. The Navy gave them a home, an education of sorts and food for as long as they survived – and many of them did very well," the Captain explained, he glanced at the Doctor, "how old did you say the one we have is?"

"At a guess no older than around eleven or twelve, younger!" he said, then added, "And the Mid called him Danny. Oh, and the other two are barely more than boys," he added looking at the Writer, "yet I should imagine that our young Midshipman was probably expected to carry a fair bit of responsibility and to lead the men he was entrusted with." He glanced at the Captain, "I wonder if we could dig a bit deeper on this. There must be some records of the battle and a report filed somewhere."

"You're right!" the Captain glanced at the writer, "Can you do a bit more digging please? Any official reports or correspondence on this incident will be very useful." He paused as a thought struck him, "I wonder, they were in a battle, the ship would have been cleared for action, the guns loaded or loading .... Did anything else come aboard with them?"

"Quite a bit I believe," exclaimed the Doctor.

The Captain keyed his link, and said urgently, "Control, alert all personnel! The wreckage in Two-Two-Three Alpha-Oscar-Charlie may contain explosives! Place the area under restriction and get the explosives disposal team down there to check! All non-emergency personnel to clear the area!"

※ ※ ※

Down on the hangar floor, Nick swore as he and his companions received the "pipe". "Damn, that's all we need!" he growled, glaring at the ugly muzzle poking from the wreckage as he and his companions retreated towards the airlock, "I wonder how far one of those damned cannon can throw a shot – and does anyone know if they had explosive shells in those days?"

"Negative to the shells, Boss," said his companion, "one of the scientists says they fired solid iron balls and could throw them about two miles depending on the quality of the gunpowder."

"Oh shit!" Nick glared in the direction of the wreckage that covered the guns. "In other words, we could have a serious hull breach! Warn the explosives boys will you! I'm going to see if I can do anything to make sure we don't have a problem in the meantime!" With that he set off determinedly in the direction of the offending cannon and took time to study the weapon carefully, examining the breech end in particular, although not at all sure what he expected to see. The second gun appeared to be equally devoid of anything which would indicate whether it was loaded or not, and he was just raising himself from where he had laid down on the deck to peer under the wreckage when he felt a touch on his shoulder and looked up to see the fully suited up figure of the Marine's explosives expert.

"I'll take it from here Commander," the figure announced through his external speaker, "but perhaps you can fill me in on how many of these things we have got?"

# Chapter 8

# A long voyage home: HMS Spartan 1804

Thomas Bell, *Spartan's* first lieutenant, greeted his Captain at the entry port, the line of Sideboys and Marines formed up to ensure the Captain received due honours in front of the Portuguese colonists and their French prisoners. It had taken a long five days to cover the distance from the sea fight, to the wide bay occupied by the Portuguese settlement and ennobled with the title Delagoa Bay. The little colonial capital rejoiced in the title of Lourenco Marques and the Captain had gone ashore to, as he put, do the pretty by our allies. "Is all arranged sir?"

"Indeed Thomas, the governor was most amenable and has offered us the use of the facilities they have while we affect repairs to our mast." He mopped his brow and said, "Let us get out of this sun and heat! I should add that we will not be venturing far ashore while here either, this is fever country – yellow jack and the like – and we cannot risk bringing any of that aboard. We will take on fresh water and I think we can certainly replenish our livestock and fresh vegetables – but I want to get the ships away from here as speedily as we can!"

By the end of this speech, they were beneath the poopdeck and Captain Blackwood acknowledged the Marine Sentry's salute as he pushed open the great cabin's door. He was relieved to see that his servant, the ubiquitous Jim Purkiss, had opened all the great cabin windows. He flung his heavy dress uniform coat with its gilt epaulettes and gold laced facings onto a chair and loosened his cravat! "By God," he breathed, "that is better! This heat and the humidity is almost as bad as that in Calcutta! I know not how these settlers stand it!" Not for the first time on this commission he wished that a dress uniform could be obtained that was made of something other than the heavy woollen clothes so sensible in the colder climes they were designed for, and so patently unsuitable in the tropics!

"I expect the body adjusts to it sir," smiled the First, "as they seem to do in India and the New South Wales colony." He waited while the Captain splashed his face with water and then settled in the seat beneath the great windows, "I have begun the striking down of topmasts and yards sir. Mr Tweedy thinks we can rig a sheerlegs using the fore and mizzen with our spare spars to draw the main and affect the repair."

"Excellent Thomas! The governor informs me that there is a wood of uncommon hardness available here. Let us arrange for the carpenter to go ashore and see to about obtaining some and to determine if it is the right timber for the repairs." He paused as the servant handed him a cup of tea and presented another to the first lieutenant. "I have a mind to send the Purser ashore with Mr Beasley to put in hand the looking out some fresh victuals for the men – and I think we had best also post a guardboat as well, some of our "guests" may be tempted to swim ashore and there are several flesh eating fish here who will make short work of any such rash attempt. Besides, there is a local liquor which we should avoid allowing aboard at all costs."

"I believe the surgeon wishes to see you as well sir, he says there are herbs available here that he can use and he is also anxious concerning the potential for an outbreak of fever. I believe he has some suggestions which may have merit in that regard."

"Very well Thomas," smiled the Captain, "pass the word for him."

The oppressive heat and the harshness of the task before them without proper facilities, kept the men at backbreaking work from first light until the sudden darkness almost synonymous with sundown in these latitudes close to the equator. By the end of the first day, the damaged mainmast had been stripped of its yards, fighting top and the topmast and royal mast. These had been lowered to the deck and now lay fore and aft along the deck. Canvas awnings had, at the insistence of the doctor been rigged to shield the men from the sun's burning rays and the gunports had all been raised and, with wind sails rigged above the hatches, some air at least circulated below decks for the exhausted men as they ate their evening meal. Extra rations of lime juice had been issued and the Purser had returned to the ship with a boat load of oranges and other fruit to supplement the men's diet. In all, the Captain reflected, the men had performed an almost Herculean task most satisfactorily and much to the admiration of the French Officers aboard.

Early the next day, the Carpenter and Mr Rae were rowed ashore to visit the Portuguese authorities and procure the timber the Carpenter required for his repair. This involved Mr Rae, who, fortuitously, spoke a little Spanish, in a lengthy and protracted negotiation, but they were eventually able to return to the ship, well past eight bells of the forenoon watch, with the news that the timbers they needed were, even then, being loaded aboard a barge to be brought to the ship. Privately the Captain felt that they might well find that the Portuguese officials may be a little slow in actually delivering the timbers. He kept this to himself as he replied, "Well done Mr Rae, best ensure that we have the tackle rigged to receive them when they arrive. It may be good to have fenders ready to protect our hull during the transfer, but I suspect that the carpenter will want to make use of the barge for some, at least, of his new construction work."

"Aye sir, so he has already intimated. I shall see to it at once!"

"It will wait while you refresh yourself with some luncheon and fruit Mr Rae," smiled the Captain, "and I think the men may benefit from a short rest as well!"

As he hurried away the second lieutenant reflected that the last suggestion from the Captain was quite probably the chief reason the seamen on this ship were so willing to carry out their Captain's every order.

Alone in his cabin, the Captain sighed and stared out of the open windows, he must soon begin his letter to Harry Heron's father, yet there was something he could not quite accept about the disappearance. With a shrug, he turned and summoned his servant, gave him specific instructions and then walked to the desk and sat, drawing out his writing block to compose a letter. He was still busy an hour later when the servant began to set out the dining table for several places and ceased only when the servant arrived to light the lamps. Then he rose and, having washed his face and neck – a gesture to the rivulets of perspiration trickling down his face and back, donned a necktie and shrugged on his uniform coat, finishing just as the sentry's musket signalled the arrival of his guests.

*Capitaine* Eugene de Villiers, late commander of the *Mistral* and

Lieutenant Jean-Marie Renault, late of the *le Revolution*, where, like their host, obviously suffering from the heat as where the other guests, Thomas Bell, the First Lieutenant, Mr Beasley the Fourth and Midshipman Tanner. All were plainly feeling the effects of the unrelenting sun and the humid heat of the bay as they sat down to the table and the servant poured large glasses of freshly squeezed fruit juice, then began to fill the wine glasses with what the Captain smilingly assured his French guests, was a product of the Loire valley and purchased rather than taken as a prize.

"Ah m'suie," smiled *Capitaine* de Villiers, "it is kind of you to afford us this invitation, the wines of the Loire are good, but those of the Rhone, my own province, are in my opinion, superior!"

"I do believe you are correct," laughed Captain Blackwood, "sadly I am not able to offer you any as I and my officers have enjoyed the last of my stock some months ago!" He bowed his head slightly and added, "Had I known I would have the pleasure of being host to a native of that region, I should have saved some!" He raised his glass in salute and continued, "Your health gentlemen, I trust the cook's efforts will not have utterly destroyed the food I obtained ashore for our pleasure!"

This raised a general laugh and the company attacked the first course. The conversation becoming general as the food was consumed and this afforded the Captain and the First Lieutenant the opportunity to discuss the events leading to the loss of *le Revolution* and the damage to *Spartan* in a less formal manner. In this way they were able to compare the device which damaged the Frenchman with the experience on their own ship and to obtain the information that the French had been attempting to force it out through the supposed 'entry' hole and had lost two of their twenty-four pounders – seemingly into thin air! Lieutenant Renault let slip that something had split the casing of the device and that this had apparently given rise to an effort to gain entry to the interior. It appeared that this attempt seemed to be connected with the explosion. "M'suie," protested the lieutenant in impeccable English, "the device was the work of the devil! It killed our men, it destroyed our ship! And you say that it was not of your making?"

"Indeed not," said the Captain grimly, "we too were struck by just such a device and it is that which has necessitated the repairs to our mainmast. By your account, it would seem we were fortunate to be able to extract it from the place it had lodged and cast it overside." He indicated the Fourth Lieutenant, "Mr Beasley and his men performed a very difficult task as two of our guns were pinioned beneath it, and it seems to have consumed three of my men!"

The French officers expressed surprise at this, but it also helped to open up the discussion and Thomas Bell, Michael Beasley and Christopher Tanner listened carefully to the details, such as they were, that could be gleaned from Lieutenant Renault. By the time the dinner was over the Captain reflected that he was now in possession of a great deal more information about the French device, but was still none the wiser as to its origin or the nature and purpose of it. As he retired to his cot, he reflected that all he could now do was record everything in his report and hope that their Lordships at the Admiralty would not consider him to have taken leave of his senses!

# Chapter 9

# A steep learning curve: Vanguard 2204

Harry awoke conscious of the presence of the man he had spoken to earlier. "Harry," said the Commander, "I think we need your help, do you think you can explain something for us?"

"Sir," exclaimed the startled Harry, he felt a great deal better and less confused, but still frustrated at his inability to move out of the confines of the thing they called a 'Medunit', "if it is in my power to do so, of course I shall!"

"Good lad," he indicated a second figure who had joined them; "This is Captain Bob Wardman of the Royal Marine Corps. He is our explosives expert and he needs you to explain something to him if you can." He stepped aside, and said, "You explain it to him Bob."

"Hi," said the new figure, a man of medium height and well proportioned build who exuded an air of competence and athleticism, "I think we have a pair of the guns from your ship on board and we need to know how they were loaded and fired and, more importantly, how we can make them safe. Can you tell me this?"

"Of course sir," grinned Harry, marvelling that these strange officers didn't know such elementary matters and yet claimed to be soldiers and sailors like himself. He explained in detail the process of loading a cannon, the placing of the powder charge in its canvas bag, the ramming home with the rammer, the placing of the wad and then the ball and finally the process of pricking the cartridge, charging the priming hole and pan, the cocking of the flint lock and preparing the firing lanyard. He then began to explain the process of running out and training using the training levers, but the man called 'Bob' stopped him.

"Thanks for that; that is really helpful and explains quite a bit! Now, how can we draw these charges out of the gun?" He paused, adding,

"And these guns don't seem to have the 'locks' and flints you mentioned. Could they have fallen off at some point?"

"I doubt that they could be so easily displaced," replied Harry. Then he thought a moment, "If they have no lock, then they may be French – they still use a match and linstock to fire – you may be able to see if there is powder in the priming hole sir!"

He went on to describe the process for coaxing the ball out of the bore of the gun, a delicate and dangerous procedure when a gun is on a ship at any time. Then the use of the wadhook to draw the wadding and finally the hook to snag and draw the canvas wrapped powder charge, stressing the need to ensure that no spark was created in the process. Almost as an afterthought he added, "Or you could simply spoil the powder if you have no need to preserve the charges. If you can draw the ball, or even if you cannot, forcing water into the priming hole will spoil the priming powder and if enough can be inserted will spoil the charge – it may then be more safely drawn."

"Thanks Harry," grinned Bob, "that's really helpful. That is the best piece of information you could give me!"

"One more thing sir," added Harry, "Danny may have been carrying his cartridge cases when we came aboard – wooden cylinders with a lid and rope handles?"

"Yes, there are two of those in the compartment," replied Bob, puzzled, "what did you say they were?"

"Cartridge cases, sir. Since we had not reloaded before we were snatched away, they will each have a powder charge inside them – for the reloading of the guns he served."

"Will they by God!" exclaimed Bob, "and we were ignoring them! Hell's teeth that could have given us a real headache! How much of this powder of yours will be in them?"

"Two full charges at eight pounds each," replied Harry, again marvelling that this officer knew so little about so commonplace a weapon.

Bob made his exit swiftly and Len returned to view to reassure Harry that all was well. "You're making damned good progress youngster, we will have you out of there in a few more hours. The Captain will want to see you as soon as you are, but in the meantime just get some more rest!" he said cheerfully.

"Thank you Doctor," said Harry seriously, then he had a further thought, and asked, "Sir, what has become of my clothes? May I have my own uniform in order to see the Captain? I think I should be properly attired do you not?"

"I will see to it that you have everything as you should, we are a little less formal than you are used to I think, and the Captain would probably overlook any lack, on your part, of the correct uniform," grinned Len wondering if he dared to allow the boy to carry his short sword into the Captain's presence. He also made a mental note to check whether or not it would be possible to outfit the lad in a new suit of clothes to the same design as he rather thought the science team, now busy taking over in his 'spare' pathology laboratory, would be reluctant to allow him to give it back to the youth. He had a sudden further thought, "Did you have any sort of cap when you went into the engagement?"

"Of course sir," Harry gave him a puzzled look, "I was wearing my round hat as required by regulations."

"I see," mused the other, "I shall have to send someone to see if it arrived when you did then!"

Leaving the boy, Len hurried into the adjacent monitoring station and called the duty MedTec. Then he linked to the ship's stores and gave some very detailed and specific instructions which the surprised stores Warrant Officer read back, then acknowledged. A few minutes later he had the information he needed and set several of his staff to work to put together the items the Surgeon Commander had ordered. Within an hour, all the items, including a hat, bearing a similar appearance to an old fashioned top hat, but rather more tapered toward the crown, were on their way to the Medlab.

\* \* \*

In Compartment Two-Two-Three Alpha Oscar Charlie, Captain Bob Wardman and his team of experts set about fitting a high pressure water line to the touch hole of the first cannon, then carefully bled in water until black and – if they had not been wearing fully enclosed pressure suits – rather smelly water began to force out the ball, which eventually dropped to the deck with a great burst of water behind it. Then they dealt with the second gun in the same manner. When satisfied that this one held no ball and no charge, they turned their attention to the two powder cartridges and opened these carefully. Sure enough, both contained the thick canvas bags described by Harry.

"Sergeant, I think we'll leave these intact for the scientists. Now we know what it is we can deal with taking safety measures around it. Best to keep it in these containers as well, so that we can be sure that it doesn't get any accidental ignition. If the old boys who designed these things thought this was a safe way to handle it in a battle, it probably is!"

"As you say Captain, should we hand it over to the science team?"

"I think so, but we had better brief them fully before we do so," Bob said, "You know," he added reflectively, "that kid certainly knew what he was talking about with these, I wonder if he's ever had to deal with something like this?"

"That lad's pretty tough according to the Master at Arms," laughed the sergeant, "sounds to me like he was prepared to take us all on to defend his lads – they were lucky he keeled over when he did! Wouldn't surprise me at all if he hadn't put up a big fight and I bet he's done something similar before – and has the madness to do it again!"

"Right," grinned Bob, "well lets go and tell 'Wings' his hangars are safe!"

✷ ✷ ✷

Two hours later, Harry was assisted out of the Medunit, discovering to his embarrassment that he was naked. But worse was to follow as the Med Technician (to Harry's relief a man) ushered him into a small chamber to one side and suggested that he take a shower and use the toilet. Handing him a towel and a small flask of something scented and rather viscous, the man withdrew, leaving Harry wondering what to do. Two items he recognised, one appeared to be some sort of commode, but fixed to the deck and apparently emptying overside as far as Harry could gauge, the other was a basin – again fixed to the bulkhead – and although there were spigots, there was no pump, bucket or jug containing water that he could see. The 'shower' the man had referred to was even more of a puzzle. There was indeed an enclosure with a glazed screen across its entrance which swung aside to admit him, but, apart from some spigots placed in the deckhead, Harry could not see how any water could be pumped to them – much less the handle which he would need to operate in order to do so. Not wishing to appear stupid he decided to try to work this out for himself, but a frustrating ten minutes later had to admit defeat and, going to the door – which slid open before he could touch it causing him to jump back in surprise – he looked out and to his relief saw that the Technician was busy assisting the man, he knew to be a Commander, attend to Danny.

"Excuse me," he said, apologetically, "but I do not appear to have access to the pump in order to draw water. May I have a pitcher please?"

"Pardon?" said the Med Technician, looking blank, "You just …." he trailed off as the Commander intervened swiftly.

"Ah, of course Harry, you will not be familiar with our arrangements. Here I'll show you how it is done aboard this vessel," said Len, stepping forward. He ushered Harry back into the small chamber which he referred to as an 'ablutions facility' to Harry's puzzlement, and swiftly showed him how to operate the thing Harry thought of as a commode, how to get water into the basin and how to operate the shower. When he was sure Harry had grasped the fact that all he had to do was stand in the shower and request the computer to provide a shower by saying the words 'Computer: Water on' and 'Computer: water off' slowly and clearly and that he could use the toilet and the basin without mishap, he showed Harry that the flask contained a soap solution to enable him to wash himself thoroughly and then withdrew leaving Harry to get on with it.

Tentatively Harry stepped into the shower cubicle and said the magic words he had been given. Instantly a deluge of fine spray engulfed him, pleasantly cool on his skin and he gasped in the sheer pleasure of it! To his surprise the water was not salt, but pure and fresh and as sweet tasting in his mouth as the clear streams and rivulets around his home as a child. He tried out the soap and managed to get it into his eyes and his mouth, but revelled in it, laughing as he enjoyed the luxury of it. Never had he known such indulgence, even at home a bath had been something requiring great preparation, here it seemed he could – and on a ship into the bargain – enjoy a luxurious shower at any time on a simple command! Even the commode was a luxury, neither perched over an evil smelling pot of turgid liquid and faeces needing to be emptied daily nor, as for the ordinary seafarer, perched in all weathers in the 'heads' over the ship's beakhead as she plunged her way across the ocean.

He emerged from the shower glowing and towelled himself vigorously dry. Never had he felt so clean and so wonderfully alive! Once again the door slid open as he approached, the towel now wrapped about his body, and he emerged even as young Danny was lifted protesting into an adjacent chamber.

The Surgeon Commander studied him with a smile playing about his mouth, "Feeling better youngster?" he asked, a twinkle in his eyes as he took in the tousled head of dark reddish brown hair and the evidence of a thorough scrubbing. "We have some new clothes for you, I'm afraid your old outfit is simply too far gone to be salvaged. I think you will find we have managed to replace everything as it should be!"

Harry thanked him and accepted the proffered pile of neatly folded clothes. Everything was arranged neatly in the order it would be needed, a pair of short legged under drawers, a long tailed shirt, with a high collar and long cuffed sleeves, a pair of white stockings, white breeches and a cravat of white material, a white waistcoat with the correct buttons of brass and finally a pair of black leather buckled shoes. With these on he looked and felt as if he was once more a Midshipman of His Britannic Majesty's Navy and almost imperceptibly seemed to age slightly to Len's observant eye. He handed the youngster a black jacket with its white trimming and button encrusted cuffs and watched the boy slip it on and adjust its hang, then, without a word handed the boy his dirk and the replacement belt and sling.

Harry accepted it with some surprise, after all he had noticed that no one aboard this ship seemed to carry or wear a sword, and had expected, as a prisoner (he had difficulty as yet working out precisely what his, or his companions', status was!) of war he had expected to be deprived of this badge of office. He carefully clipped it round his waist and adjusted the hang of it. He was even more surprised when he found the Surgeon holding out a brand new version of his round hat. He accepted it with thanks and placed it carefully on his head, crushing the unruly mop of hair beneath it. "Thank you sir, I do not know how this has been done, or, indeed, what manner of material these clothes are made of, since they are much lighter and more comfortable than my old ones," he flashed a half serious smile and said, "and they fit me better since I had grown a trifle since the coat was made in Madras!"

"My pleasure lad," grinned Len, turning as they were interrupted by the emergence of the Med Technician with a furious Danny,

"Mr Her'n sor!" the boy piped angrily, "he tried to drownded me! He put me under the washpump and poured soap on me! I near on drownded!"

"Now then Danny," smiled the Midshipman, "I have showered and there is no danger of drowning there. Surely your Messmen washed you on *Spartan?*"

"Aye, when they could ketched us'n! beggin' pardon sor!" the boy looked embarrassed, "But not often – and this'n sez I mus' do it ever' day!"

"Well Danny, if you must, I shall have to as well. We are aboard their ship and must obey their orders!" said Harry placatingly.

"But you'm an *orfitser* sor!" protested the urchin, "*Orfitsers* be different!"

"Not that different!" protested Len amused, he caste an eye at the MedTech who rolled his eyes and laughed. The man's wet uniform told its own story – one of a furious small boy sharing the 'watter' with his tormentor in protest! "Now then, we have some new clothes for you lad, so calm down and let the MedTech show you how they go." He caste an eye over Harry and added, "If you are happy with that?"

"Why, er, certainly sir, I have no objection at all!" said Harry slightly taken aback at this courtesy and nod to his responsibility for the other two. To the now slightly calmer Danny he said, "Danny, you are to do as the –," he hesitated not knowing what form of title or address to give the man trying to get Danny dry and dressed, "- Surgeon's Assistant tells you! Get dressed and perhaps we will be able to talk to Ferghal upon my return."

"You'm not leaving me sor?" cried the boy alarmed, shaking himself free of the medic and snatching back the towel.

"Only for a short while Danny! I must see the Captain of this ship and arrange for our release or return to *Spartan*." He smiled at the boy's worried expression, "I shall rely upon you to see that Ferghal comes to no harm while I am away."

With the boy's assurances that he would "look after his shipmate" ringing in his ears, Harry followed the Surgeon from the room. Entering the next chamber he brought up short at the array of flashing lights, illuminated displays and devices he did not understand and which seemed to him to be almost living entities in their own right! His gasp of surprise, brought Len's assurance that there was nothing to be afraid of, a term that put Harry very much on his mettle, and he drew himself up to his full height and assured the other that he was not, even though he found himself wondering if they had fallen into the hands of sorcerers. There could surely be no other explanation for the strange illuminations on all the various tables, bulkheads and strange machines he could see. They passed another partition and Harry saw that there were other chambers equipped like the one he had himself just left, one or two of the units apparently in use, evidently dealing with other injured men. In the room he now entered there was a small group of people, several in uniform and several more not.

"Ladies, gentlemen," smiled Len, "this is Midshipman Nelson-Heron. Harry, this is Dr Grüneland, Dr Williams and Dr Maartens. They are scientific officers and researchers attached to this ship." He said, introducing the civilians first. He watched the boy's reaction to the fact that the leading scientist was a woman and reflected that there were a few more adjustments for the youngsters to make than perhaps they realised. Putting this aside he continued, "This is Commander Gray and with him is Commander Curran our Navigating Officer. Dr Williams and Dr Maartens will want to talk to you and your friends over the next little while, but now we must see the Captain – and some things never change, you never keep the Captain waiting!" he winked at Nick who nodded sagely.

"Definitely not! Glad to meet you Mid, I expect we will see a fair bit of each other while you are with us." He grinned and held out a hand, "Welcome aboard! Now we better get up to the Captain's quarters, he'd like to meet you." There was an awkward moment as Harry first raised his hat slightly and bowed his head in salute, then noticing the extended hand, replaced his hat and hurriedly extended his own stammering a brief response. He accepted the Navigator's hand more readily acknowledging the introduction and marvelling at the almost casual approach of these strange officers.

The journey through the ship and up several decks (Harry could not work out how many as the chamber the others referred to as a 'Lift Tube' seemed to rise on what he could only surmise must be a pulley and haulage system of some kind) contained a number of surprises for him. The companionways as Harry thought of them were broad and high, more than enough room for the tallest member of the party, Commander Gray, to walk without having to duck or bend, and was one of the longest he had ever seen. It was divided by heavy doors which opened as they approached and closed silently behind them, but the route seemed thronged with people all of whom appeared to be going to or coming from somewhere along their route – a fact that Commander Gray noted wryly, saying to the Navigator, "We seem to have a lot of loungers about – anyone would think we had an alien in tow!"

This made Harry blush as he guessed that he was the object of this curiosity, and it made him realise too that there must be something unusual for a Midshipman to have three Commanders escorting him. That distracted him as he pondered the fact that this seemed to be a single ship with a full Post Captain in command, yet she also had three 'Commanders'. In Harry's experience, the title Commander was accorded the person having command of a ship, however small, and regardless of his status, whether commissioned or warranted. Thus, reasoned Harry, either this was a different order or a different navy to the one with which he was familiar. He had barely reached this conclusion when they arrived at a door which opened to reveal an antechamber and an attendant who rose from her desk as the Commanders entered and said cheerfully, "Go in gentlemen, the Captain's ready for you."

The three Commanders stepped aside and Nick Gray said encouragingly, "After you Mid, you're the guest he's waiting for!"

The door slid open and Harry did his best to stride purposefully even though his knees felt like water! He entered the apartment noting that it – in common with all those he had passed – had no windows, no openings to the sea or sky - he swept off his hat and then stopped as a tall man rose from his comfortable seat to one side and walked forward. Harry's eyes widened, first in surprise, then in suspicion and fear! What trickery was this? *"F-f-father?"* he faltered and Commander Curran caught him as he staggered and almost fainted!

He revived as he was helped into a comfortable seat and having gathered his wits, and recovered some of his spirit, found himself with a group of senior officers gathered around him in concern. The man he had mistaken for his father stood beside the kneeling Doctor, a worried frown on his face as he studied the boy. Seeing that he had recovered a little, Len Myers said cheerfully, "I wondered about that, there is certainly a strong resemblance! Now give him some room or we'll swamp him with our sheer weight of authority!" to Harry he added, "Take it easy lad. Now, may I introduce our Captain. Captain Heron, may I present to you, Midshipman Heron!"

Harry struggled to his feet, his face ashen, brushing aside the Surgeon Commander who tried to stop him, he bowed and said, "Sir, my apologies for my unseemly behaviour, I do not know what came over me, but for a moment I mistook you …" his voice trailed away.

"No apologies necessary Mid," smiled the Captain, "and please sit down, I believe we are related, so there is no surprise that there could be a mistake, especially in these circumstances." He waved a hand at the seven officers, who Harry noted all seemed to be wearing the same insignia and must therefore all be Commanders, "my Heads of Department all wanted to be here when we met – I think in the hope that some secret would be revealed. Ghouls the lot of them!" he glared in mock anger and the rest laughed.

"Thank you sir, but may I know what your intentions are for me and my men?"

"Well Mr Heron," the Captain smiled, "that is a little difficult and may take a little while to work out. In the meantime I will make you officially members of this ship's company and we wiil do everything we can to help you adjust. Commander Petrocova over there," and Harry found himself facing a penetrating gaze from a striking woman Commander, "is our Weapons Officer. She is also responsible for the Midshipmen and cadets aboard and until further notice will be your Commander. We also have a scientific team on board and they have a great deal they wish to discuss with you," he paused as one of the Commanders began to pass round a tray of drinks which Harry noted were in tall frosted glasses, and he distractedly accepted one from the small and unmistakeably feminine Commander on his left, as the Captain continued, "I want you to work with them as much as possible, and, in a day or two, we will begin to show you round and teach you about our ship and its operation."

"Thank you sir," was all Harry could think to say, adding, "But Captain Blackwood will wish to know what became of us sir – if he has survived the French ships' attack!"

*Out Of Time*

"Very well said Harry," replied the Captain gently, "I think I can put your mind at rest on that one. During the engagement *Spartan* sank the *le Revolution* and captured the *Mistral*, they also recaptured a ship called the *Minerva* of the Honourable East India Company which the French had captured during the night. *Spartan* was badly damaged, but was" - he caught the eye of Surgeon Commander Myers and hastily corrected himself, "- *Is* being repaired in," he consulted something that looked like a slate but made out of some unnatural material, "Delagoa Bay."

He turned to the others, "and now team, I would like just a few minutes with Harry here alone. Len, I'd be glad of your staying as well."

"No worries Boss," grinned Nick Gray, "Fritz here can frighten him later and so can the rest of us. Can I have my power back online in my hangar please Mary? I promise not to pull so much in future!"

The small Commander glared at him and then smiled, "Only if you can tell me that bunch of lunatic scientists and Marines have finished playing with those guns and 'cartridge' cases they found!"

"Und vy am I supposed to scare him?" growled an immaculately uniformed Commander on the other side of him, "I haf no intention of this!" His grin and laughing eyes belying the serious tone as he deliberately put on a comically thick accent bringing grins to the faces of everyone.

The group filed out, Richard Grenville the last to leave and joining in the good natured banter which had, as it was intended, distracted Harry and given him the chance to relax slightly.

Out in the corridor, Valerie Petrocova was the first to comment, "I think we will have some interesting things to learn from that young man!"

"Why do you say that?" enquired Nick, "He's going to find it tough to adjust to our technology at his age!"

"I don't know so much," mused Fritz, "He did not seem to be that phased by our presence – and the rank gap certainly isn't what worries him. I think he will be interesting to watch – perhaps he will have trouble with the tech, but perhaps not also!"

"Be interesting to see his reaction to space!" commented Mary, "That will be something he won't expect. In a way," she added reflectively, "I don't envy him or his friends!"

"He may surprise us all," commented Richard Grenville dryly. "His reaction to the Owner was certainly interesting, after that I doubt much will surprise him at all. Now, have we still got any major defects from our little transit problem?"

The team laughed and gave him a negative answer – as he had expected - and scattered to their various departments. He watched them go, glad to have the backing of such a good team. A ship of this size and type needed the best – and he knew she had them.

Alone with the Captain and the Surgeon, Harry turned to find the Captain studying him. He made to speak, but the Captain waved him to silence, saying, "Please sit down Harry, I have quite a bit to ask you and perhaps to tell you. Some of it may have to wait a while though until we have more data."

"Data sir?" asked Harry puzzled.

"Ah, of course, modern word," said the Captain half to himself, "I mean information Harry. Another glass of juice?"

"Thank you sir!" said Harry, his thirst telling him he should make the most of this.

"Right," said the Captain as Harry accepted the glass from the Surgeon, "It is very difficult to know where to begin, so you will have to bear with me and accept that we may have to explore this in small bits over a period of time."

Harry nodded his understanding, and asked, "May I speak sir?"

"Of course Harry," grinned the Captain, "Is there something you want to ask?"

"Yes sir," replied Harry, "Your name is the same as mine and the resemblance to my family is strong. May I ask sir, are you also from Ulster?"

"As it happens, Harry, yes, I am. From the same place as yourself in fact."

"Should I know you sir? I know all my cousins and their families – but I do not think I have the pleasure of knowing yours."

"Hardly to be wondered at Harry, but it is a long and perhaps difficult to understand story," he glanced at the Surgeon, who nodded, before continuing, "We are blood relatives Harry, but you were born in seventeen eighty-nine on May Twentieth. I was born in what you know as Bangor in the year twenty-one sixty two on October the Second." He

*Out Of Time*

watched carefully as Harry digested this.

"But how can that be sir?" asked Harry looking worried, "It is surely eighteen hundred and four, I am but recently turned fifteen and must serve at least another eighteen months before I can hope to sit for a lieutenants exam – but, by what you say, I must be some four hundred years your elder! That cannot be!"

"Well Harry we're not at all sure what has happened either, and we are trying to work out what, if anything, can be done about it! In the meantime you and your companions will be treated as members of my crew, we will have to take things very slowly until we can help you and them to learn how things are done in our time and in this ship but we will do it together. You are, I think an intelligent young man and a brave one, so I shall expect you to help the others to adjust to this. You are their officer and I shall expect you to show them the way," he smiled at the boy, and said gently, "and I shall hope to learn about the family from you, there is a great deal I want to know about it."

Harry nodded, still stunned by the revelation, and acknowledged the Captain's instruction and request. "I shall do my best sir!"

"Good, now, I am also informed by Captain Wardman of the Royal Marines that you were exceptionally helpful to him earlier today. Thanks to your very good advice he was able to disarm a cannon which could have caused serious damage to this ship. And he was able to identify and render safe the cartridge cases your Powder Monkey brought with him. Well done!" the Captain finished.

"I was surprised that he did not know it sir," blushed Harry.

"Harry, the technology of war moves on quite rapidly and sometimes we forget that older devices and methods are quite as lethal as our modern ones. We no longer use cannon and gunpowder, we tear things apart with beams of supercharged particles and self propelling projectiles, we have harnessed the power of the suns and can obliterate a small planet, but we can still be killed just as easily by a cannon we have forgotten how to use as by any of those!" He smiled at the bewildered youth and added, "I can see I have confused you again. Never mind, once the scientists have finished recording you as you now are, we can use some of our technology to help you catch up – I think you will find that interesting."

"Yes sir," said Harry uncertainly, and then asked, "Sir, you and all the others speak of us being on a ship, but it is like no other ship I have ever seen or been aboard. Why does it have no gunports on its decks or windows in your great cabin? Why do I feel no movement in its deck?" He looked a little pleadingly at the Captain, "Can you not look out upon the sea from inside this great ship?"

"We can look out Harry, and we can create windows, or at least the impression of them," he spoke to the computer, "Display view screen abeam one eighty degrees." The whole of the bulkhead in front of them changed colour, apparently dissolving to show a black void with a small, and to Harry's eyes, strange cylindrical object with great fins in the centre of the vision which was keeping pace with, and apparently keeping a station on, them. "There, that is why I don't bother keeping it in display while we are in transit at this speed, there is simply nothing visible to our eyes except objects travelling at our own speed – like that ship there, named *Bellerophon*. A name I think you may recognise!"

Harry peered at the object and shook his head, noting that it resembled a great whale more closely than a ship, "That is not the old *Billy* sir," he said with confidence, "I served on her and would know the old *Billy Ruffian* anywhere, and that," he indicated the screen, "is most assuredly not she!"

He looked very surprised when the Captain and the Surgeon burst into laughter! After shutting down the view screen, the Captain explained to Harry that the ship he had seen was indeed the *Bellerophon*, but a ship of vastly different design and ability to the one he knew. Little did Harry realise it, but he had passed a serious test in their eyes and they now felt certain that he would be able to make the adjustment fate had demanded of him. The Captain's comlink chirped and the Surgeon rose to his feet and signalled Harry to do the same. They stood while he answered briefly the question asked on the link and the Surgeon ushered Harry out, passing Commander Grenville, Dr Grüneland and Dr Maartens in the antechamber.

"We have received a Priority signal from the Admiralty forwarding a *'request'*," his faint emphasis on the word showed that it was thinly veiled order, "from the Confederate Department of Science and Exploration, to confine our three 'aliens' in isolation for scientific study on our return." He gave a short and mirthless laugh, adding, "It comes from the Minister himself and is at the request of a certain Doctor Johnstone

*Out Of Time*

who is apparently a self-styled 'expert' in xeno-biology and pre-industrial alien societies. He wants our 'specimens' preserved untainted until his team of 'experts' can examine and carry out tests on them and their 'preserved memories'." He paused briefly, adding, "The Admiral has endorsed it to say that since we already have a Scientific team of the highest order onboard, which includes all the disciplines Dr Johnstone refers too, the Admiralty are leaving it up to you to decide what action to take, and he has informed the Minister that our squadron cannot be recalled," finished the Commander, his face carefully showing no hint of his thoughts.

"I see," said the Captain calmly, "Thank you Richard. Dr Grüneland, have you heard of this man?"

"Not only heard of him, I'm afraid, but have – as you say; crossed swords? – with him several times. He is very influential and well connected politically but his *'research',*" she stressed the word slightly, "is the subject of some argument in the scientific community and may even breach the codes of ethics for such work!"

"Some *argument*?" snorted the Dutchman, his dark face getting even darker with anger, "he is a fraud – and his 'work' breaches every code of ethics, Silke, as we all know!" He would have said more, but the opening door behind him saw Dr Williams enter stormily.

"You cannot hand these boys over to that fraud Johnstone! I hope you can tell the Minister to go to hell by the most direct route – preferably taking Johnstone and all his people with him! I will not let anyone hand these kids over to that damned moron and his crackbrained and, frankly, little more than vivisectionist associates!" he raged. "That man's 'Research Foundation' is little more than a front for some decidedly illegal and unethical activities!"

"I have no intention of handing these boys to anyone Doctor, but thank you for your opinion," smiled the Captain grimly. "Richard, I'd like you to arrange a private link to this person at this address for me. I will arrange with him to put in train some protection for these young men. Now, I will request a face to face with the Admiral and put to him the reasons why I will not comply with this 'request', may I count on your support Doctors?"

"That you need not ask! We will support you of course! That Johnstone is no scientist – he is a fraud and as Dr Williams has said – his methods are not only unethical – they are totally unacceptable and illegal!" exclaimed Dr Maartens and the others nodded emphatically.

"I might not use such a strong term, since many of the accusations are unproven, but I have heard that some of his more recent attempts at experiments with mental and perhaps terminally ill patients have not been as ethical as he would have the world believe," agreed Silke, "but I certainly share Frederik's view of the conduct of this foundation. You may be very certain that we will argue strongly for the boys to remain under your care – and I hope ours!" She gave him a careful glance. "Have I your permission to communicate directly with my superiors?"

"Of course, Commander Diefenbach will set it up for you on a secure channel. I would far rather have your team looking after them and helping with their adjustment than this fellow." He frowned, "I have seen some of his published work and I am not sure I would allow him anywhere near these three boys – even if one were not a relative of mine!" His comlink chirped, "Yes?"

"I have a channel open to the Admiral for you sir!" came the voice of Adriana Volokova, his writer.

"Thank you; put it on screen."

Half an hour later, the Captain turned to the three scientists and said, "Thanks for your support, I think that, for the moment, we may have won a breathing space – but it's only the first round. I am sure that Dr Johnstone and his allies will try something else to get their hands on them. At least the Admiral agrees that we cannot treat these young men as if they were animals or criminals, no matter what the politicians want." He smiled, "I may have sorted out the problem by the time we get back if Richard here can get me that private channel linked through asap!"

Richard Grenville knew his Captain well, and grinned in return, "I'll have it for you in a jiffy!" He glanced at the tablet the Captain had given him, "I rather think this may blow a few heads off though!"

"Probably not a minute before time," said the Captain seriously, which left the three scientists wondering what he had given the Commander.

"If you will excuse us Captain," said Silke, "I will contact my superiors, and Dr Maartens and Dr Williams may wish to add their views to mine."

"Thank you, yes," he smiled and added, "I am sure that Fritz Diefenbach will be only too pleased to oblige you!"

* * *

Within minutes of his being alone, his link chirped and Richard Grenville announced, "I have your channel set up sir, and the privacy screening is active!"

"Thank you Richard, put it through to my desk screen please!"

"Good evening James," came the slightly accented tones which did not fit the rather austere features of the older man now on the screen, "and to what do I owe the pleasure of being hauled out of my dinner?"

James O'Niall Heron smiled grimly and as rapidly as possible told the other man what had occurred and what was now being attempted by the Ministry. He provided, through the computer, links to all the information his writer had managed to gather on the three youths and their history, the DNA data on Harry and a tape of his interview with Harry – including Harry's reaction on first seeing him. The other man listened carefully, interjecting questions and demanding further information or expansion where it was needed. "And that is all I can tell you at this moment," finished the Captain, "We need an injunction preventing interference with, or seizure of the three and an award of wardship, or some such, to me or whoever you consider appropriate."

The older man smiled, "So, it's a miracle you're wanting then! Leave this with me, I will see what I can do. In the meantime, I'd be obliged if you would get your scientific people to let me have all the information they can on the work of this Dr Johnstone – if all else fails, tying him up in legal challenges may be the better way forward. And now, my dear nephew, it is nearly midnight here in Dublin and I think I am going to have my clerks out of bed and working on this through the night! This will cost you, you know!"

"Thanks Theo, I knew I could count on you – put it on my bill and I'll add it to my list of debts to you and Niamh! Would meeting the boys be suitable part payment when I'm next planetbound?"

"You know Niamh, and yes, that will be more than enough if they are as you say they are!" laughed the other. "Good night!"

*Patrick G. Cox*

The Captain sat and stared at the blank screen for several minutes, then keyed his link, "Richard, thanks for that, now one more thing, run a check on the transmission logs since we entered transit. I want to know who sent the information that we had the boys on board!" Signing off, he checked the ship's navigation readouts and then turned in. But sleep was a while in coming to him.

※ ※ ※

Far astern a strange triangular craft, whose outer hull appeared to change patterns and texture, now fading black on black, then showing patches and strips of lighter darkness, slipped silently in their slipstream. In the Command Centre, Weapons Scan Operator (T) Ignatius De Santos, studied his scanner carefully, then touched his key pad and summoned the Officer of the Watch. When Weapons Lieutenant Commander Trevor Leonard joined him he pointed to a small image on the screen, and said, "I think we have a Foo Fighter following us, sir. He comes and goes and I can't get a decent image on him, but he stays behind us matching our speed exactly. The distortion of our wake hides him some of the time and masks my scanner frequencies."

"Well done. Tag him and I'll report it to the Captain. Notify me if there is any change of pattern or he attempts to close us." To the Communications Rate he said, "Send a signal to *Bellerophon* and to *Sydney* to see if they can get a scan fix."

# Chapter 10

# Discovering the new realities: Vanguard 2204.

Returning to the Medical Centre with the Surgeon Commander, Harry had a very pleasant surprise. Ferghal was up and dressed, very smartly, in a blue and white striped shirt, a short skirtless jacket of dark blue, wide bottomed trousers of a material of the colour of duck, but obviously much softer and of an altogether different texture. He was also fitted with a wide brimmed straw hat and ribbon which he held on his lap as he sat waiting, something that puzzled Harry as this was a form of uniform usually only seen on the crews of a barge for an admiral or a very senior Captain or Commodore. Of course, some of the wealthier Post Captains did outfit their personal Coxswains and gig crews in this manner, but Captain Blackwood had preferred a less ostentatious style and had used duck trousers, a shirt of thick cotton and a blue jacket for his boat's crew with only the Coxswain sporting a hat, similar to his own "round" hat but, having a much lower crown and a miniature of the ships figurehead as a brass badge mounted on its front. He smiled as Ferghal leapt to his feet and dragged the boy up as well. Danny was rigged out in similar style to Ferghal – and looked remarkably clean and very content with his lot!

"Well Ferghal," grinned Harry, "I see you are already promoted? The Captain did not mention his appointing you to his gig crew, so I must surmise that this is something in recognition of your talents!"

Ferghal grinned in response, "Aye Master Harry, they have done similar for you I think – or should! If my Da' could but see me now, he'd be bursting with pride I'm thinking!"

"And so he should," grinned Harry. "You'll make Admiral before we know it."

"Please sor," Danny piped at Harry, "be I in the Captain's gig wit'

Ferghal?"

"I know not Danny, but if opportunity serves, I shall ask!" laughed Harry, the thought of the small boy perched on a thwart and handling a long oar something he could picture in his mind's eye – and the consequences!

Len watched in fascination as the two older boys lapsed into the soft accents of their youth together in Ulster. The sharper accent of Danny spoke obviously of a different region and he wondered if this was what was meant when linguists spoke of "regional accents" prevalent prior to the adoption of universal pronunciation and spelling in English. He knew that the science team would be recording the conversation – and would do so with every interview – but he also knew that the boys would be entirely private when they went to the quarters he had assigned in an area adjacent to the lab and normally occupied by Medical Attendants. It also struck him from the opening conversation that their history records, from which the uniforms had been copied for the boy called Ferghal and the young Danny, might not be accurate. Obviously the boys thought that these uniforms meant they had been given some privileged status on board and he and the scientists would have to look carefully at that!

In the adjacent lab, the science team under Dr Williams had also picked up this thread and the social-historian on the team, Natalie Buthelezi, was already busily searching records to see what they might have missed or got wrong in their original search for patterns for the boys replacement clothes. She smiled as she thought of the excitement among the xeno-biologists as they had examined the smaller boy's clothes – more rags held together by some really fine needlework and patches than anything else. Apparently though, they were also somewhat malodorous and she was glad she did not have to work with them. Alongside her, Dr Williams and the linguist in the team, Georgina Curry, who despite her English name was a dark skinned beauty of Middle Eastern descent, listened enthralled as the boys used words not heard in English for centuries. Their grammar excited her as well, as they used the grammatical constructions of Shakespeare, but with a vernacular twist no doubt associated with the region in which they had grown up and their membership of the specialised world of a ship of war.

Len interrupted the discussion, with a smile, "Now then lads, I ex-

*Out Of Time*

pect you are hungry and possibly tired, I know that I am. Come with me and we'll get some food and I'll show you to your bunks so you can settle down and get some sleep – tomorrow there will be a lot of people who want to talk to you and you'll need to be rested I think. You're all still my patients for now, so let's go!"

"Thank you sir," smiled Harry, "I am certainly looking forward to some dinner, and I'm sure Ferghal and Danny will need some as well."

How quickly he reverts to command, thought Len, and smiled, "Follow me and I will show you where we have put you for the moment." He apologised to Harry as he preceded them, saying, "Of course with your having been in the Medunits, you will not have been aware of quite how long you have been aboard. It is now nearly twenty-one hundred and you will have missed the evening meal in the restaurant in this part of the ship, so I have arranged a meal for you all in the MedCent staff canteen." He stood aside to let the boys precede him into the canteen but found himself engaged in a tussle of courtesies as Ferghal stood firmly back and would not precede him, or allow Danny to do so. Even Harry found it difficult to accept this courtesy from a superior, but obeyed, treating the invitation as an instruction, he was a little puzzled by the reference to this mysterious 'twenty-one hundred' and wanted to ask, but was deflected by the protest from Ferghal.

"It's not fit sir," protested Ferghal, "We'll follow thee, if it pleases thee, sir!"

"Oh!" Len suddenly realised the difficulty he had inadvertently created for the boys and smiled, "Oh very well, this way lads." He strode into the canteen and was greeted by the half dozen or so Med Techs and Doctors seated either in the easy chairs around the bulkheads or at the small group of tables at one end. A table had been set with four places and he led them to this, saying, "Right, I hope you'll like what I have arranged for us to eat!" He pulled out a chair and seated himself, waving Harry to a seat opposite himself, indicating that Ferghal and Danny should sit between them.

Again it was Ferghal who looked shocked and objected, "I be no officer sir, we cannot sit with thee, it be against the Articles sir!"

"Now listen lads," smiled Len patiently, and to the amusement of the watching Medstaff who knew his temper to be quite fiery when thwarted or obstructed, "I am an officer, do you agree?" When Ferghal and Danny nodded, he continued, "And Harry," he thought quickly cursing his clumsiness at their affronted looks, "*Mr Heron*, is your officer, am I right?"

Again they nodded their agreement, Ferghal muttering "Aye sir!"

"Good! Now, Mr Heron, do you have any objection to my inviting your men to join us at this table to share a meal?" asked Len hovering between a smile and a frown.

"None at all sir!" exclaimed Harry, to the others he said, "Ferghal, Danny, please do as the Commander Doctor asks, we would not wish him to gain the impression that *Spartan's* crew were a mutinous and uncouth collection of goal bait would we?"

"Aye, aye sir," said Ferghal, his sense of station and dignity somewhat mollified. He helped Danny to mount the nearest chair and moved round to perch on the opposite one, his back rigid and his posture radiating his determination not to be trapped into any suggestion that he was there on anything but orders. It went even further against the grain with him when a smartly dressed Mess Steward arrived at the table with a tray of tall glasses and a jug filled with what Harry recognised as the chilled juice he had enjoyed with the Captain earlier and served first the three youths, and then the Commander who seemed to accept this apparent slight without objection! Danny watched round eyed, and obviously uncertain as to how to manage the evidently unfamiliar utensils on the table – standard cutlery to anyone brought up in most households since the beginning of the twentieth century, but totally unfamiliar to one such as Danny raised in a poorhouse or a hovel and then cast into the Navy of wooden sailing ships where he was more familiar with a wooden platter, bowl and spoon for his eating utensils.

Ruefully Len realised that they were going to have to learn to deal with both the social code pertaining in the early nineteenth century and with the fact that two of the three boys would have to learn to use a range of ordinary items such as eating utensils on top of dealing with the technology he and his fellow Twenty-third Century staff took for granted! Ferghal's face as the first plates of food arrived and were placed before him and Danny before the officers had been served, almost had him swearing in anger, but he controlled his temper – mainly directed at his own thoughtlessness - and he quietly signalled the Mess Steward and excused himself from the table for a moment to give a quick change

*Out Of Time*

of instructions to the order of serving, explaining the social etiquette that the boys were used to. The man smiled and nodded, "No problem sir, I'll take care of it. Would you like me to arrange for the two sailors to be seated separately from the Midshipman in future?"

"Probably a good idea until we can sort this one out. Tell you what," he added thoughtfully, "I'll see if young Ferghal would feel happier looking after the Mid as a sort of Messman. That may solve the problem short term."

"Good idea sir," grinned the other, "I must say it is refreshing to see someone with such a strong sense of an order to society! It's fascinating to watch them."

"Hard work," grinned Len in return, "We'll have to play it carefully!"

He returned to the table and the Mess Steward followed a moment later clearing away the plates from the first course, and having a bit of a tug o' war with Danny who felt it was his task (and perk!) to clear away the meal and feast on any leftovers. This was resolved when the Mess Steward said with a grin, "If I can't have the plates now, I can't bring the next course now can I?"

"There be more to eat?" asked Danny suspiciously.

"There better be," growled Len, "but it will have all been eaten by that bunch hanging around over there, if you keep Hannes here from fetching it much longer!"

With a furtive look behind him, Danny reluctantly gave up his soup bowl and watched suspiciously as the Steward took them to a 'locker' in the bulkhead, placed them inside and, closing the 'locker', waited a few minutes, and then opened it again to take out a tray laden with larger platters which he brought to the table. Danny's eyes widened as he saw the food arranged on each platter. Never had he seen anything like it – not even when the Captain and Officers had dined aboard the *Spartan*! For his part Ferghal struggled to maintain a proper distance between him and the officers, but even he exclaimed at the bounty on the plate placed in front of him by the Steward. There were freshly cooked *fresh* vegetables, slices of meat that looked like fresh beef, not the salt beef or pork he had eaten since he had followed Master Harry to sea. Despite himself, he ate with gusto and cleared the plate while Harry and Len talked, Harry talking of his role aboard *Spartan* and his life at home in the old house beneath Scrabo. He heard his name mentioned and looked up to see Harry explaining that Ferghal's father was his father's head groom and had complete charge of the stables and horses at the family home. 'Yes,' thought Ferghal, 'Major Heron was a good Squire and a good Master to the farm and its people. No one went hungry or cold since he had come into the land, he took care of all his tenants and they respected him for it. Harry was exactly like his father in his ability to take responsibility and to care for those under his charge.' He looked at his boyhood friend and smiled, 'these folk would do well to see how a real gentleman officer looked after his people,' he thought to himself."

There was another tense moment when the plates had again been cleared and the Commander asked cheerfully of Danny, "Well Danny, have you eaten enough, or have you some space left for a dessert?"

"Please sir," said the boy, anxiously, "why would I be wanting to eat sand?"

"Because the officer tells you to!" shot Ferghal with a shocked tone, adding to the surprised Commander, "he don't mean no harm sir, he is but a little lad and hasn't learned all his manners yet!"

"Easy Ferghal," interjected Harry, "I do not think Danny will be beaten for his cheek here. Sir, if I may explain to the lad?"

"Of course," said Len, puzzled as to why Danny was suddenly looking cowed and afraid, and the reference to his being beaten.

"Danny, the Commander wishes to know if you would like to eat a sweetmeat I think. Dessert is but another word for sweetmeats. And you should apologise for your question now ere the Gunner's Mate hears of it," said Harry carefully.

"Please sor, I dassn't know the word. Sorry sor!" sniffled Danny, obviously terrified of the potential retribution that he might incur from this at the hands of the mysterious 'Gunner's Mate'.

"No need to apologise lad," smiled the Commander, "now, would you like a 'sweetmeat'? I can assure you no one will punish you while you are in my charge!" he added giving Harry an enquiring look.

Reassured, Danny affirmed his readiness to eat and the Mess Steward produced bowls of ice cream for all four. Len found their expressions as they carefully tried this strange delight almost too much – and he hoped the historian's cameras were capturing it! Danny's face registered

*Out Of Time*

shock, surprise and then delight and within a very short space of time he had emptied the bowl. Ferghal's face went through a slightly more mature version of the same process, his determination not to give away his innermost feelings schooling his expressions to an almost ludicrous degree. Even Harry, who had encountered sorbet in the heady world of London while staying with his aunt and uncle prior to joining HMS *Bellerophon*, was a study as he discovered the delight of ice cream for the first time. His amazement gave way very rapidly to curiosity, and he asked, "Is this ship capable of conveying ice purely for the manufacture of such delights as this sir? Such a ship must be amazing indeed!"

"We have ice making equipment," explained Len without stopping to think what he was saying, "and can chill anything we need – this is something of a treat I thought you young gentlemen would enjoy as an introduction to our meals!" he finished rather lamely as their expressions told him that ice making was not a concept to attempt to explain right then!

To Len's relief the Mess Steward now stepped in and asked Ferghal and Danny to help him clear the table, whispering conspiratorially "that will give the officers time to talk."

Ferghal's face lit like a beacon at this opportunity to 'show proper respect for his officers' and he and Danny made their immediate excuses, and left to 'assist' the Mess Steward dispose of the dishes, leaving Harry and the Commander facing each other across the table. Harry said seriously, "Sir, I must ask you to forgive my people's manners, they are not used to dining with their officers and I fear we put them out of countenance once or twice."

"No Mid, I should have thought," smiled Len gently, "I am so used to our ways and our manners, that it never occurred to me that they would find it strange. Never mind, we can deal with that in the morning."

"What o'clock is it sir?" asked Harry, "I seem to have lost my pocket watch and I have not heard the bells struck since we have been aboard."

"It's twenty-three hundred according to the ship's chronometer," replied Len, again without thinking, and cursed as he saw Harry's blank expression. "Sorry, we use a twenty four hour clock so it is 11 o'clock in your terms – in the evening," he added, desperately trying to recall how it should be said in Harry's period, "that is Post Meridian or PM to you?"

"Thank you sir, six bells in the Evening Watch. I expect the Officer of the Watch will be conducting his rounds at this time. May my men be excused to their hammocks?"

"Of course, I have arranged for you all to sleep in the Medstaff Quarters until we are certain that you are all back to full health and have finished the tests we need to do. If you can persuade them to follow us, I'll show you to your beds," smiled Len amused at the quaint way Harry had phrased the request.

"If I may ask one other favour sir," said Harry tentatively.

"Ask away," smiled Len, wondering what was coming.

"I will deal with young Danny for his disrespect earlier sir. I would not wish to see him beaten for his ignorance. I do assure you it was not malice when he spoke so rudely earlier. With your permission I will let Ferghal punish him instead of the Gunner's Mate."

"Now why on earth ... ," began Len, then, slowly, realisation dawned, "Oh! Now listen to me very carefully young man," he said sternly, "there is to be no punishment for young Danny. He did not insult or cheek me deliberately and I am not offended, is that clear?" He saw by Harry's expression that his words had been a little harsh, given the youth's upbringing and the gap in social understanding of four hundred years, and continued, "You make me proud young man, I wish all our Midshipmen were half the man you are and most of them are at least five years your senior! There is no need whatever to punish Danny and I will be taking no further action on it. I may share the moment with my fellow officers on an appropriate occasion – and you will most likely be present if and when I do - and suffer their teasing as a result, but that is all." He smiled and finished, "Now, don't even think about it again. Let's find your beds!"

As they rose from the table, Len suddenly asked, "Did you say you had lost a watch?"

"Aye sir, I had a rather fine pocket chronometer given me by my father in the pocket of my waistcoat, but I fear it may have been lost when …" Harry faltered, since he scarcely knew how to describe his sudden and rather violent arrival on board this ship, "we came aboard," He finished rather lamely.

"I'll see if anyone has found it, can you describe it for me?"

asked Len.

"Oh yes sir," replied Harry, "It was about the size of a Crown in diameter and about as thick as three together, silver and with a locket lid to protect the glass. I had a leather sennet fob attached to the winder, but I fear it will have run down by now if, as you say, we have been aboard for more than a day!"

Ferghal and Danny hurried over to stand behind Harry, as Len said, "The size of a Crown you say, that's a bit too big for the pocket surely?"

"Sir?" said Harry puzzled, "Five shillings?"

"Ah, my mistake, you mean a large coin!" laughed Len, "I will see what can be found! Follow me!"

*　*　*

It was short distance along a corridor to the suite that had been set aside for Harry, Ferghal and Danny, but here again there was a difficult moment when Ferghal and Danny realised that there was a sitting room (or Drawing Room as Harry called it) and a second room in which there were four bunks and that they were expected to all sleep in the same place. Ferghal was adamant that it was not fitting for an officer to be expected to share a berth with his men and Len thought privately that he should have thought of this himself – his only concern at the time having been to keep the boys from encountering something they would find alarming or disquieting. He had accordingly made the decision to keep the smallest boy with the older two – forgetting the difference in rank would make this difficult! The moment was saved by Harry who cheerfully announced that if it was alright for him and Ferghal to have slept in a stable once when they were boys, there could be no earthly harm for them to do so again now, pointing out, "And the stable was much less comfortable than this Ferghal!"

"Aye Master Harry," smiled Ferghal carefully, "If you think so, then we will do it."

The Surgeon Commander heaved a sigh of relief as he left the three settling into their bunks, having shown Harry how to control the lighting levels. Being an entirely sealed environment, the ship's lighting was never completely extinguished, even in Night Mode, it remained at least at a level which would be normal for a room on earth lit by exterior lights such as the moon or stars. They were set to a circadian cycle so that during the day they remained at "normal" daylight strength, dimming if the room were unoccupied at sundown until they reached night status, or unless they were ordered to remain on. At night, once the occupant had gone to bed, the lighting would go to Night Mode and remain at that level until "Dawn" at which time it would gradually brighten – unless this had been specifically overridden. As he made his way to the Wardroom and his own suite he reflected that these boys would have a difficult time ahead as they adjusted to the changes in social practice as well as getting to grips with the technological matters essential to their survival aboard a starship! He ordered himself a stiff "night cap" of single malt Irish whiskey and retired to a comfortable chair to think about the day, the boys and how to help them cope with the adjustments they would have to make in the days ahead. Remembering the lost watch, he used his link to leave a message for the science team to check the Midshipman's original clothing to see if it was present and another to the team examining the materials from the hangar in case it had fallen out amongst the wreckage as the boys had tumbled to the deck. At least, he reflected as he sipped the whiskey, they would have all the help and support possible – and they were themselves tough and resourceful. "That young Mid," he thought, "is the same mould and stamp as the Owner. A man worth watching in the future!"

If he could have seen Ferghal, at work in the shared sleeping quarters, quietly, so as not to awaken 'Master Harry', erecting a screen between the berths occupied by Danny and his own, he might have been amused, but on the other hand, he may have realised that he and everyone else dealing with the boys, faced some interesting cultural challenges! Using a sheet taken from his own bedding and ingeniously fixed to the fittings so that it hung like a curtain between Harry and himself and Danny, Ferghal secured it and adjusted it carefully until satisfied that 'Master Harry' had a space proper for 'an officer' and segregated from his men. Then he too turned in, shedding only his smart new jacket, shoes and the stockings that went with them as was normal for the crew of a man o' war. After a restless few minutes trying to adjust to a bed rather than a hammock, he slowly drifted into sleep.

※ ※ ※

*Out Of Time*

At the control desk for the ship's external communications arrays, a momentary spike occurred in the otherwise flat line showing on screen indicating that the carrier signal was idle. An external observer might have noticed a brief flare along the five thousand kilometre length of the trailed array used to send high energy supra-light transmissions to the receivers at the Near Earth Gates, but there was no one to witness it and no one would notice the spike until the logs were checked in the morning watch period. Even then, it would be put down to another of the many, as yet, inexplicable anomalies encountered in hyperspace. No other shipboard system registered any change, with the exception of the computer, which opened its data storage and scanned the vast array of files for no apparent reason until it encountered the data on the three boys and their arrival aboard, then it did a strange thing – it accessed the historic records and searched for information on them and their period.

Again, the computer data access log would not be examined routinely for at least twenty-four hours, except by someone conducting a specific search. What would eventually be noticed about this entry is that it was made from no onboard access node or terminal.

\* \* \*

The 'morning', in reality the ship's computer slowly bringing the light levels back up to 'daylight' mode in all the accommodation units and areas, brought a new surprise for the boys. Used to sleeping fully, or at least in the majority of their clothes, Harry and his companions had turned in shedding only their jackets and, in Harry's case waistcoat, trousers and shoes. They awoke – Ferghal and Danny at the first brightening of the lighting – to find that the lockers at the bedside of each berth contained a full set of fresh underclothes, stockings, trousers and shirts for each of them, and a fresh towel and washing solution. Awaking to find the screen and the fresh clothing, Harry guessed that this was intended as a reminder that they must shower and dress in fresh clothes, and got out of bed to remind Ferghal and Danny, moving aside the 'screen' to do so. He found, to his surprise, that both were awake, their bedding neatly folded and rolled to be stowed away when they learned where this could be done, and both obviously already showered and dressed in their fresh clothes. "Oh! Good morning Ferghal,

Danny," said Harry, "I did not hear you rise!"

"No Master Harry," grinned Ferghal, "we was extra quiet so we'd not wake you!"

"I see," grinned Harry, "and who rigged the screen?"

"Why I did sir," frowned Ferghal, "it was only right sir!"

"Enough of the sir, you scoundrel," laughed Harry, "have you both bathed?"

"Aye sir," piped Danny, scowling at Ferghal, "I sez to 'im, that I still be clean frum, yusterdee, but he pushed me under the watter anyway!"

"I see!" smiled Harry, "But I see you didn't melt and you haven't drowned so I had better go and bathe myself!" He grinned at Ferghal, and teased, "May I use the same, er, *shower* as you men?"

Ferghal frowned and then smiled, struggling not to let it become a laugh, "Master Harry, you may be as careless as you please of your dignity, but we only wish to show these people that you're our officer!"

"I know, Ferghal, I know, but you were my friend through many a scrape ere ever we had to follow our stations in life and I would hope we'll see this one through as friends as well! Our stations may be different, but we are in this together and we'll sink together or swim together!"

"I dasn't swim, sur," exclaimed Danny in fright.

"A figure of speech then youngster," laughed Harry as he headed for the shower, "Oh, and Ferghal, you might want to strike the screen, I feel sure we will not need it again!"

They breakfasted on a meal they found already prepared for them in a servery to one side of the living area, having followed their noses to discover this bounty, their stomachs grumbling at the delicious scent of food, wondering at the luxury of the ship and its facilities – and the apparent ability of their hosts to provide for their every need before they had themselves begun to consider it. Ferghal insisted that Harry ate in solitary splendour waited on by himself, and then he and Danny sat at the far side of the room to eat. While they did so, Harry tried an experiment, recalling the Captain's ability to apparently open a window by a simple command. He thought carefully, and then looked at what he considered likely to be an external bulkhead and said carefully, "Computer, display view abeam one eighty degrees."

*Out Of Time*

A voice apparently from the air around them made him jump and Danny squeak in fright, as a panel suddenly darkened giving a view of a strange looking ship, which glowed with a ghostly blue white light, suspended in a black void. There was nothing beyond it, nothing below it and certainly nothing above it! The three boys stared at it carefully and Harry advanced and touched the surface, feeling a slight tingle in his fingertips. Next to him Ferghal whispered, "What devilment is this? And what manner of craft is that?"

"I fear that we will discover that this is something well beyond our understanding Ferghal," mused Harry, "but as to yonder ship, the Captain yesterday named her *Bellerophon*, though she is nothing like our old *Billy Ruffian*!"

They stared at the strange looking ship for a long moment, noting its blunt snout, its tapered after end with the strange looking pods attached at the extremities of what appeared to be fins, with even greater fin-like structures at its midships point rising and descending and apparently similar structures in the lateral plain as well. From this vantage point it looked less like a whale to Harry than some sort of fantastic creature of some even stranger deep, but it fascinated him all the more.

"Can we shut the port Master Harry?" asked Ferghal, "that void looks uncommonly like Father Murphy's description of Hell!"

"For shame on you Ferghal!" smiled Harry, "You know I am not supposed to know of your Papist persuasions!"

"Aye, sir, I know," Ferghal crossed himself, "but that void makes me uneasy and yon ship looks uncommonly like a whale or a ghost! Could she be the Flying Dutchman?"

"I doubt it Ferghal," said Harry, "I do not think these are his waters – if indeed they are waters!" He looked around and saw Danny hiding behind a seat, "No need to be afraid Danny, this is just an image, see" - he struck the panel with his hand - "it is not a true opening. But perhaps I should close it before anyone comes." He tried to recall the Captain's commands for the closure of the port and tried "Computer, close port!"

The voice responded, "Command not understood. Do you wish to shut down viewscreen?"

"That's it," exclaimed Harry, and when nothing happened, tried, "Yes?" and heaved a sigh of relief when the screen turned opaque and returned to the previous bland colour of the other bulkheads. He had barely sat down again and Ferghal was coaxing Danny out of his hiding place, when the door slid open and the Surgeon Commander strode in accompanied by two newcomers in what the boys recognised as civilian clothing. Harry stood politely and gave a small bow to the Commander since he did not have his hat, while Ferghal hauled a trembling Danny to his feet and forced him to stand to attention until Len said kindly, "At ease lads, I want you to meet our scientists and they are very keen to meet you! Harry you will remember briefly meeting both Dr Williams and Dr Maartens yesterday?" Receiving an affirmation of this, he introduced Ferghal and Danny to the newcomers. Then he fished in a pocket and produced a small fat silver disc with an attached piece of intricately knotted leather cord, "Harry, is this what you were asking for last night?"

Harry beamed in delight, "Thank you sir! My watch! It was given me by my father when I went to sea. It is the very best timekeeper – but I fear it will have stopped as it must needs be wound at least daily!" He took it eagerly and the Surgeon and the scientists watched as he held it first to his ear, then touched a small lever and the lid popped open to reveal a clock face. "As I feared," he grinned, carefully winding a small spindle with a backwards and forwards motion between finger and thumb. As he did so, a faint ticking sound began and he nodded in satisfaction, "Now it will be right as rain! May I ask the correct time sir? Then I may set it and we shall be able to keep to proper time keeping."

Len, without thinking, keyed his comlink and said, "Give me the ship's time please!"

The voice the boys had heard earlier when the viewscreen activated, said "Ship Standard Time is now Zero-eight hours, twenty-one minutes, forty-two seconds."

"There you go," said Len cheerfully, then realised his mistake as Harry and the others looked puzzled. He thought frantically how the time would have been stated in their day, but was saved by Doctor Williams.

"I think that Commander Myers means it is now twenty one minutes past eight o'clock!" he said.

"Thank you sir," replied Harry concentrating on setting the watch, "so it wants but a few minutes to one bell of the Morning Watch. Do you have any assignment for us today sir?"

"Assignment? Well, I think you could call it that," smiled Len, glad to see the boys relaxing again, "Doctor Williams and his fellow scientists would very much like to take the opportunity to talk to you about your lives aboard the *Spartan* and possibly before that."

Harry looked a little surprised that anyone should be interested, but nodded and said, "Then we are at your disposal Doctor," giving a small bow in the direction of the two scientists as he did so.

\* \* \*

Further forward and several decks above the Captain stared at the images on his repeater screen relayed from the scanner manned now by WSO (T) Hsu Li Ching who was monitoring the alien craft shadowing them. Several hours earlier, the WSO's predecessor had reported that there were now two unidentified craft, both elusive to scan and both apparently matching their course and speed. So far, both had evaded any attempt to lock a scanner beam onto them and obtain positive type identification, but the weapons team under Commander Valerie Petrocova were now actively engaged in using all the technology at their command to do so.

Watching the wavering and distorted images they could get, the Captain had an uneasy feeling that he and the rest of the Command Centre were being watched, but could not pin this down to anything other than instinct – the instinct of prey which warns them that a hidden predator has spotted them. Yet, studying the image he was also very conscious of the fact that these ships, labelled Foo Fighters by the scanner operators in deference to long dead fighter pilots in an almost forgotten European war, had never done more than shadow them and had certainly not showed any signs of aggression. He could thus afford to wait and see.

\* \* \*

The sense of being watched was stronger for Harry, Ferghal and Danny, because they were being watched, by a team of scientists. Dr Williams had brought several of his fellow linguists and historians into the large laboratory Commander Len Myers had made available to them. As Len looked on, the team conducted a number of interviews with each in turn. From time to time, Dr Maartens or one of his team would appear and ask one or other of the boys to allow them to measure, weigh or examine them and he marvelled at how well the three youngsters accepted this treatment. He had to admit that this was largely due to the fact that the scientists all treated the boys, even the youngest, with respect and cheerful apology. From time to time one or another would rush off to check something with the computer (they were always careful not to let any of the three see them do so) and return with the same excitement of discovery normally seen among scientists who have just discovered the secret of life, the universe or something equally earth shattering!

As the day progressed, each boy's particular abilities slowly emerged, with Ferghal showing an aptitude for delicate, even surgical, work with small detailed pieces of equipment. Danny surprised everyone by his musical ability and managed to play a fairly wide repertoire of sea shanties and country dance music on a soprano recorder and then an alto version when this was produced by the ships replication system from specifications found in the historical data files. Harry amazed his interviewers with his ability to memorise detailed images, charts and diagrams and in his recall of things he had read or seen. His sketches too attracted a great deal of interest, particularly when he was asked to explain what he had described of Port Jackson and Port Phillip in New South Wales and produced sketches of the Heads to Sydney Harbour and its environs which showed the area as it had been in eighteen oh two – a state of natural vegetation long since disappeared as the human population expanded.

It was Danny who let slip that they had seen the strange glowing ship in the black void, and asked if it was the "Flying Dutchman". The scientists were puzzled by this, until they realised that he could only have seen this if a view screen had been activated in the quarters he shared with the others. There was a quick conference, and then Rhys Williams approached Harry, interrupting his explanation of the method of navigating by means of the sun 'sights' at noon and the manner in which the calculations would be done manually, again something not seen for almost two hundred years. "Excuse me Harry," said Rhys, "but Danny has just told us that you all saw a strange glowing object you told him was a ship earlier today. Did someone activate a view screen for you?"

"Why yes doctor, we did see a ship, one I think the Captain told me was the *Bellerophon*, except she is unlike the *Bellerophon* on which Ferghal and I served," answered Harry, "I hope we have not committed an offence – I merely tried to see if I could operate the port on this ship and used the command I heard the Captain give when he showed me the outside from his quarters." A look of concern crossed his face, "It frightened Danny, so I closed it again just before you fetched us from our quarters."

"Did you now," exclaimed Rhys, wondering why he was surprised so intelligent a youth would have so quickly discovered how to make something as simple as this function, "no, you haven't broken any rules by doing it, we were simply not expecting you to have discovered how since you hadn't asked and no one had thought to tell you! Good heavens, this is terrific!" he nodded to the person who had been interviewing Harry and said, "I'm sorry to butt in like this Piotr, but I feel I have to know! Harry, could you tell us what you think of what you see out there?"

Harry thought for a moment. Then said carefully, "Well sir, I think it may be that what I am seeing is unreal, but it looks much as a fish does swimming beneath the sea. I saw some when we swam on the coral atolls in the South Pacific. This ship appears like a great whale, or perhaps even one of the great sharks. It may be that we are below the ocean, though I do not know how such a thing could be managed – although it is said that such a submarine boat was made and rowed from Westminster to Greenwich beneath the surface of the Thames in King James' time – and the glow is caused by the phosphorescence in the water as she makes headway?"

The scientists looked at him in some amazement, and Rhys smiled, "Harry, you keep surprising us. That is probably the best explanation anyone" he almost added, 'from your time', stopping himself just as the words formed in his mind, and finished, "could have produced. In fact, that's pretty close to the reality." He looked thoughtful and then said, "Do you know, I don't actually think I know how to open the screen! Would you show me please?"

Harry did as he was bid and used the same command he had given earlier, facing the bulkhead he thought most likely to be the position. In fact he was ninety degrees out and had the screen open to his immediate left, and to his surprise, it showed a different ship! This he noted immediately, and the scientists wondered how he could be so certain. "It is in the detail sirs," he explained carefully, puzzled by their inability to see immediately that it must be so. "This ship has shorter fins than the other, her bows are finer and seem to have a greater sheer – and aft those great remora like sections attached to her tail fins are a different shape and size to the other ship!" He studied the ship again, "Ah, I see the difference," he exclaimed, "we are on the Larboard side now and our quarters are to Starboard, the *Bellerophon* must lie on our other beam."

"Have you seen this ship before?" asked Rhys.

"No sir, only the *Bellerophon*," replied Harry.

"And you have seen the – *Bellerophon* – how many times?"

"Just twice sir, from the Captains quarters and from our own," Harry studied the faces of the two men carefully, "Is something amiss?"

"Amiss? Good heavens no!" exclaimed Rhys, "You have just surprised us a little with your ability to see totally unfamiliar things and yet to make such a detailed observation!"

"I see sir," replied Harry politely, wondering why this should be thought unusual, after all, it was an essential ability if one was to survive at sea! He asked, "If this is another ship in company with ours sirs, may I know the name of it?"

"Er, yes, of course," replied Rhys, "I think that is the *Sydney* – and do you know I would not have been able to tell the difference between her and our other consort without comparing the two!"

"Thank you sir; named for Sir Phillip Sydney no doubt?"

"No, named for the city now occupying the shoreline around the places you know as Port Jackson and Port Phillip. It is the largest commercial centre on the Pacific Rim, and stretches right down the coast almost to the Australian Continental Capital at Canberra." Seeing that this puzzled Harry, he quickly changed the subject and, having got him to shut down the viewscreen, left him to the mathematics of navigation with Lieutenant Piotr Łopata.

✸ ✸ ✸

For the scientists and the boys the next week was a steep learning curve as they continued to surprise their observers with the way in which they coped with the strangeness of what had happened to them. The manual, physical and mental abilities they seemed to think ordinary, but which had been all but lost under the technological revolution which accelerated from the mid twentieth century onwards fascinated and excited the scientists, while the youths seemed to think there was nothing special about them. As Rhys Williams remarked, it was the loss of these abilities in the Twenty-first Century that had led to the collapse of almost all non-tech related skills dependent crafts. The data gathered by the scientists far exceeded their expectations and the xenobiology team had become engrossed in tracking and unravelling genes from the boys DNA that had been bred or engineered out of the human race almost a hundred years previously. The trio carried antibodies, identified in the initial scans, to protect them from viral and bacterial infections not seen on earth for almost two hundred years and which the scientists were now studying to see how these could be adapted and used to deal with the many new viral and bacterial threats the human race was beginning to encounter as it spread out across the stars. To say that they were excited by this, is to understate it, Dr Grüneland found herself having to, on the one hand, deal with a flood of demands for access to data or reports of 'potential breakthroughs" in virology, bacteriology and gene technology, and carry out a daily brief for the Captain on the other.

Not unnaturally by this time, the three 'time travellers', as they had become known, were the subject of many conversations in every department and the Captain discussed this and the effect it might have on the boys when they were eventually able to start to be incorporated into the crew as he was sure they would have to be. The two older boys were not a problem in this regard, provided they could be brought up to the required levels of understanding to be assigned roles within the crew. Danny, on the other hand, was far too young to be placed on the ship's books in any capacity. In the end, it was decided to put out a briefing note explaining as much as necessary to the crew without compromising the boys or the scientists. This decision allowed the Captain, on the advice of Surgeon Commander Len Myers, Dr Silke Grüneland and Doctors Williams and Maartens to decide to 'accept an invitation' from the Gunroom to dinner and to 'invite' the Gunroom to include in their 'invitation' the three boys and the three scientists. This technical device – in effect an order – allowed him to introduce the three boys to the ship's Midshipmen in a way that gave them an opportunity to begin the absorption process and to acquaint Harry and his companions with others nearer their own age, although, he thought ruefully, the youngest of his present crop of Mids, twelve in all, was nineteen!

He was interrupted by a message from his duty Writer. "Sir, I have a personal call for you on a top security private channel."

"Thank you, I'll accept it," he responded, wondering who it would be.

※ ※ ※

Moments later he smiled in pleasure as the face of Theo LeStrange appeared on the screen looking relaxed and slightly pleased with himself. "Theo," he smiled, "I hope this means you have some good news for me?"

"What? When you have stirred the most horrendous hornets nest? My dear fellow," smiled the other, "I have had quite an interesting week sorting out your three young men I can tell you! But I have the papers now duly signed, by the Chief Justice of Ireland himself."

"Theo, I am in your debt my friend. How have you arranged matters?"

"Well, it's a little complicated, but I will forward the records to your data banks and you can take it from there. Essentially Henry Nelson-Heron is now your ward as a direct relation and you have full guardianship of him. Ferghal O'Connor is assigned to your wardship by virtue of your being the heir to an estate and the will of Harry's father which required his heirs and dependents to 'have a care to the dependents of the estate'. As Ferghal is such a dependent – at least the Chief Justice accepted my argument, as did the Court of Rights in Aachen – he is also assigned to your wardship until he reaches his majority. The youngest boy has proved more difficult and, I have to say, much more interesting. You are made his guardian subject to there being no living relatives. As yet there has been no trace of any close DNA match among the living on any European Federation database, so it may well be that he will be in your care for some time to come."

"Theo, I don't think I can ever thank you enough!" exclaimed the Captain, "and any further news of Dr Johnstone?"

*Out Of Time*

"Ah, yes! I should warn you that he has a 'research' facility on the planet you are heading for. I have," he added seriously, "placed certain information in the hands of some very interested people so he may not be a threat in future – but you should exercise great care for the duration of your cruise! One simply does not know with people of this type!"

※ ※ ※

In the Communications Centre Commander Diefenbach studied the log entries on his screen carefully. One showed the message that had gone out to an address in the Department of Science and Exploration, and most worryingly it had gone out from one of Surgeon Commander Myers' labs, the originator being one of the Medical Technicians, although the person had also made quite a sophisticated effort to hide the origin and content of the signal by routing it through several onboard channels and then disguising the message as an attachment to a routine return on Med Centre activity. The recipients address had also turned up some interesting diversions when he had called in a favour from an earthside friend. So now they knew who the leak was, what they did not know was why. Earthside, the military police and espionage branch were already busy and Fritz was reasonably sure that it would be dealt with very efficiently and swiftly – he knew the head of the investigations branch and had a great deal of respect for her methods and her ability to track down and bring to trial anyone who threatened the security of the Confederation's military.

More worrying, was the fact that his logs indicated that a signal from an unknown source had entered their system and apparently disappeared. The receiving equipment all showed an incoming signal, but nothing anywhere in the system had recorded it. In parallel with this, he had run checks on the computers and other electronic systems under his control and discovered that these had all been accessed by someone or something which used no terminal on board and, as far as he could see, no other interface either verbal, visual or, using the still secret, 'mental link' technology. This last was still highly classified and available to a very small and select group including the Captain. It involved a small implanted loop circuit linked to a microchip implanted at the base of the skull at a point where the ganglia joined the spinal cord. It used a range of microscopic fibres to sense electronic waves generated in the brain at certain key centres. It was very secret micro-technology, which worked extremely well, if installed carefully and correctly, allowing the user access to certain computer data files and routines. Of those equipped with it aboard *Vanguard* only a dozen or so actually had full access to the computer and these were all in the Command team with a smaller number among the pilots in the interceptor squadrons where the links to weapons, communication and navigation systems were fairly straight forward and allowed 'hands free' operation of crucial systems. Aboard the *Vanguard* herself, the access was more restricted but still extremely useful.

He keyed his link and spoke to the Captain, passing to him everything he had found and adding his suspicions. The Captain was in thoughtful mood as he closed the link and spent several minutes deep in thought as he considered the first part of Commander Diefenbach's information. Then he keyed his link and gave Surgeon Commander Myers' specific instructions concerning MedTec de Vries. When he had done this, he sat very still for a moment then followed the mental routine to activate his computer link, the sense that he was being watched stronger than ever. His mental command to the computer was simple; "Survey this compartment for any anomalous energy sources." When a few seconds later the computer reported back, his command was simple. "Show me!"

Aloud he said slowly, looking at a point in a corner of the room, "Who are you and what do you want on my ship?"

# Chapter 11

# The learning begins

Sub-Lieutenant Petroc Trelawney, as his name suggested, a Cornishman, in his capacity as senior of the Gunroom, briefed the collected dozen Midshipmen on the Captain's expectations for the coming dinner. In deference to the fact that one of their guests would be an officer and two not, they had decided to include two Warrant Officers as guests. They had considered inviting some ratings but even in this day and age, some barriers existed and the idea had been dropped when the Junior Ratings Mess Association had pointed out that their members felt slightly uncomfortable at sitting down with their future officers. "So," announced the Sub, "Jellico, you will be responsible for hosting the Owner, and you Hearn, will host the Exec. Murphy and Zimmerman, you will take care of Midshipman Heron and Hardy you will see that Warrant Officer (Communications) Kelly and Warrant Officer (Weapons) Carolan have everything they need to keep Seaman O'Connor and the boy comfortable." He grinned at the group and added, "I will play host to Commander Petrocova as our Head of Midshipmen and Hardy, you and Battenberg will look after the scientists. Oh, and the Owner has said he'll pick up the tab for the Gunroom – in recognition of your willingness to host our guests."

There was a ripple of laughter – some of it relief, since entertaining certainly strained a Midshipman's credit allowance – and questions began to flow.

"I heard the Mid is quite sharp at maths and a chess player," said Ute Zimmermann, "is it true he does trig calculations on a writing block?"

"He does, and he uses logarithms – the science team had to search the data bases for a set so they could test him – and he's a demon at a game he calls Whist. The scientists had to do quite a bit of research to find out how it was played. But he hasn't got two heads and he is just like us – just from four hundred years ago!" He frowned slightly and said, "We have to accept that he and his companions aren't used to us or our ways of saying and doing things so take care when talking to them to keep it to things they are likely to be able to understand. The Owner is putting the Mid in the Gunroom in a few days time and we will be helping him to adjust and catch up. I know that you'll all be keen to help, just take it easy and we'll see how it goes."

"What about the other two?" asked the senior Mid, John Jellico, a pleasant faced twenty one year old due for the first step on the promotion ladder.

"The youngster is a bit of a problem as he is well under age to be signed on, so he will in all probability be quartered with us as well so as to keep him with someone he knows as his officer. The older one is going to be quartered in the Junior Rates Mess with the Electronic Rates and will come under Commander Diefenbach's department so he'll be working with you Mr Ng and Miss Sarbutt. Apparently he is absolutely fantastic at working with delicate and intricate equipment so they think he'll fit in there with his skills. He'll be rated as a trainee Electronic Technician as soon as he has enough knowledge to be able to start the training."

The others digested this, and then Ute Zimmermann asked, "How will they be brought up to date?"

"Ah, we have a stroke of luck there! Although it will be tough on them, the older two will get special 'immersion' lessons with the help of some of the science team, the younger one will get a more normal education approach," he paused, then added, "One or two of you may be needed to help Mr Heron adjust to it, apparently it can be quite confusing – even for people who are not four hundred and fifteen."

One of the others chipped in, "Rather him than me then!" and the others laughed.

Paula Sarbutt, a tall and rather wiry young woman, asked, "I've been wondering, is this Mid any relation of the Captain?"

"Funny that," responded Petroc Trelawney thoughtfully, "according to the rumour mill, he is. One of the Owner's direct family – only from four hundred years ago."

✳ ✳ ✳

In the Med Centre suite the boys shared, the news of the invitation to dine in the Gunroom with the Captain and the Midshipmen was received with mixed feelings. Ferghal was plainly uncomfortable until it was pointed out that he would be joined by two Warrant Officers with whom he would in future be training and working. Assured that he would also soon be assigned to a proper Mess with people learning their skills and helping him to learn something new as well, Ferghal felt reassured. He was much more comfortable about the arrangement and relaxed even further when told that he would be placed on the ship's books and given a new uniform to wear to reflect his new status. Harry too, was informed that he would retain contact with Ferghal as they would be undergoing quite a bit of their re-training together and he was even more assured of the position of his companions (the scientists noted with interest that he never asked about his own position, always about the two he had assumed responsibility for) when told that Danny would have a berth in the Gunroom under his care.

"The biggest problem we have Harry," explained Len, "is in how we bring you all into this age in terms of knowledge and skills. You have some skills and knowledge we have lost and there is a whole range of new knowledge that you will need to acquire quite quickly in order to become useful members of our crew." He gave the youth a quizzical look, adding, "You will have to acquire them or become rather anachronistic specimens in a museum somewhere!" he finished seriously.

"I think I understand sir," said Harry with equal seriousness, "there is much about this ship I do not understand and which I know frightens Danny and worries Ferghal, but quite how we are to begin to understand it unless we are taught I do not know."

"You have summed it up very well Harry," said Len speculatively, "That is not the only problem, the gap in technology is one thing, the gap in the underpinning knowledge that you will need to bridge it is another. Fortunately if we cannot do it conventionally, we do have a system and a means to do it in an accelerated way, but it will involve a very delicate piece of micro surgery, and you will have to decide whether you are willing to undertake it. It will need to be cleared by the Captain as well before we can even consider it. We will try everything else first I think."

"I will be guided by you sir," said Harry carefully, "but I cannot accept such a risk for Ferghal or Danny unless I am sure it is safe to commend it to them."

"Well said young man!" interjected Rhys Williams, "Len, I think we may be able to test the technique first without surgery. One of my colleagues has been involved in a long running study which may provide an alternative solution. If you agree we could run a trial, if it works it might provide a simpler solution."

Harry did his best to follow the discussion that resulted but found it difficult as it was conducted using terms and expressions and concepts totally outside his knowledge. In the end it was agreed that a simpler and non-invasive system would be trialled first, but then it was time for the three boys to prepare for the Gunroom dinner and the scientists took their temporary leave assuring Harry and his friends that it would be an enjoyable meal. Len remained and was now joined by two newcomers whom Len informed the boys were from the ship's Supply Branch.

※ ※ ※

The newcomers brought several containers with them. On being opened these revealed a full set of new uniforms for the boys, all exactly regulation Confederation Fleet. Harry found himself fitted into a pair of high waisted trousers of fine soft blue-black material that fitted perfectly on his boyish frame, having first changed himself into new underclothes which sat with an unfamiliar snugness and comfort on his person. This was followed by a white shirt with a standing collar and finally a skirtless jacket of the same blue-black hue as the trousers. The jacket had a standing collar and white patches almost the image of his old uniform – except smaller and somehow finer. On the left breast of the jacket was a badge showing the ship's crest and below this a single metal bar just over four inches in length with a single dark blue line along its length and a device superimposed which resembled a sextant. In response to his enquiry, he was informed that it meant he would be joining the Navigation Officer's team when he was ready.

He looked across to see Ferghal looking anxiously resplendent in a simpler version of the uniform he wore, the main difference being the fact that the collar had badges of a strange design and the short bar below the ship's badge on his chest was plain metal with a lightning flash linking two objects. Next to him stood a proud Danny immaculately turned out in an identical rig except it lacked the collar badges and any insignia of service other than the ship's crest. He spoke, his voice filled with pride, "These'ns sez I'm the ship's mascot sor! 'N I'm to stay with you in t' Gunroom!" he looked at Ferghal proudly, "Ferghal sez it's all Bristol Fashion if'n you sez so sor!"

"Of course it is Danny," grinned Harry, he looked at Ferghal and smiled, "Well Ferghal, you're too smart for a Cutter's crew now! Very fore and aft," he nodded, "I think all will be well with us now."

"Aye Master Harry," beamed Ferghal, "we'll be right once we learn the ropes and the rig, see if we aren't!"

"We will Ferghal, we will," said Harry, adding with a grin to Danny, "and if you're the ship's mascot Danny, you'd better begin to learn to recognise your betters!" He moved a little closer and added in a loud whisper, "These'ns as you called them, are next to Boatswain's Mates, so best not get too cheeky!" he winked at Danny who grinned. But it obviously registered because Danny looked at the pair of grinning Supply Rates and saw the badges on their sleeves. He looked at Harry's patches and at Ferghal's collar, then at the watching Surgeon Commander's insignia. Then he nodded, and whispered to Harry, "I'll get t' knack of it sor, but I don't see no starters wiv' 'em."

Harry laughed, "Right you are Danny, they don't need them – but take care you mind their orders just the same!"

The door slid open and two young people, in uniforms identical to that worn by Harry, entered the cabin just as Harry finished speaking. The leader was a square built young man of slightly above average height with a round open face and a slightly squashed nose, red hair and a wide smile. His insignia bar showed the pale blue line of a flight trainee and the wings on his sleeve showed him to be already a qualified atmospheric pilot. Behind him came a tall and slender built young woman with short cropped blonde hair and a laughing face. Like her companion she wore a Midshipman's collar patches but her insignia bar showed a single dark line and this was crossed with a slender shape which Harry would soon learn to be representation of a missile. They acknowledged the Surgeon Commander, and the young woman said, "Midshipmen Zimmermann (She pronounced the name with a "Ts" sound – the only indication in her accent that suggested Euro-English was not her first language) and Murphy, sir! We are here to escort Mr Heron and his companions to the Gunroom."

Len nodded, "Good. Let me introduce you then." He smiled at Harry and said, "Harry, may I present your new messmates from the Gunroom, This is Ute Zimmermann, who has the privilege of working under Commander Petrocova our Weapons and general destruction Head and Paddy Murphy our rugby player and ship's middle weight boxing champion who is, as you can see, from our Flight Commander's section and is occasionally allowed to fly some of the ship's atmosphere craft – usually when his Commander thinks he can't damage anything." He grinned as the other two smiled at his slightly irreverent descriptions of their roles and abilities, and turned to them saying, "Meet Harry."

The three shook hands the newcomers smiling warmly and doing their best to make Harry feel at ease. The Surgeon Commander in the meantime collected Ferghal and Danny and now brought them forward saying, "And now I shall ask Harry to introduce these gentlemen."

Harry smiled at this courtesy and looked at Ferghal's anxious expression and Danny hanging slightly back like a frightened cat, ever ready to take flight, and said seriously, "I have the privilege of the company of Ferghal O'Connor, Seaman and Danny, a Powder Monkey and Ship's Boy, both from His Britannic Majesty's Ship *Spartan*." He smiled at Ferghal and placed a hand on the older boy's shoulder drawing him forward, "Ferghal and Danny I'd like to present you too," he hesitated a second as he tried to recall the pronunciation then managed 'Oote', and Paddy."

The two boys raised their right hands and stood rigid as they touched their forelocks, while the two slightly bemused Midshipmen held out their hands expecting to shake them. There was a moment of confusion while Harry frantically signalled Ferghal to accept the proffered handshake, which he did uncertainly and Danny followed suit with even greater reluctance. Len watched this little interplay trying hard not to smile as the gap of four centuries of cultural change collided head on.

"Welcome aboard," rumbled Paddy, his voice a deep baritone with a slightly musical lilt to it, as he solemnly shook Danny's small hand, "I hear that you are quite a musician, I hope that you will join our choral group and teach us some of your songs."

Like a small animal dazzled by the headlights of an oncoming juggernaut, Danny gulped an unintelligible reply, faring only slightly worse than Ferghal who found himself shaking hands with a young woman who quite took his breath away – one moreover who seemed to consider that wearing trousers rather than full skirts was perfectly natural. He blushed and stammered "H-o-o-onoured!" in response to her welcome and was relieved when Len suggested that Ute and Harry should lead the way and that Paddy Murphy might like to escort Ferghal and Danny to the Gunroom.

Harry found dealing with the questions about his home and the life aboard the *Spartan* much easier and he was soon at ease in the company of the attractive Midshipman as they made their way along the corridors leading to the Gunroom. Behind him, Ferghal relaxed under the easy charm of the big Irishman, made easier by the discovery that he came from Ulster, having been born in Armagh. Unlike the arrangement aboard the *Spartan*, the Gunroom aboard *Vanguard* was on the same deck as the Wardroom, itself on the same central deck as the Command Centre, but in a different compartment. As the boys would soon learn, the internal divisions of the ship and the separation of the various Control Centres, power generating plants and even the accommodation for key officers, ratings and functions were all designed to ensure that the ship could sustain damage and the loss of some areas but would not lose all her officers or all her power and weapons from the loss of a single compartment. Thus the Gunroom was located on the same central Deck – known as Deck 0 or the Main Deck – as the Command Centre, the Engineering Control Centre, Flight Control and Weapons Control, but each of these was located in a separate compartment and would be, in battle, sealed off from every other key compartment.

The Gunroom proved to be a large space with a comfortable communal lounge area at one end and a dining area, currently laid out for slightly formal meal with the tables arranged in a large hollow square, at the other end. Along the sides a series of doors evidently gave access to sleeping cabins and from the number of doors Harry judged that the ship carried slightly fewer Midshipmen than she had accommodation for. As they entered the compartment Ute announced to the assembled group; "Midshipman Harry Heron, Seaman Ferghal O'Connor and ...," she hesitated briefly, "*Powder Monkey* Danny of His Majesty's Ship *Spartan*!"

There was a guffaw of laughter as the others glanced at Danny and then at Ute's face as she realised the import of what she had just announced, but noted with relief that Harry, Ferghal and even Danny were apparently oblivious of the reason for the laugh as they tried to take in the scene. Sub-Lieutenant Trelawney stepped forward, smiling, "Welcome to the Gunroom Mr Heron, and you Mr O'Connor, Master Gunn," he noted the puzzled looks on their faces at this last name and hastily corrected himself, "I mean Danny!" he grinned as Danny's face cleared and smoothly continued, "I am Sub-Lieutenant Trelawney, the Senior of the Gunroom. Ute and Paddy will introduce you to the others, but first, what would you like to drink? The Captain and the Executive Commander will be along shortly to join us so we have a few minutes yet. I believe you already know the members of our science team?" he indicated Silke Grüneland, Rhys Williams and Frederik Maartens, "and of course Commander Petrocova." Who acknowledged Harry's bow with an inclination of her head and a smile.

"Thank you sir, I do indeed have that honour," Harry bowed slightly acknowledging the introduction, "May I have some wine? Perhaps Danny should have some of the excellent juice we have enjoyed."

"Certainly Mr Heron," grinned the Sub, signalling the Mess Steward, "We have some very good dry white or some equally good red. Which do you prefer?"

"My father's cellars always had Beaujolais or Burgundian sir," smiled Harry, "I'm afraid, our stocks aboard *Spartan* were not very broad and often spoiled! If you have a claret, I would enjoy that, thank you."

"Well, I hope our stocks will be better kept! Is it true that your water supply was often tainted with salt?" He consulted the Mess Steward and added, "Try a glass of this, it is a Cabernet and quite a nice balance between dry and fruity."

Harry accepted the glass gratefully, responding to the question, "It is true sir, the water butts could not always be purged of the salt water placed in them to maintain our trim at sea when they were emptied. So the fresh water was usually very salt. Mind you," he added seriously, "it probably, at least according to our surgeon, prevented the water from becoming foul with disease. It is such a luxury to have so much fresh water aboard this ship that one may bathe daily – even our Captain must needs use salt water drawn from overside for that!"

"Really?" exclaimed the Sub, interested and suddenly aware of just how much he and his fellows took for granted now. After all, it was only a hundred years since the introduction of systems for recycling and purifying water had been introduced aboard space stations and barely sixty since the first large ships had begun carrying the same systems out into space. He grinned as he recalled stories of ship's returning after several months away with their atmospheres so 'ripe' with body odour that it required full decontamination to make them fit for further use.

Harry watched as Ferghal and Danny were surrounded by the other Midshipmen and was pleased to see that Ferghal was soon relaxed and at ease in the company while Danny was fussed over by two attractive women Midshipmen that he would later learn were named Jean Hearn and Sophie Xavier. He too was soon the centre of a small group of Midshipmen and found himself trying to recall names as they were introduced, meeting Paula Sarbutt, George Singh, Phillip Ng (pronounced as Ong – something which confused his attempts to think of how it was spelled for some time!), Hans Dinsen and Ashley Battenberg before the arrival of two Warrant Officers, Andy Kelly from the Computer and Communications Systems Branch and Paul Carolan from Weapons signalled the start of further introductions. The watching scientists and Commander Petrocova took careful note of the various interplays as the three newcomers dealt with their new surroundings. These latest introductions were barely completed when the door slid open and the Captain strode in with the Executive Commander in company.

Acknowledging the Sub-Lieutenant's welcome with a warm smile, the Captain said, "Thank you Mr Trelawney, it's good to be able to join you. Mr Heron," he greeted Harry, "I hear you are a man of surprises. I hope you are settling in with us? Perhaps you would introduce me to your people?"

"Thank you sir," said Harry bowing automatically, "We have been made very comfortable." He indicated Ferghal and Danny, both standing stiffly to attention, and continued, "If I may present Seaman Ferghal O'Connor and Powder Monkey and Ship's Boy Danny Gunn?"

The Captain gravely acknowledged the knuckled forelocks and smiled as he said, "I am glad to make both your acquaintance, I hear that you have some considerable skill in working with delicate equipment, Ferghal. Are you a model maker?" he asked, "It is still a hobby of mine when I have the time to indulge it!"

"Sir!" responded Ferghal, despite Harry's having told him of the Captain's remarkable likeness to Harry's father, he was more than slightly disconcerted by the resemblance as he replied, "Aye, sir, I make models as Mr Tweedy showed me and Mr Benson the Boatswain taught me how to do the rigging sir!"

"Well, Ferghal," smiled the Captain, "perhaps you will one day show me how it's done?" He turned to Danny and said, "And you, Danny, I hear are a musician? I hope you'll join the ship's music group, I hear that they are keen to hear you play."

Danny made a strangled response, awed at being in the exalted presence of this imposing figure and a little afraid – a fear based on the harsh discipline of the Navy he had been thrust into three years earlier.

The Captain smiled encouragingly and said to Harry, "I gather Commander Grenville here has assigned you and Ferghal to ship's departments and mapped out a learning programme for you with the scientists and the Surgeon Commander. Danny will have to wait a few years to join you if he wants too, but we'll start his education now – I have assigned him to my Writer so she can start him off and keep an eye on him until we can work out a proper plan for it."

"Thank you sir," said Harry gratefully, "I hope we will not disappoint you!"

"I am sure you will not," smiled the Captain, accepting a drink from the Mess Steward as he made his apologies and moved off to talk to several other Midshipmen, while the Executive Commander took his place and engaged Harry, now joined by Ute and Paddy in conversation.

A few minutes later the Sub-Lieutenant invited the assembled company to take their places at the table and Harry found himself seated opposite the Captain between his earlier escort while each of his companions was similarly bracketed by one of the Midshipmen and one of the Warrant Officers. He was pleased to see that Ferghal had relaxed into the company and that Danny was being treated kindly by the Midshipman named Sophie Xavier, a dark skinned and raven haired Spaniard on one side and the Weapons Branch Warrant Officer Paul Carolan on the other. Reassured that the pair for whom he felt a personal responsibility were being cared for, he relaxed a little himself. Across the table Captain Heron and Silke Grüneland watched him carefully without making it obvious and were struck by the way he handled himself in these strange and disquieting circumstances, but most particularly they were struck by the care he showed for the two 'other ranks' he regarded as his responsibility in this situation. Similarly Executive Commander Grenville and Commander Petrocova watched from either side of Rhys Williams as the three settled into the company, the scientist fascinated by the old fashioned manners, but the two Commanders watching with interest the interplays between Harry and his 'men' as they constantly looked to him for signals. But, noted Valerie, it was often Ferghal who initiated exchanges with those around him. Interesting, she thought, and worth seeing how he develops.

The dinner was in all respects a huge success, not least due to the efforts of the Chief Mess Steward who ensured that Danny and Ferghal always had a 'little guidance' by surreptitious signals on what to do with which utensils and how to indicate they were finished with a particular course. By its end, Harry and his friends felt that they had been accepted into this new company and crew. Ferghal in particular was much more relaxed after having the opportunity to talk to the two Warrant Officers and learning that he would be under their tuition and supervision for training. Danny found himself telling an enthralled audience what his task aboard *Spartan* had involved and just how fast he and the other boys had had to run to keep the guns supplied with powder. His description of the scenes below decks during an engagement stilled all conversation at one point and left several of the Midshipmen – and their Captain and Commander – astonished at both the candid observations of this child and the conditions in which he had lived and worked during his short life.

\* \* \*

The next morning Harry was summoned to the Executive Commander's Office, presenting himself carefully turned out in his new uniform, expecting to be assigned some task. Instead Commander Grenville invited him to sit down and handed him a tablet. It was the first time Harry had held one of these although he had seen a number of people using them since his arrival. Now he saw that it had a glass-like surface which glowed and that it appeared to hold a document of some sort.

"I think you should read that Mid," smiled the Commander, "it is the report submitted by Captain Blackwood of the *Spartan* on the engagement in which you and your people disappeared."

Harry studied the unfamiliar script carefully. It took him several minutes to realise that, although many of the letters had changed their form slightly, it was, once he had recognised the alternative form, quite easy to follow. He read swiftly through the rest, of how the one French ship had apparently been destroyed by an explosion and the other, engaged first by *Spartan*, had surrendered to boarders from the *Rajahstan* and *Swallow* when the *Spartan* had turned and begun to close on her to board. He learned too of the damage to Number Eight gun and the mainmast, of the repairs in Delagoa Bay and of the long voyage home. As he finished reading, he looked up and said, "I do not understand how we may be here sir, or how I can be reading this," he indicated the tablet, "on this device, but I hope I may one day know these things."

"I think you will," smiled the Commander, "Now, look again at the tablet please, do you see a series of tabs along the bottom of the screen?"

"Aye sir!"

"Good, now touch the second from the left!"

Harry did and the document he had been reading was instantly replaced by another, one he immediately recognised as his Warrant as a Midshipman! He expressed his surprise and was told to touch the next tab. This document showed an extract of the *Spartan's* Watch and Quarter Bill with his own name and those of Ferghal and Danny highlighted. Next to each were the initials 'DD' – naval shorthand for 'Discharged Dead'. He looked up, his expression serious, "I do not understand sir, according to the Captain's report and the ship's Muster Book we are dead, yet we are here and very much alive!"

"Exactly. You *are* alive, that record is four hundred years old Mr Heron. Try the next tab, I think you'll find that we have some new information on that situation."

Harry touched the next tab and read the document that appeared. It showed his name and his correct place and date of birth – and declared that he was now the ward of one James O'Niall Heron, Captain and Commodore North European Confederation Space Fleet, of Scrabo Manor, County Down, Kingdom of Ulster! To his amazement it went on to state that the "*said Henry Nelson Heron, having been displaced in time/space by a malfunction in Near Earth Gate Southern Hemisphere Indian Ocean, and having been erroneously declared dead, and is hereby declared to be alive...*" He looked across at the Commander in amazement, "Sir, does this mean that I am, I mean the Captain is ...?" He trailed off, lost for words.

"If you are asking if you are now in the care of the Captain, the answer is yes. You, Ferghal O'Connor and Danny." The Commander smiled, "you are very fortunate young man, not only because the Captain is a direct relative, but because he is also a man who knows when to use his connections. There are a number of people back on Earth who would dearly like to get their hands on you three for their own ends. The Captain has taken on these legal issues and ensured that you have a legal existence and therefore the protection of the law, but he has also undertaken to give you all a chance to fit into these most unusual circumstances."

"I see that sir," said Harry, still amazed at the turn of events. "Sir, if I may ask, do the others know this?"

"If you mean O'Connor and Gunn, the answer is no, I shall leave it to you to tell them. My fellow heads of Department know of course. There is no need for anyone else to know unless you decide to tell them. I should point out to you that the Captain will not intervene on your behalf if you are in breach of any of your duties when we decide you are ready to take them on or if you commit any offence under the discipline codes."

"I understand sir," nodded Harry seriously. He glanced at the tablet again and noted the Captain's address with slight pang, "I hope that he will allow me to see the old house again some day," he said sadly.

"I'm sure he will Harry," said the Commander gently, "he has to be careful for the moment that no accusation can be levelled at either of you of favouritism or of nepotism on his part. Nor can there be a suggestion of your having taken advantage of your relationship. I am sure you can see the danger in that!"

※ ※ ※

Two days later the three said farewell to the MedCentre quarters they had occupied and Harry and Danny moved into the Gunroom with adjoining cabins, a small shower and toilet unit shared between them. Ferghal moved two decks down and a full compartment forward of the Gunroom to a small but comfortable cabin off the Mess Flat for Junior Technical Rates in the Computer and Electronics Department headed by Commander Diefenbach. He found himself under the watchful eye of Warrant Officer (C) Andy Kelly and in a Division headed by Lieutenant Elizabeth Pascoe. Despite the change in quarters, the three boys still faced a challenge in acquiring sufficient knowledge and understanding of the science and technology they now had to master to be able to take their places in the crew. All too often initially the boys found themselves up against a gap of understanding or of essential knowledge in this modern world. The support they got from their mentors and new friends was tremendous, but they found it both intimidating and frustrating to be so ignorant of so much that others took for granted. Yet, on the positive side, their new companions found their eagerness to learn and some of their skills and somewhat old fashioned powers of reasoning and deduction in solving problems not only intriguing but refreshing. For people used to asking the computer it came as something of an eye opening revelation to see Harry sit down and perform a mental exercise to solve a tricky problem, frequently coming up with a better solution than that suggested by the computer. Ferghal's skill in understanding the relationships between components, even though he did not fully understand their function amazed those trying to teach him, and both youth's powers of observation and memory stood them in very good stead.

Danny was perhaps the most fortunate in this respect as Adriana Volokova, the Captain's Senior Writer, was a qualified teacher and she had immediately set up a programme for him which started with language and reading. It wasn't long before he was advancing in leaps and bounds, most amazingly in learning how to use the equipment and the computer to aid his studies. Harry found himself assigned to Commander Curran's team and directly under the care of Lieutenant Case, a large man who cheerfully accepted his charge and immediately began to push him to master the various aspects of the computers he would need to use in future. One problem soon became evident for both Ferghal and Harry – neither had sufficient understanding of the science of electronics or of the various theories underlying much of what they would be required to use in future – to be able to fully develop

*Out Of Time*

their skills in this regard. Even so they soon mastered the art of accessing data and being able to retrieve information. They also tackled with fierce determination the mastery of some of the uses of the computer for the various tasks their respective roles demanded, but this again was hindered by their lack of background knowledge on the science and technology which made the entire process functional and this led to some frustration on both their parts. A large part of the problem was, quite simply, the knowledge gap on a very wide range of subjects. The young men had little or no knowledge of the concepts of space, electronics, advanced physics, environmental management or even that most basic force in the universe – gravity. It quickly became apparent that using normal educational approaches and even the 'immersion' technique suggested and supported by the science team, could not give the pair the 'catch up' they needed in the time available. The problem was discussed at length between the officers, the scientists and the medical team. As a result both Harry and Ferghal were instructed to see Surgeon Commander Myers.

The two reported to the Surgeon Commander's office promptly the next morning slightly worried that their ignorance was about to cause their dismissal from their new posts before they had even begun. They found themselves being shown into a conference room with Silke Grüneland, Rhys Williams and Frederik Maartens, Len Myers and another officer, a Lieutenant Commander, also present. Len greeted them with a smile, "Harry, Ferghal, please sit down, we need to discuss something very important with you and you will need to decide what you want to do."

The two boys seated themselves and smiled nervously at the assembled team. "We will be guided by you sir, if it will help us gain the knowledge we lack we will do whatever you advise."

"Well, that will be a first in my career!" laughed the Lieutenant Commander, "and yours Boss!"

"I should think so too!" grinned Len, "After all, none of the victims we usually have to patch up have much choice in the matter." He indicated the assembled company, "Harry, you both know all our friends from the Scientific Office, but you haven't met our Neurologist before. This is Lieutenant Commander Thomas Blakewell and he is an expert in cyber implants." He saw that the two boys were looking puzzled and explained, "There are two ways we can give you the knowledge you need to adjust to our age and technology. The first we have been trying; it will take far too long and creates a number of difficulties for you and for us. The other is to attempt to set up a neural network and download the information directly into your heads. It can be done by setting up a sort of cranial cap which interfaces with parts of your brain. It requires resetting every time we do it and it is unreliable. The other way is a permanent implant in your cerebral cortex."

Both boys looked alarmed at this, and Harry asked carefully, "Do I understand you correctly sir, you wish to open our heads and place some device inside our brains?"

"Almost correct Harry, only we don't need to actually open you cranium," interjected the Lieutenant Commander, "I can make the connections I need to make at the base of your skull. He nodded in the direction of the Surgeon Commander, "Both the Boss and I have these implants and so does the Captain and several of the other Commanders. It will require making a small incision here," he indicated a position at the base of his skull and on the back of his neck, "and exposing the spinal cord. The procedure is extremely safe, but it does require you to be awake and alert while I make the connections and interfaces."

"What precisely will this do for us sir?" asked Harry fighting down his fear.

"It will allow you to access information directly from the ship's data banks Harry," replied Rhys Williams quietly, "If set up correctly you will be able to learn everything you need to know or understand almost instantly and as you need it."

"That is correct, and it has another advantage, you can learn and download other information while you sleep, which allows you to expand your knowledge base into non-essential and non-technical areas when you want to," added Len, adding, "and Dr Bischof from the science team will continue working with you to make the adjustment and help you cope with the extra stress the more rapid expansion of knowledge can bring."

"Could we try the other mechanism first?" asked Harry, "Meaning no disrespect sir, but I have seen our former surgeon, Mr Watson, attempt to repair a man's head and have some reluctance to having mine opened up."

*Out Of Time*

"Understandable Harry," smiled Len and the Lieutenant Commander nodded in agreement. "OK, we have the kit here, so perhaps if Dr Williams and Mr Blakewell can fit it to you, let's see what we can achieve with it."

A frustrating and uncomfortable hour later, Harry and Ferghal were seated in front of a pair of terminals wearing what looked like a forest of wires sprouting from their scalps and held in place by elastic caps which fitted tightly. Asked what it felt like and whether it was comfortable, Harry had replied that it was not, in fact putting him in mind of what it would feel like to have someone using his head as a pincushion. This raised a laugh as the experiment continued. "Try it again please Harry," said Tom Blakewell, "I think I have now got the sensors lined up on the neural paths we need. You chaps are a little different to the way us modern types function!"

Harry concentrated on the thought routine they had given him and suddenly he could 'hear' the computer inside his head. He tried to focus on a question – "Newton's third law of motion?" he thought carefully, and heard the answer "Newton's Third Law of Motion states 'For every action there is an equal and opposite reaction.' And he nodded his confirmation, and then tried again, thinking carefully, "What is Phlogiston?" The answer surprised him. "Phlogiston was a term used to describe a non-existent element believed by many in the Eighteenth Century to be the linking agent which was destroyed in the combustion process and was supposedly the binding agent holding all solid materials together. It is now known that this substance does not exist and that the essential bond in solids is the electro-bond between atoms."

He opened his eyes wide in surprise, "It works! At least I think it does, it answered two questions, but one I know to be correct, the other I am not sure of – my uncle took me to hear a lecture at the Royal Society and the speaker told us about Phlogiston and its role in binding the universe! The computer says it does not exist!"

"Then the computer is correct," grinned Silke Grüneland, "I shall explain it to you when you have time, try asking the computer about Relativity and Tachyons."

Harry tried it, and received two surprising answers. The first explained that a man named Albert Einstein had developed a theory of relativity based on a mathematical formula. The maths filled his head and suddenly he was able to see the logic of Normal Physics and the rules that the universe obeyed concerning the relationships between mass, gravity, matter and the physical universe. The second question yielded even more exciting information, explaining the theory of hyperspace and the particles which existed there and which could only exist very briefly outside of that realm. Again a wealth of information seemed suddenly available to his mind – as if it had always been there.

Next to him Ferghal sat transfixed as he too experienced the opening up of an exciting new realm of knowledge. He found himself immersed in miniaturisation electronics and circuitry. He found it exciting and exhilarating, but, no sooner had they acquired each bit of this new knowledge than they realised that there were gaps, bits of the information that they were unable to capture or unable to access fully – the 'voice' seemed to stutter from time to time and it was frustrating in the extreme to have something they only half understood and could not capture the rest. Harry explained this to the watching scientists and Ferghal confirmed that he too was having trouble with it.

The team exchanged glances. Then Tom Blakewell said, "I was afraid that would be the case. Even when it is working perfectly this interface technique relies on the contacts on the scalp being exactly right and immovably fixed which is very difficult if the scalp is secreting its normal oils. OK guys, we have a choice," he said to the boys, "we know that you can master the access to the computer, but we now also know it isn't going to work as well as we need it to. The second drawback is that these caps have to be set up every time and that they have to be connected to a terminal – in other words you can't use them if you are asleep. So, the choice is yours – struggle on with this or allow me to insert the implants so you can access the information whenever you need to?"

Harry looked at Ferghal and raised one eyebrow. Then he nodded, "Very well, I will do this – but I must ask that you allow Ferghal to see what is involved and if anything happens to me as a result, that he and Danny be spared the risk."

"Agreed!" The Lieutenant Commander gave Harry an appraising look and continued, "And don't worry Harry; the routine is relatively simple – much easier than trying to match up those caps in fact." He looked at Len and said, "given that we know we have a spy in the camp

I suggest that we use the Emergency Medical Station right aft – and I'll get Fritz Diefenbach to put a block on access to the records from that Station for this."

"Good thinking," replied Len, "and I'll give her an assignment that will keep her so busy she won't have time to wonder about this."

"When do you want to do this?" asked Silke Grüneland.

"Ideally I want to start immediately, can we do it?" he asked Harry as much as Len.

"I'll clear it with the Owner if Harry is up for it," replied Len, "and I will make sure you have the right people around you for it. I need about half an hour to get everyone in place without arousing our spy's suspicions." He smiled at Harry, "Are you sure you want to do this?"

Harry nodded, "If it will help us to catch up with everything and fit in better, I see no alternative sir," replied Harry carefully, "but I think I should first ensure it is safe and works, and then if Ferghal wishes to try it he should be allowed to make his decision on how it affects me."

"Bravely said Harry," said Rhys Williams, "but what is this business about spies?" He asked Len Myers.

"Ah, sorry," exclaimed Len looking a little uncomfortable, "we have discovered who sent the boys data to your colleague and we'd like to keep that under wraps in case we can use the same channel to our advantage later."

"I see, but I must protest at your calling any of that party a colleague!" snapped Silke Grüneland with both Rhys Williams and Frederik Maartens rumbling their agreement.

Harry and Ferghal listened to this exchange in bemusement, which showed on their faces and Len realised that the conversation needed to be explained to the pair.

Turning to face them he explained, "Harry, Ferghal, your arrival onboard has caused quite a stir in scientific circles, some of them not quite as ethical as our friends here. You are considered prime specimens by certain parties – as indeed they see any life form we encounter in exploring space. It is known that they have people they can get information from on all ships in the fleet, but we underestimated the skill in getting messages out when we 'acquired' you. I am sorry to say that there are people who will stop at nothing to get their hands on you and Danny so they can carry out some tests and experiments on you for their own purposes. *But,* we have identified the person and have taken steps to limit the risk that poses to you. You don't need to know the details, just that you are safe as long as you are with this ship and under the care of our Captain and Exec." He looked at Tom Blakewell and continued, "Once the computer link is installed we will have another back-up which, as long as the other side don't know about it, will enable us to find you anywhere, provided you are near a computer network, should they manage to do anything to grab you."

Silke Grüneland watched Harry's face and saw the worry cross his young features, she intervened, saying, "Harry, you should not worry, I and my colleagues will do everything we can to help you and Ferghal gain all the knowledge you need and we are already working to reduce the threat of this other party." She turned to Len, saying, "I think I have the answer to your problem for the spy, send her to Frederik's team and leave her to Frederik and Thomas Scheffer, I know that they have several fairly complex and involved procedures they will need a Medical Technician to help them complete, *nicht wahr, Frederik?"*

*"Ja!"* exclaimed Dr Maartens, his face breaking into a wide grin as he guessed her intent, "Give Thomas and I ten minutes and we will have a series of medical trials for her from our data which will all be very time consuming and very pointless, but completely convincing! Let us see what she does with the information after that," he gave a bark of laughter, "or what our 'colleague' makes of it!"

❋ ❋ ❋

Two hours later Harry was seated in a strange back to front seat in a small operating theatre, his chin resting on a special support and with his head secured in a clamp. This held his neck and the base of his skull exposed allowing Thomas Blakewell completely unobstructed access. Controlling the array of equipment in the theatre from a console to one side was Senior Med Tec Dick Hopkins, a rather cheerful man of spare build who kept Ferghal amused as he ran through the routine checks of all the equipment to be used on Harry. Picking up on Ferghal's era he showed his understanding of the old saying 'Aft the most Honour; Forward the better men' adding that the implants simply improved the officer's memories – suggesting that once he had one Ferghal would have to become an officer since there was no need for an ordinary rate to have

*Out Of Time*

such a memory! This kept Ferghal distracted as the preparations on and around Harry continued so successfully that the boy almost forgot what was about to happen to his friend.

Next to Harry sat another of the Medical Team, Surgeon Lieutenant Commander Bridget Jepson, a cheery woman who explained that her task was to make sure Harry felt only what he was supposed to feel and to make sure he didn't mess up Tom Blakewell's handiwork! Harry listened as Tom Blakewell spoke to the computer, "Computer, isolate all records for this Station, no access unless on personal authorisation of myself, the Head of Medical Centre or the Captain. Commence recording offline from ship, but show on online systems that this lab is idle. Confirm instruction!"

The ethereal voice of the computer responded, "Instruction confirmed, this lab shows as idle on all ship's systems. Lab is isolated from system and recording is offline, restricted access only to authorised code holders."

"Make it so!" confirmed Tom. Turning to Harry and the others, he grinned and added, "That should keep prying eyes out! I have got Fritz monitoring all attempts to access any records relating to the boys as a precaution – and anyone attempting to access anything on these records is in for a visit from Eric the Red and his merry men!" He gave the boys a thoughtful look and added, "And I need hardly tell you two, but I will anyway, that you must not, under any circumstances, tell anyone you have these! Clear?"

Bridget laughed as she positioned a screen in front of Harry, commenting, "I should imagine that the Master at Arms and his team will make life very unpleasant for anyone prying where they ought not! Especially if the Owner might be annoyed by said intruder!" To Harry she cheerfully pointed out that he would be able to watch the entire procedure – in fact he had to watch because he needed to be able to tell them what was happening when they did certain things to connect his implant to his cerebral cortex! To Harry's amazement – and the anxiously watching Ferghal's – the implements the surgeons laid out did not contain a single knife, saw or any of the other 'tools of the trade' they had so often seen the surgeon use aboard *Spartan*. The most amazing piece of the equipment was a large microscope whose function had to be explained as it was totally unlike anything they had seen before

– and Harry had, on occasion, seen and been allowed to peer through the small one used by *Spartan's* surgeon who was something of a biologist. Tom Blakewell insisted that he should see the device that was to be implanted in his head through this, it was explained that the chip was so small they needed the microscope to actually see it. To Harry it resembled nothing less than a very small sea creature with a mass of fine tentacles radiating from its periphery.

"Ready Harry?" asked Tom Blakewell, and received an affirmative response. He glanced at Bridget and got a confirmatory nod from her, and then said to Harry, "OK Harry, now I'm going to insert this needle. I'd like you to watch the screen and tell me if there is any sensation." He slipped the needle under the skin and watched carefully as the minute camera it carried showed its passage through the various layers, gently manipulating it around obstacles and through the minute passages he needed to negotiate until finally, almost an hour later; it was exactly where he needed to be to begin. He checked again with his colleague and received a nod as she kept Harry busy explaining exactly what he was seeing and how the implant would now be attached. Harry watched in fascination, amazed that he felt nothing, but even more amazed at what he was actually seeing. Ferghal watched, on a separate screen, equally enthralled, listening with complete engrossment to the commentary Bridget provided as Tom now began the process of inserting and attaching the implant.

As each tiny interface was attached to a different section of Harry's ganglia he was asked to perform some mental task, each one different, each one simple in itself, yet crucial to identifying the areas of his brain the device needed to work through. On screens around them, Tom and Bridget followed carefully the computers responses to these exercises, while the boys watched in amazement as the computer screens showed the result as Harry called it up.

Harry was exhausted by the time Tom Blakewell finally declared he was satisfied and wanted nothing so much as to sleep, but the two surgeons insisted that he had to learn a simple routine to control the device and, rather grumpily he did so. He soon cheered up though when he found he was able, through a very simple mental exercise, to access the computer and open up any information he required. He was jubilant, "It works!" he exclaimed, "It's fantastic – I can read the theory of FTL travel and the Relativity Parallax!"

"Great stuff Harry," grinned Bridget, "now; I think your system needs some sleep and a recovery period. Ferghal, do you want to go through this?"

"Aye, Mis… er Commander!" responded Ferghal, "that was amazing to see! I wish I could work on circuits like that – only I'd rather work on a machine than a man!"

"Do you now?" the two surgeons smiled at him, "Well, that's a distinct possibility once we have your implant inserted. But that will be a task for tomorrow – Tom you look exhausted! Let's get our victim off to bed and you and I can get this sorted out over a stiff refresher!"

❉ ❉ ❉

The following morning Ferghal underwent the same procedure, under the same tight security, with Harry watching anxiously, and the real learning process for the pair began soon after. To everyone's relief the implants showed an immediate result, neither youth now had trouble grasping difficult technical concepts since a few minutes reflection and a quick mental search of the data banks generally bridged the gaps in their understanding – but there were a few amusing misunderstandings due to language and phraseology, and sometimes due to accessing the wrong information! Starting that very evening, the two young men began the process of 'catch up' on technology, by the relatively simple process of the automatic download of packages of knowledge, converted to 'memory' in the unique chemical-electric process of the living brain while they slept. Each 'package' being carefully selected so that it built their knowledge upon the foundation of the last piece of data. By this means the pair were soon able to build understanding of their new environment and even began to acquire the necessary knowledge by more normal means, swiftly coming up to the required level in order to deal with the new world they found themselves in.

While none of this activity could be read or registered by anyone without a special access code, currently restricted to just six people, one entity watched the boys with increasing interest. Unknown to either of them, their progress was closely monitored by more than just their mentors on *Vanguard*. A factor the Captain was considering carefully since his encounter with the alien presence in his quarters – despite the very clear impression the alien had given him that it intended no harm.

※ ※ ※

Aware of his Captain's concerns and of the encounter with an alien presence, Commander Ben Curran had, for several days, been engaged in attempting to use the ship's remote exploration probes to get a good look at the following ships. To his and Valerie Petrocova's frustration nothing they had tried had so far succeeded. "Damn it Val I've tried launching them and leaving them dormant in our wake, and all that happens is that as soon as the aliens get anywhere near them and they activate, the probes are deactivated until they are astern of the aliens and all I can get is a view of their tails!"

"Have you tried angling them out abeam and dropping them astern?" asked Val, certain that her friend would have done this.

"Yup, tried looping them ahead and out to extreme range then closing them from abeam as soon as the direct approach failed. This is all I got for my trouble!" He called up a series of long range and very indistinct images which showed strangely shaped appendages sprouting from the roughly triangular main body of the nearest alien craft. Bright flares along these seemed to indicate power transfer of some sort, but the probes' sensors could not read the frequencies or get a firm analysis of the hull material. "It's almost as if they are screening themselves in some way – or the hull is some sort of organism," mused Ben.

"What about the visual approach?" asked Val, "have you tried using the deep space telescopes in the fin observatories?"

"Hey, that's a thought! Thanks, for suggesting it, I'll get up the North Cardinal observatory post right away – if that 'scope can see them, we can lock the other 'scopes on to them from there!" He grinned and gave her a friendly thump on the shoulder, adding, "I knew you were more than a pretty face attached to some awesome fire power!"

The Captain's comlink chirped. He acknowledged the call and the clipped accents of Fritz Diefenbach said, "Captain, our leak has just sent another package to an earthside receiver. Interestingly it has been relayed immediately to our destination. I have decoded it; it contains the data the Science Team has tasked the source with."

"Thank you Fritz. I take it there is no suspicion we are monitoring this?"

"None sir. The target has used a similar attempt to disguise source and identity but I have in place a programme which unravels that!"

"Good – and Fritz. Thank you."

※ ※ ※

Harry slept deeply, but with a troublesome dream. He found himself in a world surrounded by light, a world without any form or shape, and yet he did not feel any physical threat. Instead he felt that somehow he was being examined and that his examiners found him satisfactory. The trouble with the dream was that it seemed to him that he was being assessed for some task, something that would only be revealed in time, and he woke up in the morning with the distinct feeling that the dream had not been a dream, that he was now linked to something in some way he could not quite understand.

# Chapter 12

# Getting to grips with a chimera

It was once said that a man who thought he understood the universe, didn't understand the question. Commander Ben Curran felt like that man as he studied the images of the alien ships the powerful telescopes mounted at the extremities of the four great fins recorded. With some difficulty, since communications between ships in hyperspace always had to pass through signal boosters and relays, he had succeeded in speaking to his opposite numbers in the *Bellerophon* and the *Sydney* and they too had trained their optical imagers on the shadowing ships. "It's the damndest thing," he told Val Petrocova and Nick Gray in exasperation, "as soon as you get a good focus and start to record, the damned things shift in some way and we lose the definition. It's almost as if they know we are watching them!"

"Perhaps they do," mused Val, "Fritz was telling me that we have something accessing data and systems in our computers without using the usual interface tech. Could it be we have a 'ghost' in the system?"

"If we do I'm sure Fritz will find it and scare it straight back out of the systems! Nobody messes with his system and gets away with it for long," laughed Nick, "There has to be a rational explanation. Do you want me to get authority to launch an interceptor to attempt to close with them?"

"Well, that's the mystery," grumbled Ben, "the bloody telescopes don't use any sort of emitter, so there's nothing to detect or measure for any sort of scanner to lock onto. They're the oldest bloody technology we have on board! The only damned thing in them that uses any sort of power – besides the training and focusing gear – is the image recorder! How the blazes do they know we are looking at them?"

"Anyone would think this is a personal thing!" remarked Valerie, "You should take a more pragmatic approach. In the old days of the twentieth century period called the 'cold war' the various super powers used to attempt to shadow each others submarines. The technique involved getting into another submarines wake – a blind spot." She grinned at him, and continued, "The Russian Commanders developed a technique for surprising their shadowers – a tight circle to Port or Starboard with all their sensor arrays focused behind them. It was a manoeuvre called a Crazy Ivan – you should consider trying it!"

"Hmmm, you may have something there!" exclaimed Ben, "a three-sixty degree jink by all three ships could just catch them off guard. I'll have to do a check on what it would do to our exit point though, a few thousand klicks in hyperspace translates into a few million in normal space!"

* * *

In the Briefing Room an assembly of Midshipmen, Lieutenants, Warrant Officers and selected reps from all ships' departments were gathered for a briefing on the destination. Harry found himself seated with the other Midshipmen and to his delight noted that Ferghal was also present in the next row. The briefing was conducted by the Executive Commander with a number of others giving a part, each a specialist in their own particular field. He was interested to note that Dr Grüneland was also seated with the briefing team.

"The planet we are soon to visit is a fairly recent colony – it was settled eighty years ago by people jointly from the European Confederation and the North American Federation. Since then there has been a considerable investment by a number of Earthside Corporate investment groups. Not all of that has returned quite the profit the bureaucrats predicted," He paused as a ripple of laughter ran through the room, "but now the political situation seems to have become unstable. There is one principle settlement with a number of smaller towns and communities. Recently there has been a shift away from the colonist's interests to those of a non-government organization. The Corporate interests have sponsored what is to all intents and purposes a *coup d'etat* – or so the messages smuggled off world are saying – and have installed a Governor who was actually rejected in an election. They have also installed a 'Civil Guard' – effectively a mercenary army – and are using them to control the populace and suppress protest. We have recently obtained information that they are using the planet for research of an unethical nature and dissidents are reported to be disappearing. These disappearances have been ascribed to 'alien abduction', but in fact we have credible evidence that this is not the case. Our orders are to land a force of Marines and Infantry and take control of the Colony until such time as a civilian government can be re-instated following an investigation and elections under the aegis of the World Treaty Organization. It should not involve a shooting war, but the Marines will be deployed to the surface to take control and if necessary to use force to do so. Colonel Kernan's teams will deploy using the ship's landing craft. They will be supported by forces landing from the *Bellerophon* and the *Sydney* and by a larger force arriving aboard the *Fort Belvedere*. Once the objective has been achieved, the ship's science team will also be landing to carry out a range of tests on the flora, fauna and the geological formations of this planet. I shall leave it to Doctor Grüneland to explain the planetary side of things." He smiled and nodded towards her as he said this, continuing, "Each Department will be supporting this activity and a rotation will be worked out to give everyone possible the opportunity to go planetside. I have to stress that the political situation is highly sensitive and will be receiving the attention of a team led by the Captain who has a specific brief for this. I must also inform you, that under our present orders, Captain Heron will formally assume the rank of Commodore for this deployment from the moment we 'drop out' of hyperspace. I will be assuming the position of Captain of this ship for the duration of that exercise, with the other Commanders sharing some of my present duties between them. Colonel Kernan will assume the rank of Brigadier on the commencement of the deployment to the planetary surface and will be the Military Governor until relieved by a civilian government. Your roles will be to maintain a stabilising influence and to gather data, not, under any circumstances, to be drawn into supporting or refuting any argument with any faction." He paused for a moment then added, "As we are about to enter a zone where we could be attacked or fired upon, all personnel will be required to undergo refresher survival training. Off duty watches will be required to turn out for this on a rota which will be posted shortly. I'm sure I don't need to remind you that being able to don your survival suits in a hull breech situation correctly and quickly may mean the difference between living and dying rather unpleasantly."

The Commander was followed by Captain Bob Wardman RM and who explained that there were indications that sporadic outbreaks of fighting apparently between dissidents from the now virtually dispossessed colonial settlement and the Governor's Civil Guard. These were a matter for concern, but were not expected to hinder the landings. While it was hoped that the landings by the Marines would be unopposed it remained a possibility that they could be resisted by the Civil Guard. It was not intended for the landing forces to become involved in the skirmishes between factions, but if necessary they would to restore peace. They would be carrying out an in depth reconnaissance to determine the extent of operations by the Civil Guard and would be disarming them and any other forces they encountered. In this they would be supported by several flights of Commander Gray's atmosphere strike craft and transports, complimented by squadrons from the other ships as well and by several of the orbital survey craft the ship carried.

By this stage Harry and Ferghal had begun to get to grips with the concepts of space travel and of the idea that some craft could land and leave the planet's surface while others could not. What they had not, as yet, actually physically seen was any planet from space. They both listened carefully to the briefing as it progressed, hoping that they too would be allowed to see this strange new world at first hand. Not even the medical briefing could put them off, after all, in their own age, death from disease, accident or enemy action had been a constant feature of life. The thought of exposure to strange infections hardly registered in their eyes, even when the Surgeon Lieutenant giving the briefing made a passing reference to the fact that some of the antibodies which formed the basis of the vaccinations everyone going planetside would receive had come from Harry, Ferghal and Danny which got Harry a playful punch on the arm from Paula Sarbutt who whispered, "You must have lived an interesting life to pick up all these strange bugs – you sure you were never off-world before?"

Harry acknowledged this with a grin and a whispered response, but then his attention was taken by the images Dr Grüneland was now calling up on a large display screen. Harry listened enthralled as she spoke.

"The planet is named Pangaea and is, in age, roughly equivalent to the Devonian Period of the Earth's development. The arrangement of landmasses is unlike the pattern we are used to on Earth and the continents are all clustered in one quadrant with the largest continental mass located just south of the equatorial region. The seas separating the five major continental masses are relatively shallow and harbour most of the naturally evolved life forms this planet has produced – until human settlement." She paused as the pictures changed to show some large and rather clumsy looking animals, "Do not be deceived by appearances, this is the largest animal encountered to date and it is extremely fast in its natural habitat, the open oceans. It is one of the most vicious predators we have encountered anywhere. They are also capable of attacking prey – essentially any other life form – short distances from the water. Fortunately they do not seem to be very numerous, but great care must be taken near any large body of water. As far as we are aware there are no longer any natural land-based predators, most of them having been rendered extinct during the early phase of settlement. The remaining land based fauna are vegetarian or omnivorous scavengers and their only real threat to humans is their size." She called up a series of pictures of strange looking animals. "The planet is the major source of several ores and minerals which are now very scarce on Earth but are essential to world industry. It is likely that control of these deposits may underlie the current tensions." Again the images changed and showed a range of plants, as she continued, "The naturally evolved plants on this planet are quite primitive relative to Earth's biosphere, again roughly equivalent to those found on Earth during the Devonian Period. One of the tasks my team will be undertaking is an assessment of the impact of introduced flora upon the natural evolutionary process." It became apparent as she continued that the Science Team would have several major scientific projects to conduct during their stay, and it was equally apparent that the *Vanguard*'s crew would be fully involved in these activities.

※　※　※

As they left the briefing Harry received a comlink instruction to report to Commander Curran, and hurried to obey, somewhat surprised to find Ferghal hurrying in the same direction. "Hello Ferghal," he greeted his friend, "what brings you to the Command Centre?"

"I am instructed to report there," he grinned in response, "not for me the reason – just the requirement!"

"Well, I expect we shall soon know!" grinned Harry in return, "The life of a Midshipman is not so very different you know – we too are not always told the reason why! But, how does it go with you lately, it seems a while since we last met."

"Why it goes very well Master Harry. I am soon to receive a change of training I am told. It seems I have surpassed the expectations of my tutors," grinned Ferghal justifiably pleased with himself, "but I would truly like to study the micro-circuitry technology once I am finished my present task. And how does your training go?"

"Well, I think," laughed Harry, "at least Commander Curran seems satisfied with my learning!" They stepped out of the corridor and into the airlocks that protected the access to the Command Centre and then entered the Centre itself, Harry leading the way to the Navigation Station where he saluted Commander Curran and reported their attendance.

"Right Mr Heron," smiled Ben Curran, noting Ferghal's interest as he looked around the various control stations, he said, "I expect this is a bit different to what you are used to seeing Tec O'Connor. Harry, explain the stations to your friend while I collect a couple of things."

Obeying the instruction with a smile, Harry gave Ferghal a quick tour of the Centre showing him the helm station, the Owner's Command Station and the OoW's station from which the ship would normally be commanded on passage, or to use the term more commonly applied to ships in hyperspace, 'in transition'. He finished finding the Commander waiting, a broad grin on his face, as he said, "Ready Mr Heron? Now we have something completely different for you both! Follow me please I have something to show you and a task for you both which is best done manually – and you two are probably the only people on board who could do it!"

Mystified, Harry and Ferghal followed the Commander out of the Command Centre and across the adjoining flat to a transport lift. Entering this the Commander gave an instruction to the computer and the cabin ascended rapidly, finally opening its doors in a large space housing a collection of equipment which the boys could not identify. Leading them to a large tube at the after end of the space the Commander explained it was part of a large optical telescope, the functional part of which was external to the ship and thus free of the interference of any atmosphere. Both boys now understood the concepts of atmospheres and the interstellar 'vacuum', but did so purely from the knowledge acquired from their access to data and information systems.

"This telescope can be trained and focused by remote control using electrical motors, but these give off electrical emissions," the Commander explained, "and what I want a look at is a bit coy and very quick to detect any sort of emission." He looked at the two boys and then said, "Harry you are used to focusing a telescope quickly by hand aren't you?"

"Aye sir," Harry nodded, "but only the signal telescope."

"True, this one is a bit bigger, but," the Commander indicated a small tube protruding from the body of the larger tube, "that is the sighting tube, and these," he touched a series of vernier control wheels, "are the focus adjustments." He drew Ferghal closer and said, "Your task Ferghal, is to keep the telescope pointed at the target. You will have to follow the cross wires on this sighting scope here." He indicated the controls and the manner in which the target could be brought into the crosswires and then tracked using the controls. When he was satisfied that both boys could perform the tasks necessary for controlling the telescope he gave Harry the final piece of the task. "Now Harry, once you have the telescope on the target and the focus, I want you to use your eyes to note everything you can about it. We can't risk using the cameras as they generate emissions so you are going to have to memorise what you see and then sketch it for me. Clear?"

Mystified Harry confirmed his understanding, adding, "Perhaps if Ferghal could look as well, he could make a model of it?"

"Good plan, yes; we can try that if we can hold the target long enough!" He looked at both of them then said, "Right, here we go. Ferghal lift the 'scope out of its housing as I showed you, and then bring it to this bearing." He held out a tablet with a directional bearing and an angle of depression. "Harry, watch the sighting 'scope. You are looking for several small triangular objects. As soon as you see them, take the 'scope to maximum magnification and get a good look at whichever one you pick. Got that?"

"Aye sir," said Harry bending to place his eyes to the sighting tubes.

*Out Of Time*

For the first few minutes the view remained black, then the flicker of a glow swam into view followed by another and another as Harry quickly adjusted the focus and the magnification and suddenly he was looking at a strangely shaped object which reminded him strongly of the fiendishly painful 'Portuguese Man o' War' jellyfish they had encountered in the Great South Sea. He studied the ship in the telescope for as long as he dared then signaled Ferghal to take his place and allowed his friend to take a long look as well. When Ferghal withdrew his eyes, the Commander stepped in and said, "Thanks both, let me have a quick peak!"

Placing his eyes to the eyepieces he took a long look, drawing a sharp breathe as he got his first good look at their elusive shadowers. To himself he said, "Right you buggers, didn't know we still had the means to look at you directly did you!" Turning to Harry, he said, "Have you seen enough to do a decent sketch of it?"

Harry nodded his confirmation, "I think so sir. What is it?"

The Commander grinned, "We call them Foo Fighters. Elusive blighters, this is the first time we have had a good look at one, they seem to be able to sense any attempt to use electronic equipment to get a look at them, so I wondered if they would be able to evade a manual approach – and it worked. Can you do a sketch for me now? What do you need?"

"Why, paper and a pen sir. Have we any here?"

"Good, it took a while to get the replication system to get it right, but will this do?"

"Oh yes sir," beamed Harry accepting the proffered pad and the pencil. He found a flat surface and set to work while the Commander and Ferghal took the opportunity to study the strange ship in the telescope's sights. When Harry finished the sketch he handed it to the Commander who studied it for a moment then took another look through the telescope before giving Harry a broad grin, saying, "Fantastic Harry, absolutely spot on! Right Ferghal, house the 'scope and I'll show you lads possibly the most amazing sight you will ever see!"

When the telescope had been secured Ben Curran led them forward and into a semicircular area right at the forward end of the space. Overhead the bulkhead curved upwards from the deck to meet above them forming a half dome. With a grin, Ben positioned them at the centre of the curve and said, "Ready lads? This is the only place on the ship where you can get this view." He gave a command to the computer and the bulkhead and domed cover above them became completely transparent. They stood amazed; high above the great ship, her vast bows and forward end bathed in the luminescence they had previously seen enveloping the ships now visible on either beam. Enthralled they gazed at the huge fins extending on either side of the great ship they stood above, then Harry lifted the pad he had used earlier and rapidly sketched the scene beneath him, flipped a page and as quickly drew the ship to Starboard and then the one to Port. Fascinated, Ben watched as he did so, noticing that Ferghal was also apparently making some measurements, using his hands and fingers to estimate sizes and distances. When the pair had evidently seen all they could, he stepped forward, and said, "When we drop out of hyperspace, I'll bring you up here again so you can see reality – the whole of creation laid out above, below, behind and on both sides of you. That, my lads, is probably the most beautiful sight anyone can ever see! But, time to get back to work!" He gave a command to the computer and the view vanished as the bulkheads and deckhead returned to their opaque state.

* * *

Captain Heron studied Harry's drawings carefully as he listened to Commander Curran's explanation of how they had deployed the optical telescope mounted at the very peak of the great 'north' cardinal fin. He gave his own description of how Harry and Ferghal had trained the telescope with precision and then studied the ships, Harry to make a sketch and Ferghal to produce a model which now lay on the Captain's desk. The Captain studied it carefully noting the organic appearance of the hull and the delicate trailing tendrils that Ferghal had created using monofilament and resin. "Well done Ben, now at least we know what they look like, but we still don't know what they are, who they are and what they are capable of." He looked up and grinned, "Good thinking to use the telescope manually and without any of its systems powered up, I expect they must be able to sense any electronic activity in any of our scanning equipment. Using an optical 'scope and training and focusing manually will have ruled that out."

"Well," said Ben, "I have to thank Val Petrocova actually. She mentioned the twentieth century manoeuvre called a 'Crazy Ivan' and that got me thinking about detection gear. If our chief means of detecting someone else's presence while staying hidden ourselves is to use electronic sensing gear, what if we reverted to manual optics? I doubt I'd have thought of using the telescope that way without her Crazy Ivan idea."

"Even so, I'm glad you thought of using Harry and Ferghal – those boys have a real eye for detail!" he held up the model and compared it critically to the drawings on the desk, "the details they have picked out are quite amazing! You saw this yourself?"

"Yes, and Harry has captured the image exactly – even the shifting patterns on the outer hull. They looked almost as if the thing was breathing, or as if something inside it was moving about." The Commander added thoughtfully.

"Hmmm," responded the Captain, a far away look in his eye, half to himself, he said, "I wonder?" then fixing his visitor with a serious look, he said, "Ben, I want you to scan this drawing into the ship's record and get the model imaged in as well. Can you get Harry or Ferghal to help you get the image as realistic as possible – I want it in the logs looking as if we have managed to image the real thing."

"Can do Captain, I'll get onto it straight off."

"Do that, and then let me know as soon as you have it done. I'll want you to send an image transmission to Fleet Command with a request for ID." He grinned mischievously, adding, "I'm betting that our friends will either clear off or try to make contact. One way or the other I mean to find out more about them, preferably before we reach Pangaea."

When he was alone again, he stared at the space near the bulkhead and murmured softly, "I think you may want to talk to me sooner rather than later!"

\* \* \*

Harry was busy trying to capture the view from the upper fin observation deck with his recently acquired water colours when Jean Hearn, John Jellico, Phillip Ng and Ashley Battenberg came in off their watch stations. John Jellico looked over Harry's shoulder and exclaimed, "Hell Harry, that's good! Any chance I can get a copy for my bulkhead – it needs something decent to look at!"

The others clustered round to look and Jean said, "You lucky dog! How did you get to use the Observation Dome? I've never even seen that deck!"

"Not surprising Jean," chipped in Phillip, "you're always buried in your beloved Hyperdrive generation station!"

"Or the gymnasium!" laughed Ashley dodging a playful punch. "Come on Harry, how did you get a visit to the dome?"

"Commander Curran took me there. He wanted me and Ferghal to use the telescope and wanted us to do it manually so we could look at some strange ships following us." He picked up his pad and flipped the pages back to show them the rough sketches, "He didn't want to use anything electronic because these ships can sense it," he grinned at them and finished, "so he got a pair of old fashioned sailormen to do it the old fashioned way!"

"*Touché!*" laughed John Jellico, "There'll be no living with you now I expect! Here, I am serious; can I have a copy of your painting?"

"Sure," said Harry, "I'll paint you another."

"Why?" asked John, surprised, "Won't the replicators reproduce it?"

Harry looked surprised. "Oh! I forgot that. Yes of course, you're welcome to copy it."

As a result of this conversation the small watercolour was soon to be seen all over the ship, almost every cabin being decorated with it. In Ferghal's mess his fellow Junior Tec Rates watched in amazement as he carefully created models of the *Sydney*, the *Bellerophon* and finally the *Vanguard* herself. To them he seemed to be pulling the details out of his mind as he sometimes sat, his eyes closed as he recalled the vision from the fin, then he would once more attack the blocks of resin he preferred to use for his models. The details seemed to grow from his fingers. Most prized of all were the small animals he carved for fun, squirrels, hedgehogs and otters. Ponies, great draught horses and even cattle, all created out of the hard resin using the point of a knife and his keen eye for detail. These too found their way into the replicator and became prized ornaments for everyone who heard of them or could obtain one to replicate.

✳ ✳ ✳

*Out Of Time*

The Captain's signal did not get quite the response he had expected, but it did get a response. Firstly, Fleet Command sent back a sheaf of reports of sightings of these ships and a demand for as much information as he could gather on them. It transpired that Harry's sketch and Ferghal's model were the first reliable images anyone had acquired. Secondly, monitoring the activity on the computer Fritz Diefenbach had immediately recognised the fact that the images had been accessed by something or someone not using a normal interface – in fact it seemed to have originated in the file itself. When this was reported to the Captain he had smiled grimly and ordered that the files be protected and monitored for any attempt to tamper with them. But the strangest response had come from Harry.

※ ※ ※

Harry found himself trapped in a dream. It was not a frightening dream, just a strange one. He was seated in an empty cold space devoid of features. He was aware that he was not alone but could not see anyone or anything else in the space with him. Something seemed to be trying to reassure him, but seemed unable to find the right words or the right images. Finally he said 'you are from the strange ships. What is it that you want of me?'

A feeling of relief flooded through him and he half felt, half sensed a 'yes'.

'Do you mean us harm?' Harry thought in his dream.

The answer this time was a feeling of alarm and revulsion.

'So you do not mean to threaten us?'

Again the feeling was positive.

'Why do you talk to me and not the Captain,' thought Harry.

This time the feeling was one of confusion, almost a mixture of sorrow and remorse.

'You have tried and couldn't make contact?' thought Harry surprised.

Again the feeling was of failure. Then a strange thing happened, Harry suddenly saw the surrounding space filling with binary code. He watched for a moment and then slowly began to make sense of the mathematical patterns swirling across his dreamscape. Realisation dawned; these creatures relied on a language of numbers! He thought of several natural logarithms and was rewarded by a sense of relief!

He tried again, thinking carefully he tried to convey the idea that if they needed to communicate with the Captain that they should do so through the computer system, perhaps using imagery.

The response was a feeling of alarm. Harry tried again.

\* \* \*

In Commander Diefenbach's office an alarm began to flash and Fritz Diefenbach did three things in rapid succession. He locked a tracking programme into the system access, he called the Captain's link and summoned the Medical Centre. Then he left the office in a hurry. He met the Captain and the Surgeon Commander at the entrance to the Gunroom and the three made straight for Harry's cabin. Harry lay on his bunk in absolute stillness, barely breathing and his eye's rolled back. Len examined him quickly, and then nodded to the others, "he seems to be stable, his bio-rhythms are slowed right down, but stable." He ran a portable scanner across Harry's head and gave an exclamation of surprise! "My God! His brain activity is off the scale!"

"I'm not surprised!" frowned Fritz, "According to my tracers, he's currently scanning every part of our database that uses mathematics. At the rate of search he's using he'll either burn out or wake up with a planet sized headache!" He consulted his tablet to see the readouts repeated from his control station. "This is unbelievable; something else must be doing this! It is not possible for the implant to do this!"

"You're right," frowned the Captain, "Damn, I should have thought of this possibility! Right, Len, can you stay here and monitor him, Fritz, you and I have work to do!"

In his office he watched as Fritz Diefenbach ran a series of commands through the computer. When Fritz indicated that he was ready, the Captain activated his own implant and addressed the computer carefully. 'Harry, I hope that you can hear me. Please acknowledge my presence if you can.' For a moment nothing happened, and then he felt rather than heard, Harry respond. 'Harry, this is very important,' he thought using the computer, 'is there anything with you?'

Again there was a pause, then the clear feeling of an affirmative response.

'Can I speak directly to them?'

A longer pause ensued, then a feeling of relief and a rush of binary maths. He reeled under the onslaught, managing to convey a sense of confusion. The rush slowed, to be followed by a sense that he would find the answers in the computer – and, strangest of all, an access code and storage address! This was followed by a great surge of relief and then of something having left. Moments later his eyes snapped open as his comlink chirped, and he heard Len Myers saying, "Harry's awake and a bit confused – he has one hell of a headache, but that's it! By the way, he says you were in his dream sir, talking to the alien?"

The Captain gave a snort of relief and laughed, "Flattering I'm sure! Well, if he's going to be OK, maybe you would care to join Fritz and me? I think we may have another piece of this little mystery to explore." He looked across the desk at Fritz and said, "Can you get Richard, Ben, Val, Nick and Mary to join us please? I have to access some files our visitor has created in your system!"

# Chapter 13

# Information from unusual sources

"Well team?" asked the Captain as the images contained in the alien data file closed and the laser projection ceased in his Briefing Room. "What do you make of it?"

"If I may sir?" Valerie Petrocova was the first to speak, "It seems to me that they are conveying three separate pieces of information. First, they are trying to tell us that we are in danger from our own kind. Second, that there is a race of reptilian hominids which is being destroyed by the same group that threatens us – I don't fully understand how, but it does seem to be somehow connected with mining operations, and third, they seem to think that we might need to decipher the reptilian language? That," she gave a grim smile, "might be very useful – but the language scientists are probably the only ones who can do that!" She looked around the table, "Human enemies I can deal with, but my Russian fatalism tells me that I must be very uncomfortable about anyone with the ability to access directly our computer systems and plant or remove data at will!"

"Not at will," growled Fritz Diefenbach, "but I agree, I will need to put in place a few traps and blocks to protect our system."

"I'm concerned about one aspect," interjected Nick Gray. "If I understood that bit on these *supposed* enemy ships right, they appear to be a previously unknown type manned by our own people. And they are apparently equipped with some jamming device which can block our scanners rather like the way our 'friends' seem to be able to achieve. If they can do that, they could have the capability to block our targeting system as well!"

"Good point," exclaimed Valerie, her face grim. "Some of my weapons systems can be manually targeted, but the new primary weapon, the heavy emplacements and missile arrays rely on our main targeting system. If we can't use that, we have a major problem!"

"Likewise, my strike craft need to be able to lock onto the target," said Nick looking thoughtful. "It is possible to use visual targeting but that means getting up close and much too personal – well within range of their short range equipment!" He frowned, "And if they can lock onto us while we can't return the favour we will have trouble even getting close!"

"OK," said the Captain, "let's break this up into smaller parcels." He swept the table with his steady gaze. "First, Fritz, send the reptilian language package down to the Scientists, as far as I am aware this is a new species to us and not, according to our databank, native to this system at all – but our intruders seem to think we need to have this. Then share the information on the enemy and their screening system with *Sydney* and *Bellerophon* – and get a conference call set up with their Command teams as well. Now, while we are waiting, let's take another look at the clips on these ships!"

They reviewed the images again, slowly, replaying them several times as they checked details and calling for enhancement of features visible on the hulls at some points. In appearance similar to the Confederation's ships, there were some significant differences, not least the fact that they bore a strong resemblance to freight haulers but with weapons 'pods' fixed to the hulls, something they all noted with interest. While they were doing this, first the *Sydney's* and then the *Bellerophon's* Command teams linked in, all able to see each other on the conference projections in the briefing rooms. "Thanks for joining us Wes, Jon," Captain Heron greeted the Captains of the *Bellerophon* and *Sydney* respectively. For form's sake the teams introduced themselves briefly and then Captain Heron shared the alien information with the other ships. "From our review of this data we can see that we will have two problems. If our main weapons cannot lock onto their ships we will be sitting targets. If we are also unable to scan for them, they may well be on top of us before we know they're there." He let the other teams digest this, and then added grimly, "and I'm afraid that we must anticipate their having our full specifications at their disposal. This is the confirmation we needed of the reports we have had of ships being built for a Fleet under the control of some non-government organisation and it does suggest that this goes right to the heart of our own governments." He added seriously, "I think we must accept the fact that we may well have agents onboard all of our ship's in the pay of that organisation. I suggest that we start to look carefully at our security."

Once the other ships had had an opportunity to comment on this, a moment made easier by the fact that they too had seen the information now flowing from Fleet HQ in a steady stream – with security intelligence reports to the Captains showing that someone had indeed penetrated the Fleet's most sensitive information. The Captain/Commodore skilfully guided the debate, probing promising suggestions and drawing out even some of the more unconventional ideas. Finally he drew the conference to a close, saying, "OK. We have a little time at least and we do have the ability to use a visual only scanning system to check the system on arrival. I am going to task you Val and you Fritz with collaborating with Commanders Breckle of the *Sydney* and Wenceslas on *Bellerophon* to come up with a way of targeting our main weapons without the scanners. Fritz, I want you to work with the E Warfare Officers on *Sydney* and *Bellerophon* – Lieutenant-Commanders Hsi and Paterson I believe?" He nodded as this was confirmed, "Gentlemen between you I need you to come up with a way to disrupt their interference screen!" His fellow Captains nodded their agreement and he finished, "There has to be a way to beat this system – if their side can come up with it, I have every faith that you folk can find a way to beat it! We have a week before we drop out of hyperspace, so let's make the most of it!"

The meeting broke up even as the conference screens winked out. The Captain looked around the table, "Well team, to work. I suspect that if we ask the right questions we may get a little more help from our visitors. He indicated the amazingly accurate watercolour Harry had created of the alien ship – one used in the ship's computers to create a three D image of even greater accuracy. "That seems to be the key. If we can find a way to get their attention – they may provide us with a little more information!" The team rose to leave, but the Captain called to Valerie and said, "A moment please Val – and you had better stop too Nick."

When they were alone he said, "Visual targeting may be the only way we can hit these scum, so I want you to look at every option and make sure that if we have to go down that route we have everything possible available to us. I have no idea whether we have a week or a month – whatever it is it won't be long enough. So I know I can count on you to think the unthinkable and the unconventional."

"Thank you for the confidence sir," smiled Nick, he glanced at Val, "there is one thing I do plan to do right now, I want a word with Midshipman Heron, I have a feeling he may have some tips on using visual sights!"

Val nodded, "I'm with you there. I'll talk to him later. Now I think I want to go and run a check on the specs for our scanners and see if we can do something with the frequency. It's a long shot and Fritz may shoot me down on it, but if it's some sort of interference screen, changing the frequency may just sneak in the back door."

\* \* \*

The remaining days in hyperspace were ones of feverish activity for key members of several departments. Two things made this difficult; not least the knowledge that the indefinable enemy had spies aboard and secondly their lack of real intelligence on the screening system. The first real breakthrough came when Valerie, using a combination of manual/visual location managed to lock a scanner array onto one of the shadowing alien ships. To do this she used a specially created programme which controlled a triple frequency emitter to scan across three separate band widths rapidly changing the frequencies up or down in a random and very erratic pattern. The biggest problem was the length of time it took to visually locate a target in order to lock the scanner onto it, since the variable frequency scatter made wide pattern scanning unreliable.

After talking to Harry about the method of sighting a gun in the Napoleonic period, Nick and his team tried a number of designs for sights based upon Harry's sketch of a blade foresight and notched backsight as fitted to a musket or swivel gun and which could be lined up on a target. Their first models were rather too crude and some simple trials soon showed the flaws. One of his Warrant Officer's took it away and refined it so the Mark Two version as Nick dubbed it, was much more functional but still flawed. It was Harry who provided a simple answer when he innocently mentioned that it was sometimes necessary to 'aim off' and 'lead' or 'oversight' a target. The Mark Three version of the visual sight with an 'oversighting' ring for the interceptors worked.

* * *

While the Command teams worked feverishly on the problem of targeting and scanning an enemy with the ability to hide their presence or confuse an enemy's targeting arrays, another and, for them, more urgent problem absorbed Harry's and Ferghal's attention. Early in their time aboard *Vanguard* the trio had been given instruction and training in the donning of the emergency survival suits provided for all personnel in case of a hull breach. Now Harry and Ferghal had to learn how to don and work in a fully enclosed space suit. Effectively these suits were miniature space ships in their own right, completely self contained and capable of supporting the occupant's life for up to forty eight hours, it could be donned swiftly and without assistance, but the user had to be able to operate the suit's systems and, in emergency, diagnose and correct any fault. It was this aspect which gave both youths the greatest difficulty. The second difficulty arose, not unnaturally, from the fact that, in order to function inside the suit for two days, the suit had to allow for the wearer to use a toilet. And this function had to operate in Zero G. Neither young man had yet experienced this and attempts to let them do so gave rise to some heated exchanges between the training team and engineering. In part this arose as a result of a misunderstanding between the operator on duty in Engineering Control and the Training Officer on their very first full suit exercise down in the training bay, under Lieutenant Bart Erasmus. Harry and Ferghal saw the funny side of the situation when the gravity in the wrong training compartment was shut down without warning and an entire group of Marine 'Squadies' undergoing unarmed combat training, were suddenly bouncing off the bulkheads, deck and deckhead while the two boys, fully rigged in the Extra-Vehicular Activity or EVA suits, remained firmly deck bound. As Harry later remarked, "In the absence of gravity, Newton's Third Law really bites!" After an intensive week of this, they were finally passed "fit to deploy on EVA; accompanied." Fleet shorthand for "under supervision."

Harry's version of the Marines situation – and Lieutenant Erasmus' subsequent confrontation with Captain Wardman – had the entire Gunroom in fits of laughter. For some time after this the subject of gravity and unarmed combat mentioned in the same breath as EVA training could reduce the Midshipmen to laughter – usually to the annoyance of their RM counterparts in the adjoining Mess for the junior officers of the Marines.

* * *

The problem of targeting the missiles – entirely reliant on the missiles ability to 'see' the target – remained to be solved. A number of different approaches were tried and rejected. Then Commander Hsi Lu Wan of the *Sydney* came up with an answer.

"Commander Petrocova," he smiled, "the screen, if it is electronic, must have an emission band. If we attune our passive sensor arrays to detect those emissions we may be able to use that as a targeting device."

"Now there's a thought," grinned Valerie, "I think I have a target we can try it on as well!" She keyed her comlink, "Targeting Plot!"

"Commander?" responded Lieutenant Helen Pascoe.

"I want you to lock the after passive scanners on the Foo Fighters. Then run a scan with the targeting array!" she ordered, "I want to know if the passive array holds the signature!"

"One moment Commander," responded the lieutenant.

Her fingers danced across the terminal, first activating the passive scanners; effectively a receiver which detected and interpreted emissions from another ship's electronics or scanning system. Then, once she had a lock on the small group of Foo ships, she activated the after main weapons targeting arrays and tried to lock these onto the same targets. Immediately the Foo ships seemed to vanish from the targeting screen – she glanced at the passive screen and let out an exclamation of surprise, "Commander? The Foo ships have disappeared off the targeting scan – but I can see they are still there on the passive scan. It's gone very fuzzy, but they're still there!"

"Yes!" she heard the Commander's whoop of joy! "Thanks Helen! That's just the news we needed." She broke the link and spoke again to the *Sydney's* Weapons Commander, "You were right Wan! The passive scan does hold them – it's fuzzy and doesn't give us any great detail but it's enough to lock a weapon onto it!"

This breakthrough gave Nick's team another edge – the combination of what had become known as the 'Harry Sight' and a passive scanner array meant that the pilots could find a target even when it was screening its emissions, lock onto it and then take more accurate aim using the 'Harry Sight' for no other reason than that, at its heart, lay the 'blade' and notched 'V' first sketched by Harry for Commander Gray and embellished by the 'aim off' rings. This was shared between the ships, elaborate precautions being taken in an effort to reduce the risk of betrayal of this vital edge.

※ ※ ※

Two days later the ships dropped out of hyperspace, Captain Heron choosing to do so on the outer rim of the system in which Pangaea was the fourth planet from the yellow/white sun. The 'drop out' was always a risky procedure when not using a gate, partly because it was possible that some uncharted object could lie in the path of the decelerating ship, but also because, if it occurred too close to a large body and its gravity well, a ship could be pulled off its intended course or pulled into a death dance with the planet. Normal freight services tended, as a result of this, and the fact that a ship making its own 'singularity' needed an enormous amount of power, to use gates when these were available. Power meant that energy had to be generated, and the engines which generated it were big and needed a lot of space – space that could be used more profitably. Ships of the Fleet were equipped with the plant to make their own entry and exit singularities, but, again, conserving power usually used the gates. There was a gate near Pangaea, but Captain Heron had good reason to believe that ships entering the system using it were also being monitored by unfriendly forces.

'Drop out' went without a hitch, Commander Allison's power plant ran up smoothly, the energy pulse opened the singularity exactly as required and the ship flashed into normal space with her retrograde braking engines flaring spectacularly. On either beam, the accompanying *Sydney* and *Bellerophon* appeared on schedule and on target, slowing perceptibly in company with the senior ship. At his assigned watch station, Harry shadowed the actions of the Navigation Scan Officer, Lieutenant Piotr Łopata and followed the results as they appeared on the screen in front of him. Apart from the obvious tension in the Command Centre as the ship passed through the singularity, Harry felt almost nothing, but the display screen in front of him was suddenly filled with data concerning planets, large bodies on near trajectories and two ships in orbit around a planet. Having no active role, he was able to simply watch and listen to the flow of commands, responses and actions as the huge ship sped onwards toward its destination. For him it was exciting, interesting and amazingly satisfying to be a part of the team controlling the ship in this crucial manoeuvre.

Captain Heron, from his command desk, ordered, "Complete system wide scan please, Weapons."

"System wide scan, in operation. No hostile contacts detected. Two Type Three-Four-Seven Freight Lifters in orbit at fourth planet, power plant on both in stand by mode!"

"Good," the Captain addressed Commander Petrocova, "Now let's take another look. Kill the active scanners and use passive only. Link to our consorts and ensure they do the same."

"Done sir," responded the Commander on receiving the acknowledgements from the operators, "all scans negative – no, there is a small echo coming from the asteroid belt between the sixth and seventh planets. Appears to be an unmanned surveillance station sir, but it's not one of ours!"

"Hmmm, I had a feeling there would be something watching. Is it sending any signals?"

"Yes sir, three short Hyperspace Transmitter Extra High Frequency band bursts were registered from that location as soon as we used the wide scan."

"Right, so somebody knows we are here. The question now is who – and who do they have as a doorman?"

\* \* \*

Commander Curran remembered his promise to Harry and Ferghal and took them up to the Observation Dome at the top of the 'North' cardinal fin. As a special treat they had been allowed to bring Danny and they were joined by the other Midshipmen as well. As the dome became transparent the blaze of stars spread out above, below and on every side drew gasps of amazement from the assembled company, even though, with the exception of Harry, Ferghal and Danny they had all seen the view of space from training ships in the Earth's own corner of the universe.

For the trio the view was astonishing. Harry's first thought was

"How can I draw or paint this?" and for the first time in many days he wished he could write about this to his family, or even be able to tell them of the wonder of it when he could once more sit in the drawing room with his parents and siblings just to describe his experiences and the wonders he was now seeing laid out before him. Next to him Danny stood spellbound, while Ferghal, like Harry, just stood and stared at the wonders around him. They caught each other's eye and smiled, "My Da' would not believe this," sighed Ferghal.

"No more would mine," whispered Harry, "but he'd want to see for himself all the same."

Watching them, Ben Curran smiled, enjoying their wonderment, but he also detected a note of sadness in Harry's face and Ferghal's response to his friend confirmed his opinion that, for all the boys' resilience, they felt their separation from their familiar surroundings perhaps more deeply than anyone had considered. He determined to have a word with the Science Team's psychologist. Moving to stand next to the boys he asked quietly, "Everything alright lads? Sort of thing you really need to share isn't it?"

Harry gave him a lopsided smile and said, "I used to write to my family every day about the things I'd seen and done – now I cannot." His face closed, and he said softly, "I have no family to write to any longer."

"Not strictly true Harry." Ben paused thoughtfully, and then said, "I believe you should start writing your letters again. I think I know of someone who would be interested in suggesting a person who would enjoy receiving your letters – in fact would be delighted to do so." He placed a hand firmly on Harry's shoulder, "I won't make this an order, but I do want you to start writing your letters again – and I will check that you are doing so," he smiled at the surprise in Harry's face.

"But, to whom should I address myself?" asked Harry.

"To me, to the Captain, to anyone you like – the important thing is to share your thoughts Harry, otherwise you risk becoming cut off from the world outside this ship or any other." He smiled and added, "As it happens there is someone the Captain knows who I think would be delighted to receive your letters. If you will undertake to start writing letters home again, I will check with the Captain and get the address of a person you can write to for you. Do we have a deal?"

Harry thought for a moment, and then nodded, "Thank you sir,

I will write, but I will need to know the proper name and style of the person I am addressing."

"You'll have it within a day or so." He gazed at the vista of the universe laid out around them, and said softly, half to himself, "I would love to see how you will describe this!"

Harry heard him and grinned, his mood lightening, "Perhaps you would care to act as censor for my letters sir? Check that I am not revealing the Fleet's closely guarded secrets?"

"Where the blazes did you hear about that?" laughed Ben and Ferghal and Danny both looked up sharply at his question.

"It was in one of the histories prescribed for our studies. In wars of the twentieth century the soldier's, sailor's and airmen's letters had to be censored to ensure they did not reveal any secrets which could help their enemies," Harry explained.

"Ah, of course!" laughed Ben, "No we don't do that anymore – but I'd be very pleased to be allowed to read the letters." His link chirped and the informality was over. Minutes later they were all returning to their duties, the observation dome once more opaque.

*　*　*

In the Captain's office, Commander Grenville, Commander Gray, Colonel Kernan, the Captain and the Captain's Writer faced the Communications screen occupying half the bulkhead. Currently it displayed the image of a rather florid faced man dressed in an expensively tailored suit whose blustering protests at this 'unnecessary exercise' based on 'falsified documents and outright lies' were beginning to get on the Captain's nerves. For some little time now he had been watching the other figures visible on either side of the 'Governor'; two rather heavyset men in dark clothing seated to one side of the desk and another female seated on the other side who had introduced herself as the legal representative of the Interplanetary Development Consortium. He listened politely to Governor Carl C Kodiak, watching the responses of the three "advisers" as he did so. The Governor was clearly, in his view, a small time politician who had used his commercial and political connections to ascend to a position of power, only to find that the real power lay with those pulling the strings, the people who had put him there.

The Captain tried a new approach, "Governor Kodiak, as you know,

I am authorised to take control of the space port and both the Planetary Docking Stations. I would appreciate your ensuring that, in order to avoid any unpleasant incidents, all of the Civil Guard personnel you have stationed at these facilities are withdrawn before I commence disembarking my garrison troops."

"Impossible Captain!" squeaked the Governor, "the minute I did that the dissidents would sabotage them! I keep trying to tell you – and the Parliamentary Committee - that we are not the perpetrators of this situation! Our investors have been more than generous to the original settlers but they persist in destroying corporate property – and quite a lot of Colonial Government property as well in their ridiculous demand for control of assets and of the future development of these! Ms Ceausescu here has done everything she can legally to represent their interests, but they refuse to act reasonably or rationally!"

"Very well Governor, I take note of your concerns. Our garrisons will land and take control of the facilities before your people leave – but the moment my people are in place, your Civil Guard forces are to lay up their weapons in the facility Guardrooms." The Captain watched the reaction of one of the two men in the Governor's office and continued, "It would, of course, also be advisable, in the circumstances, for your people to remain in the facilities until we are satisfied that no sabotage attempts are likely to arise during the handover period. It would be most unfortunate if anything where to happen during that time wouldn't it."

"Captain I must protest at your suggestion!" spluttered the Governor. "The suggestion that the Civil Guard would actively allow anyone to sabotage these essential facilities is a serious slur!"

'Got you, you little creep,' thought the Captain, "You misunderstand me Governor, I am sure that nothing will happen to the facilities while your men are in them – what concerns me is that something might be attempted or intended to happen after the handover." Again he watched the exchange of looks and facial expressions of the other three people on the screen as he said this, and decided to toss in another hand grenade, "As a precaution, I will be landing the planet-side facilities garrisons using the landing barges and not the lifts. I note that there are two freighters in dock at the present moment. We will want to inspect their cargo manifests and cargoes before they are permitted

*Out Of Time*

to depart and in order to facilitate that I am ordering that they remain in the dock until I give authority for their departure."

At this the larger man interjected, "You haven't the authority to do that! The *IPD Greenplanet* is a freighter under charter to Interplanetary Development and she is fully loaded and ready to ship out! A delay could mean a loss of cargo as she is carrying perishables!"

"Mr Cromwell, I am well within my authority to impound that ship and her consort. You have a copy of my authorities in front of you and am sure Ms Ceausescu has already been through them thoroughly," he smiled, "I note your concern, but I will have no option but to impound or have seized or disable any ship that attempts to leave the dock without authority." He let them digest this for a moment, and then added, "By the way, I am sending an investigation flight of interceptors to look at an unauthorised station in the asteroid field. We spotted it as soon as we 'dropped out' of hyperspace and it appears to be an unauthorised surveillance station." He noted with satisfaction that the three men exchanged shocked looks as he said this, adding, "Of course, if it is Confederate property it will be moved to a more open position."

The Governor's look of fear, and the looks of consternation on the faces of the two 'aides' as he said this, told him more than enough. He let Colonel Kernan take the lead to arrange the landings and carefully monitored the Governor's companions' faces as he did so, glad that the Captains of both the *Bellerophon* and the *Sydney* were watching this conference from their own ships and that the entire proceeding was being recorded.

The 'conference' wound up, with the Governor reluctantly agreeing to stand down the Civil Guard and accept the suspension of his authority as soon as the ship's entered orbit over the planet. Turning to the others and calling up his fellow Captains, Captain Heron said, "Well gentlemen, what do you give as the chances that that hidden satellite will shortly self-destruct?" He waited as they laughed and added, "Even if it does, I will be sending a team to recover every piece we can, the more we know about them the better!"

\* \* \*

The searching interceptor squadron eventually succeeded in obtaining a visual sighting of the device lurking in the asteroid field, a large automated surveillance satellite on the edges of the field, its configuration undeniably human – but whose? One more useful piece of information came from this exercise – the combination of the passive scanner and the 'Mark Three Harry Sight' worked on their human device as well as it had on the Foo targets!

# Chapter 14

# Planet fall:
# Lies, Damned Lies and ....

Ever since they had 'dropped out' into normal space, Harry, in common with almost everyone who had access to a view screen, had kept his live. The blaze of stars, the planets and even the asteroids visible to him in its display fascinated him and spurred him to access even more information about the star patterns and navigational data for the planet. His interest amused some of his fellow Midshipmen and he was regularly teased about it in a good natured way. Harry, used to much worse aboard the *Spartan*, actually enjoyed it, realising that it was a sign of his acceptance. Danny had become something of a mascot for the ship, but the boy was still a little afraid of the black void outside – even though it was now filled with the incredible star fields – and frequently sought out Harry for company. He was involved in a number of activities, the chief one being the ship's band and orchestra, with the bandmaster having undertaken to teach Danny to read music – something that came almost naturally to the him – and to train him in a modern clarinet, again something Danny adopted with a natural talent – but his real talent was exposed when he discovered a keyboard. Suddenly all the music in his head could be made to sound simultaneously to the delight of the other musicians who were soon engrossed in copying him. Sadly, the return to normal space meant that everyone was pre-occupied with the task to be achieved on the planet and Danny found himself at something of a loose end. However, he was at the very centre of the action as he sat in the Commodore's anteroom attempting to concentrate on the lessons set for him by Adriana Volokova, his attention wandering as he listened to her fielding requests and instructions from a variety of departments and even the other ships. The view screen display was another distraction as he watched the formations of strike craft as they weaved around the great ship and its consorts.

Having entered the system on its outer edges deliberately, the ships needed a further day to reach the planet and to enter a geosynchronous orbit. This was achieved by making a second short "jump" through hyperspace, in real time for the ship a period of just over an hour which dropped them out just inside the asteroid belt and less than a day from the orbital position they wanted as they decelerated. The Commodore's determination to be ready for any eventuality had seen the ship's interceptors and strike craft launched in a great swarm as soon as the singularity closed and *Bellerophon* and *Sydney* had been similarly surrounded by their own strike craft as they approached their targets. The first assignment for these craft had been to locate and recover the unidentified satellite. Commander Gray had ordered a flight of six strike fighters out to the satellite's location, one of the large general purpose craft was despatched as well. To no one's surprise the satellite first began to send a stream of high energy band signals, then it received just one – and detonated. "Target has self-destructed," reported the Flight Leader, Lieutenant Bjørn Pedersen, "quite a big bang – I doubt there'll be much left to find!"

"Do your best. Anything that looks like it might be interesting – particularly anything that tries to hide itself. You never know, some working component might have survived!" Commander Gray instructed. He grinned at his second in command, Lieutenant-Commander Karl Pedersen, "You Viking types just have to wreck everything don't you?"

"It runs in the family!" laughed the other even as his brother responded from the asteroid cluster.

"Will do – but the debris field is spreading like crazy! A least it all shows up on the scanners now!"

Four hours from the target and a second swarm of larger craft began exiting the great launch bays that pierced the leading edge of the lateral fins. From his Flight Control Centre, Commander Nick Gray watched as the great 'barges' each loaded with its full complement of troops and their equipment formed up and began the descent towards the surface of the now rapidly nearing planet. He nodded as his launch controller said, "First wave of Landing Barges clear, estimated time of flight, five hours twenty two minutes."

*Out Of Time*

"Very good, maintain tracking. Load and launch second wave in thirty minutes!"

"Yes sir! Second wave loading."

"Order up Combat Escort to cover the entry zone, we'll insert Squadrons Seven-Three-Seven and Eight-Four-Seven into the atmosphere to provide air support and recon for the Brigadier as soon as we're at optimum launch range. Tell handling crew to bring them to the launch ready state in an hour from now!" He paused as an indicator flashed, keying the link he acknowledged the signal, "Yes Mr Pedersen?"

"Thought you'd want to know sir, the Barge has recovered a device which wasn't showing on their scanner – almost ran into it in fact. We have collected everything else we can find as well, mostly stuff that bounced into the asteroids around it and didn't reach escape velocity."

"Well done, come on back to the barn, I think we'll soon have another job for your flight. Report as soon as you're aboard." He keyed his panel and spoke briefly to the Commodore, then returned to the task of launching the landing parties.

Barge Number Six-Six Golf-Papa landed on two hours later and was immediately surrounded by a Security team led by the Master at Arms. Commander Diefenbach himself supervised the initial unloading of the mystery device, although his technicians would eventually be tasked with trying to dismantle it, he insisted on inspecting it himself before they did so. He immediately noticed several things about it, not least that it had been attached to what appeared to be an antenna array, and secondly that it appeared to be powered by a storage cell. The third was that it did nothing until any form of active scanning device was activated near it – then it set up a distortion field.

\* \* \*

At his Control Desk in the Flag Command Centre, Commodore Heron monitored the progress of his forces as they deployed. His secret orders having become active on entering the system appointing him Commodore of the soon to be enhanced Squadron, operational and tactical command of the ship now devolved upon the Executive Commander who assumed the rank of Captain in the process. Open channels with the commanding officers of his two consorts allowed them to keep each other informed of every development as their strike craft, landing barges and boarding parties deployed. *Sydney's* objective of taking over Orbit One went without a hitch, but *Bellerophon's* boarding party found the Civil Guard on Orbit Two spoiling for a fight. Commodore Heron addressed a disgruntled and evidently frightened Governor, over the open channel he had insisted on, demanding, "Governor, your troops on Orbit Two have attempted to prevent the boarding party disembarking. Is there a problem controlling your forces?"

"My people say they were fired on by the boarders and have simply taken up a defensive position," protested the Governor, looking uncomfortable.

"That is complete nonsense, our barges were prevented from docking," said the Captain of the *Bellerophon* on the secure link to *Vanguard*, "We have it all on image recorders if they want to try and argue the toss later."

"Governor, someone at your end is giving you false information," the Commodore continued, "as you know we record all situations such as this and our records show that the station was locked down and the barges prevented from docking. They cannot have fired on your people. I insist you order them to stand down immediately or I will instruct my people to take the station by whatever means are necessary."

"I will do my best Captain," wheedled the Governor, "I'm sure it is all a misunderstanding." He looked decidedly uncomfortable as he turned and addressed someone out of the range of the link's imager. There appeared to be a rather awkward exchange and then the man was facing them again, looking flustered, "It seems that the communications with the platform are not functioning Captain. Perhaps you can give us a little more time to try and restore communications?"

"Governor, again our checks show that there is nothing wrong with the platform's antennae and certainly nothing wrong with the tether cable for the lifts. That suggests that you have a rogue commander aboard that station – or are deliberately attempting to delay our boarding for some reason. My patience is running out, order your men to stand down and accept the boarding party or we will board and take it anyway. Anyone attempting to use the lift will be stopped and any attempt to fire on our boarding party will be regarded as a hostile act! Please make that clear to your Civil Guard. You have four minutes!"

*Out Of Time*

He glanced at the screen on which the *Bellerophon's* Captain waited and nodded, pleased to see the other ship's commanding officer turn away and issue a stream of orders. "One more thing Governor, please advise your people that I will take an extremely serious view of any little surprises they may be attempting to arrange for when they have been evacuated."

Now looking very worried indeed, the Governor turned away from his screen and began an apparently heated debate with what appeared to be several people off screen. With three of the four minutes expired the Governor reactivated his voice link and said in a resigned voice, "Captain, my officers on the Docking Platform will surrender to your invasion forces – but we do so under protest. Orbit Two is wholly owned by the Interplanetary Development Consortium and is private property. The Consortium has every right to defend its property from illegal seizure!"

"Governor Kodiak, as you well know, this is not a seizure, Fleet is acting under legal orders from the Confederation of Northern Europe and the World Treaty Organisation. The orders are perfectly legal within the terms of the current interstellar treaties. Your protest is noted and rejected! Any further attempts to frustrate the execution of my orders will be regarded as an act of hostile intent and will be dealt with accordingly."

A glance at the *Bellerophon's* Commander's screen and he saw with satisfaction that the other had already placed his boarders in position, ready to take the platform by storm – then the docking platform's bays showed that they had been unlocked and were ready to receive the barges. In a very few minutes the platform was in the hands of *Bellerophon's* Marines and the Civil Guard occupants had been herded into a holding area while their subsequent fate was decided. Much would depend on what the security teams discovered as they swept the platform for indications of sabotage or any sign of delayed action devices or programmes which might subsequently affect operations.

※ ※ ※

On a screen in the Commodore's anteroom, Danny watched spellbound as the swarms of fighters, barges and strike craft spread out on their tasks, below them the world seemed to hang suspended in the star filled blackness. The planet below them fascinated him, blue oceans filled most of it as far as he could see, with great rafts of clouds drifting across these and the green, brown and yellow swaths on the land clustered beneath them. From time to time he asked for and was given an explanation of some particular action he could see. He supposed that Harry and Ferghal would be in the thick of this, and while part of him wanted to be with them, another part was grateful that he could watch in this manner and not be directly involved. In fact Harry was in the adjoining compartment monitoring the ship's approach parameters with the Lieutenant in charge of manoeuvring, Lieutenant Piotr Łopata, and Ferghal was manning a monitoring post routing comlinks and communications between all the various fighter leaders, two decks below him and one compartment aft.

* * *

Slowly but surely the Marines and other troops began to secure the key positions and installations. In some areas they met a warm and enthusiastic welcome, but, wherever the Consortium's supporters held sway, the welcome was somewhat less enthusiastic. In the initial landings there were few serious challenges to the landing forces and only one serious exchange of fire, curiously at an apparently insignificant installation located outside the capital. The resistance was quickly suppressed and the troop commander would have secured the remaining prisoners and wounded and moved on to his primary objective had he not noticed that the place appeared to have a disproportionately large power supply for the apparent purpose – a local television relay. He called up support and when it arrived, began a difficult penetration of the facility. It proved to be a very large and sophisticated communications centre, but it was hard won. The value of the capture would not be appreciated for another twenty four hours – when it was discovered that they had captured signal records that would prove very interesting and even more useful in the weeks that followed.

A more serious situation erupted when the landing force from the *Vanguard* arrived to secure the spaceport. The Civil Guard unit was heavily armed and well dug in. And they were led by a Commander who had evidently trained his troops well and knew the ground they were defending very well indeed. The resulting fire fight was made more complex by the fact that there had been a large number of civilians in the spaceport when the troops arrived. It did not take long to establish that the civilians were not there willingly, but had been forced to provide a 'cover' for the Guards. The Major of Marines in command had had no choice but to pull back and call for support when fired on by the well prepared Guard defenders. Their purpose in trying to hold the port would not become apparent until much later. With reinforcements in place the Major initiated a diversion while a special troop infiltrated the buildings and evacuated the hostages. The short and vicious battle for control of the facility which followed, finally secured the spaceport after the remaining guards surrendered when they found themselves surrounded by the highly professional and extremely determined Marines. The guards had taken heavy casualties, losing roughly a third of their number and the survivors were secured in a hangar as prisoners where they were given medical attention for their wounds. Not one of the assault force had been wounded in the fight – a tribute to their training and professionalism.

This fight was still in progress when the Commodore received a very welcome message. His comlink flashed at his Command Station and on acceptance, he found himself looking at the image of Captain Mark Boland, CO of the cruiser *Penelope*. "Commodore Heron," he said smiling broadly, "It's my pleasure to report the arrival of *Penelope*, *Phoebe*, *Aurora* and *Ariadne* in system. Our ETA is eighteen hundred Standard Ship Time."

"Mark; you rogue, welcome to our little dust up," he grinned, "I'm going to spoil your fun a little, I think we may get some visitors soon who have a bit of wizardry to give them an edge. I'll arrange for you to get an upload on it in the next hour. I want you to take up a patrol line beyond the sixth planet – the blue gas giant. For now switch to passive scan only – active scanners may give away more than we want to at the moment."

"Understood," Captain Boland became serious, "We have been updated by the Admiral. Your order is being copied by *Phoebe*, *Aurora* and *Ariadne*. How is the landing going?"

"A couple of small fire fights - one in progress at the moment at the space port – but so far fairly smoothly. The Governor has not yet stood down, but I don't think it's going to be much longer, we control both the

Orbit Stations, and their lift anchorage stations and we have garrisons going into all the major population centres." He grinned, adding, "And a couple our friends were trying to deny existed. I expect the Governor will be considering his options at the moment!"

A few hours later the Governor and his staff formally renounced office and vacated the Government Buildings leaving Brigadier Kernan in possession. "Commodore," he reported, "we now hold all the key installations and the Governor has handed over all the Access Codes to the planetary defence and communications controls. I have to report however, that either there was a massive overestimation of the strength of the Civil Guard or a considerable number of them have gone to ground." He glanced at a tablet and continued, "We have found no trace of the Corporate Legal Adviser, Ms Ceausescu, or the man reported as the Commander of the Civil Guard. But we have found the reason they were so keen to hold the space port – a nice little package of freight they were trying to get off site before we could find it. I'll upload the content to you later."

"Well done Mike, you and your fellows have done a fantastic job. Nothing has left the surface so our fugitives must be hiding in a facility somewhere down there. I suggest that you try an appeal to them to turn themselves in and we'll run a sub-surface scan – although I suspect if there are underground installations, they will be shielded." He paused as the other answered a comlink message, and then continued when the Brigadier signalled he had finished, "What about the weapons? Have you rounded up the full inventory?"

"On the heavy calibre stuff; yes. Small arms no, there is a hell of an inventory unaccounted for. The Governor swears that people have a need for it to defend themselves against these aliens he keeps on about, but he's as vague as all hell about who they are and what they look like. I don't think they actually exist!" He gave a tight smile, "We'll put out a warning that weapons are to be registered within forty-eight hours or handed in. I'm not going to have enough weapons for an army just vanish like this. If I don't get a response, we'll know there's something afoot!" His link bleeped again.

When he returned to the Commodore, he said, "Well, I think we have solved one of our mysteries. I have just had a report that one of my Tactical Squads has found a huge underground Coms Centre equipped for off world and hyperlink coms. The OC tells me there is a very large cache of arms there as well, and access to an underground complex which is being defended by some well trained and equipped troops!" He gave a bark of mirth as he added, "I'm ordering up a full assault team and a recon of that entire area, there will be more than one entrance that's for sure. I'll keep you updated as we find out more. This is the first bit of serious resistance we have encountered, so there's something they don't want us to see hiding there."

Breaking the contact, the Commodore linked to the Flight Control Centre and spoke briefly to Nick Gray. Within minutes a further two squadrons of atmospheric strike craft were on their way to the surface.

\* \* \*

Twenty four hours later the Brigadier was able to report that the centre had been taken, its defenders surrendering after the Marines, having reconnoitred the area very carefully, aided by an aerial survey carried out by a flight of slow moving rotary wing craft, had located several entrances to the facility. The Marine Major in charge of the operation had simply secured each entrance, and then offered the occupants the option of surrender, or of having their power supplies eroded until they did surrender. There had been a brief skirmish when a body of the trapped defenders had attempted to fight their way out, but it had been short-lived. The superb training of the Marines had easily made up for the difference in numbers and a relatively small squad – ten in number – had taken the survivors prisoner, some forty men and women in a uniform not registered as belonging to any earth based forces. Their surly refusal to identify themselves or the authority under which they were acting earned them no favours from their captors. The final count showed that the defenders had suffered some fifteen killed and a similar number wounded. The reason for their determination to escape the facility became evident when the Marines penetrated it and found that almost every piece of equipment had been sabotaged or booby trapped to kill or maim anyone attempting to examine it. They also found a number of prisoners held in appalling conditions. "The people we have released are all among those listed in the Governor's so-called Alien Abductees," reported the Brigadier, "We are still unable to get any useful Int out of the prisoners we took down there, and they have done quite a job on destroying the data banks!"

"I'll send down a team of data recovery specialists if you can make the place safe for them to examine it," said the Commodore, "I'll get Fritz Diefenbach to sort it out."

"That will be very useful," agreed the Brigadier. "Some very positive news. The locals have suddenly decided to throw their weight behind us and have turned in a number of people we wanted to talk to. The response on weapons has been good as well; you'd be surprised what has turned up!" He grinned and added, "It's early days yet, but I think we have a lot of support from the populace. Mind you, I won't be the first commander on the ground to have misjudged that!"

"Well, let's hope you're right this time!" laughed the Commodore. "That satellite has turned up a couple of interesting items which Fritz is getting quite excited about. With a little luck he'll be able to come up with some counter measures for it." After a moment, he asked, "How has the Governor reacted to your latest capture?"

"He seemed very worried when I told him, there's obviously something he's not telling us, but I suspect he'll make a decision soon!"

"Well, when he does, perhaps you'd better get him sent up to me," responded the Commodore thoughtfully. "There is something about this whole situation which doesn't make sense, and I rather think our friend is a very frightened man at the moment."

"It'll probably make even less sense when I tell you that we have a fellow here claiming that he has the support of the colonists to set up a 'Commonwealth' – by which he means set up some sort of communal system of shared ownership of everything. His name is Bert Lowe and according to the files on him in the Governor's office he's been a political activist for some time, although he's managed to stay out of the clutches of the Consortium and the Governor's Civil Guard somehow. He seems to have some grandiose scheme to turn this place into a 'workers commune' and apparently heads up some sort of private army. So far we haven't had any trouble from him – come to that we haven't actually run into him, but he is out in the hills with a transmitter of some sort and is broadcasting on the civil news channels trying to whip up support. As soon as we can I plan to round him up and find out what the hell he's trying to achieve!" the Brigadier finished.

Two days later he had an answer of sorts from the now ex-Governor.

A request was passed up from the planet surface from the very frightened former head of the government, for political asylum and protective custody aboard the *Vanguard*. Commodore Heron ordered immediate security isolation for him and sent down his personal launch with a full fighter escort to bring the man aboard.

* * *

Harry and his fellow Midshipmen found themselves on a rotation in support of officers sent planetside on a variety of tasks. Harry's first such rotation had been a very short trip in company with Lieutenant Case to assist in re-instating a series of navigation beacons disabled by the now disarmed and largely imprisoned Civil Guard. They were escorted by a squad of Marines on all expeditions as there were still units of the Guard on the loose and causing disruption among some of the outlying farming and mining settlements, but the Marines were keeping up the pressure - chasing them and driving them further away from population centres.

On a second expedition, with Ferghal also assigned to the landing party, Harry had a brief encounter with a large herbivore, the beast having a large head and awkward looking body on short legs and a beak-like mouth. The creature seemed harmless enough except that it was very large and totally unafraid of the human party. Efforts to chase it away had no effect at all. Ferghal's skill in the stables at Scrabo had come to the rescue as he had hit on the idea of cutting some of the more succulent fronds from a plant he had seen the creature eating earlier and then tempting it away from the party by holding out these offerings for it to take as he slowly led it clear. On this occasion it was Lieutenant Helen Pascoe in charge and she spotted the obvious solution – the creature's favourite food grew around the beacon. Closer inspection revealed that much of the damage seemed to have been caused by animals. The beacon was relocated to a less tasty salad bar as she later reported to Commander Curran. It was also a source of fascination for Harry that the vegetation was familiar yet somehow unfamiliar. It seemed to be of a limited variety, trees having fernlike leaves or wide fronds, low scrubby bushes with small leaves and low growing herblike plants. Grasses seemed to him to be very coarse and not at all like the grass he knew and strangest of all there were no birds. All of this was poured into the letters he was now writing and illustrating, letters addressed "Dear Theo and Niamh," continuing in the first, *"I hope this finds you well, I am in good health, as is my dear friend Ferghal and our mutual charge Daniel. I hope that Captain Heron's suggestion that I write to you as I was used to write to my parents and my brother and dear sister does not impose too great a strain upon your good opinion of us ..."*

※ ※ ※

Several light years from where Harry sat in his small cabin to write his letters, a meeting was in progress. An observer would have thought themselves to be attending a meeting of a company Board of Directors, and, in practical terms this was the case. Chairman Ari Khamanei was not someone known, by those who had had the opportunity to meet this shadowy man, for his tolerance of failure. Several of those now sat at the table in this meeting were all too aware that matters in their portfolios had clearly not brought the results the Board required.

"The situation on Pangaea must be retrieved! Our investment in the mining there is far too valuable to allow the Confederation or their World Treaty Organisation to control it. Besides which it is essential to our long term goal!" the Chairman stabbed his index finger on the table to emphasise his point, "You, Mr Dien, assured the board that our facilities on the planet were well concealed even from scanners – yet they have now uncovered two of our key installations!"

"But Chairman Khamanei, both were discovered by ground forces due to the carelessness of the local commanders who left the power and supply access exposed!" protested the small Asian featured man addressed by the Chairman.

"True, but it does not reassure me that this error was not detected!" The Chairman turned to another member of the Board, "And I am extremely concerned at the latest voting record in the Parliament and Senate! Our spokespeople are obviously losing influence. Did we not specifically instruct them to block the motion for this expedition?"

"We did Chairman," replied the large man seated on the right of the table, "but it appears that many of the recently elected members of both chambers are not aware of the benefits of supporting our members. A temporary reverse, but not irretrievable."

"I disagree!" snarled the Chairman, "The recent arrest of Dr Johnstone puts our entire investment in the research his Foundation is conducting at risk! In fact, my sources tell me that a number of our key people are already under investigation and there will be a move against others in the next few days! I do not consider that a 'temporary reverse'! It has taken us years to get to this point and we needed only a matter of another year to bring off our first objective – to gain control of the Ministries of Security, Interstellar Trade and Science and Exploration. With those under our control we would have controlled all the key Ministries and would have been in a position to take over the government completely! Your inability to prevent this intervention has now ruined the work of several years!"

"Surely not Chairman! Our new ships and the anti-scanning equipment they carry must allow us to intervene now and force the Confederation and its allies to accept our proposals! We know the Fleet ships are unable to see ours and will be sitting targets for our gunners!"

"I agree, but we will not have the full number we had planned for another year. It is too soon to show our hand until we have all the forces we will need!" interjected another member of the group, a small man with a nondescript face, but cold eyes. "This reverse could expose our controlling interest in WeapTech! So far we have been able to build our ships at Fleet expense," he gave a mirthless laugh, "thanks to the very generous terms of the outsourcing sell off of Fleet's own weapons and development divisions we have been developing and building ships for our own account in parallel with Fleet orders – and at their expense!"

"Agreed, Mr Gollen, there is a serious risk of this being exposed" purred the Chairman, "but I am afraid we have no choice. You see, there is a deep facility on Pangaea. It has a complete backup for our Boardroom, including every record – and Ms Ceausescu has taken refuge there. Unless we go to her rescue she is very likely to fall into the hands of the Marines eventually – and that would be fatal for every member of this Board." He swept the table with his gaze, "We have no option gentlemen, but to send our available ships to attack the seven Fleet ships currently in the system and to take back the planet."

"But Chairman," protested the large man, "The *Vanguard* is reputedly the most powerful starship in the fleet!"

"She is also unable to see ours! Thanks to our control of WeapTech we have been able to acquire technology being developed for Fleet and have diverted it to our ships - telling the ignorant bureaucrats that it doesn't work," snapped the Chairman. "Our ships will 'drop out', strike hard and disable her and her consorts then bombard their ground forces. I have already arranged to ensure that her weapons will not be fully operational! I, at least, consider these things. It will be at least a month before the next nearest Fleet force can reach Pangaea, more than enough time for our people in Brussels to seize control, we already own all the key bureaucrats, a factor you seem to have overlooked!" He glared at the now sweating man, "This will not be allowed to fail! Now, give the orders! We will be aboard this vessel to witness the first strike against the Fleet, one I have no doubt will do much to recover our losses."

※ ※ ※

Aboard *Vanguard*, the former Governor of Pangaea was a frightened and worried man as he was shown into Commodore Heron's office. "Captain," he said as soon as the door closed, "We are all in very grave danger – the Consortium has some very powerful ships and they will be sent to recover the data and resources they have hidden in another base on the planet!"

# Chapter 15

# And the truth is?

"The Consortium has some very powerful ships," the former Governor repeated, "They are fitted with a system which interferes with the targeting equipment of Fleet weapons! And I heard them say that your main weapons are inoperable because they have people onboard your ships who have fixed them." The words seemed to pour from the man, who looked as if he was deflating as he poured his information out to the assembled group of Commanders. Commodore Heron had been joined by his Captains from *Sydney* and *Bellerophon* and an open link on a secure channel set up by Fritz Diefenbach brought the four cruiser Captains into the conference as well. As they listened the mood changed subtly from anger to controlled fury. It was obvious that the events they had been sent to deal with ran far deeper than anyone had imagined, treachery which penetrated deep into the Fleet itself, with key individuals on their own ships aiding the still mysterious enemy and committing acts of sabotage. The ex-Governor knew of two facilities on the planet which the Consortium had built and staffed, but he was not able to tell them where these were located or what their purpose was, only that they were protected by the same technology that the Consortium's ships used and that they had garrisons of some strength – who sometimes wore the uniforms of the Civil Guard and carried out activities in the name of the guard.

"It was all run by Ms Ceausescu and the Consortium's Security Chief, Mr Stan Welling …." He trailed off and looked pleadingly at the Captain, "You have to get me to a safe place! They'll kill me if they know I've talked!"

"By the sound of it," said Captain Heron, "we may well all be in some danger," a slight edge of sarcasm in his voice. He nodded to the Lieutenant who had escorted the former Governor from the secure quarters allocated to him and said, "Thank you for bringing this to our attention. Now I hope you will excuse us as we discuss our strategy?"

As the door closed behind the pathetic figure and his escort, he looked at his Commanders and said, "Right, we know we have at least one spy aboard and there are probably several more, I want the rest of them identified and neutralised. Val, we need to have the assurance that our primary weapons and all your emplacements are fully functional and operational, but we have to check this without alerting the saboteur. Can you do this? Fritz, we will need to make sure no word of our alternatives to the targeting problem leaks and that the device your people and the scientists are studying is unravelled asap, both of you, draw any assistance you need from the other departments." He addressed his fellow Captains, "Gentlemen, I think the same needs to be done your end. If we have infiltrators, you will have them as well."

"We're on it already!" agreed *Sydney's* Captain, Jon Wright, "With your permission, we'll head back to our ships and get things moving."

"I'll have my people tie up with your security officer as soon as I am back aboard," agreed Wes Orkadey Captain of the *Bellerophon*, "This explains a number of things we have been trying to bottom out – and I have a damned good idea of who and how now!"

The conference broke up swiftly, with Commodore Heron escorting his fellow Captains down to the Hangar Bays and their waiting launches. As he shook hands with them, he said, "I shall be damned glad when that trooper gets here and we can land the troops she's carrying, there are a number of things we need to get on top of and Colonel Kernan is spread pretty thinly. His troops are scattered and if they were attacked in strength could be vulnerable. There are whole areas down there we simply have not examined and won't be able to until the extra troops arrive and the *Ramillies* joins us." He gave a tight smile, "then I think we will have to carry out a full sweep and survey of the surface and find out exactly what is happening down there!" He returned their salutes and watched as they boarded their launches for the return to their respective ships. Then strode back to the transport lift as they disappeared into the launching bays, his Writer almost running to keep pace. One more worrying piece of information had arrived while he had been in conference. This message had come up from the surface passed from Colonel, now temporarily promoted to Brigadier, Kernan's ADC and contained the news that a delegation had presented itself at the Government House and demanded an audience. It had been led by a representative of the self-styled "Spokesman" for the Colonists who was demanding that they be allowed to hold an election and to establish a "commonwealth" in the fullest sense of the word. Unfortunately, the Colonel reminded the Commodore, this individual, named Bert Lowe, was also the leader of a group the previous governor's records showed as being behind a number of sabotage attempts and bombings. The Colonel reported that he had returned a 'holding reply' and placed the group under surveillance.

It was a relief to receive, an hour later, the news that the troopship, NECFA *Fort Belvedere* and her escort of three small frigates, NECS's *Lion*, *Tiger* and *Leopard* had arrived in the system and would begin disembarkation within four hours. Welcoming them over his comlink, he ordered the frigates to extend the defensive patrol and arranged for them to be given the information he had received. The solutions his team had devised to overcome the expected enemy were also transmitted under high security coding. He was now very conscious of the fact that the enemy could be expected to strike at any time – and that they still did not know who they were! With that in mind he went to see the Surgeon Commander and then summoned the Master at Arms and the Executive Commander to his office.

※ ※ ※

At her console in weapons control Commander Valerie Petrocova rechecked her readouts, her face white with fury at what she was seeing. Then she contacted Commanders Diefenbach and Allison and relayed to them the information she had in her system.

Mary Allison let out her breath slowly, "Phew, I think we can be very glad you found that before attempting to initiate that system! Just a quick look suggests to me that it would create a shunt which, if we were lucky, would only burn out the power cells and the supply system – if we were unlucky, it would blow away our fore end!"

"Exactly what I thought!" growled Valerie Petrocova, "The bastard who did this is going to wish they had never even been conceived! Fritz, I know I can fix this and I have an idea of who did it, but I need to create the illusion that it is undetected and still in this state. Can you set that up for me?"

"Of course! It will be easy to do that, but how will you disguise the physical repair?"

"Leave that to me! One more thing, can we arrange a little trap for anyone making an unauthorised access to any part of my weapons arrays? I want the traitor caught red handed – so I can personally fry him – or her!" she snarled, her fury at this betrayal giving her an icy focus.

"Yes, it will be done, I will see to it immediately," Fritz replied, "and I shall advise the Captain of our findings."

"Thanks, that leaves me free to deal with this – and to search for any other little alterations to the system." She gave Fritz a brief smile and then said to Mary Allison, "Can you run a full set of checks on all the power systems for the weapons emplacements without alerting anyone to them?"

"Tricky, but I think so," was the reply, "I'll have to find an excuse to cover what we are doing, but I think I know a man who can be inventive in that line!"

"Great. Look, it will take a couple of hours to get this fixed, do me a favour and don't run the power up on the primary until I give an all clear?"

"You got it." The Engineer Commander grinned, "The Owner might be a little annoyed if I fried his Weapons Commander – and I'd rather keep you both on my side!"

That drew a laugh as they blanked their links as they got to work at the various tasks now ahead of them.

Commander Petrocova now faced a dilemma, who should she get to help her with the work of correcting the sabotage? Quickly she ran through her list of staff – she already had a pretty good idea of who the culprit was and knew that it could not have been done without at least one other person to help, therefore there had to be at least two people on her team who were in the pay of an enemy, but who was the second candidate? She reached a conclusion and called up the Master at Arms office. When the square face of the ship's senior Warrant Officer appeared on the screen, she said, "Go to secure channel!" Watched as the screen flickered and then said, "Mr Suddaby, I need to know, very quickly please, everything we have on file for the people on the list I am sending now!"

She saw his face flicker with surprise as he read the list, and he nodded his confirmation, "I'll have it for you in a few minutes Commander. Will you be at your command station?"

"I'd prefer you bring it to me in person; and Chief?"

"Yes Commander?"

"Please make sure no one else has access to this – or knows that I asked for it!" She accepted his acknowledgement, and added, "I will be taking it to the Commodore and he will no doubt have a job for you when I do. That is all." With that she blanked the screen and used her comlink to call three of her staff, two lieutenants and one of her technicians. After briefing them she left Lieutenant Commander Trevor Leonard running further checks on the other weapons systems, while she and Lieutenant Jay Williamson went forward to the secured compartment in which the generator for the primary weapon was located. Here she met the Master at Arms and Weapons WO (T) Martyn Howell. Operating the necessary key codes for access, she explained briefly what she had discovered and what they needed to do to correct the problem.

"This is unbelievable," growled Martyn Howell, "whoever did this knew exactly what would happen if we attempted to fire this!"

"Dead right they did, now we have to get it sorted out and make sure they don't know it's fixed!" snapped their Commander. "Jay, I want you to record exactly what has been done to it before we change it back. Then I want a false unit put in place. That's your task. WO Howell, you and I are going to relocate that unit and rerun the cables so they are concealed and can't be rejigged."

The Warrant Officer grinned, "Got you Boss, right, piece of cake really," he opened his toolkit and began to open another panel, "I always said this would be a better place to put the flux controller, plenty of space and no bastard is going to think of looking for it in here!"

While he was busy, she checked the data tablet the Master at Arms had brought and quickly scanned the information on it. She nodded, and made several swift entries, then handed it back to him. "Thanks Mr Suddaby, please carry out the instructions I have entered – and I must stress that this remains absolutely confidential for now! I suspect the Commodore will have a view in due course!" she laughed "and I think I know what I would like it to be!"

An hour later the weapon had been modified. A check of the circuits and the system from her portable diagnostic terminal confirmed that the weapon was once more fully functional and she communicated this to Fritz Diefenbach who confirmed that his dummy readout would go into place immediately and so would the monitoring system. Anyone accessing any part of the primary weapons control system would now raise an alarm at his personal console and he would be able to lock a trace onto it. Someone, she reflected, was going to get a very nasty surprise!

※ ※ ※

For Harry and his fellow Midshipmen the days were full of tasks assisting various officers as they prepared the ship for a possible attack, ferried supplies or equipment to the surface, shuttled officers between ships or helped install new beacons on the surface or in space. The ships were occupying an orbit inside the smallest of the planet's three moons, each of which had a different orbital period. The innermost, for some obscure reason named Pocahontas, was the smallest and Captain Heron had decided that it should be the site of a surveillance and recording observatory. This was fully automated, its power supplied by solar arrays, but Harry and Ferghal found themselves, for different reasons, included in the crew which set it up. For both boys it was their first excursion in EVA suits onto alien soil and they found it fascinating to be walking on a planetisimal so small that its gravitational pull was almost too weak to hold them on its surface. To be able to stare downwards at the beautiful planet beneath them, while at the same time, to be able to gaze in wonder at the great ship which had become their home in such strange circumstances simply filled them with wonder. The actual installation and setting up of the observatory was quite easy, the unit had been manhandled out of the landing barge and then the bracing and levelling gear extended, solar arrays deployed and the equipment activated and checked. Ferghal's task had been to make a number of delicate adjustments to the optics and then secure and close up the housing.

The sensation of being able to 'walk in the void' and to be able to see planets from the skies was still a novelty to them both and they enjoyed every opportunity to the full. Danny could only listen in awe as Harry told him about it – and poured his experiences into his letter and the sketches he was making to accompany it. So it was with some pleasure that he heard that he and two other Midshipmen would be allowed some shore leave on their next sortie to the planetary surface. His pleasure was increased when he learned that Danny would be allowed to go with them, but it overflowed when he learned that Ferghal would be on the surface for another task and could join them as well. The three began to count the hours to this treat!

* * *

The politics were beginning to annoy Commodore Heron. All organisations have some form of politics; after all it is a human trait to have personal and corporate agendas running side by side. It was said; he reflected morosely, that most nations or governments only advance when the corporate and the personal agendas of the majority coincide. Pangaea seemed to have more factions than a Mandelbrot fractal! For a colony world with just over two million inhabitants it seemed to have as many politicians as it had of anything else. In fact, he thought, it was no wonder the corrupt governor and his henchmen and paymasters had been able to take over so easily. He had no doubt at all that as soon as he withdrew his forces, the government of this place would become unmanageable and be left to the first man or woman who arrived to take it over backed by another army! And in the midst of all this, Colonel – or more correctly Brigadier – Kernan's troops were starting to uncover some very unpleasant evidence of what had been happening here. One puzzling find had been the partially decomposed remains of a reptilian hominid, hastily buried with a number of human corpses. No creature like this was to be found in the databases and the xenobiologists under Dr Maartens were convinced that it was not a native species. This opened the question; where did it come from and how did it arrive on Pangaea?

Inspiration came to the Commodore as a result of a throw away remark made by Surgeon Commander Len Myers. He had said casually, "Call a conference – that ought to keep them all talking for months!" Shortly after his next discussion with Brigadier Kernan, he had seen the germ of an idea in this, and next morning called the Brigadier and said, "Mike, I think you should set up a conference and make sure every last one of your would be 'leaders' is invited. Make it clear to them that if they don't attend they could be excluding themselves from any future governmental structures! That ought to give them something to do. Tell them they must sort out the process by which they can decide their own future and they must come up with a solution which can be put to a vote."

"Good idea, that should tie the silly buggers up for a couple of months," laughed the Brigadier, "As an added incentive, we'll make sure its televised and broadcast live to the rest of the colony – I reckon that should make sure the rest of the colonists make their feelings known as well."

Satisfied that he could now safely leave this problem to the surface teams, the Commodore looked again at the problem of the threatened strike by the star ships reportedly possessed by the Consortium.

Here the science team led by Dr Grüneland and in co-operation with Fritz Diefenbach, had made several surprising discoveries while examining the device recovered in the asteroid field. The most important being that it worked by creating a localised disruption of any scanning signal. Equally importantly, they discovered that it also disrupted, or at least restricted, the 'view' of any scanner within it! Fritz Diefenbach's team had then taken this information and modified a scanner, but this had not produced quite the effect they had hoped for. By chance, in carrying out that check, they had discovered that a high energy focussed pulse disrupted the energy field the device created – and rendered it fully visible on all their scanners! Now began a race to create a generator capable of projecting such a pulse over long range – and then to fit this to the Fleet ships! Teams from all the ships were called aboard *Vanguard* to carry out the work – and to ensure that the reason for the work remained confined to as few people as possible.

With this in progress the Commodore could once more turn attention to the situation on the surface of the planet, and learned that the conference was well in hand, with much useful work coming out of the deliberations so far. He thought nothing of it when he was advised that Harry, Ferghal and several of the Midshipmen had been flown to the surface to assist in setting up the systems for broadcasting the conference under the charge of their Gunroom Senior, Sub Lieutenant Trelawney. Reassured by reports of returning normality in the capital he also approved surface leave for some personnel and, at Danny's pleading request, had approved the boy's joining Harry for the projected forty-eight hours they would be on the planet. He almost reconsidered this

*Out Of Time*

decision when Commander Nick Gray received a report from one of his long range interceptor patrols that the Foo Ships had made a reappearance. As usual with them, they had appeared and evaded investigation, but they had left a message. It was simple and consisted of two numbers with the second enclosed in a circle.

The second sighting of the Foo ships was of a single one, close to the planetary surface. It was fleeting and very early one morning, the pursuit interceptors reported that it had "dropped out" above the centre of Pangaea City, lingered briefly, then disappeared as the intercept flight approached. It was to have a profound affect on a number of events and in particular upon the lives of Harry and his companions.

※ ※ ※

Fritz Diefenbach studied the strange looking message on the Commodore's screen. The first number was clearly an eight, and it overlaid an image of a ship. The second number lay within a circle, but the circle was clearly representative of something revolving. The number itself was easy enough; it was the single digit five. The question was, what did it represent? Fritz, the Commodore and Ben Curran had been working on this for several hours, when finally, Ben Curran asked, "I wonder if that leading dot on the circle is meant to represent something in orbit?" He looked embarrassed, and added, "I know it sounds simple, but it occurred to me that this place has three moons, Pocahontas, Hiawatha and Gitchigume. The innermost of them has an orbital period of exactly seventy-two hours, the next has an orbit of three hundred and forty-seven hours and the last has an orbital period of thirty days. Perhaps they are trying to signify an orbital period as a measure of time?"

"OK, if we suppose that to be the case, which one are they indicating as the period?" asked the Captain.

"And why have they not shown all three moons?" demanded Fritz.

"I think maybe they don't need to," mused the Commodore staring at the circles as it was traced and retraced by the small mobile dot. "Can we calculate the rotation of that dot?"

"What?" the question surprised Fritz out of his usual punctilious politeness. He stared at the dot and the way the circle illuminated and darkened as it passed. "Yes, of course!" He tapped a command into the keypad and then waited, when a prompt appeared he gave a series of instructions to the computer while Ben Curran ran a series of calculations of his own on his tablet. They both stared at the answers for a long moment.

"Well?" asked the Commodore. "I think I would be prepared to bet that the period of rotation in this circle is exactly equal, in scale, to the orbital period of one of the moons – at a guess the innermost one!"

"Spot on sir," grinned Ben Curran, "It is exactly seventy-two seconds in period, and my guess is that we should read the circled number as the number of circuits the moon will make before these visitors will arrive!"

"Well gentlemen, I think we need to run a few more checks before we decide we have all the answers, but it certainly looks as if our mysterious 'friends' are trying to tell us that we will have a visit from nine ships of unknown intent, in five standard orbits of Pocahontas. By my reckoning that gives us fifteen days to prepare for them." He looked at the two men in front of him. "I think we have a lot of work to do in that time!"

※ ※ ※

Sub Lieutenant Trelawney, at twenty-two, the grand old man of the Gunroom and due for promotion in a matter of months, was glad to be going 'ashore'. His task was, on the surface, reasonably simple, they had a new television digital booster to install and another signal relay for the ground troops. His team consisted of two Technical Ratings, Midshipmen Murphy, Dinsen and Heron – and the boy Danny Gunn as a passenger. Danny would be looked after by a member of the Brigadier's staff until he could join Harry on the 'shore' leave, the boy's pleas to be allowed to 'see the new world' with the support of the Surgeon Commander and the scientists had resulted in his receiving permission from the Captain for this treat. The Technical Ratings were to be Ferghal O'Connor and WO Tech Siobhan NicDaied, the latter to be detached from his group as soon as their immediate task was complete, in order to join another team assisting the Marine Division. He and the five young men would then have a twenty-four hour leave on the surface before they had to return to the ship.

He grinned ruefully as he thought that there wasn't much to do or see on the surface. Pangaea City, as the capital had been imaginatively named, was a collection of domed 'business and industrial' centres and several fairly low rise accommodation domes with a small hotel and recreation complex nearby. There was a small harbour as well, but maritime activity was, he believed, minimal. But, he reflected with a smile, at least it was in the open and on a planet and not inside a lump of metal whizzing round in a vacuum! He checked the kit lists and the equipment load sheet again, then he nodded to his eager party, "Right, we seem to have everything! Board the launch and let's get down to work!" He grinned at Danny's eager expression and said, "Mr Heron, I shall leave Mr Gunn in your charge! Make sure he doesn't get under anyone's feet and doesn't get lost when we transfer – Mr Gunn, you make sure you stay close to Harry, OK? Mr Murphy, Mr Dinsen, you'll ensure all our kit is secure. Let's go!"

Boarding the launch, Harry reflected that the entire process could not possibly be compared to the process involved in *Spartan*. There was nothing whatever of the 'boat' in the vehicle they were inside, there was no requirement for two dozen men hauling on falls rigged to the yardarms to lift the boat from its cradle on the boat tiers and swing it outboard. Instead he settled Danny into the padded seat and then strapped him in, checking that the boy's helmet was properly sealed and his air supply correctly set, before seating himself and securing his own straps. Around them the rest of the party settled into their own seats while the Load Master checked and secured their baggage and equipment. Then, with a hiss and the sound of the heavy locks engaging, the hatches shut and the craft began to move slowly from the loading bay into a launch bay. Danny's excitement bubbled up as he watched the operation desperately trying to see everything at once. For Harry and Ferghal this was their fifth excursion, yet even so, it was difficult not to show that they were almost as keen to see it all as Danny!

The pilot gave a warning over the flight comlinks and then a brief count. There was a sensation of acceleration followed by the feeling of weight loss. Startled, Danny let out a squeak as he clutched Harry's arm, "I'm floating out of the seat Mr Her'n," he said in an alarmed tone, raising chukles from everyone on the voicelink.

"Don't worry Danny," Harry assured him, "This launch hasn't got AG, so we'll be weightless for a bit. That's why we have to strap in."

"It don't feel right!" sniffed Danny, but already his attention was on the viewscreen and he gasped in wonder as he saw the *Vanguard* for the first time from the outside as the launch dropped away and circled back towards the Orbit lift platform station. Then he gave another gasp of amazement as he saw the beautiful planet below them, "Oh Mr Her'n," he gasped, "Ain't that beautiful? Is that where we're going?"

"Yes, but first we have to disembark at the Orbit Station and then go down in the lift from there," Harry grimaced, "That's the bit I don't like!"

※ ※ ※

The transfer went smoothly, personnel and equipment disembarked from the launch and moved across to the centre of the station where they were loaded into a large five-storey lift shuttle. Harry and the others now found themselves seated in the uppermost deck of the shuttle together with a party of medical technicians from several ships. Harry immediately recognised the attractive MedTec Patricia de Vries chatting to another person he recognised as being one of the weapons specialist rates. He rather liked her, finding her attractive, despite the disparity in their ages, and she always seemed to have a joke or a pleasant word to share with him when they met. As on his previous trips down to the surface, he did not enjoy the descent, but was glad to find that he was not alone in this. The downward journey took a little under an hour with the deceleration and braking accounting for almost half of that and they were all glad to disembark, find their ground transport and head for their accommodation in a small hotel on the outskirts of the capital. Here Danny was taken under the wing of one of the ship's Administrative Staff, a young Writer named Heather Bare. She was attached to Brigadier Kernan's staff, but would take care of him until the Midshipmen's shore leave commenced.

The installations proved swift and easy, which left the midshipmen and their senior with spare time on their hands. Having checked by secure link that there were no further tasks, they were authorised to extend the 'leave' period by commencing the break immediately, but to stay within the area designated as safe for their recreation unless escorted. Effectively this meant staying in the hotel or within a very small area around it, something of a disappointment for them all. Fortunately for the party, another member of the Brigadier's staff was also quartered in the hotel and offered to arrange for them to visit a nearby reserve where they would be able to see some of the aquatic life as well as some of the more common animals escorted by a group of Marines also due for a rest. Sub Lieutenant Trelawney, conscious of the briefing he had received before leaving the ship regarding the safety of Danny in particular, but, by inference, of Harry and Ferghal as well, checked privately with the ship and was given the necessary clearance. The result was an extremely memorable tour for all concerned.

For Harry the aquatic life on display in the aquarium was astounding. Like the fishes he had seen on the Great Barrier Reef, everything was new and unfamiliar, but here it was doubly so since the evolutionary process was still in its infancy in terms of the planet's natural development. They saw amazing fish-like creatures that breathed air and controlled their buoyancy by apparently swallowing stones collected from the bottom, a range of jelly fish that seemed even more primitive, and yet, as they learned, more deadly than any similar animal on earth. In one room they gazed in awe at the stuffed remains of a huge creature the curator referred to as a 'Pleurodon', that Ferghal dubbed "the Kraken". Measuring at least fifteen metres from its hideous tooth filled snout to its tail; its flat head and short neck connected to a slightly bulbous body and then tapered to a thick tail. Four long flipper fins protruded from its body and the curator told them that this creature was the most dangerous animal on the planet, attacking anything and everything it came upon, including the colonist's solidly built watercraft. It had, he told them, been known to beach itself and seize prey venturing too close to the water in some instances, adding that this had made bathing in the seas very unpopular!

Back in the land transport the party soon found itself admiring strange vegetation and some of the large lumbering animals, more reptilian than anything they had ever seen before, and yet, according to their guide, monotremes and proto-mammalian in the main. They returned to their hotel tired, stimulated by what they had seen and done – and, in the manner of youth everywhere – hungry! Harry again noticed MedTec de Vries in deep conversation with a local man, one he did not recognise, but, while the midshipmen's party was eating a well prepared meal, he saw that a Weapons Master Tec had joined her. He asked Ferghal if he knew the man.

Ferghal glanced across at the other party and nodded, "Aye Master Harry, that is Master Technician Dupré, he looks after our primary weapons system. Strange to see him here."

For no reason he could identify, Harry felt suddenly very uneasy.

※ ※ ※

Harry's unease would have been further increased had he been able to hear the conversation taking place over a comlink between the head of the Johnstone Foundation and a member of the Board of Interplanetary Development several light years away in the headquarters of the Foundation. "I tell you these boys are a gold mine! Their DNA and the antibodies they are carrying hold the key to a major breakthrough! We must have them, and now is the absolutely perfect opportunity! They are on the surface of Pangaea in a low security resort. We have several of our people on the staff and in the area and can grab them and get them down to our secure facilities without any trouble and well before the military can react. Then it's merely a case of waiting until the Chairman's fleet sweeps that damned landing force and its support ships away!"

"Oh very well Doctor," the speaker sounded bored, "I'll authorise our people to secure them for you. As you say, it is only a matter of time before we destroy their forces anyway and the research will certainly be useful."

A few minutes later a secure link channel carried an instruction to several individuals in Pangaea City, including several wearing Fleet or Forces uniforms.

※ ※ ※

Above Pangaea City, an atmospheric interceptor took evasive action and then called in a sighting as a large Foo ship seemed to drop out in front of him, lingered a moment, then vanished as swiftly as it had appeared.

# Chapter 16

# Third Party Interests

Waking suddenly in his hotel room Harry felt strange. At first he thought he was reacting to some allergen, his limbs seemed to be outside of his control and he felt by turns dizzy and then cold. A quick check of his medlink showed that his metabolism was normal – but he felt really strange. Then he realised that something seemed to be trying to speak to him. Recalling the 'dream' he had experienced on *Vanguard* several weeks before, Harry tried to see what or who might be doing this, but, apart from a slight shimmer surrounding everything he looked at, he could see nothing. Then he felt himself lose complete control of his own body and slumped to the ground.

Trapped inside his own head, Harry felt angry and alarmed at his helplessness! But, almost immediately felt someone was attempting to comfort, and then sooth him. And then he began to dream.

He awoke refreshed and with the knowledge that he needed to tell Sub-Lieutenant Trelawney what he had learned from the alien urgently! He dressed quickly and made his way to the Gunroom Senior's 'cabin', knocking gently. The door opened and the tall figure of Petroc Trelawney filled it, "Problem Harry?"

"Yes sir, I think so!" blurted Harry, "Can I talk to you privately?"

"Is it that urgent?" frowned the Sub-Lieutenant.

"It is sir," said Harry urgently.

"OK! Then you had better come in – but this is irregular you know!"

"I know sir, but it's rather tricky."

Admitting Harry, the Sub-Lieutenant shut the door and turned to wave Harry to a chair. He remained standing leaning against the entertainment centre. "Well Harry, what's the problem?"

"Sir, you may remember a few weeks back something happened to me aboard the ship? Well it's happened again, only this time I know I have to tell the Commodore that there are ships approaching this system to attack us." Harry said in a rush.

The senior frowned, "Slow down Harry. How did you get this information?"

"It's difficult to explain, but, if I may use something from the beliefs of my own period – I think it happens when the – whatever it is – takes possession of me? Then I have a sort of dream. This time I saw ships similar to ours entering this system. I recognised the planet we are on at the moment as if I was stood on the *Vanguard's* observation deck, and these new ships come straight at us and open fire. I think it is a warning from the aliens everybody calls the Foo, but I don't know who the enemy is – I think they do, but don't know how to tell us," he paused and the Sub-Lieutenant noticed a change come over him. When he spoke again, it was as if it were from a long distance and his voice sounded strange, and slightly strangled, "They are allied to the former governor and to certain interests on Earth, these ships have been built in secret in a system where they have enslaved the population. They will be here sooner than we anticipated. They will be here in ten," there was a slight hesitation before Harry's voice continued, "planetary rotations."

Surprised and more than a little puzzled, the Sub-Lieutenant hesitated, then saw Harry's glazed look and exclaimed, "Right! That does it! Harry?" Trelawney was momentarily nonplussed as Harry slumped from the chair. Then he moved quickly, checked that the boy was still breathing, in fact found that Harry was apparently asleep, then picked up his Surface to Ship comlink and put in a call to the Captain - Commodore's office. In a very few sentences he conveyed to his commanding officer exactly what had just transpired.

"Well done Mr Trelawney. Ten days is a lot less time than we anticipated, something must have changed!" responded the Commodore. "Now listen very carefully; your orders are to get those people to the nearest RM barracks immediately. As soon as you have them there Brigadier Kernan's men will ensure their safety. According to my data there is a barracks established half a kilometre from your location. Get your party there now and report to me as soon as you have done so!"

"Very good sir!" responded the Sub, "I have Heron, O'Connor, Gunn, Murphy and Dinsen with me. Oh, and MTec de Vries is also in the hotel, should I take her with us?"

"Negative! We have reason to believe she's working for the other side! Just the Midshipmen, O'Connor and the boy Gunn. And try not to attract any attention as you leave, I suspect you are already under surveillance!"

"Very good sir," acknowledged the Sub as Harry stirred awake at his feet. Harry sat up looking confused, and Petroc Trelawney reached down to take the boy's hand, "Well Harry my friend, you do seem to have stirred a right old mess with your visions! Don't move from that chair while I dress!"

"I'm sorry sir! What happened? I recall coming in and trying to tell you about the enemy – but then something else took over again sir! I'm really sorry to have caused you trouble!" said Harry looking worried.

"No trouble Harry, but we have to move quickly. The Captain – I mean Commodore – was quite definite on that score!" he finished dressing and grabbed his weapons belt, comlink and a small bag with his personal things stuffed into it, and said, "Right, follow me and stay close, we have to get the others roused and ready and we have to do it without raising the house!"

The next few minutes saw Harry and the Sub-Lieutenant move swiftly between the four remaining rooms, rouse the occupants and get them ready to move. Danny proved to be the easiest as he was already, for some inscrutable reason sat on the end of his bed, wide eyed and fully dressed. Harry had no time to ask why this was so, but just made sure the boy had everything he needed and then ushered him out to the corridor where they met the others pulling on jackets and securing their weapons belts. "Right lads," said the Sub softly, "dead quiet now, we have to get out into the street without raising any suspicions and get to the Marines."

"Sir," said Paddy Murphy, "I suggest we split up and go out in pairs. There are three routes and if we all go different ways there's more chance we can get out without arousing any excitement!"

"Good thinking! You and Heron go out the poolside way, Dinsen you and O'Connor, through the main lobby, Danny, you are with me. Let's go!"

Paddy Murphy sauntered off with Harry in tow heading for the pool patio – a reasonable move as there was a breakfast bar set up at one end where the group had eaten several times. This early in the day there were few other people about apart from hotel staff, but Harry had an uneasy feeling about this, especially as he did not recognise several of them. They had almost reached the street exit when MTec de Vries strode through it.

"Good morning gentlemen," she smiled, "going for a walk this early?"

"Morning MT," grinned Paddy, "Just a quick errand to the Barracks for the Sub. Then we can get some breakfast. Work before pleasure and all that!"

"Really?" she smiled broadly, "perhaps I better go with you then!"

"As you please," shrugged Paddy, "but we won't be long I'm sure and you've already had your jog!" he finished indicating the fact that she appeared to be dressed in sports gear.

"Oh well," she grinned, "I don't mind the exercise," and turned to accompany them. Out of the corner of his eye, Harry caught what looked like a signal to one of the waiters, but he could see nothing alarming in the response and so followed Paddy onto the street, with MTec de Vries moving between them with an unusual familiarity. His instincts were sending warning signals to his brain even as she began to ask about the nature of the 'flap', and he returned a neutral reply saying that they had only been told to go to the Barracks and would get more instructions there. On the other side of her, Paddy's cheerfulness was, he sensed, covering the fact that neither of them could see any sign of the other members of the party, but just as he was about to question this, he saw the Sub-Lieutenant and Danny emerge from a side street on the other side of the road. As they did so, the Sub caught sight of them and signalled for them to run for it!

Even as the two Midshipmen responded, camouflage clad figures burst from the roadside shrubbery behind the Sub and Danny and from several hiding places ahead of Paddy and Harry. Before he could react and draw the weapon he had so recently learned to use, he felt something sharp penetrate his upper arm and turning saw MTec de Vries withdrawing a syringe! She grinned at him and said as his knees buckled, "Got you kid! My retirement from the Fleet is about to take effect!"

✳ ✳ ✳

Harry drifted in and out of consciousness, confused and disoriented. Later he would recall being roughly manhandled at several points, being transported and restrained at others, but eventually he awoke in strange surroundings, stripped of his clothes and strapped to some sort of bed. His body ached and he could feel several small wounds evidently held closed by dressings on his abdomen and chest. He struggled futilely against the restraints holding him but could not free himself. He took stock of his surroundings and realised that he was in a small windowless room lit by strip lighting directly above him. The only opening he was able to see restrained as he was, was a ventilation grille to one side of the lighting. He gathered his breath and shouted at the top of his voice; "Let me out of here!" When there was no response he tried again, and again until at last there was the sound of a door opening and a large man entered, looming into Harry's limited range of vision to say savagely, "Shut up! Or I'll give you another dose to shut you up!"

"How dare you do this to me!" stormed Harry. "I demand you release me immediately! I am a Midshipman in the Confederate Fleet, not some crofter you can treat as you please!"

"I said shut up!" growled the man. "You're a bloody alien specimen in my books and I don't care if we carve you up alive or dead, conscious or unconscious! Now shut up or I'll knock you out until we are ready to take you apart!"

"You wouldn't dare," began Harry, and regretted it as he felt the sharp jab of a needle. As the darkness engulfed him yet again he could not know that his friends had heard his cries from their own cells a little further along the corridor he could not see from his position. Nor could he in any way suspect that the former Medical Technician Patricia de Vries was among those preparing the laboratory in which her new paymasters were planning first to test a number of drugs on him as his system was, as yet, relatively unchanged by modern living and had antibodies that might produce different responses. A large number of samples had already been taken of his tissues and were already in use in a number of experiments, some of which would lead to further samples being required, and others which had already born fruit for his captors, one including the splicing in sections of alien DNA to that of a human. Their second set of 'trials' were of an altogether less moral standard – not that their first were either – and included some active vivisection to test the effect of mind control drugs under extreme trauma and the effectiveness of the genetic tinkering they planned.

It was intended that eventually they would extract samples of all his and his two friends major organs as part of their 'research' to determine what evolutionary differences separated Harry and his friends from their modern counterparts. By then, the research leader postulated, they would have all the useful samples and data they needed and the three could be disposed of before there could be any chance of their being traced. A range of equally unethical tests were planned for Ferghal and for Danny, but these would not begin until they had extracted all the information they could from the trials on Harry. He could not know that it was the apparently friendly MedTec de Vries who had selected him as the first of the trio for this purpose, for no other reason than his rank. The first part of the proposed programme included testing a number of psychotropic drugs on him as part of a longer trial intended to find ways of controlling slave workers by inducing a state of drug controlled autonomic obedience.

For Harry the humiliation and torture was only just about to begin, but it would also have a very unexpected result – one which would bring an end to the activities of the Johnstone Research Foundation and the downfall of a very large number of rich and powerful people.

❈ ❈ ❈

The disappearance of the three Midshipmen, the newly trained Ferghal O'Connor, their Sub-Lieutenant and the boy Danny Gunn was noticed as soon as they failed to arrive at the Barracks within the expected half hour the Commodore and the Barracks Commander had allowed. In fact, so serious was the news the Commodore had transmitted to the surface, the Marine Captain had sent out a patrol with the express intention of meeting and escorting the group within twenty minutes of receiving the it. Arriving just minutes after the last of the group had been subdued and thrown unceremoniously into a stolen transport, they had found the signs of the abduction and immediately raised the alarm. More worrying was the fact that the implants carried by Harry and Ferghal seemed to have become inactive since all attempts to trace them had thus far failed! No one was to know that this was in large part due to the fact that the boys were being held under a close electronic screen which prevented any form of electronic scan – that and the fact that, drugged as they were, neither of them was in a position to activate their implants while they were being moved. Now that they were in the carefully concealed 'Research' Centre, the complete blockade of any scan was concealing everything.

In fact the operation had been planned with great care and the boys and their officer were separated and drugged before being concealed in several different vehicles. Their captors then moved them from place to place just ahead of the searching troops until they could be loaded aboard a submarine transport docked in a subterranean cave system accessed through a mine. Even though the mine itself was shown on all the charts available to the searchers to be 'worked out' and listed as 'exhausted', it was all part of an elaborate ruse created to conceal the fact that the former Governor and his associates had been engaged for some time in asset stripping the Colony and creating a dependent economy over which the Consortium could exert full control. This in turn was providing funds and resources to a group of powerful and power hungry bureaucrats and corporate interests in order to develop the resources necessary to seize control of the Confederate government and the colony worlds for their own ends. In this way Harry and the rest of the party were transported to a secret facility located on a medium sized island, part of a chain straddling the equator and situated roughly halfway between three continents. For them all the entire episode would remain a confused and uncertain gap in their memories.

Brigadier Kernan reported to the Commodore by videolink, saying, "We have tracked the route and vehicles used by the abductors and captured the vehicles. We took several prisoners as well and have found a very interesting submarine harbour designed to handle several submersible vessels in a mine that is marked on the official maps as worked out. The interesting thing is that it is far from worked out, in fact it is producing a hell of a lot of very high grade ore. Even more interesting is the workforce."

"Right, we suspected that something like that was happening! I take it the workforce is the supposedly 'alien' abductees?"

"No, that's the interesting part – they are hominid but appear to be evolved from a reptilian species – and are certainly not native to this planet! Their appearance accords with that skeleton we found a few days ago," advised the Colonel. "I think it might be a good idea to get the Science Team, particularly the linguistics experts and the xeno-biologists to widen their remit and take a look at this. There is plenty for them to study here and I could use some help in communicating with these people, they are intelligent and have a language – but it's not one our translators can handle!"

"Good idea, in fact I'll get Dr Grüneland to sort that out immediately. Perhaps the prisoners can shed some light on the Sub-Lieutenant's party's whereabouts!" said the Captain.

"Unfortunately, no. The prisoners we have taken are all 'grunts' and know very little about where the subs come from or go to. I wondered if an IR scan of the seas might pick up a trail if they haven't gone to ground already!"

"We'll do a scan and let you know. Now, I have some more intel. There are several ships of unknown class and force due here in roughly eight to ten days - or so we are led to believe. I plan to leave *Sydney* in close orbit and to take *Bellerophon* and *Vanguard* out to a holding position so that we are in place to strike back if they prove hostile and wanting to fight. I will leave the atmospheric squadrons under your command and we'll land extra troops from *Sydney* for you. Your main task for now will be to track down and isolate, neutralise or capture any of the former regimes people. I rather think it may become a bit of a guerilla campaign, but I know your people can deal with that. As soon as we have the situation stabilised on this end, we'll be back."

"Clear and understood. We have this end in hand, just make sure you bag the bastards coming your way!" growled the acting Brigadier, "I don't particularly want to spend the rest of my natural sat on this dirt pile – it's far too bloody volcanic for my taste for a start!"

"Don't worry Mike, I plan to give them a very warm reception. Just find those youngsters will you – or, if you don't; find me the bastards that are responsible for their abduction. I'll see you when we've sorted out the visitors!"

Three hours later the Brigadier watched the landing barge touch down and welcomed Silke, Thomas Scheffer, Georgina Curry, Natalie Buthelezi, Frederik Maartens and Rhys Williams, driving them straight out to the underground complex where the reptilian miners were being held. High above them, the *Vanguard's* great manoeuvring engines flared into life as she and the *Bellerophon* moved out of orbit leaving the *Sydney* scanning the surface and searching for any signal that might betray the whereabouts or intentions of the enemy. The Brigadier's estimation of the task facing the scientists had been right – there was enough to keep a team twice the size they had available busy for a long time!

* * *

For Harry hell had become reality. The drugs coursing through his veins left him unable to resist as his tormentors ordered him to perform tasks without a break. Throughout he was fully aware of his surroundings, but unable to take control of himself or to refuse to do whatever he was told to. Each time he began to regain control, they administered another dose and forced him to return to whatever task they had set him. What he could not know was that they had already carried out a genetic splice, implanting a gene taken from an alien which they hoped would allow his body to regenerate damaged tissue more swiftly and allow it to continue functioning for extended periods without rest. Periodically they allowed him to drink water or fed him some nutrition in the form of a thick soup. Several times during his ordeal he thought he recognised the face of MedTec Patricia de Vries and struggled to understand why she was doing this to him. At other times he was restrained and samples of skin, urine and blood taken, then he would be dosed and returned to some mindless task. He was allowed no sleep and no rest, the intention apparently being to see how long he could be kept under this control and still carry out the tasks. When eventually his system could take no more he was secured, hallucinating, in a strait jacket, muzzled to still his rambling cries and dumped in the bare cell in which he had first recovered consciousness and from which he had been taken for this torment. As he was removed from the test laboratory, the man in charge, a small and rather cold man, stripped off his mask and said, "Get this place set up for the next set of tests on that one. We'll let the drugs work themselves out of him over the next twelve hours, then start on phase two." He smiled mirthlessly, adding, "I am told that people in his time underwent operations without any anaesthetics, well, we will have an opportunity to put it to the test and see what his system does with systemic shock! It will also give us a good idea of whether the RNA splice has taken and if it helps repair human tissue."

* * *

While Harry had been undergoing his ordeal, Ferghal and Danny had been singled out from the rest and forced to undergo a number of examinations, including the taking of blood and other samples. The examiners treated them as if they were nothing more than laboratory animals to be manhandled, used and presumably discarded at some point. Danny was terrified by this and Ferghal was furious – a fact which attracted even more ill-treatment to him. Fortunately for them both, the experiments on Harry seemed to provide what the people abusing them wanted for the moment so, with Ferghal heavily restrained, they were eventually dumped back in the cell with Sub-Lieutenant Trelawney and the other two midshipmen. Once Ferghal had been released from the medical restraints by the others he was able to tell them something of what had been done to them and did his best to comfort Danny while fretting over Harry's whereabouts, little realising that the subject of his concern was occupying a cell a short way away.

* * *

Harry huddled in a corner, fighting the demons in his head and the voices whispering in his fevered ears. Eventually he must have slept because he started awake, still exhausted but with his mind surprisingly clear – except that the 'voices' were still whispering in his head. He listened carefully and then realisation dawned! He was 'hearing' the computers in this terrible place. Feigning unconsciousness in case his cell was monitored and his tormentors returned to force him to return to their torment, he focussed his mind and soon found himself exploring the computer's data files. He found the files they had created on him and took a few minutes to see what they had done. Anger burned in his heart as he left these and explored the system further, suddenly realising that he could now see the operating system, which, on *Vanguard*, he could not!

For a several minutes he explored and found that he could 'see' Ferghal, so he attempted sending an image – and was almost betrayed into dropping his pose of unconsciousness as Ferghal responded. Quickly Harry tried to send several more images and ideas, and once again was delighted when Ferghal indicated that he had understood. Leaving

Ferghal to communicate his idea to the others he now knew to be with him, Harry tried to discover the security system and stumbled across the formulae for the drugs this fiendish place was creating. It gave him a sense of tremendous satisfaction to instruct the computer to send these to the food and refreshment replicators for the staff and guards, and, when he detected that these were now sufficiently contaminated, to erase the formulae from the system entirely. He pushed further and found the security system at last, carefully searching it for monitoring of the cells. One by one he found what he was looking for and carefully instructed the computer to show only what it could see at that moment. Then he returned to Ferghal's link and dared to think of an escape. Ferghal responded positively and Harry allowed himself to return to the exploration of the computer looking for a communication channel that he could use. He had just found it when things started to happen – and he suddenly realised that the computer had suffered damage to several parts of its network! He explored and found that it was in fact being attacked physically, as if people were attempting to destroy it! Quickly he tried to contact Ferghal, but now without success. A noise above him brought him back to reality and he looked up to see the worried face of Danny peering down at him through the ventilation grille.

He tried to speak but the muzzle prevented him. He indicated to Danny that he would have to force his way out to the corridor and attempt to open the door and the boy apparently understood, because he vanished along the duct and a few minutes later Harry heard the sound of a grill being pulled into it. He tried to explore the computer again, but now many of its several parts were registering as non-functional or inaccessible. He had just managed to struggle to his feet when the door burst open and Ferghal rushed in ahead of Paddy Murphy and the Sub-Lieutenant!

Ferghal's face registered his horror at Harry's condition, and he strode forward with a face transformed by fury. In seconds he had the muzzle off and joined Paddy and the Sub-Lieutenant in releasing Harry from the strait jacket. No one said anything as they worked, and Harry did his best to maintain his dignity even though his legs hurt with exhaustion and he wanted more than anything else to burst into tears. As the strait jacket was flung aside by Ferghal, the Sub-lieutenant broke the silence, "Wait here while I find you something to wear! Ferghal, Paddy, find him somewhere safe to sit down. I don't know what's happening here at the moment but whatever it is, it's going to get a lot worse when I find some weapons!"

Ferghal's face was a mask of fury as he hissed, "No sir! I'll find Master Harry some clothes – and when I finds the scum that did this to him, they're mine sir! Mine!"

He left the cell before anyone could stop him and a few moments later there was a shout from the other end of the corridor. There was a momentary burst of weapon fire and then silence. The Sub-Lieutenant darted out and ran to the now open door where he realised that Ferghal had short circuited the door controls. The visible evidence suggested it to have been a rather unorthodox method! A weapons burst had partly melted the door frame and he stepped beyond half expecting to be met with another burst. Instead he found Ferghal stripping the clothing off a man whose neck was clearly broken. Without a word he took the clothes Ferghal removed and carried them back to where Harry was now propped against a wall and watched as the others helped him dress. From the guardroom he could hear Ferghal busy doing something, but did not care to check what this was for the moment, hoping it would not be something they would regret.

Taking stock as the others tended to Harry, the senior realised that they would soon have to move out of the cell block and get clear. But, which way to go and what forces would they face when they left this area? Clearly the facility was under some sort of attack, but from whom? Harry provided the answer. In a voice hoarse with fatigue, Harry said, "Sir, I think most of the people in this place may have been affected by the drugs I made the system divert to their food and refreshment system. Their computer seems to have been damaged because I tried to get a message out, but the system is now malfunctioning and no longer responds when I access it!"

"Harry, I don't even begin to understand how you did that, and I don't think I want to!" he nodded to two of the Midshipmen, "Right, we'll move out. Hans, Paddy go and see what Ferghal is doing and if there are any weapons there that are serviceable. I think Ferghal has gone fighting mad Harry - I pity anyone who gets in his way. Now lad, I want you to walk with Danny, I'll bring up the rear. Has anyone checked the other cells? OK, wait for a moment while I do it!"

The first two cells proved to be empty, but the third revealed a prisoner like no other that Petroc Trelawney had ever seen. The figure was man shaped and bipedal, but that was where the resemblance ended. The head was clearly reptilian and the skin, though damaged and showing signs of abuse was covered in small iridescent scales. The hands and feet were equipped with talons at their extremities and the creature hissed a warning and adopted a defensive posture as Petroc opened the door! "Easy, easy!" he said as he held up both hands, palm outwards in a gesture of peace, "I mean you no harm, we are trying to escape from here and you should as well!"

The creature eyed him suspiciously, evidently uncertain, so Petroc backed away and said to the waiting boys, "move slowly and don't make any threatening gestures. Let him see you mean him no harm!" He moved to the next door and opened this to reveal another of the creatures, this one clearly injured, one arm a mutilated mess. "Oh shit!" he exclaimed, "Now we have an injured alien as well!" he was thrust aside as the first creature leapt past him making guttural hissing and growling sounds to which the injured creature responded. "OK, I guess we leave now and these guys can come or stay – their choice! Move chaps, I rather think Ferghal may not be the only person around here with a determination to do a lot of damage to anyone who gets in the way!" Turning to the aliens, he said, "I don't know if you can understand me, but this officer has accessed the computer for this place and caused the food replicators to be contaminated. We must escape and you can come with us or stay – it's up to you!" He made to back out, but the injured alien made a gesture to stop him, hissing something to its companion and he realised that the creature was staring past him to where Harry stood just beyond the door. He indicated Harry and said, "This officer has been tortured, I must get him to the surface and away from here." Then he turned and ushered Harry and Danny out of the corridor.

On reaching the guardroom however, the Sub-Lieutenant saw an Emergency Med Kit and had a sudden thought. "Wait here! I think our friends next door may have a use for this!" He grabbed the kit and darted back to the cell where the two alien creatures remained locked in a fierce debate. He opened and placed the Med Kit on the floor and said carefully, miming as he did so, "You may find the things you need in this to help your friend." He backed away carefully as the first alien stared at him and then at the open kit. Carefully it reached out and drew the kit closer, then made a gesture which could have been thanks or a dismissal. The second creature gave the same gesture rather restricted by the damage to its arm, but the expression seemed rather more grateful and the Sub-Lieutenant backed away and returned to the waiting group. "Right, Ferghal and Paddy take the lead. What weapons have we got? You have the guard's personal projector Paddy? Ferghal?" he looked at the boys stony expression then at the strip of shiny metal and its improvised handle as Ferghal held it up. Somehow the youth had found something and given it an edge and a point, Petroc Trelawney didn't like to think how. He nodded, "Let's go."

The party explored the corridors adjoining the guardroom and found the laboratories in which the experiments were conducted. In one they surprised three of the facilities technicians. It was an uneven struggle and the three were soon cowering prisoners as Ferghal, his face a mask of hatred, stood menacingly guard while one of the three did his best to apply a dressing to the wounds he had inflicted on the only one who had attempted to resist. Sub-Lieutenant Trelawney watched with a detached interest as the wounded man was bandaged, then turned to the third and said, "Now, my friend, you have a choice. This lad is from a time and a place where the words 'no quarter' meant no rules of engagement apply. You can tell me the way out and the numbers of people here and where you have the rest of your 'specimens' locked up – or I'll simply walk away and let Ferghal finish what he has started on your friend there – but on all three of you!"

The man shot a glance at Ferghal, and then tried to bluff, "You won't get away with this! The guards will be here any minute now – these labs are under constant surveillance and recording – and they will already be alert to your escape!"

"Funny you should say that!" replied Petroc smoothly. Without taking his eyes off the man he said over his shoulder, "Harry, can you still read the computer?"

From where he had been lowered into a seat next to a terminal, Harry replied, "Yes sir. It's easy from here, this terminal has a loop system installed."

"Good, then show this gentleman," he laid an ironic stress on the last word, "what you can do to their system."

*Out Of Time*

Harry concentrated and felt himself link to the computer, he probed around looking for surveillance records, and then found the data storage of the laboratory activities. He picked a record at random and said, "I'm going to put one of their experiments on the viewing screen sir."

Across the room a screen lit up and there was an angry growl from the Midshipmen as the picture showed a naked man strapped to the examination table fully conscious but apparently paralysed as the assembled 'medical' team busied themselves removing a part of one of his organs. The expression on the victim's face told the watchers exactly what the victim could feel as this was done! The whimper of fear from the man in front of him brought Petroc Trelawney's attention back to the prisoners.

"Kill that Harry!" he ordered, "But we will want to retrieve all of those records. A court will want to see them rather sooner than these bastards would like!" He fought to control his revulsion and fury as he said, in a voice filled with loathing, "For the life of me I can't think of a single reason why I shouldn't let Tec Rate O'Connor do to you what we have seen in that screen! You aren't even worth scraping off my boot! The only thing restraining me is that I *will not* sink to your level, and I won't allow any of these fellows to either! Now, tell me what I want to know – or, there are a pair of reptilian creatures back there who would probably do it better!" He glared at the man, with a look of such loathing that the man actually backed away, and said, "Now you bastard, start from the top – what is happening here right now, who is in charge, where are they and how many of you pieces of filth are there?"

The words began to tumble out of the man, his companions nodding in confirmation as he spilled names, exits and guard positions. From the torrent of words the group learned that this was a secret facility set up by the Johnstone Research Foundation to study interspecies breeding, mind control and commercial cloning of bodies for sale as spare body parts. The full staff ran to about sixty workers of whom roughly twenty were guards – but, and the captive did not know how it had happened, it seemed the guards had turned on each other and there was a running fire fight in progress in some areas of the base. To add to the confusion several of the scientific staff seemed to have been dosed with the psychotropic drugs they had been experimenting with and had run amok. "It's a bloodbath outside this level" pleaded the wounded man, "we were trying to access the computer to try and reverse the contamination but all the files on the formulae have been erased and the computer is not responding to some commands!"

"So you tell us," snarled Paddy Murphy, visibly shaken by the short vision he had had of the hell these people inflicted on fellow beings. "Well I sure as hell don't know how it's happened, but I hope it lasts a long, long time!"

The man cowered away from the hatred blazing in the youth's eyes and whispered, "Please? I've lost a lot of blood, can I have some water?"

Sub-Lieutenant Trelawney considered this request, knowing what the water was likely to contain, and its probable affect, he faced a difficult choice. He made it, "Do you see the man at that terminal?" he asked quietly, "Until he collapsed, he was in one of these labs being used to test one or more of your mind-bending drugs. As you have just seen, something you bastards did to him has enabled him to talk directly to your computer. The reason you can't find the antidotes or the formulae is that he destroyed them – and told the computer to feed what it already held in stock into your food and water supply. If you drink the water, you do so entirely at your own risk. You may get lucky, I have no idea how long lasting these chemicals are!" He signalled to Paddy Murphy, "You brought those manacles from the guardroom Paddy? Good, join these gentlemen by the ankles and then we are leaving." He smiled viciously at the trio and said, "See you later gentlemen, we'll be back to fetch you as soon as we can raise the Marines! I am looking forward to your trial – it should be very interesting!"

He watched as the trio were hobbled then said to Ferghal, "Ferghal, I want you to take that terminal apart as creatively as you can and make it so that anyone attempting to fix it is in for a nasty surprise!"

Ten minutes later the group climbed a long staircase and emerged in an accommodation area. Making their way cautiously along the empty corridors they found a trail of destruction, as if the inhabitants had all run away, desperately trying to escape some terrible attacker. Along the way they discovered several bodies, all in the uniforms of the guards, and recovered a number of weapons as well. On the next level they found several survivors, but it was obvious from the paranoia these wretches displayed that it would be useless to even attempt to question them so they were chased into a convenient lounge and the door immobilised, sealing them in. This was to be repeated at several more levels until at last the sound of weapons fire and fighting told them they needed to exercise a great deal of caution. As they waited outside a door listening to the sound of explosions and weapons discharges above them, Harry suddenly said, "Sir, I think the main computer core is here. If we secure the core we can preserve the evidence of this place's fiendishness for the Captain."

"Good thought Harry, but how?" responded the Sub-Lieutenant, "It sounds like a full scale war up there and we still have to get past it!"

"No sir, the computer is here!" said Harry urgently, "I can hear it – and all the records are here, if we can but secure them?" He looked about, "Ferghal! Ferghal, you know how to do this?"

"Aye Master Harry," nodded the other, looking from Harry to the Sub-Lieutenant.

"Oh, very well you two, I don't know what you think you can do, but let's try it! What the hell, we're in this up to our stupid necks anyway! Murphy and Dinsen, take the weapons and guard this room. No one comes down here! Clear?"

"As daylight," said Paddy Murphy and Hans Dinsen nodded his agreement.

The room Harry and the others entered was circular and the walls were lined with computer terminals. In the centre of the chamber a solid core of servers, cables and electronic display panels rose in a tall column to disappear into the roof structure above. Ferghal followed a staggering Harry across the floor to this core and then waited while Harry apparently linked to the computer again. Sub-Lieutenant Petroc Trelawney watched as they held a whispered conversation, then Ferghal shut his eyes and seemed to be praying silently before he moved across to a panel and removed the cover. A few minutes work and he saw the youth withdraw a part, then a series of small sealed components, replacing them with others Harry passed him. The removed items were placed in a pouch on the youth's utility belt and then the panel was again closed and the boys returned to where he stood looking pleased.

"We have the storage discs sir. And the ones we have fitted in their place will lock anyone who attempts to change anything in this computer out of the system – disabling all terminals unless our code is entered." said Harry, the exhaustion showing in the sunken appearance of his eyes and the hollowness of his face.

"Do you know Harry," smiled Petroc gently, "you two are a constant source of bloody amazement to us all! Two months ago you had never seen a computer and now you are controlling the damned thing just with your mind?" He laughed, "Well, let's hope your magic works. Now, can you get us out of here? There is a full scale war going on upstairs as I think you may have noticed?"

"I think there may be sir," grinned Harry, his tiredness ageing his face, "there is a tunnel through which all the service cables run over there," he pointed to a blank panel against the wall, "According to the plan of this place in the computer, that will take us out to the surface since it is also the intake for the cooling system for all this," He finished indicating the mass of computer equipment.

"Right, then that's the way we'll go! Get it opened up while I get the others in and secure the access to this place!"

"One thing sir" asked Harry, "There is a replicator here. May I try and get myself a proper uniform from it?" He indicated the dead guard's clothes with an expression of loathing, "I don't want to wear this if I can get a proper uniform!"

"Harry, you've earned more than that! Go for it, get yourself kitted out – just make sure it's free of the stuff you shoved into their food OK!" He turned his attention to supervising Ferghal as he opened up the panel they needed to gain access to the tunnel. When he finally turned his attention back to Harry it was to see the exhausted youth dragging on a new Fleet jacket evidently copied from one loaned by Hans Dinsen. There appeared to be some other item at Harry's waist, but he could not identify it and turned back to recall the others and seal the entrance they had used. While he was busy Ferghal used the replicator to create something with which he replaced the improvised weapon he had been carrying, and then helped Harry and Danny into the tunnel to be joined a few minutes later by the Sub-Lieutenant and the others. Hans accepted his jacket with a nod to Harry and slipped it on, while Ferghal and Paddy closed the access panel with some difficulty and secured it from within.

A little over an hour later the party emerged cautiously into the open air at the mouth of what appeared to be a large natural cavern. Situated in the shoulder of a small mountain, it was screened from above by an overhanging cliff and the approach from below was steep and open. Some distance away they could see what appeared to be a huddle of houses and a small harbour, but the Sub-Lieutenant decreed that they would rest first and move at sunset. Fortunately there was a fresh clear stream tumbling from the cliffside about fifty metres away and several trees bearing fruit they recognised, from having eaten them at the hotel, were also dotted about the hillside. There was a general feeling of relief once they had all slaked their thirst and eaten a little fruit, but the Sub-Lieutenant also recognised that now they faced another challenge. Until they knew the situation in the village they could see below them, and determine whether the food and water there was safe to eat and drink, they would need to have access to, or carry with them, items they knew to be safe. Once again it was Ferghal who provided the answer to this problem. Finding a tree bearing a gourd-like fruit he carefully extracted the seeds and the soft innards of it, then scoured it clean and flushed it several times with clear water. Apologetically he explained that it should ideally be rinsed out with boiling water or baked in a hot bread oven to ensure it hardened and that any poison was destroyed, but, as he had seen these being eaten by both humans and animals he thought this would be safe. It was the work of another hour or so for everyone to be equipped with an improvised water bottle. Harry's exhaustion being all too evident and despite his attempts to stay awake and to remain active and cheerful, it was becoming increasingly evident that he could not keep going.

Petroc Trelawney found a dry place out of the sun and ordered Harry "to get some rest". It did not take long for the youth to fall into a deep and exhausted sleep, and the Sub-Lieutenant left Danny to look after him while he tried to learn the techniques Ferghal was showing the others as he fashioned the water flasks and then began to assemble staves and other items he described as useful. It proved to be a very educational afternoon for the group, and as the sun sank beneath the distant horizon, he reluctantly woke Harry.

"I'm sorry sir," Harry apologised as he rubbed the sleep from his eyes and eased himself into a sitting position, "I hope I have not slept for too long!"

"Long enough Harry," grinned the relieved Sub-Lieutenant, "Ferghal has been teaching us some of his skills, but now we must move on. As soon as the moon rises we will be under way!"

"Which one sir?" grinned Harry, "This place has three of them and two are up already," he laughed, "though I doubt we'll get much use from them!"

"Cheek Mid? So early?" the Sub grinned, "The larger one, Gitchegumee, should rise in about twenty minutes if my estimate is right, and it was almost full the night before we were grabbed. I think it's about four days since we were taken. All we have to hope for now is that there are no large predators hereabouts and no one with night vision helmets!"

The journey down the mountain side was harder than expected and painfully slow. No one and no animals disturbed their progress however, and some six hours later they reached the outskirts of the small settlement and discovered, when they spotted one of the inhabitants using an optical viewer from a concealed spot to watch the entrance to the facility they had escaped, that it was in fact home to a cowed and terrified group of settlers who lived in fear of the installation under the mountain. Carefully weighing up the risk, the Sub stalked the man's position cautiously and then distracted him in order to allow Paddy Murphy to leap out and grab him before he could raise an alarm. There followed a brief interrogation from which they learned that there were several collaborators in the village who kept the others in order by threats and coercion. However, when the Sub-Lieutenant pointed out that the support these people could expect from the facility would be a little erratic unless the occupants could overcome the contamination of their food and water supply, he became more cheerful and talkative. They swiftly learned that there was another camp nearby that housed a few reptilian hominids and a small group of guards. "How many?" asked the Sub-Lieutenant, and received the intelligence that there were never more than six, changed once a week from the main facility.

Trelawney took stock. He had four young men, a child and himself, a few weapons and a local population clearly in thrall to the operators of the base – or at least under their control. Against him were ranged the unknown collaborators, an unknown number of surviving guards and staff from the facility they had escaped, a camp full of beings he wasn't sure would be friendly towards humans of any description and six heavily armed guards. He called a council of war.

* * *

Half an hour later Terrien Hurker, Chairman of the Village Council appointed by the Research Foundation, opened the door of his house, angry at having been disturbed from his comfortable bed. The angry demand died on his lips at the sight of a hard faced youth, holding a lethal looking sword, who placed the point of this weapon against the Chairman's bobbing Adam's apple and forced him to retreat into the house. Behind the sword wielder another young man darted in and swiftly shut the door, making a rapid search of the room for any weapons. He heard his wife enter the room and her gasp as she drew breath to scream. He shut his eyes as the boy with the sword hissed, "If she makes a sound, you're dead Mister!"

"Hush Mellia – don't make a fuss!" he pleaded, relief flooding his heart as he heard her stifle her intended scream – unable to see that Hans Dinsen had stepped into her line of view holding a weapon.

The pair herded him and his wife to a closet and the first boy expertly tied them with strips of cloth torn from the robes hanging there. Then, having gagged them he thrust them into the closet, and shut the door! They heard his companion say, "Right Ferghal, I have their com-links! And another Personal Plasma Projector! Do you want it?"

The pair in the closet listened as the sword wielder said almost contemptuously, "No thank ye! My cutlass makes less fuss and is more effective up close!" there was a sound of footfalls and they heard the first voice say, "I'll signal Mr Trelawney then!"

This scene was repeated in six more houses, only in one did a fight ensue and the householder would regret this error for the rest of his life. Ferghal's wild Irish temper had flared as all his anger at what Harry had been subjected to boiled to the surface. The man would live the rest of his life without the use of one arm and only the partial use of one leg. Ferghal's replicated cutlass had almost removed the man's arm as he tried to raise his plasma weapon, and the second backslash intended to take out his entrails had only narrowly missed as he fell back, but Ferghal's final slashing thrust had impaled his thigh and torn away muscle and flesh, exposing the bone and severing the major muscles. The man had collapsed in agony and shock, blood pouring from his wounds. Ferghal would have finished him off, but for the fact that the man's wife had thrown herself between him and his enemy. As Ferghal hesitated he had seen the terrified face of a child peering from the open door and the bloodlust drained from him. To the woman he snapped, "Tend to your man! But make a wrong move and I'll kill you both!"

"Easy Ferghal," said Harry as he followed the Sub-Lieutenant into the room and surveyed the scene. He dropped to the floor next to the sobbing woman and opened the MedKit he had brought with him down the mountain. He looked at the pulsing blood and recognised, having perforce helped *Spartan's* surgeon several times, that the major blood vessel was intact. He set to work and packed the wound with dressing materials and then told the woman to bind it tight. The almost severed arm gave a greater problem, and in the end, he simply cut away the remaining tether and, making a pad bound the stump. To Ferghal he said, "I am glad you are my friend and not my enemy! I think this fellow will live, but he may be wingless and his leg will not be much use either!" He gave the wary youth a smile, "I think Master's Mate Treliving taught you the cutlass drill well."

"Aye Master Harry, that he did," a flicker of a smile crossed Ferghal's face.

"Where the hell did you get that from?" asked the Sub-Lieutenant watching the easy manner in which Ferghal held the weapon and recognising for the first time that Harry had a dirk slung at his waist.

"Why, I used their replicator – the one in the computer core!"

"But," began the Sub-Lieutenant, "replicators can't …" he trailed off as realisation dawned, "Idiot!" He exclaimed, "That bloody thing doesn't need plasma generators, fuel or anything else! It's just a piece of bloody steel and whatever! Of course a replicator can make it! Damn, why the hell didn't I think of that before?"

The woman next to Harry listened to this her eyes wide with fear as she watched the group now occupying her home! She looked around at them and realised for the first time that one was a child. Her own child suddenly filled her thoughts and she said frantically getting to her feet, "Illia! My child! What have you monsters done with my child?"

"Nothing madam," replied Sub-Lieutenant Trelawney, sharply, "Calm down please and we will find him." To Paddy Murphy he said, "Check the rooms again, the kid may be hiding! Danny, you go with him."

Moments later a wail of fright told them the child had been found and Paddy emerged with a struggling boy in his arms and thrust him at the woman, Danny's impish grin told the tale of one small boy having known where another would be hiding. "Safe and sound!" he grinned, "we don't fight kids' ma'am, unlike your friends up the hill it seems!"

A tap at the door sent the group into action, but the door, when opened, revealed a party of the villagers and the bound and now somewhat bedraggled collaborators collected from where the group of Midshipmen had secured them. The leader smiled as he advanced to where Sub-Lieutenant Trelawney stood, "We wanted to show our appreciation for whatever you've done to the research station. They seem to have gone completely mad up there and the snakeheads are having fun with whoever they can find. What do you want us to do for you? We'll deal with this lot," he waved at the cowed group of prisoners, "we have a number of scores to settle with them one way or another!"

"Well, I can't let you dish out vigilante justice I'm afraid," said the Sub-Lieutenant seriously, "if they are guilty of any crimes then they must face trial in a duly constituted court of law. And as the only legitimate authority around here since the declaration of Martial Law a week ago, I must insist that you hold these prisoners and keep them in good health until a full investigation of all complaints can be held and a court assembled to try anyone charged."

"You've got a nerve! Who'll stop us? You and these kids?" asked one of the men at the back of the group.

"I'm afraid so. Ferghal show them your, er, cutlass. Harry; let them see what Ferghal did to the last man that attacked him."

There was a long moment of silence as the group looked at the bandaged stump and the mutilated thigh of the man lying on the floor in a now congealing pool of blood. Sub-Lieutenant Trelawney reflected momentarily on how much cleaner a kill from a plasma projector was – the cauterising effect meant you didn't see the blood – or smell it! The villagers looked at Ferghal, his expression stony, and they looked at the weapon he was holding. Then they looked again at the young Fleet officer and realised that he meant exactly what he said. The leader surrendered, "OK, we'll play it your way. What do you want us to do?"

"Well, we need a comlink station and transport back to the capital," began Trelawney.

"Can't help you with either of those," growled the man who seemed to have assumed the role of spokesman for the villagers, "Our 'governors' have confiscated all power craft and comlinks – the only one was up there!" He indicated the mountain, "and I doubt it is still working. The guards used submersible craft to shuttle their 'guests' to and from the facility."

"Submersibles? Why would they use them? And where is this place anyway?"

"Because they didn't want anyone seeing who or what they brought here," the speaker shrugged, "a lot of people have 'disappeared', supposedly abducted by the snakeheads – but they're just slaves used by the Consortium. Where are you? Welcome to our island – at least it was ours until the Johnstone people arrived with their Consortium troopers. This is New Caledonia, we're only a day from the mainland by power skimmer – if you can get past the Pleurodons in our ocean!" he gave a short laugh, "another reason the Consortium use submersibles. At least with our wave-piercers we could move fast enough to outrun them; now? Well we have some boats, but nothing powered!"

"Well, we'll take a look in the morning," decided Trelawney, "right now we need food and sleep.

As he arranged a rest rota and sentry duties Sub-Lieutenant Trelawney had the uneasy feeling that he was being watched. Try as he might, he could see nothing, but the feeling persisted. He posted his sentries with care, and then took the first watch himself, allowing the younger men to sleep after a light meal prepared and shared with them by one of the villagers wives. He was slightly concerned at this and would have preferred to have one of his own party do this, but was reassured by the fact that the villagers joined in the meal without hesitation, and to his relief, dawn eventually found them all rested and still at liberty. It also showed a plume of hazy smoke issuing from several points on the mountain and brought the news that the guards at the camp had apparently been overwhelmed and the reptilian slaves they had been guarding were gone.

# Chapter 17

# Unequal forces

Like the Earth's solar system, the Pangaea Alpha system had several planets and some proto-planets. The innermost orbits were taken up by three medium sized planets, the innermost being about a third the size of the habitable planet and the remaining pair about half that size and sharing the same orbital path. Scientists had already calculated that these two would eventually collide, but at some distant point in the future. All three were too close to the system's sun to be habitable, in fact they seemed to be in a constant state of reformation as their surfaces erupted and heaved under colossal forces. Beyond Pangaea a small planet occupied a steady orbit along the edge of a wide asteroid belt, rather like the planet Mars in the Earth's system, it may once have had the potential for life, but no longer, its atmosphere stripped away by the next planet in the system, a huge gas giant almost large enough to become a proto-sun, constantly circled by a swarm of moons, some large enough to be considered planets. Two more worlds orbited beyond this giant, both frozen and roughly twice the size of Pangaea itself, water, carbon dioxide and frozen methane locked in the thick crusts of frozen gas as they rolled along their orbital paths.

*Vanguard* and *Bellerophon* held station inside of the gas giant's larger moon. The giant ball of glowing gas raged and swirled below them, its electrostatic emissions causing a storm of background interference on their passive scanners, a situation made acceptable by the fact that it also made their presence extremely hard to detect. It had a second advantage, in that it was only a few minutes hyperjump from the position held by *Sydney* and the *Aurora* both of whom now carried enhanced strike and inceptor squadrons. Aboard *Vanguard* Commodore Heron had set up his Staff in the Flag Centre, several compartments away from the Command Centre, leaving the ship's manoeuvring and management to

Executive Commander Grenville, now effectively Captain.

Studying the disposition of his forces, James Heron considered the positions of his remaining three cruisers, *Penelope*, *Phoebe* and *Ariadne*, and was satisfied that the enemy would not be able to locate, target and fire on all his forces immediately on 'dropping out', unless, of course, each ship had onboard some spy set to betray their presence. He thought with an edge of sadness of the purge the Executive Commander had carried out just a few hours before on his own ship – a purge precipitated by the discovery of several other sabotage attempts on their weapons, and by the defection on the planet of a Master Weapons Technician, suspected of sabotaging the primary weapon, and of the Medical Technician de Vries, now known to have been instrumental in the abduction of Sub-Lieutenant Trelawney and the party that included Midshipman Heron, Ferghal O'Connor and the boy Danny Gunn. He frowned as his link chirped, promising himself that if any of that party had been harmed – and he meant any of them – everyone responsible was going to regret whatever part they had played, however small.

"Commodore," he replied to the link.

"Sir, all our ships are in place and the minefield you ordered has been laid. I have reports from *Sydney* and the cruisers that they have arrested several members of their crews caught out by Fritz's spy programme. All of them are now in the brig and they have also identified and isolated several 'associates' just to make sure," said Richard Grenville.

"Thanks Dick, I know this is a tough one, but if the 'int' is correct, we have a force of eight principle ships with probable hostile intent inbound against our seven and they will probably have some frigates as well – I can't afford to allow them any edge at all! I see that *Fort Belvedere* is now on station and out of the way on the outer rim and the *Lynx* and the *Lion* and *Tiger* have arrived on station with the *Sydney* and *Aurora*. Their fire power isn't great, but they may take down a few of the enemies strike craft and keep them off *Sydney* and *Aurora* while we get into position. They will also have the Marine boarding parties aboard and the boarding sleds rigged – once we jump to the positions for attack they will swing in under our lee and then come up astern of the any enemy ship and close so that they can launch boarders. *Sydney* and *Aurora* will hold the enemy's attention until we drop out behind them and then jump to our support. Strike squadrons will launch as soon as we drop out and those already in position among the asteroids will attack as soon as the enemy shows his intent!"

"Agreed," came the response, "but another bit of good news is that Fritz and Val have come up with a way to project one hell of a burst of disruption for their interference screen emitters as soon as we are ready to engage. It's an EM Pulse that will knock out all scanning transmissions in its path. That will shut down their screen while we lock onto target and let them have it."

"Better and better, have the others got this kit as well?"

"Yes, I let them have the information as soon as they'd cleaned house!" the Commander replied, "We couldn't risk it getting to the enemy through any leak they had onboard."

"Good, then there's nothing left to do but wait. *Ramillies* is on her way, but is still at least two days from 'drop out' according to her ETA., we'll have to hope she's managed to clean out her subversives before she gets here." He paused briefly and then asked, "Any news on the missing party?"

"Sorry sir, I'm afraid there's nothing on that front. The people we have taken in the mine base either won't say or can't say. We know only that they were all taken aboard a submersible and shipped to a secret base – one that even the people at the Minehead Base don't know much about." There was a pause, then, "If we can sort out this little assault fleet problem, we'll be able to go back there and take the planet apart until we do."

"Thank you Dick, you know my mind far too well!"

\* \* \*

"Chairman," the speaker was nervous, "we have lost touch with the research station on New Caledonia and the facility at Minehead has been taken by the Marines."

"I see," the Chairman was dangerously calm. "And what other news of incompetence and bad planning have you got to report?"

"We have suddenly lost all communication with our people aboard the Fleet ships at Pangaea. We think that they may have been compromised by the operation to snatch the youths involved in the reported time slip." The speaker gulped as the Chairman's face darkened and his brows snapped into a terrifying frown.

"What?" he demanded his voice one of controlled fury.

"Doctor Johnstone was particularly insistent!" the messenger gabbled, "He demanded the operation and we thought it …."

"He demanded?" the Chairman's rage exploded. "You *thought*? You may have compromised everything we have worked for and you have the audacity to say you *thought*? None of you are capable of thought, if you were, you would not have allowed Johnstone and his ambitions to have compromised our operation on Earth and elsewhere – instead you let him pursue *research*," he spat the word as if it was some sort of curse, "which was bound to result in an investigation!"

"But Chairman," protested a slightly overweight member of the Board, "that research has paid immense returns to both the Consortium and to Interplanetary Development as we all agreed it would! Our returns on his research into mind control and work enhancing drugs is paying handsomely – so is his technique for cloning replacement organs and the DNA he is hoping to recover from these time travellers the Fleet has captured – well, the potential profit is enormous!"

"Mr Hsu, I agree it has paid the dividends we hoped for to date – *but it should not have been conducted anywhere where the Fleet or the European Confederacy or their allies could find out about it!*" Although his voice dropped to a level of quietness just above a whisper, it brought a chill to the room. "Overconfidence and incompetence; those are the hallmarks of failure! That is why we must strike now and strike hard against this force the Fleet has sent to Pangaea. Yes, it is a declaration of war, but we have weapons and tools superior to theirs – thanks again to the bureaucrats and their 'outsourcing' ideology! We have also had our people at work on their ships for months quietly arranging for their weapons to malfunction – those were *my* orders and they are being affected by *my* people," his finger stabbed the table, "and I have personally placed special agents aboard those ships – agents with the training and the expertise to disable them. Thanks to your incompetent meddling and greed in allowing Johnstone to demand and get his way, our entire plan is now in danger. We now have no choice but to destroy these ships and to destroy this colony world as well as a warning of our capability." He glared around the table, his eyes resting for a moment on an empty chair, before he continued, "Anyone who wishes to leave has my permission to do so – Mr Aspery, whose incompetence in authorising this snatch for Johnstone has compromised us, has already gone, I arranged his departure myself this morning."

The other members of the board glanced nervously at one another. These departures were not frequent occurrences, but, since Ari Khamanei had become Chairman, no one who left the board was ever seen again. It was as if they had vanished completely from their home worlds or any other corporate activity. There were rumours of course, but nothing could ever be substantiated.

The Chairman glared at the assembled board members for a moment longer, and then said, "Fortunately for the success of our enterprise I have other sources of information and operatives! This morning I have learned from my own agent that the main Fleet is now required for another task, which will leave *Vanguard*, *Bellerophon*, *Sydney* and some frigates there with a transport ship supporting the ground forces. The *Ramillies* is supposed to join them, but our people are to take her over and join us when she arrives. I have decided that this will give us the perfect opportunity for a strike at the heart of Fleet's reputation. If we strike now, we can overwhelm these ships before any others can be sent to their aid. It will go some way to wiping out the failure to prevent the loss of our Pangaea bases and the exposure of some of our operations." He gave the cowed members of the board a cold stare before continuing, "We have a powerful group four starships and four heavy cruisers against their three starships and four cruisers and this opportunity will enable us to begin the process of reducing the Fleet's resources in small groups, avoiding serious opposition. With our frigates as well we are an overwhelmingly superior force"

"What if the intelligence is not accurate, what if the Fleet is simply waiting to spring a trap?" asked a member of the board.

"Our forces are sufficiently powerful to overwhelm them even if they are – which, I can assure you, is not the case! My source is extremely reliable and, in any case, our ships are equipped with the device which prevents their targeting us." He permitted himself a thin smile, "It will be a massacre and a warning to the rest. I anticipate that we will receive the capitulation of the World Treaty Organisation governments within days of our final annihilation of their main fleet – which will be soon." His smile was anything but friendly as he stared at each member in turn, daring a challenge to this plan. Finally, when there was no demurral, he said, "If none of you has anything to say, this meeting is closed. We will assemble at ten hundred ship's time in two days. From this Board Room we will be able to watch as the Fleet Squadron is destroyed! I expect you all to be here promptly." He rose from his seat and stalked from the room.

The remaining members stood and nervously made their own exit carefully avoiding each others eyes and refraining from making any comment.

※ ※ ※

Some thirty six hours after the ship's taking up an orbit against the gas giant, Commander Nick Gray, in his Flight Control Centre, checked the results from his latest practice sortie. In setting one wing against another he was exercising the flights as much as possible, allowing only rest and refreshment while the craft were refuelled and serviced. His pilots were muttering about 'slave driving' but he was impervious, snapping at Lieutenant Commander Pedersen, "Tell them they can complain all they like –either they are better than anyone the other side send in to bat – or they're dead. Their choice! Now get them out again and tell the leader on Six-Five-Two Alpha to get his Flight tightened up or I won't be looking at poor scores in a computer game, I'll be writing letters of condolence – and I'll hate them for it!"

"Yes Boss!" said Karl Pedersen well aware that what fretted his Commander more than anything else was the fact that he was cooped up in the Flight Control and not outside in one of his beloved fighters. He conveyed the message, careful to phrase it as an order from himself, and equally aware of the fact that he was talking to his brother Bjørn as he did so. A few minutes later the launch controller was requesting launch clearance for two more flights and, when given, passed the order in one word, "Launch!"

On the view screens Nick watched as the nimble craft were flung about the exercise area – an area chosen because it offered a screened position behind one of the planet's moons – and was a little more satisfied when they eventually requested landing instructions. He listened as the Controller gave them permission and then tracked them as they followed one another into the giant landing bays located in the lateral fins. "Right Karl," he said, "let them rest a full watch now, I'll want them in the ready room at O-Six hundred tomorrow!" He keyed his link and said, "Patch me to Maintenance." A moment later he had the Maintenance Master Warrant Officer on the link, and continued, "MW, I am resting the strike craft and Fighter Squadrons Six-Five-Two, Six-Five-Three and Seven-O-One, I'll want them all refuelled, rearmed and ready to launch at O-Six-Thirty."

"You'll have them Commander," came the reply. "O-Six-thirty launch ready. What about our Combat Patrol sir?"

"The patrol craft will be coming in on rotation, get your people to turn them round as fast as possible, I want two squadrons on patrol at all times."

"We'll do our best sir."

"MW, your best is always good – but tonight I want better than best."

"Understood, Commander."

"Good – and MW?"

"Yes sir?"

"Tell your people I said thanks in advance!"

"I'll tell them sir."

※ ※ ※

After the scare of discovering that her primary weapons had been sabotaged, Valerie Petrocova was taking no chances, everything was being checked and rechecked. Her team were being driven as never before, no matter how well they did, she demanded better – and the surprising thing was they found they were delivering it. Several, Weapons Scan Tec Ignatius De Santos in particular, were still feeling anger at the betrayal of their Master Technician, Jean Dupré. There was a general feeling that he had somehow betrayed not just the Fleet and the ship, but something more personal, he had betrayed his friends – rigging the weapons so that it could have killed them all while he had 'jumped ship' and gone on the run.

"Right!" said Commander Petrocova, "Mr Jellico, target acquisition for the primary again please! Target is the small asteroid coming onto your screen in five seconds. I want that lock in fifteen from the moment it appears!" She watched as he ran his scan up, then spotted the asteroid and began his target tracking routine, her timer said twelve seconds as he declared "Target locked, ready to fire!"

"Excellent!" she grinned at her team, "Now that is how we knock down the skittles!" She looked at their surprised faces and asked, "What's so amazing? That he can do it?"

"No ma'am," gulped De Santos.

"Er, Commander," asked Lieutenant Helen Pascoe, "I don't think any of us know what a skittle is?"

"What?" It was Valerie's turn to be surprised, and then she threw back her head and laughed, "Damn! Of course, this is Harry's fault!" She laughed, "He talked about skittles – wooden pins you stand in a triangular formation and roll a heavy ball at them. The idea is to knock down as many as possible with a single ball and each player has three balls to roll." She sobered suddenly, "I hope they're alright, those bastards seem to have them very well hidden."

\* \* \*

Commodore Heron looked around the battle control room and at the 'Flag' staff he had assembled, Lieutenant Chris Case from Weapons, Lieutenant Callaghan from Engineering, Lieutenant Commander Albrecht Bär from Communications, Lieutenant Piotr Łopata from Navigation and Lieutenant Dick Maclean from Flight Control. A good team, he reflected, watching them at work, already shaken down and working together. Interspersed with them were a number of other Technical Rates managing the plots, tracking the interceptors and strike craft and monitoring all coms traffic and scanners. The Flag Control buzzed with pent up energy as they prepared for the battle ahead. He made a decision on a matter that he had been pondering all day and rose from his Command chair, "I'm going to my quarters, ask all the Commanders to join me there."

Arriving in the anteroom to his quarters he spoke briefly to Adriana Volokova, then entered his sleeping cabin and pulled on a fresh shirt and replaced his jacket. Returning to his office space he found it already being transformed, the long conference table already covered by a white cloth, the cutlery laid and the glasses set out. One by one his Commanders arrived, surprised to find themselves served with a small glass of wine and slightly puzzled by the Commodore's sudden interest in social activity.

When they were all assembled, he ushered them to the table and Chief Mess Steward Huw Powys began to serve an *hors d'oevre*. With a smile, Temporary Commodore James Heron raised his glass and said, "In case you're wondering whether or not I have finally tipped over the edge, I think I had better enlighten you to the truth – it's far too late to be wondering that! The reason I have asked you all here is to say to you that I know I can rely on you all to do whatever it takes when the enemy arrives, and to say thank you in advance. A famous Admiral once, on the eve of a battle that changed the course of history, invited all his Captains to dinner. I would have liked to do the same, but distances out here are a little more difficult to manage than the sea in the days of sail." He paused while they gave the expected laugh and continued, "The purpose of my invitation is quite simple, you have all done the impossible in the last few days, and done it well. We are as ready as we will ever be; it is now up to the enemy to make the first move. Thanks to you, we have slight edge, but it is slight. I will be following an illustrious lead tomorrow or the next day when our expected visitors arrive and will send a signal round the Fleet – after that it will be up to each of us to make the best use of what we have and to use it to the best advantage. Now, it's time to relax and enjoy a dinner Mr Powys has created at very short notice!"

The dinner went extremely well, all things considered. Chief Steward Powys had excelled himself and the company enjoyed a great meal. They were in relaxed mood as they parted to go to their quarters, each conscious of the uncertainty of the day ahead. Without exception and buoyed up with confidence, they were all at their action stations a little over eight hours later when Weapons Scan Tech De Santos keyed his alarm and reported, "I have eight large ships and escorts on passive scan dropped out inside the asteroid field!"

Seconds later the optical watch from the observatory deck reported, "Four Starship Class ships, four Heavy Cruiser class and four Frigate class ships on visual approaching *Sydney's* position."

※ ※ ※

Aboard the Consortium flagship Chairman Khamanei watched the huge boardroom viewscreen with satisfaction as the planet of Pangaea and its moons leapt into view. The shining jewelled dots of the two equatorial docking platforms showed plainly, as did the slightly smaller bright stars that were two of the ships he had expected to see. He turned to the rest of the Board and said, "Sitting targets. Gentlemen, I do not think this will take long at all." He touched a key pad on the desk and said, "Admiral Hung, you may commence the attack, it seems we have fewer ships to deal with than you thought."

"Chairman," came the reply, "there is something not right here. That is the *Sydney* and the second ship is a cruiser, one of the 'Goddess' Class – but the other ships we expected do not show on our preliminary scans. The anti-scan device limits some of our scanning ability as well as theirs."

"Admiral," said the Chairman dangerously, "do not offer me excuses – destroy those ships and hunt down the others!" To the rest of the board he said, "As soon as we have destroyed these, we will be in a position to destroy the *Vanguard* and her consorts when we locate them!"

He had barely finished speaking when one of the heavy cruisers out on the flagship's Port beam was illuminated by a great plume of fire, then a second, and the frigate on her quarter suffered three explosions in rapid succession, leaving the ship a shattered wreck. "What …?" the Chairman began, interrupted by another frigate vanishing in a vast flare of fire.

"A minefield Chairman," exclaimed the Admiral on his link, "I suggest we withdraw until we can ascertain its extent!"

"Nonsense Admiral, do not give me excuses! The fleet ships have been alerted already and will be calling for reinforcements," he snarled, "I insist that you commence the attack immediately – these losses will be avenged!"

# Chapter 18

# A voyage in strange oceans

The small bay and its jetty was some distance from the town and surrounded by a huddle of sheds and working areas. There were several craft there, but only one in a condition to remain afloat, the others having obviously been deliberately damaged to prevent their use. Sub-Lieutenant Trelawney looked at the large boat moored alongside the jetty. It lacked any sort of engine and was evidently designed to carry containers of equipment or goods from the island to the capital. At least that is what it had originally been intended to do, but, as the leader of the village, one Marcus Grover, told him patiently, although originally intended to be powered, the discovery that it would be too slow to outrun the Pleurodons had meant it had never been finished as intended, instead being used in the harbour as a storage unit or as a lighter to carry containers to waiting wave-piercers. Since the arrival of the Johnstone facility on the island none of their produce had left and only what the Johnstone people allowed had been brought in by their submersibles. "Thanks Mr Grover," sighed the Sub-Lieutenant, "as he turned away from the jetty, "But I can't see how we could use it."

"I agree Mr Trelawney, but you did ask to see what ships or boats we had here!"

"Well, I guess I had hoped that there would be something we could use." He paused at the sight of Harry Heron explaining something to Paddy Murphy and Hans Dinsen. Half jokingly he asked, "Well Mr Heron? Have you some marvellous solution to convert this boat into a starship?"

Harry looked surprised, "A starship? Oh no sir! But we could rig her and sail her to the mainland!"

"Rig her? Sail?" it was the Sub-Lieutenants turn to look surprised, "I think you'll have to spell that out for me!"

"Sorry sir?" asked Harry caught off guard by the colloquialism.

"Explain what you mean by 'rig and sail' it please Harry," grinned the Sub. "Us modern types aren't quite with you on some of these concepts of yours you know!"

"Oh, my apologies sir," smiled Harry, "that hull is about the size of a small brig, and seems to have the lines of one, although a little finer in the bow and stern. There are a number of large spars we can use to give her a mast or masts and there are also some large sheets of cloth which can be turned into sails. If we give her a simple rig, perhaps as a gaff cutter, I think we can sail her to the mainland and find our troops."

Sub-Lieutenant Trelawney looked at Harry, then at the lighter. He looked at the expectant faces of the rest of his party and then took in the puzzled expression on the villager's face. He made his decision, "OK! Harry, you've surprised us again I think, but none of us knows anything about ship rigging so you're going to have to explain everything carefully and supervise the whole thing. Here, Paddy, Hans, are you fellows up for being skivvies and labourers?" Receiving their cheerful acknowledgement, he turned to the villager, "Mr Grover, I suspect we are going to need a lot of help for this, can you organise some volunteers to assist us please?"

Under Harry's guidance over the next two days, the ship built 'lighter' was transformed, with a mast stepped and a topmast fitted, stays and ratlines, crosstrees and a gaff boom rigged. Ballast in the form of stones, packed down with shingle and then secured by a platform of boards laid over it, settled the hull a little deeper and gave her a steadiness that surprised everyone except Harry and his two companions for whom this was all much more normal than the technology they had had to adapt to. The work went swiftly, aided by the use of modern tools and equipment which made it easier to adapt things, fabricate parts and hoist, lift or fit them. The villagers had become quite enthused by the work, and several of the women helped with the cutting and stitching of the sails that Harry and Ferghal had drawn out on a cleared piece of ground so that the large weatherproof sheets – of a much lighter and more durable material than any sail cloth they had previously encountered – could be laid out, marked and cut and then stitched and reinforced as needed.

While that work was being done, others were searching for containers in which water could be carried, food stored and kept dry. The hold area was covered over to create a large living space in shelter and a steering position was also rigged. By chance, one of the villagers had a map of the continents and the seas around them, which, even though it was not a sea chart, at least gave them some idea of the shape of landmasses, the position of Pangaea City itself and the distances to be covered. As far as Harry was concerned, its best feature was that it showed the land in relief, colour graded and had the lines of latitude and longitude superimposed. It also provided some vague ideas of sea depths by showing shoal water in lighter shades of blue and even marked some of the larger areas of shallows quite clearly. Looking at it, Harry felt that it would do as a rather simple chart – better than the complete absence of one as he told the Sub-Lieutenant.

Another of Ferghal's hidden talents came to the fore as they pondered how to create a compass, when he cheerfully borrowed a magnet out of a damaged generator and used this to turn a piece of soft iron into a straight magnet. With this suspended in a cutaway dome and an improvised compass card, drawn by Harry, fixed to it, they had a crude compass, but they soon discovered that it swung a little too readily. Even so it was still sufficient to give them a good directional indication. The swing was damped somewhat by suspending the bowl in improvised gimbals and by filling the lower part with water, attaching some simple fins to the underside of the plastic card. This and a digital clock provided the first basics of their navigational equipment, but Harry realised they would need something more to determine position. He had wracked his brains and then remembered that he had observed a fairly bright star that seemed to hold a pole position. If that could be used as a navigational mark, finding Pangaea City would be relatively easy, he thought with all the confidence of youth. A check of his theory over three nights confirmed his idea – at least sufficiently to give him the confidence to hope it would work.

The Sub-Lieutenant watched all this with keen interest and began to ask Harry to explain and to show the rest exactly what he was doing and how. This took a lot more effort than Harry had realised – especially when it came to explaining the tools he was planning to use to navigate the little ship to their proposed destination! For one thing, his improvised sextant could read only three angles, it being a metal sphere filled half with water and two holes drilled at its 'equator' to allow him to sight the horizon, with three more at different altitudes above one of the equatorial openings. Patiently Harry explained that lining up the horizon across the lower pair of holes allowed him to line one of the other three on his 'Pole Star'. He had carefully calculated the angles for his prime navigation points along his improvised 'chart' so that he could work the ship down to the latitude of Pangaea City – and then run down the westward distance along the appropriate parallel. When asked if this was how he had navigated on *Spartan* he had looked surprised and then laughed, "Lord no, we had proper sextants for that and a good chronometer! No, this is something I saw the South Sea Islanders use in the Pacific, but it was much easier for them, all the islands they visit lie in open waters and along a narrow parallel. We will have to go south along this line," he sketched the route along the blue space of the coast of the island, then, when we reach this point, the star should be in the second hole and we turn west along this line and sail South by West until the star is in the third hole. We should then be able to see Pangaea City – or at the very least its coast!"

By the end of the fourth day the exhausted crew were able to stand on the jetty and feel pride in their creation. To everyone's surprise the lighter now looked like a trim little ship riding steadily in the water, her sails furled neatly (Ferghal's insistence that she must be made to look shipshape and like a proper man o' war saw to that!). Danny had found plenty he could contribute, being very good at his knots and even smaller splices in some of the lines they had used. An even bigger talent was his ability to assemble the running blocks they needed and which had to be created piece by piece in the replicators. Like Ferghal and Harry he seemed to have suddenly become less a child and more a man as he found tasks and carried them through with a thoroughness completely belying his years. It was his idea that the little vessel should have a name and even more importantly, an ensign. Harry was not sure how the boy persuaded one of the village women, or even how she had made the flag or from what pattern, but he found himself being presented with a white ensign that would not have looked out of place on the gaff of a First Rate! He handed it to Ferghal, saying to the Sub-Lieutenant, "With your permission sir, may we hoist our colours?"

"Harry, since I find myself unable to sail this vessel of yours," smiled the Sub-Lieutenant, "I think you had better assume command – if you wish to hoist your colours, it is your decision, and not mine!"

Harry nodded, considering this, "That is generous of you sir, but I don't mind acting as the Sailing Master, under your command."

"OK, you're right of course," grinned the Sub, "Whatever happens now, I'm the man in the firing line if I lose any of you! Somebody think of a name for our ship?"

"If I may suggest something," interjected the village leader Marcus Grover, who had proved himself an invaluable helper in organising and fabricating much of what they had needed, "my family used to be seafarers on Earth many generations back and one of them talked about a famous ship preserved in a place called Portsmouth – a ship called *Victory*. I suggest you name yours after her!"

Harry looked surprised then remembered the history he had explored of his own period – the bit he had missed – and nodded, "Admiral Nelson's flagship! It would be a good name sir, although," he laughed, "our little *Victory* would be rated a cutter and not a First Rate as the old *Victory* was."

"*Is* Harry, she's still preserved in Portsmouth although she's been rebuilt a couple of times now!" the Sub-Lieutenant considered, "OK, *Victory* she is! Now Harry, if you will take charge and sail the ship then let's get settled – Ferghal, what are you waiting for, get that flag up!"

The ensign, its great red cross dividing the field of white into four quarters with the upper quadrant filled by the long forgotten flag of the defunct United Kingdom, made an amazing transformation. Suddenly the little ship looked like she was ready to go to war, something, the Sub-Lieutenant reflected, that they probably would be doing! But the day held one more surprise and it showed itself as they began to file aboard. There was a gasp from the assembled visitors and a rapid reaching for weapons as two figures emerged from the gathering shadows and stood in full view, their clawed hands clasped to their chests and their heads held low. Sub-Lieutenant Trelawney stepped forward quickly placing himself between the people and the reptilian figures. Thinking quickly he imitated their gesture and speaking slowly asked, "We mean you no harm, what is it you want?"

One of the creatures straightened up and advanced slightly. With a shock, Trelawney realised it was the same creature he had left in the cells under the mountain, the one with the damaged arm. The arm still looked damaged, shorter and seemingly deformed, but no longer covered in the angry looking wounds. The creature gestured with its good arm and hissed something slowly and carefully. Trelawney hesitated, his hearing was excellent and it seemed to him that the creature had attempted to say something in English. "I am sorry, I don't understand you?" he replied carefully.

The creature tried again, repeating the gesture which now seemed to indicate the little ship, and hissed, "we go wissss youssssss!"

"You want to come with us?" Trelawney's surprise filled his voice.

"Yesssss!" the creature made another gesture, "impossshible sssshtayy! Helllpssss usssss, now helpssss you wisss ssship, wisss you and wisss him." This time the gesture took in the Sub-Lieutenant and Harry stood to one side, "Isss massser of..." it appeared to search for a word, "honour."

"Wait a minute please!" Sub-Lieutenant Trelawney looked at his small group of midshipmen and did a rapid calculation. From the way in which the townspeople had withdrawn he suspected that they might have a reason to do so, but he also had a duty to protect everyone who asked – and that included, in his view, these strange creatures. He called over his shoulder, "Harry? I don't know whether you need help to sail this ship or whether they could actually help us. You seem to have been included in their interest. We know almost nothing about them" He mused to himself adding, "What do you think?"

Harry looked at the creatures and considered this. "Well sir, a few extra hands won't go amiss especially if we have a bit of a blow at sea and have to take in some of the sail. Is it just these two?"

"I don't know," replied the Sub-Lieutenant, "let's see." He addressed the creature again, "How many of you?" he asked slowly and clearly.

The creature made a gesture behind him and suddenly there were ten of them in sight! The creature tilted its head and hissed, "Theeessse a'e allll survivesssss."

Looking at the group, Trelawney realised that all the creatures seemed to be nursing injuries or to be showing signs of damage to their bodies. He gave the group a long and thoughtful look, assessing their postures, their appearance and trying to gauge what, if any threat they posed. Again he made his decision, "Very well," he nodded, "we will make a place for you." To Harry he said, "Have we enough water do you think? And food?"

The creature made a gesture which could have been gratitude and then hissed something to its fellows. The others vanished silently for a moment then reappeared carrying carefully wrapped bundles, "Weee bring ffooood." Hissed the leader, indicating himself and the others, "Help sssssave, we helllpssss you."

"Well," said Trelawney to no one in particular, "I guess that answers that question!"

Suddenly the hold space they had fitted out for their stores and accommodation seemed crowded. Up close the reptilian hominids proved to be quite lizard-like, their heads were slightly flattened and tapered to a sharp snout with a large mouth and wide set eyes with vertical pupils while their ears were small ridges almost at the base of their skulls. Their bodies were covered in small iridescent scales over a leathery skin which seemed to be uniquely patterned and although largely a silver grey, appeared to change to blend with their surroundings. They wore no form of clothing at all. All of them were marked by scars and other signs of what they had endured in the facility they had escaped. They proved to be incredibly lithe and very strong and seemed to have a quiet dignity and very disciplined order to their group. It was clear that the spokesman was their leader and he interpreted the Sub-Lieutenant's orders to the others. It did not take long for the contents of the hold to be rearranged and the newcomers settled into the fore part quite comfortably. Their linguistic sibilance was just one part of their strangeness. The other was the fact that, despite their nakedness, it was not possible to tell whether they were male or female and they had a faintly musky, but not unpleasant, odour to them. Their diet, Harry and the others were somewhat relieved to note, was not unlike their own, a mix of meat and vegetables, carefully prepared and served. It very soon became apparent that these were not some primitive people or animals, but a society with a developed social sense and order. Sub-Lieutenant Trelawney felt himself ashamed for the fact that human beings had obviously treated them as if they had no civilised rights at all.

The night was spent in uneasy watches as the two groups adjusted to each other. During the night Trelawney learned to his surprise that the reptilian leader knew what had been done to Harry and something of how Harry was linked to their escape. They seemed to regard the youth as somehow 'special' and wanted to remain with him – and the party he was with – for reasons he could not determine but seemed to be connected to something in their cultural lore. That they regarded his party as having rendered some service to their people seemed to play a large part in their behaviour towards him, secondly, they felt that this demanded a debt of honour. In short he and the rest of his party, but especially Harry, were regarded as having some sort of life debt owed to them. The language barrier made any discussion of this decidedly tricky so the Sub-Lieutenant wisely decided to let it drop for the moment. He slept on it and on how they would manage the next stage of this little enterprise, and the dawn found the little ship as ready as she could be for what was to become a legendary voyage.

"Mr Trelawney," rumbled Marcus Grover, "we think you are completely mad to attempt this especially with the snakeheads! No one knows anything about them. They give us the creeps, always moving silently and suddenly, and they can stand absolutely still for hours – you can't see them half the time until you're on top of them! And this trip of yours – you do know about the Pleurodon? Those brutes attack everything they meet and they have been known to try to board ships like this. Most of our original sea going craft were that fast they could outrun the damned things, but I think you're going to be fair game!"

"Thanks for the advice Marcus," replied the Sub-Lieutenant, "I know this sounds crazy but we'll be OK with our passengers I think." He asked, "How much actual contact have you had with these people?"

"Not a lot," shrugged the townsman, "but the guards used to talk about them. Every now and then one would escape – they're quite strong as you'll discover – and the guards used to think it was good sport to hunt them because they were so good at hiding. The guards always got them in the end. Heat sights and goggles help!"

"I see," said Trelawney, a little distantly, he looked at the other thoughtfully, and changed the subject, "I believe we will have to take this Pleurodon as it comes. We are at least aware of the thing, which I understand is more than the first settlers were. We do have a bit of protection as well, we'll be rigging some heavy netting outboard to hamper anything trying to get inboard – Harry and his friends call them 'boarding nets' for some reason, and we've rigged up some of the strongest we could find. It may not stop the beast but hopefully it'll slow him down long enough to kill it or injure it."

"If you do encounter one, make sure you kill it outright." Grover produced a heavy weapon from a bag and said apologetically, "You had better take this with you; we got it at the compound this morning, but make sure you get a good shot! Pain maddens those brutes and they go into a frenzy, also the blood will attract more of them so kill it and make sure it stays and you move!" The Colonist offered his hand, "Best of luck, you're going to need it – and don't worry, we'll not take our revenge on your prisoners – old Terrien is all bluster now his pals have gone and the old fraud is spilling the beans on everyone. Even Stepan Glinka is recovering as well as can be expected when someone's taken your arm off and damned near a leg as well!" He grinned, "They'll be here when you get back with the soldiers!"

※ ※ ※

The breeze was light as Harry and Ferghal directed the others in hoisting and setting the great gaff mainsail and the foresail. Then Harry used the backed foresail to swing the bows away from the jetty and, once the swing had begun, sheeted it home and called on Paddy Murphy and Hans Dinsen to haul in the mainsail sheets. Almost immediately the little ship began to gather way, moving easily away from the jetty and heeling gently to the pressure in her sails. As soon as they were clear he apologetically asked the Sub-Lieutenant to take the helm, a great tiller rigged with lines through double sheaved tackle blocks onto a wheel with the compass mounted in front of it. Going forward he steered some of the reptilian crew and his fellow Midshipmen towards the halyards for the topsail and then supervised its being set. Immediately the ship heeled a little further and gathered way, increasing this again when he had them haul up the flying jib and set the jib on the short bowsprit. Spray soon began to shower them as the little vessel thrust her bow into the slight swell as she cleared the shelter of the bay and, with her great ensign streaming from her gaff peak, began to shoulder her way into the short swell.

※ ※ ※

Even as Harry and his companions were setting out in their cockleshell of a ship, and launching upon a voyage in unknown seas, the

Commodore and his commanders were sitting down to dinner. The next few hours would bring new challenges for both parties.

* * *

Harry held the *Victory* on a course that would give them plenty of sea room, noting with pride that the little vessel held her heading well despite having almost no depth to her long keel. She handled very well, thanks to his having ballasted her down slightly by the stern, with only a small tendency to want to work her way to windward. This meant having to correct her with a touch of rudder to keep her head off the wind. By now she had settled into a comfortable motion – comfortable that is for Harry, Ferghal and Danny, but less so for his companions who began to discover the misery of sea sickness. The reptilian creatures seemed unaffected by this, so Harry had them spread and drape the boarding nets, a precaution he would be very glad of in due course!

By evening they had made a good day's sail – an improvised Logline cast every hour showed an average 'run' of eight knots, good sailing with a slight head wind over the Starboard bow. Harry had tried to estimate their likely leeward movement, but found that he could not gauge this effectively. He watched with Danny and Ferghal from the helm position as the first of the moons rose and then the second, noting their angle relative to the ship and recording this on a pad he had managed to acquire, thinking that later he would try to work out a table to assist in navigation if he could get enough observations of the moons and the relative motion. He glanced at Ferghal and then at the compass card, checking that they were holding the course and heading he had set, he grinned at his friend and said, "Does it not feel good to know how to do something the others cannot?"

"Aye Master Harry," laughed Ferghal, "They fair boxed the compass trying to hold a course – mind, Mister Murphy almost had it right – then he got sick!"

"That too!" laughed Harry, "But remember how ill we both were on our first voyage?"

"Me too," grinned Danny, "I wist I could die then!"

Laughing at the memory, Harry said, "Hold her steady. I wish to climb to the cross trees and see if I can get a fix on the land before we lose the daylight fully. I will indicate the bearing if I can and must rely on you Danny, to mark it on our compass!"

With that he walked forward and swung himself outboard and began the climb. He had barely started to do this, when one of the reptilians joined him climbing just below him and always between him and the water, merely indicating its intent to remain there when he protested that he did not need an escort. Reaching the crosstrees he hauled himself upright on the yard and looked about him. He took time to study the surface of the sea to windward, noting the swell patterns and the surface texture as the wind ruffled across it. Then he looked to the eastward and tried to make out the shoreline as it caught the setting sun. He noted the line of the hills that formed a spine running south along the eastern side of the long island and searched for the headland he knew from the map should be a marker for the halfway point on the southerly run. He was on the point of giving up when he spotted it as the little ship lifted to a larger than normal sea and quickly he pointed and called to Danny, "Mark my direction!" Hearing a cry of affirmation he took another look at the seascape, now rapidly darkening as the sun dropped below the horizon and, just as it vanished, leaving a brief twilight, saw a sudden eruption and disturbance in the sea far to the west. Thoughtfully he descended, climbing swiftly down the ratlines, his escort still between him and the sea, wondering what the disturbance had been and secretly afraid it was the dreaded 'Kraken' Pleurodon.

He wrote up the bearing on the headland and now faced another difficult task. None of the others could be trusted to steer a proper course – vital if they were to avoid running ashore in the dark – even if they weren't suffering the effects of seasickness. He knew the reptilian people were not affected by this, but did not think they could be relied on to steer safely either. That meant that he or Ferghal had to remain on watch while they let someone else steer. He was still pondering this when one of the reptilians approached and in their strange hissing language indicated that it should relieve Ferghal. Harry considered this carefully, then nodded, "Very well, Ferghal, do you take Danny and find us something to eat. I shall take the first watch, and you shall take the next, we shall rotate until we can get the others to understand the helming!"

"Aye, aye, Master Harry, but if this…" he hesitated, "..man, cannot steer properly, call me!"

"Fear not Ferghal, You will know immediately I need you!" he turned his attention to the newcomer, and showed him carefully how to keep the Lubber's Line on the mark showing the direction on the compass card. To his surprise, the reptilian face showed amusement and then the creature indicated that it understood him – and demonstrated this by taking the wheel from a reluctant Ferghal, then adjusting the course, first bearing away from the wind, then returning to the bearing with precision – or as much as the crude compass would permit! "Right," breathed Harry, "you have done this before?"

The creature seemed to grunt and then indicated that it had steered a vessel. Communication seemed to be exhausted at this point so Harry ordered Ferghal and Danny below to find food and to rest. He watched the seas around them carefully and was glad to notice that the light from the moons at least provided a sort of twilight which gave them good night sailing conditions. They sailed on in silence for a while, and then the reptilian's leader emerged and approached Harry. The creature nodded to him in greeting and spoke carefully, "You wissshhhh for…" it seemed to be searching for a word, then made a gesture of peering out over the sea.

"Lookouts!" exclaimed Harry, "Yes!" he nodded his head vigorously, "Yes, we need some lookouts."

The creature went to the hatch and hissed something to its companions and two more emerged, spoke briefly to their leader and then positioned themselves where they had a good view of the seas ahead and on either beam. Harry touched the leader on the shoulder, jumping back as the creature whirled to face him, conscious of a sudden chill, "I'm sorry!" he exclaimed, holding up his empty hands, "But I think we should tell them to stay away from the gunwales?" The creature cocked its head and stared at him quizzically, "Tell them," Harry indicated the pair of lookouts, "to stay inboard – not at the sides like that. There are creatures here that attack ships," he ended desperately. For a moment the other stared at him, seemingly weighing up what he had said, then it seemed to grasp what Harry was trying to say, and said something to the others. Instantly they moved away from the gunwales and stationed themselves nearer the mast. Harry relaxed again as the leader made a gesture of enquiry about the new arrangement and Harry nodded, adding "Yes, that is safer!"

## Out Of Time

Looking out to seaward a short while later he saw again the disturbance of the water some distance from the ship, this time catching the flash of a huge flipper as it rose momentarily above the crest of a wave. He shuddered and was about to say something when he realised that the reptilians had seen it too and evidently recognised it as a threat. Their leader looked at Harry thoughtfully, and then said something to the others which made them look his way as well before returning to their scanning of the waters around them. Ferghal appeared on deck some four hours later looking well rested and moved to stand next to Harry, "Shall I relieve the helm Master Harry," he asked.

"No, I think we can leave it to our friends. Stay away from the gunwales and make sure everyone else does. I think there is one of those Pleurodon creatures out there and I have no desire to test our boarding nets in the darkness," said Harry. "Keep our course as it is at the moment, south by south-south-west and a quarter west and call me in two hours. I think," he added as Ferghal made to protest, "that we shall have reached the southern end of the island by then and there may be reefs, that map," he indicated the 'chart' attached to the cover of the steering winch, and covered in a waterproof sheet, "indicates shallower waters there and I want to make sure we do not run aground!"

Going to the reptilian leader he made their greeting gesture and said carefully, "I am leaving my man Ferghal in charge. Do your people need relief?"

The leader looked at Ferghal and then at Harry and nodded an acknowledgement returning his greeting gesture. Harry used signs and gestures to show that he was going below and that Ferghal would remain on deck. The reptilian nodded its head gravely and hissed an instruction to its own people. Harry watched as the helmsman's place was taken by one of the lookouts and the helmsman dropped into the hold. A few seconds later another emerged and went forward to take up the lookout. Harry had the distinct feeling that he was in the presence of people who knew as much or more than he did of the sea, and went below to catch a little sleep.

At midnight he was again on deck, this time with his improvised sextant. He was relieved to find that the sky was clear and that despite the moonlight from the three moons, now in various positions overhead, he could still pick out his navigation star. Carefully he tested his instrument and found to his relief that he could line it up successfully on the horizon, and with a little difficulty, get the right line on his star. From the angles of the holes he did a quick estimate of the declension he still needed and then did some figuring on his pad, all of this watched with keen interest by the reptilian leader. Then he moved to his improvised 'chart' and measured off the distances run and checked his calculation for the distance to run to his next point. To his annoyance he noticed that, if his calculations were correct, they would arrive at the turning point just after sunset, much to early for him to get a proper sight on the star. He was about to go below and get a little more sleep when the sky above them began to blossom with great bursts of light, greens, reds and occasionally brilliant white. For a moment he thought it might be a meteorite shower, then fireworks and finally, as he noticed that it seemed to be concentrated in groups across the sky, he realised that he was witnessing a titanic battle in the heavens above them. "Quick Ferghal," he said urgently, "Get below and rouse Sub-Lieutenant Trelawney! I think this is something he needs to see immediately!"

Sub-Lieutenant Trelawney stared aloft with a growing sense of unease. He knew all too well what the brilliant streaks of light were, and what the great flashes represented. He felt completely helpless as he watched, desperate to know who was attacking and more importantly, who was gaining the upper hand. By this time everyone was on deck, all staring aloft, even young Danny gazing in awe at the titanic display of light overhead. Quite suddenly there was a brighter than usual flash, followed by a comet tail of light as something large entered the atmosphere and trailed a blazing path across the night sky. Other smaller trails told of smaller craft burning up in uncontrolled re-entry and testified to the savagery of the battle.

The sudden clatter of the sheet blocks brought Harry back to earth as the ship's head came dangerously to wind and almost into 'irons' he leapt back to the wheel and snapped at the embarrassed reptilian helmsman "Watch your course man! Steer small or you'll have us all aback!" The helmsman's reaction showed that it understood his intention even if it did not understand his words, and the motion of the little ship settled quickly back into its steady movement. Harry moved back to stand next to the helmsman where he could watch the trim of the sails and the compass card as they dipped and surged steadily on their course. Glancing aloft again, Harry saw that one of the 'ship stars' as he thought of the orbiting ships when they were visible to the naked eye through reflection of the sun, seemed to be emitting a series of flares. Others seemed to be getting brighter or to be flickering and he prayed silently that *Vanguard* and his friends and protectors would be safe!

For several hours the battle continued to rage overhead, gradually contracting until it seemed to be confined to an area near the southern horizon – and recognising the distances involved, the watchers on the tiny *Victory* realised that it was a long way out into the system. Overhead debris continued to collide with the atmosphere and occasionally larger pieces blazed trails across the sky and once or twice actually crashed into the sea below the horizon. By now no one, human or reptilian, spoke.

The Eastern horizon was just lightening when, with no prior warning, a great new star blazed briefly into existence, and just as suddenly winked out. For several minutes nothing more happened – and there were no further indications of battle either. Sub-Lieutenant Trelawney looked around the deck in the growing light and said quietly, "Let's hope that our side has won – or we are in very deep trouble!"

It was a very subdued party that prepared for the day ahead, sea sickness still making occasional attacks on the Sub-Lieutenant and the other two midshipmen, but this was becoming less and less of a problem and all three began to take as keen an interest in Harry's calculations and navigation as the reptilian leader. Later the wind began to increase in strength and the little ship responded by heeling a little more steeply and increasing her motion. This seemed to help, and certainly diverted attention from the sometimes flaming contrails that still scarred the skies above them. Towards sunset the wind began to back round on them and Harry laid the little *Victory* on a new tack, taking them westward and away from the island's southern shoals. This took them into deeper water as well and the motion changed as the swell got longer and the interval between them increased.

"This will delay our passage sir," Harry explained to the Sub-Lieutenant, "since we will have to put in a long run to the west before we can turn south again and make our next change of course to run towards Pangaea City. It will mean running extra miles – and may increase the chances of meeting one of those sea monsters we saw."

"Can't be helped Harry," shrugged Petroc Trelawney, wearily. He had spent a part of the day trying to think of ways they could ascertain who had won or who had lost in the battle they had witnessed, and come to the conclusion that one way or the other, their eventual arrival would be a small event if their people had been victorious and downright unfortunate if the other side had triumphed. He smiled encouragingly at the youth's serious expression, and said, "The important thing is to get there Mr Sailing Master Heron! A day later or earlier will not make any difference one way or another at this stage!"

"I'm glad you think so sir," replied Harry, "I think we can probably make up the time if this wind holds." More seriously he asked, "Do you think our ships have been successful Mr Trelawney?"

"Harry, if there is a God and he is just, I hope so!" he sighed, "If only we had some monoculars or anything that would give me a decent magnification of those satellites I might be able to guess! Now," he said firmly, pulling himself out of his moment of doubt, "to ship's business Mr Heron! We need to have a proper watch system; I can't have you, Ferghal, Danny and these fellows doing all the watchkeeping. You'll have to *'show us the ropes'* as I believe your expression is, so that we can be useful as well. I will take the watch with Ferghal and Paddy Murphy can stand watch with you on the first watch now. Hans can stand with Ferghal for the next watch and we'll do that until we are able to do our own watches and relieve you two. Does that suit you?"

"Why, yes sir, that will be a pleasure," smiled Harry, adding, "I will have to be called or be on deck at midnight to check our position sir, but if Mr Murphy or Ferghal call me a half hour early I can be ready to do so before taking over the watch."

Impressed, Sub-Lieutenant Trelawney nodded, "Good. Then let's make a start. Send the others to get some food sorted and some rest. We'll take the first period."

"Aye, aye sir!" replied Harry, reverting to the acknowledgement he was best used to. He turned away and called to Ferghal, quickly explaining the proposed system and what was required. Petroc Trelawney listened as they discussed his order in an almost foreign language. He caught references to First Dog Watch, Second Dog Watch, Middle watch and Morning Watch, Forenoon and Afternoon, then heard Harry tell his shadow, as Trelawney now considered Ferghal, to get some rest and food and to report at "eight bells in the first Dog Watch" to relieve him. 'And I need to get to grips with who our aliens are – and if they have names!' he thought, running up a list of things he needed to consider if he was to command this strange ship and crew.

At midnight Harry checked their latitude, again noting the distance between the star's angle and the angle he had calculated, and, after some work on his pad, arrived at a position. Having marked it on the 'chart' he noted that they would need to change tack again at the middle of the watch in order to make more Southing. He examined the chart again wishing for the umpteenth time that it contained more detail of the oceans instead of simply different shades of blue! He had guessed correctly that the lighter blues indicated likely shoal water, so had planned a course which should keep them away from the shoals apparently lying in a long chain from the southern tip of New Caledonia, which he hoped would also keep them away from what he had been told was the hunting ground for the terrifying Pleurodons.

At O-Two hundred – or four bells of the Middle Watch as he thought of it – he called all hands and, when he had everyone ready and in the positions he needed them, ordered the helm up and brought the little ship neatly round onto the Starboard Tack, settling her on her new course, still beating to windward, on a heading south by east south east. The wind had dropped a little but remained obstinately from the south south west – the direction he wished to go! By his estimate this wind and their present rate of sailing would see them taking another day to reach the position from which he could safely turn west and run down the latitude in the hope of striking land at Pangaea City. Relieved on watch by Ferghal and Hans he turned in tired, a little anxious that his navigation was so reliant on such crude instruments and at the outcome of the great conflict they had witnessed above the planet.

# Chapter 19

# A clash of Titans

With the enemy ships visible as fuzzy blobs on his passive scanners, Commodore Heron, keyed his comlink and said deliberately, "All ships, execute orders as directed. Good luck!" Around him his staff tensed as their screens blanked momentarily as the ship accelerated into the hyperjump.

Aboard the Consortium ships the energy surge from behind them as the two starships 'went hyper', was detected by their scanner plots almost immediately. Seconds later three more bursts were picked up as three smaller ships also vanished into hyperspace. Their attention now diverted to scanning for a drop out near them, they failed to notice the swarm of strike craft firing up from the asteroid field which formed a broad swath between Pangaea and the gas giant which lay in fifth place in the system. They also missed the fact that the four ships in orbit above the planet were running their hyperdrives 'hot' and ready to jump. They were thus caught very much off guard as the *Vanguard* and the *Bellerophon* 'dropped out' above and below them, immediately releasing swarms of strike craft. And seconds later the three cruisers also 'dropped out' immediately astern of the Consortium ships.

Their weapons controllers, however, were not slow to react and the Fleet ships were rapidly targeted in response to the deliberately mis-aimed opening shots from the Fleet ships. A heated exchange of fire commenced – the Consortium ships convinced that the Fleet ships were unable to lock and target them until, just seconds after commencing fire, a massive electro magnetic pulse washed over them – followed immediately by a frighteningly accurate burst of fire from the all too efficient ships of the Fleet. The close engagement coupled with the juxtaposition of friendly ships  – and the darting presence of the swarms of interceptors and strike craft from both sides – made the use of the new primary super weapon (designed as a 'stand off' weapon for long ranges) non-viable in the initial phases, especially since, being as yet untried in battle, no one knew with any certainty what the likely effect would be on other ships in close proximity. It was therefore, and by agreement with all three Fleet Captains and their Commodore, kept in reserve should opportunity present itself to take a clear shot with it. The close engagement and the heated exchange made it difficult for the Consortium units to employ the usual tactic of mini-jumps, so they fell back on the strategy of making sudden accelerating manoeuvres using the hyperdrive to achieve short bursts of speed which moved them large distances in minimal time spans.

Forced onto a defensive posture, the Consortium ships manoeuvred skilfully and attempted to spread into a fighting line. In this the Fleet ships proved to be more than a match – it was, after all, something most Fleet navigators practiced as a routine battle manoeuvre – and they matched hyperdrive burst for burst, preventing the enemy ships from escaping into hyperspace. The swarms of interceptors and strike craft engaged one another like angry wasps and the space between the great ships began to be filled with bursts of flame as little ships exploded or weapons bursts found their target on a larger hull. *Vanguard* shuddered as one of the larger Consortium ships found its target. Valerie Petrocova coolly called her targeting team to respond, selecting weapons and targets as she assessed the threat each posed. Her team began to score and the enemy attempted to break away simultaneously trying, once more, to hide behind its interference screen. She called up Fritz Diefenbach, "Fritz, another big pulse please? The bastards are getting their screens up again!"

Again the huge energy burst knocked down the Consortium ship's screens, but their weapons were also beginning to cause damage. Valerie selected one of the biggest Consortium ships as her target and passed the order to targeting, "Take out his hyperpods. Disable him and we can finish him off later!"

"Hyperpods. Aye, Commander," responded Helen Pascoe, her fingers skimming over her targeting console, "Weapons locked," she called.

"Fire!" Valerie watched as the plasma projectors pulsed their lethal bursts of ionised plasma across the gulf between the ships and saw with satisfaction the flares as the other ship's drive pods disintegrated in a great flare of energy. "Shift target! Hit his main weapons arrays!"

"Shifting target, aye," called Pascoe as her team reconfigured their screens and seconds later the great pulses were again striking home.

In his Command Centre the Commodore watched on the vast display screen as the fight intensified. In seizing the initiative, he was gambling on the Fleet squadrons' ability to maintain a superior rate of target selection and destruction and to be able to shift targets more rapidly and more accurately than their opponents. In this he seemed to have been at least partly vindicated. Calmly he received reports and listened to his squadron's Captains as they kept him informed of their manoeuvres and battle damage. Manoeuvring such big ships in close proximity – in space anything under a hundred klicks with ships of this size was very close – meant that battle, once joined, tended to develop into slugging match as the larger ships exchanged fire and tried to knock out each others ability to manoeuvre or escape. He noted with satisfaction that the ship targeted by *Vanguard* appeared to have been badly damaged and her fighting capability reduced. He keyed his comlink, "Captain Grenville, engage the big Consortium ship targeting *Penelope*, she appears to be their Flagship and I want her knocked out!"

"I have him sir," came the response. From his Command Centre, Richard Grenville quickly gave the orders to the manoeuvring team and navigator, then relayed the change of target to the Weapons Commander. "Try to give him hell as we jump in close Val!"

"Will do!" Commander Petrocova, turned to her weapons targeting team and gave a string of swift orders for a change of targets. As she finished the ship surged into a micro hyperjump.

The *Vanguard* leapt forward and, forewarned, Valerie's team were ready as the ship slowed, their weapons already focusing and locking on, their first burst of fire tearing a vast opening in the other ship's hangar spaces venting atmosphere and debris, including personnel and interceptors as it did so. But the Consortium ship's Captain was a man of some skill and he moved his ship swiftly, jumping out of range, and then returning to face the *Vanguard*, his own weapons doing damage as they came. Now it was *Vanguard's* turn to make a rapid shift of position and try to return the compliment, beginning a cat and mouse exchange which gradually drew them away from the main body of ships locked in mortal combat.

*Sydney's* Captain, a man known for his bold handling of his ship, jumped from his orbit into a position close beside one of the Consortium ships and engaged it in a deadly hail of fire as soon as his targeting system locked. Desperately the other ship attempted to disengage, but the *Sydney* was magnificently handled and the Consortium ship was rapidly reduced to a wreck left to the interceptors to pick off at leisure. The frigates *Lion* and *Tiger* had managed to jump in close beside the *Bellerophon* and the *Vanguard*, the big ships' bulk providing a vital shield from the Consortium's scanners. Once in position they then used their manoeuvring capability to close with the nearest pair of Consortium ships, heavy cruisers of a type the Fleet had long wanted to build, and launched their boarders, having the satisfaction of seeing both parties of Marines successfully landing on the ships they had targeted. This was to be the first stage in a battle of skill and wits as the frigates used their size and their ability to manoeuvre swiftly to cause enormous damage to their opponents, targeting hangar docks, weapons mounts and scanner arrays, while the boarders planted their blast charges on propulsion and manoeuvring pods, including the hyperdrives. Their withdrawal was the signal for the frigates to make a running recovery and withdraw, but as their larger targets attempted to turn and bring their forward weapons to bear, the planted charges began to detonate, crippling them and leaving them unable to manoeuvre without assistance.

An attempt by one of the other enemy ships to return this favour, targeting the *Vanguard*, failed when their boarders were met by a Marine company who engaged in a short, sharp and deadly engagement on the hull casing. Little damage was done by this and the survivors surrendered to be secured, stripped of weapons and suits, in a holding area.

*Bellerophon* found herself locked in a deadly game of leapfrog with two enemy ships and at first seemed to be struggling to survive, but the engagement allowed *Aurora* to drop out close to the more dangerous of the two and the fight very rapidly became a more even contest as a lucky hit from *Aurora* destroyed the enemy's forward plasma cannon mountings. This left *Bellerophon* able to deliver a deadly series of blows on the second of her enemies, reducing the ship to a helpless wreck closing the planet without propulsive power. As the battle now moved closer to the planet and its moons, the battle between the strike craft and fighters became even more intense. The darting small craft hurled themselves at each other and at the larger ships. Some, caught by the fire of an enemy or partially destroyed by defences of the large ships and the orbital docking platforms began the death spiral towards the planet's atmosphere. From *Vanguard's* Control Centre, Acting Captain Richard Grenville watched this engagement with satisfaction even as he gave the orders to jump his own ship in and out of danger. His calm concentration on the intricacies of the manoeuvring kept the ship in optimum position as they engaged in the deadly dance with the enemy.

Two Consortium ships, having broken away from the main battle, had succeeded in closing one of the orbital stations and launched boarders, their interceptors delivering a damaging covering fire against the Fleet interceptors attempting to prevent their assault. The raging dogfight that ensued could be seen from the planet surface, the dying wrecks and damaged craft crashing into the atmosphere to burn as they fell towards the surface. Seeing this, the Commodore ordered *Ariadne*, *Penelope* and *Phoebe* to support the platforms and watched as the three dropped out behind their bigger foes laying down a devastating fire as soon as they were able. With satisfaction he noted that one of the Consortium ships had lost its hyperdrive pods and then a great flower of flame burst from its after section as one of its reactors ruptured. What remained of the ship was clearly no longer capable of fighting and the cruisers immediately switched their attention to the second ship, leaving the wreckage of the first ship, still riven by internal fires and explosions to shed large chunks of itself into the upper atmosphere of the planet. The second ship, now furiously attacked by the three cruisers, hyperjumped clear of these determined enemies, taking a hit even as it did so on one of its lateral hyperpods, causing it to 'drop out' close to the larger moon's surface. Only the use of full power on normal drive engines saved it from becoming yet another wreckage strewn crater on the moon's pock-marked face.

※ ※ ※

Aboard the Consortium Flagship the Chairman was furious. He watched the battle on the screen with, in contrast to his companions whose fear was palpable, a burning fury, convinced that his ships had been betrayed and that their apparent inability to destroy an enemy that was supposed to be helpless and unable to target them was proof of this. He had the sort of mind that could not admit to being mistaken or to being overconfident, thus, in his mind the lack of success must be due to betrayal by one or more of the Board and the incompetence of the Captains commanding his own ships. It would never occur to him that it might be down to the superior discipline and training of the Fleet ships and officers and crews, or to the inspired leadership of its Captains!

He watched the death throes of a third of his ships as it was torn apart by the concentrated fire of two cruisers co-ordinating their attack from either bow of the larger enemy and saw two more apparently disabled with the blossom of explosions on the outer hull testifying to the fact that they were under attack from boarders. He keyed his link to the Command Centre, "Admiral," he said, his voice ice, "break off the attack and take us out of here!"

"But Chairman!" Protested the Admiral, "If we leave now, the other ships will be lost!"

"We, the Board, are more important than those incompetents! You will do as you are told! Get us away from here, take us to the headquarters at Solaris. And I want a secure link to IPD HQ in Brussels, I can only hope," he said with venom to the cowering board members, "that matters there have gone to plan! Incompetents; all of you!"

No one present dared to remind him that it had been his insistence, based on the information from his 'reliable' source, which had led them to attack and through it, to this debacle. Several of the board members were already considering how best to use this to their advantage, it was just possible, they reasoned to themselves, that this reverse might provide the very opportunity they needed to recover at least some of their own power and status.

※ ※ ※

"Commander," John Jellico's voice filled with urgency as he called for Commander Petrocova's attention, "Their Flagship is preparing to go hyper!"

"Oh no he won't!" she checked her scanner, "He's at optimum for the primary! Lock it to target while I get firing permission!" She called the Commodore and rapidly apprised him of the development, "Sir, if I can target him and knock him down with it, it may convince the others that it's time to quit!"

"Agreed," replied the Commodore, "I am entering my firing code now! You may fire at will."

"Target locked," called Jellico, "he's entering the singularity!"

"Like hell he is!" snarled Valerie Petrocova, her fingers dancing as she entered her code, "Primary hot! Fire!"

The Consortium flagship plunged into the singularity her hyperdrive engines had just created, her battle damaged hull groaning as it slipped over the event horizon. Behind her the *Vanguard* swung slightly, then an intense beam of dark light lanced from her forward battery, at last revealed by the opening of the great shields that concealed them, and bathed the Chairman's ship in a green/black light. What happened next stunned everyone into silence. There was a flash, many times brighter than the system's sun and a shockwave that should not have existed erupted as a perfect sphere from the space where the ship no longer was. For a brief moment a miniature supernova flared brilliantly – then slowly collapsed and winked out of existence leaving a spreading shell of ionised radiant gas expanding into a vast cloud that swept past the still embattled ships causing instruments to flicker, screens to blank and then clear and, in engineering control, to show as a power fluctuation on their generating systems.

✳ ✳ ✳

In his Command Centre, Commodore Heron stared at the spot where the ship had vanished for a long moment, then jerked out of his reverie to say to his Lieutenant-Commander, "Albrecht, give me an open channel link to the enemy!"

"You have it sir!"

"This is Commodore James Heron of the North European Confederation Ship *Vanguard*. I order you to surrender your ships immediately; your flagship has just been destroyed by our primary weapon. Two more of my ships have the same weapons capability and will use it on any ship that continues to fight or attempts to escape. Those who surrender can expect to be tried as pirates and rebels. You will receive the full benefit of a legally constituted court and a fair trial. If you continue to fight, my squadron will have no choice but to destroy you. You have two minutes to decide." He signalled for the link to be closed and leaned back in his chair, his eyes momentarily closed. He opened them again as the voice of Captain Wes Orkadey came from his open link to his ships, "I am receiving surrender signals from three of the remaining ships Commodore. They're all in pretty bad shape, I think I'll have to evacuate them and destroy what's left."

"Thanks Wes, do it." To his staff he added, "Get *Fort Belvedere* in to take survivors, but make sure they're disarmed and held secure!"

"I have two more surrenders," came the voice of Jon Wright, Captain of the *Sydney*, "reckon they're a bit better off, but I don't want to leave them with their own crew, someone might get ideas." He paused and added, "We also have some damage to the hyperdrives and have had to shut down the fusion reactors supplying them. I can still manoeuvre on normal propulsion, but we need assistance to sort out the hyperpods."

"We'll get some assistance for you as soon as possible. In the meantime it's a good idea to break up those Consortium crews, distribute prisoners as you can." To his Acting Captain, commanding the ship while the Commodore fought the fleet, he added, "Richard, we have two definitely destroyed and five surrendered. One is still in the system somewhere, I want him found please!"

"We're already scanning sir, Weapons and Flight have everything they've got looking for him and so have the cruisers."

Further calls to the frigates *Lion* and *Tiger* and to the cruisers *Penelope*, *Phoebe*, *Aurora* and *Ariadne* brought confirmation of the surrender of the remaining frigate and the rounding up of interceptors and strike craft. It also brought the news that several of these had apparently escaped to the planetary surface. A check with the ground squadrons however, soon allayed this fear and brought the assurance that although many had tried to escape retribution in this way, they had been intercepted and destroyed or forced to land and arrested. This left one enemy starship unaccounted for and the scanner teams on *Vanguard*, *Sydney* and *Bellerophon* were working hard to locate it. A message from *Lynx*, escorting the *Fort Belvedere* soon gave them a pointer to the fact that the missing ship was using the background of the same gas giant that had helped *Vanguard* and *Bellerophon* hide, to cover her escape.

The Commodore's intention to order his ship out to deal with this enemy was interrupted when his Lieutenant-Commander said, "Ship dropping out at the enemy location sir! She's firing on the enemy!" He was cut off by the voice of a newcomer.

"My apologies for a late arrival Commodore! *Ramillies* reporting as ordered, I regret we had a little internal dispute to settle first, but I see you have left us something to take our frustration out on!"

"Welcome Bruce, you old rogue!" laughed the Commodore, "Glad you made it. Deal with our runaway will you and join us when you can for the clean up."

"That we will and with pleasure. Then I must ask you to relieve me of some unwelcome passengers – including my ex-Executive Commander and around three hundred more of his supporters. I don't think I can stand the stench of them for very much longer!" reported Captain Bruce Wallace of the newly arrived *Ramillies*.

"Deal with that ship and bring them in, we have a secure place for them!"

※ ※ ※

As the reports trickled in concerning damage, defects and prisoners taken, Commodore James Heron found his mind dwelling on the carnage around him. All about the system the scattered remains of small interceptors, and frequently their pilots, drifted in a macabre dance. Even the torn and battered bigger ships lay amid a cloud of debris, here and there the telltale jets of escaping atmosphere showing where the life support systems were failing as well. It would be a long time before the full cost would be known and even longer before all his ships could put right their damage. In the meantime the search began for surviving pilots adrift in the debris of their craft, while down in the emergency medical centres of all the ships the med teams began the task of dealing with the wounded and the dead. Suddenly weary he opened a comlink and said, "Computer, open a ship wide broadcast." For a moment he paused, and then he said, "This is the Commodore. We have won the battle and I am proud to have had the privilege of being your commanding officer and the Commodore of this squadron. You have performed magnificently today and I thank you for it. Today we have confronted an enemy which comes from within our own ranks and from within our own society. We have won this round, but there will be a bitter harvest and an even more difficult time ahead. We must at all costs maintain our vigilance and our efficiency." He paused and then continued, his determination apparent, "We have lost many of our friends today and we have seen many brave acts, we must not let that sacrifice be in vain. Thank you all for your loyalty and your bravery!"

For a moment there was a silence throughout the ship, and then a cheer began to roll through the compartments finally penetrating the Commodore's Command Centre. Temporary Commodore James Heron was not a man given to showing his emotions, but this moved him. It was some minutes before he was able to trust his voice sufficiently to call the Captains of the other ships in his victorious squadron and convey much the same message to each ship.

* * *

Commander Nick Gray stood in the Upper Hangar deck of the Starboard fin and looked around the depleted squadrons, still slowly trickling back to the ship. All bore the marks of carbonising where they had taken damage or near misses. So far, he thought, they had been lucky. Their losses were far lower than he had privately thought they might be. Fifteen percent casualties were very low indeed, and might easily have been fifty percent. He looked to where Lieutenant Commander Karl Pedersen was talking to a small knot of pilots, and felt a cold hand clutch his heart. Lieutenant Bjørn Pedersen had not returned and only fragments of his fighter had been located. Nick walked across the where Karl had just turned away from the now dispersing group and gave his second a brief touch on the shoulder. "We'll keep looking Karl, if we can, we'll find him."

"I know Boss, but I have a feeling the kid has gone for good this time."

"Well, don't give up hope just yet, he may still be out there somewhere. If he is, we'll find him." He surveyed the damage to the hangars, and moved across to the Port side fin passing through the transfer and maintenance bays located in Compartment 223 Alpha Oscar Charlie and wondered as he did so what had happened to the three youngsters so suddenly plucked from their own period in time to be dumped here. He reflected briefly that even their previous experience of battle could not have prepared them for something like this. The Port side fin had taken several serious hits and the damage to one section meant that a third of the space was now sealed off by the huge atmospheric seals. Beyond the seals he knew would be the bodies of many of his 'ground crew', the essential maintenance teams whose expertise and dedicated work kept the strike and interceptor craft fit to fly for the pilots. Any inspection beyond them would require full EVA suiting. More to get his own adrenalin levels down to normal than for any desire to survey the damage – he already had a full assessment from the Damage Control Officer – he walked to the EVA Dressing Station and fitted himself into a suit, then joined the Damage Control and repair parties cycling through the airlocks to enter the damaged area. At least, he thought as he did so, he could see for himself and lend a hand where it was needed.

※ ※ ※

Commander Mary Allison and her deputy, Lieutenant Commander Stuart Browne ran through their defects lists again. "Right," said Mary, "Priority One is get the environmental systems back in operation in all areas where we have had damage. Areas where there is a hull breach will have to wait until we have the breach sealed, but the replacement of ducts and feedlines can go ahead while that is happening. As soon as the salvage teams have the area cleared out and ready for repair to begin, we can get started." She paused while several of her team made entries in their tablets and then continued. "Priority Two is to get the generator plant in Turbine Room Four back online as soon as possible. The damaged steam lines must be repaired and tested asap, then we can test run the turbines. I know Number Three generator has a burned commutator, so that can be stripped and the whole thing checked while maintenance rebuild it. Stuart, get your team over to Number Two Reactor room, there was a lot of damage in that area and I want that reactor checked from top to bottom." Turning to her next group, she continued, "Lieutenant Khalifa, the Port lateral hyperdrive pod took some near misses and one definite hit. The damage doesn't seem to have affected its operation yet, but I want your team to go over it with a fine tooth comb and make damned sure it isn't going to come apart on us in hyperspace under continuous burn." She checked that everyone was clear on their tasks, then nodded, "Right get to it, anyone needs more muscle or more assistance with sorting things, call me, I'll be right here!"

※ ※ ※

In her Weapons Control Centre Commander Valerie Petrocova leaned back in her chair, the tension draining out of her as she listened to the chatter of relief among her staff. She had seen the primary weapon fired several times, yet she had never seen the response it had evoked on this occasion. She thought deeply about it and wondered if the fact that the target had been about to drop into hyperspace had had any effect. If so perhaps it should be studied further – after all they really ought to know what could happen if it was repeated with the firing ship closer to the target. They had fired at extreme range – but what if they were closer? What would the affect have been?

"Commander?"

She snapped alert, "Yes?"

"I think you should see this," said Lieutenant Commander Trevor Leonard. He handed her a tablet.

Scanning the information it contained she paused and reread it slowly, and then she looked up and said thoughtfully, "Just as well we didn't try to fire it any closer to other ships. I doubt anyone thought of that when they were testing it. So; the use of this weapon near a singularity increases its disruptive power to by a minimum of $10^{10}$. We had better keep that in mind for the future! I wonder what the effect was in hyperspace?"

In two days she would get an answer to her question, but for the moment could only wonder as other tasks demanded her immediate attention.

※ ※ ※

As crews began the task of shoring up and securing damaged areas they were sometimes surprised to find their Commodore among them, even occasionally lending a hand. Here and there he stopped to talk to his crew and to compliment them on their efforts. Following him on this tour, Lieutenant Helen Callaghan and Midshipman Hardy found themselves beginning to understand the man who commanded them. He might appear remote, but he believed in staying in touch with 'his people' and they soon discovered that there was no part of this vast ship that he did not know. Everywhere he left behind him parties of ratings and technicians working even harder than before and more determined to get their ship back into full readiness as swiftly as possible.

The Med Centres also saw his presence, despite the fact that his comlink seemed to be constantly calling as reports came in for his attention or decisions had to be made. Those who could be talked to in the Med Units he talked to, a few words here and there, a word of encouragement to the personnel and thanks to the med staff and he would move on. His 'doggies' as the pair shadowing him were dubbed were exhausted by the time he dismissed them and had seen parts of the ship they had never visited before!

*  *  *

In orbit once more above Pangaea the *Vanguard's* scanners lit up two days after the battle as a fleet of large ships dropped out and entered the system. "*Vengeance* to *Vanguard*," the hail on the Captain's comlink began, "Admiral Cunningham asks that you will receive him when we arrive in your orbit." The speaker continued.

Recognising the voice as that of the Fleet Flag Captain, Commodore Heron replied with a slightly amused tone, "I shall be delighted to receive him – and yourself of course. Andy, what brings you out this far off the diplomatic circuit?" Despite his light-hearted response, he was rather intrigued by the unusual nature of the 'request' – Captains and Commodores usually visited their Admirals, not the other way round!

"Well, I think I'll take the opportunity to tell you in person. In fact the Admiral would have liked to tell you we were on our way around two days ago – but somebody let loose with a nova in hyperspace and fried all the hyper signal transmitters. No one you would know of course!"

"Well I might, but that depends on whether you want to give them a medal or a court martial!" he laughed and continued, "I hope you have a repair ship in tow, we have several ships quite badly damaged and need at least partial docking ourselves."

"Well you're in luck there then," came the reply, "we just happen to have two along with us and a host more troops and fighter squadrons. How does it feel to be the man who has toppled a commercial empire, caused a political upheaval of earth shattering proportions and exposed the corruption in Brussels? You're a hero old friend – among some sections of the population anyway!"

Three hours later the Command Team were assembled in the Starboard Lateral Hangar with Marine Guard of Honour and 'Side Party' as the Admiral himself disembarked from his barge. Returning the Commodore's salute he held out his hand saying, "Well James, you've certainly brought the house down around some people's ears this time! You and your squadron have performed magnificently – a real credit to the Fleet!" He smiled as they shook hands adding, "But you had better tell me what the hell you sent into hyperspace, the shockwave is causing havoc!"

Commodore Heron grinned and said, "I think it may be the remnants of a certain enemy ship. It reacted rather badly to being hit by our primary as it entered the hyperspace singularity!"

The Admiral gave a short laugh, "That so! Well, that would certainly explain the disruption cloud we encountered! Your Weapons Control hit him as he entered the singularity?" He gave a penetrating glance at Commander Petrocova, adding, "That is damned good targeting – the disruption field is tremendous and you have only a couple of microseconds to fire!"

"I agree sir. May I suggest we go to my quarters and I can give you a full report," said the Commodore.

"You may, and we won't," the Admiral gave him a long look, "I have come to see your ship and to tell you that you are promoted. Full Commodore as of this moment, so you will be eligible to appoint a Captain to take full command of this ship – which I assume you will wish to keep as your Flagship? I have also come to meet and congratulate your team. You have achieved something really remarkable here James, you and your people, Fleet are fully aware of it and I am here to tell you that you will remain in Command here while your ships are repaired. I am taking the main fleet on to deal with the bases the Consortium has set up in several locations. We will hunt down their ships and destroy them, we will find their bases and secure those too. Thanks to your team and the innovations you have applied to finding ways to beat the screening system they have developed, we can now hunt them."

"Well, I have to say sir; that it was team effort – all my people have performed remarkably."

"Yes, I know. Just one thing," the Admiral turned to Commander Gray, "who came up with that visual targeting system? I'm told it's more effective than the computers!"

"Oh," laughed Nick Gray, "the Harry Sight! Our Napoleonic Navy Midshipman gave us the idea, and it's pretty effective according to my crews."

"And who is this Napoleonic Navy Midshipman?" began the Admiral, then his memory clicked into place, "Weren't there three of them?"

"Yes sir," replied Commodore Heron gravely, "unfortunately they have been abducted on the surface. We are trying to discover their whereabouts at this moment."

# Chapter 20

# Fallout and other debris

The two days following the great battle in the heavens, saw the little ship and her strange crew inch her way to the position from which Harry hoped to run down the Westing and find the coast of the principle continent, somewhere in the vicinity of Pangaea City. Given the crudeness of his chart and of his instruments for navigation, he knew he could be anywhere within a hundred miles North or South of his target. He hoped that he would be able to recognise which it was from the features shown on the maps he had, in order to be able to make the correct call and turn along the coast in the right direction. The time spent together had allowed the him and his fellows to learn something of their reptilian fellow travellers, discovering that they called themselves Lacertians, and to develop a great respect for their abilities – their diet was being well supplemented by a daily capture of fish, some of them very strange indeed, that these strange fellows seemed very good at finding and catching. The Lacertian language defeated every attempt at communication, being extremely sibilant and filled with clicking sounds which overwhelmed the human's tongues as they tried to at least learn some of the individuals' names!

By contrast, the human crew watched and learned as Harry and Ferghal patiently explained the trimming of the sails and the art of holding a ship on course. Each day, there was a further dimension as Harry tried to explain the mathematics for navigating using the angles of the sun (hampered here by not having a sextant!) or the angles of known stars – again a tricky aspect since he had only his own rather crude observations and choice of star to guide them. In the cool of the first evening Danny had produced a simple pipe he had obviously been carving for himself since their escape from the research station, and, with Harry's permission, began to play it. The tune was a slightly melancholy one and all those onboard listened in silence – Harry noticing the Lacertian folk taking a particular interest. Danny played for some while, several tunes being hymns and others dances. When Ferghal found a cylinder about two feet in diameter and some thin membrane material which he could stretch tightly across the open ends, he began to accompany the crude fife with a Celtic drumming rhythm, using a pair of drum sticks to beat a sometimes hair raising tattoo.

"Ferghal," grinned Harry, "Yon drumming of yours is like to have us clearing for action! Will you not show us how to dance the hornpipe properly?"

"Aye Master Harry," responded the other, his face breaking into a wide grin, "Danny, give me a hornpipe now and let's show them how it was done on *Spartan*."

Danny beamed and raised the pipe to his mouth, with a quick count he started a brisk tune with a lively lilt. After a few bars Ferghal launched into an energetic rendition of the dance, his feet now slapping down and now sliding as he made the forward and backwards movements of the dance, swaying his upper body, now this way and now that, as he moved. Not for the first time, Harry thought his friend a very talented dancer and wished he could do this half as well himself.

By the end of the second dog watch the Sub-Lieutenant, Paddy Murphy and Hans Dinsen were all trying the dancing while Harry and three of the Lacertians kept watch. To Harry's casual interest he noted that these strange creatures seemed fascinated by the music and the dance, yet seemed to have none of their own. This supposition was confirmed when he asked their leader at the change of watch. After this first evening, it became the pattern for relaxation during the dog watches during the remainder of the voyage.

The language remained a serious barrier between the human crew and the Lacertian group, although their leader showed himself to be very able in understanding what was said to him and in passing this on to the rest of his people. His name at least they did master – albeit in a humanised form. The nearest they could get to it was 'Sersan' and it was immediately apparent that this small courtesy had a profound impact on relations. One rather strange aspect of their behaviour, one which worried Ferghal at first, was that, while they treated the Sub-Lieutenant with courtesy and deference, they never let Harry out of their sight. One of them was always close to him and careful to stay between him and the ship's side. In addition they showed a degree of respect and courtesy to him quite out of proportion to his apparent rank – even as Sailing Master and navigator. When asked, the reply from the Reptilian's leader made no sense at all to the Sub-Lieutenant or to Ferghal, being along the lines of their having recognised Harry as the navigator and therefore, in their culture the most important person on board – a statement that made Harry blush crimson in embarrassment. Pointing to Harry and then to Ferghal Sersan added an even more puzzling statement, "weee sshhaaareee bloooodd!"

Their sailing efforts were rewarded as dawn broke on the fifth morning of the voyage. The wind had become rather variable overnight and Harry had just decided to abandon his attempt to hold a course due West and allow the ship to fall off two points to a more Northerly course when a large landing barge passed almost directly overhead, on a bearing which almost mirrored his proposed heading! Signalling the helmsman to follow the barge's course, he raced for the weather ratlines and scampered to the cross-trees in the hope of a glimpse of land. Moments later he was joined by one of the Lacertians who gave him a rather hurt look, apparently put out by the fact that Harry had moved quickly enough to avoid being accompanied.

To the west the darkness was still lingering, but, even as he watched the sunlight began to penetrate the gloom and, as the ship lifted lazily on a swell, he caught a sudden glimpse of a hill or mountaintop. He watched as the ship dipped and then rose again and this time got a good glimpse. He shouted joyfully to the group on deck "Land ho! Fine on the Starboard bow!" Even his Lacertian companion seemed to catch the excitement and called to its companions on deck. Harry paused to take another look as the light cleared the night shadows a little more and tried to get a picture in his mind that he could match to the maps on deck, and then began his descent to the deck. He was halfway down the ratlines, when a monstrous shape reared out of the sea right alongside and slashed its jaws at the deck, only to encounter the boarding nets!

Entangled, the beast fell back, its weight dragging the ship to windward as it thrashed alongside. Harry almost lost his footing on the ratlines and had to cling tightly to save himself from falling. On deck pandemonium broke loose as the crew dashed to defend themselves and to shed the dragging load of the beast which was now pulling the ship's head round and threatening to cause them to come about! Ferghal and Sersan both dashed to find a way to release the nettings. They worked feverishly, dangerously close to the thrashing beast's fearsome jaws, still slashing this way and that. Sub-Lieutenant Trelawney found the weapon given him on the island, and unpacked it as rapidly as he could. Shaking it clear of the covers at last he feverishly armed it, noted that it was fully charged and activated the targeting device. Shouting to Ferghal and Sersan he yelled, "Get back, I need to have a clear shot!"

They jumped away and with that the nets began to tear loose from their anchor points as the beast's struggles overstressed them. Petroc steadied himself, got his sighting lock on the brutish head and fired. The result was not quite what he expected, the weapon certainly fired and the pulse certainly smashed into the huge head, but apart from a brief moment of stillness, and a darkening of the area where the pulse had struck, it appeared to have no other effect. Swiftly he shifted his aim, trying to aim for the junction of the neck and skull and fired again. This time he was rewarded by seeing a huge wound torn into the flesh, exposing muscle and blood vessels which showered those nearest in the creature's blood. This seemed to send it into a frenzy so that its thrashing now threatened to capsize them. Desperately the Sub-Lieutenant fired again - this time severing the creatures head completely – and the great head crashed to the deck still snapping and trying to grasp a victim while the thrashing body finally tore the nettings from their moorings and fell away astern.

Briefly the helmsman struggled to recover the ship's course while everyone else tried desperately to avoid the slashing jaws of the severed head. It fell to the Lacertian crew to finally ensnare it and drag it to a position where it could be thrown overside, still wrapped in a tangle of torn net and lines. It was then that Ferghal and the others realised that Harry was still aloft, pinned to the ratlines and secured firmly in place by the Lacertian who had simply recovered him, and then pinioned him to the rigging. "Thank you," Harry wheezed, his breathing difficult under the pressure of the creature's grip, "but I think I can manage to climb down now!"

The creature hissed something in response and Harry looking aft, suddenly realised that there was another of these ghastly monsters closing on them. But his shout of warning was strangled by a sudden roar of power as an atmospheric fighter craft rushed across their bows, banked in a tight turn and dropped several metal objects into the sea between them and the oncoming beast. The sea erupted around the monster, lifting it clear of the water and as it crashed back into the sea, a second fighter swooped and delivered another crop of the bombs. This time, when the sea erupted, it changed colour as the beast's life blood stained the sea.

Harry descended to the deck as the first fighter returned and took up a hover position just on their quarter. There was a click as the craft's hailers were turned on and the voice of the pilot said, "Identify yourselves!"

Cupping his hands, Harry bawled back "*Vanguard*! On the cutter *Victory*!"

He gesticulated at their streaming colours as the Sub-Lieutenant stood up and shouted, "Sub-Lieutenant Trelawney and party, returning to duty!"

The hailers clicked into life again and the metallic voice boomed, "Sub-Lieutenant Trelawney? And all your party? God, the Squaddies have almost torn the planet apart looking for you guys! Welcome home, hold this course, an escort will be out to collect you in an hour! We'll ride herd and make sure none of those damned Pleurodons attack you again, this area is full of them, must be something around here they hunt."

Then Sersan, somehow managing to ensure he was between Harry and the bulwarks, hissed, "Isss their mating groundssss."

"Their what?" asked Sub-Lieutenant Trelawney, surprised.

"Thissss isss the mating placssse for the ...," Sersan made a sound which Petroc Trelawney could not interpret, but he understood what the creature was saying.

"How amazing," he said thoughtfully, realisation of their unwitting error dawning. He hoped that would not complicate matters, but in the event it did not. The earlier bombs seemed to have driven the creatures away from the little ship as she made her steady way towards the shore.

An hour later it became somewhat academic as three heavily armed fast patrol catamarans came out to meet them. The first closed and

Captain Bob Wardman of the *Vanguard's* Marine Corps emerged on her open deck to hail them. "Mr Trelawney, glad to see you have all survived. Who are your companions?"

"Thanks Captain. These folk are the Lacertians, prisoners we released from the facility on New Caledonia. They have helped us sail this vessel – frankly I don't think we would have managed without them." The Sub-Lieutenant replied.

"OK. We found a few more down a mine! Well, I'll take you all off then and get you back to the City. There are a few folk who are anxious to see you all!"

The Sub-Lieutenant looked around the little ship that had served them so well, he looked at Harry's somewhat disappointed expression and at the Lacertian crew standing around expectantly, and called back, "If its all the same to you sir, I think it would be better if we complete the voyage as we started it! I don't think it would be right to simply abandon our little *Victory* at this point, besides, I think it may make quite a statement in certain quarters!"

Bob Wardman looked surprised, then he nodded, "OK, I'll make a signal to that effect! How long do you think you'll need to bring her in?" He paused for a moment and then asked, "It is the wind you're using to drive her isn't it? Or do you have a motor of some sort?"

"Just wind power," laughed Trelawney, "Our old fashioned sailor men have been giving us quite a few lessons these last few days!" To Harry he asked, "How long will we need to get to the harbour?"

"Difficult to say sir, how far precisely is it?"

"How far is it to the harbour," called the Sub-Lieutenant and watched as the question was relayed to someone inside the catamaran.

"About sixteen miles in old money!" came the reply.

"Then, if the wind holds steady and we can keep this speed, we shall reach the port in a little under three hours sir," announced Harry.

"My navigation officer tells me we will be three hours," called Trelawney with a big grin.

"Does he indeed!" laughed the Marine Officer. "OK, we'll ride herd and keep the beasties at bay then, but I'm going to move in close and drop a comlink aboard for you, my voice won't hold up to all this shouting!"

❊ ❊ ❊

In the event it was a little over three hours later that the little converted barge, dubbed *Victory* by her human crew, her oversized white ensign from a bygone age streaming proudly from her gaff, eased her way into the bay that formed the harbour of Pangaea City. Concentrating on conning the little ship to the berth allocated to them, Harry was too busy to notice that the pier was packed with onlookers as the sun began to dip towards the horizon. He had the sail reduced, the first time he had done so since they had set them, furling the large mainsail and the jib and foresail, using just the flying jib and topsail to keep her underway and manoeuvring. He swung her round in a tight circle until she luffed, then allowed her to drop gently onto the quayside with the jib and topsail aback. As she touched the quay, he yelled, "Let go sheets, let go halliards and brail up!"

The onlookers watched in interested silence as the crew of reptilian hominids and humans jumped to obey and in seconds the triangular topsail was furled to the mast above the gaff and the flying jib was dropping to be caught by waiting hands on the bowsprit, leaving just the large white flag with its great red cross and blue, white and red upper quarter flicking above the waiting figures on the quayside. Commodore Heron and the Admiral stood side by side and watched as Sub-Lieutenant Trelawney and the two senior midshipmen joined the reptilian beings and a boy in lashing up the sails and making the deck neat and tidy under the direction of another youth, a tall and well set young man in the uniform of a Fleet Technical Rating. At the compass, Harry turned to the Lacertian helmsman and smiled, giving a short bow, he said, "Thank you Helmsman, your steering has been exemplary."

The creature made a gesture and returned the bow stiffly, making a hissed response. It was only as he turned to look forward at the rest of the crew that Harry noticed the two figures standing apart from the crowd and directly opposite him on the quay.

Hastily he stepped forward to the rail, saying as loudly as he dared, "Captain! My apologies sir, I did not see you before. I shall call Sub-Lieutenant Trelawney to welcome you aboard!"

To his immense relief the Sub-Lieutenant heard him and came aft swiftly, greeting his Captain as he did so, but his greeting faltered when he saw the Commodore's companion! He stopped and snapped to attention beside Harry, "Admiral! We didn't expect you sir!"

Harry looked at the man his Senior had just addressed and noticed the extra insignia for the first time. Excusing himself he signalled Ferghal and the others to form a Side Party, even managing to convey to Danny that his fife was required. Ferghal leapt into action and pushed, pulled and manoeuvred the Lacertians into a formal line, placing the two bewildered Midshipmen at its head and himself and Danny at the point at which the senior officers would have to step from the quayside onto the deck. Harry joined the Midshipmen having steered his officer to a point in front of them as the Commodore and the Admiral watched in some amusement while walking the short distance to the point they were obviously expected to board this strange little ship.

The Admiral stepped onto the rail, and jumped lightly to the deck. Immediately Danny began to play an unfamiliar tune on his pipe and Harry raised his dirk's hilt guard to his chin, then dropped his hand to point the blade downwards while his Senior raised his hand in salute. The Admiral recognised the honour accorded him by this and stopped, raising his own hand in a stiff response. Behind him, Commodore Heron, stepped to the deck, his eye's on the young man whose dirk now flashed in a reverse of the salute as the music stopped, the blade vanishing into its sheath. The Commodore stepped forward and said to the Admiral, "Sir, may I present Sub-Lieutenant Trelawney, who seems to have acquired an unusual vessel and an even more unusual crew in the course of an extended absence." He smiled at the Sub-Lieutenant and continued, "I hope you will introduce your crew to the Admiral, Mr Trelawney!"

The Sub-Lieutenant gulped, and said, "Yes sir!" He fell in beside them and introduced each in turn; explaining when he introduced him, that it had been Harry's idea and design that had created the little ship they were stood upon, and Harry's skill in navigating that had brought them safely from New Caledonia. The Admiral was fascinated by this rather abridged account, asking Harry for several explanations and finally for a look at the dirk. As he returned it to Harry he said, "I believe you are also behind the weapons sighting equipment which overcame the jamming device young man. And this demonstrates some unusual talents." He gestured round the deck, adding, "I am very pleased to meet you Mid – and to have you in my Command!" Sub-Lieutenant Trelawney then introduced the Lacertian leader, Sersan, explaining the circumstances in which they had encountered the party and how these folk had helped them.

Finally, the Admiral reached Ferghal and Danny. For a long moment he studied Ferghal as the youth's actions and bravery were recounted. Finally he said, "Young man, as I have just said to Mr Heron, I am very glad you are in my Command. I think you have earned something, but I will have to discuss this with your Captain. In the meantime, show me this 'cutlass' of yours." Ferghal looked at the Sub-Lieutenant for permission to go and fetch this, and receiving a nod, went below. While Ferghal did so, the Admiral asked for and was shown the boy's pipe and was told that he had been welcomed aboard with the tune 'Hearts of Oak'! Ferghal returned just as the Admiral asked, "And what flag is that you're flying Mr Trelawney?"

"With respect sir, it is the Naval Ensign of Harry, Ferghal and Danny's navy – the White Ensign I believe it is called?"

"The White Ensign? Good God, I don't know when last that was seen at sea!" exclaimed the Admiral, "But it looks absolutely right!" He saw Ferghal holding the cutlass and studied the weapon speculatively. After a pause he said, "So that is your cutlass is it Mr O'Connor?" He held out a hand and Ferghal passed him the hilt. Holding it carefully, the Admiral looked from the blade to Ferghal, before passing the weapon to Commodore Heron, and said, "James I think you have some remarkable young men in your command. This weapon," he added, taking it back from the Commodore and handing it back to Ferghal carefully two handed, "Must have given several people a very nasty surprise. Thank you Mr O'Connor." Turning back to the Commodore he said, "We need to talk about several things Commodore, but first I think these remarkable young men need to be allowed to rest and to have a once over with the Med Staff. And this," he swept a hand around the little ship, "I think needs to be preserved as a monument to ingenuity and resourcefulness, something your ship seems to have plenty of!"

As the Admiral made to lead the Party ashore the Sersan stepped forward. "Plisssss, we sssssstaayyy here. Keepp ssshhhhiippp for himmm!"

Nonplussed, the Admiral glanced at the Commodore and at Sub-Lieutenant Trelawney. Trelawney said, apologetically, "It's something to do with Harry I think sir. They seem to have a very high regard for people who navigate – and Harry has done all of it to get us here, using some interesting instruments."

The Admiral looked at the reptilian face and at Harry, who was looking embarrassed and nodded, "Very well; are they safe here from those Pleurodon things?" On being assured that they were, he nodded and agreed, "Look after her for us, but I think our people will want to talk to you in the morning!" With that he led the party ashore. The crowd broke into applause as the five young men and their Sub-Lieutenant walked grinning through the crowd to the waiting ground transport, several people calling out to them and one young lady even dashing forward to plant a kiss on an embarrassed Danny's cheek!

※ ※ ※

It was three days before all of the party were passed clear by the Med Team headed by Surgeon Commander Myers who insisted on running a very thorough series of tests on them all. Dr Grüneland's team were also interested, particularly in Harry, Ferghal and Danny once it became known that they had been subjected to some experiments while in captivity. It was a matter of some concern to Len particularly that the ship's scanners, which should have been able to detect Harry's and Ferghal's cyber implants, had been unable to do so until they had already been found by the surface forces patrolling the approaches to Pangaea City. In Harry's case there was further cause for concern when the full details of what he had endured emerged, but they could find nothing either in his system or in the numerous samples of tissue and blood they took from him to show any lasting damage. Neither could anyone explain why the Lacertians seemed to be convinced that he was important to them, or, even more interestingly, why he could now access and manipulate any and every computer he came into contact with. "There is something about both Harry and Ferghal O'Connor which is showing up on our analysis, but we can't pin it down. Something in their DNA or RNA has changed very slightly, but, apart from this ability to access the computers, nothing else seems different," Len Myers complained to Lieutenant Commanders Blakewell and Jepson. "Damned if I know what it is but we'll keep looking. I don't know exactly what they did to Harry, especially as he isn't ready to talk about too much of it, but he seems to have recovered well, at least physically."

At least they now had a more information for Harry and his friends on the Lacertians who were in fact native to a planet designated in human charts as Sinoia, a name conferred upon it by its 'discoverer', a Romanian astronomer named Sfarlos almost two hundred years earlier. Although it had been visited by humans at least once, a search of the Fleet records found that the reports of the visit had apparently been heavily and rather clumsily altered to reflect a vision of the place at odds with an earlier record discovered in a search of encyclopaedia entries. These described the planet as having extensive oceans and a moderate climate with little seasonal variation – at odds with the Fleet record which stated that it was a barren and waterless world of little interest to humans!

The Lacertian language took a little unravelling and it was not until the science team established that, just as human communication contains a large element of 'non-verbal' communication, that they began to make progress. In the event, the translating machine remained a crude device, because the Lacertians relied in part on a form of telepathic linking as the non-verbal element of their speech communication. Even with this handicap and the sometimes hilarious misinterpretations of the language translator, the scientists found themselves tapping into a huge resource of knowledge and culture – and discovered that the beings referred to by the Fleet as 'Foo Fighters' were also known to the Lacertian people – by a name which didn't translate and was rendered as '*Sidhiche*' in human tongue, but, beyond the fact that the Lacertians knew of them and apparently had encountered them occasionally on their own world, learned little more. The only thing of real interest to emerge about them was the fact that, in Lacertian legend, it was these beings who had brought knowledge to the Lacertian race. Georgina Curry was surprised to learn that the leader's name translated to mean something approaching 'The One Who Leads', although in his own more complex tongue it was rendered quite simply as Sersan, suggesting, as she told Rhys Williams, that it was title rather than a name. It was also very obvious that the group that had accompanied Sub-Lieutenant Trelawney regarded themselves as having a blood debt or some sort of blood link, to Harry and Ferghal in particular, and their human companions for their release – and that their regard for Harry as a Navigator rode above even that.

There was excitement too among the xeno-biologists when they learned that these strange new allies had another remarkable property buried in their genes. They could replace damaged or lost limbs, a fact borne out by Sub-Lieutenant Trelawney's report that, when first encountered, Sersan's left arm had been all but destroyed, yet had been almost completely restored by the time they had reached Pangaea City – as the medical staff confirmed. Examination of other Lacertians who had been suffering from serious injuries when they had joined the desperate little crew of the *Victory* showed that they too had been healed or regenerated leaving almost no trace of the injury. "This is the most fantastic thing I have ever seen," said Dr Maartens as he reported to the leader of the science team, Dr Grüneland. "The nearest thing to this in our previous medical knowledge is the lizard *familia* on earth that are able to shed parts of their bodies to avoid capture and can regenerate the lost part. But that is usually confined to a tail or to parts of the skin, not as these people seem able to do, whole limbs and possibly even organs!"

Re-united with their fellows rescued by the Marines from the deep facility labelled Minehead, the Lacertians proved both willing to co-operate with their human rescuers and to provide information to the Fleet officers who questioned them. An important point that rapidly became clear was that these were not a space faring people at all. In fact they had only left their planet as slaves aboard the Consortium's ships and been used to work in environments hostile to human and Lacertians alike.

"They are clearly evolved from a warm blooded reptilian ancestor," reported the xeno-biological team, "Very probably amphibian in origin, but admirably adapted for land dwelling. Omnivorous, their diet is similar in variety to ours, but with considerable bias towards marine dwelling animals and plants. Interestingly they need little water to sustain them."

"Their language is extremely complex," added the linguistic team. "It combines some sounds more akin to numeric expression with gesture and," Georgina Curry paused, "there is almost definitely an element of telepathy involved. The translator misses meanings in a number of areas, even when it is able to identify and record the exact words used."

The Lacertians did make one request – repeated at every interview - which gave the Commodore some cause for careful consideration when it was brought to his attention. The Lacertians wanted the crew of the *Victory*, specifically the Sub-Lieutenant and Harry, whom they referred to as 'Navigator', to spend time among them – and for Harry to return to their world with them. "I don't think I can permit that," said the Commodore when this was put to him. "I expect I can allow them to spend some time with these people if it won't be detrimental to the service, but I certainly cannot allow Harry to go and live with them." he added after a moments pause, " And I think they should be accompanied by the Science team."

In the event, when the request, and the Commodore's reservations were explained to him, Harry, still confined to the Med Centre on Pangaea, readily agreed to the Commodore's restriction. He joined the rest of the party at the Lacertian's quarters they had now established near the port, flattered to be treated as an honoured guest. It was to be a remarkable and memorable time for him, one more experience to write into a letter to the mysterious Mr and Mrs L'Estrange to whom each of his carefully handwritten letters was addressed.

# Chapter 21

# 1805: A sad homecoming; 2205 A new lease on life?

A light rain was falling as Captain Blackwood brought HMS *Spartan* to her assigned mooring off the entrance to Fareham Creek. The late spring rain seemed to fit exactly the mood as the sails were swiftly brailed up and the great anchor splashed down on his signal. Ahead of the ship the guard boat curtseyed gently as the port mooring officer resumed his seat in the stern sheets and without fuss the oarsmen gave way, swinging the boat about so that she idled down the side of the weather beaten seventy-four as she settled to the pull of wind and tide against her anchor. As he watched the busy figures snugging down lines, harbour stowing the great sails and preparing the boats for lowering overside, the Captain reflected that, though sadly depleted in numbers by the toll of sickness, battle and accidents his crew were still able to perform their duties with great professionalism. They had left this same port together in the brief interlude of peace brought by the now defunct Treaty of Amiens, and they returned to it again in a war resumed and, perhaps, more bitter than before.

He turned as his coxswain coughed politely behind him, his dress sword and boat cloak held ready. Already the ship's one remaining Midshipman stood at the entry port carrying the despatch case for the Flagship where she lay at her anchors a quarter mile away. Even as he threw on his boat cloak, the midshipman descended into a waiting boat which cast off immediately to make a swift round of calls to the Flagship, the Port Admiral and the Dockyard. He thought briefly of the letters in the mail pouch for the Dockyard post office, the one's to the families of the officers and Warrant Officers who had died during the long commission, either from sickness or in battle, and of the other letters, the ones written by the likes of Midshipman Heron to his family. At least they would now have these last lines from their loved ones he mused. Nodding to his First Lieutenant, he said, "I shall be with the Admiral for about an hour I expect Thomas, then I must ashore to convey our requirements to the Dockyard. I expect the Purser will need a boat to arrange our replacement stores."

"I will see to it sir," smiled Thomas Bell, "I expect we will have to find some replacements for the Wardroom and Gunroom, and I should think we will have to take whatever the poorhouse and goals can provide to fill our quota of the men we need!"

"Indeed! I shall make representation to the Admiral for some Lieutenants to assist you as soon as may be. I regard the work you and the other officers have done since the engagement in the Indian Ocean as of the first order; I do not have to tell you that! I expect too that the Admiral will confirm Mr Bowles as Lieutenant. Perhaps Mr Tanner will also have a chance if a Board of Examiners can be arranged." He walked towards the entry port, acknowledging the trill of the side party's pipes and the salute of the Marine guard. "And perhaps Thomas, a command for you? God knows you have earned it!"

The interview with the Admiral lasted a little more than an hour. Captain Blackwood was well received, the Admiral in an expansive mood and much inclined to dwell on the positive achievements of the small squadron. The mystery of the lost Midshipman and two young seamen seemed of little interest to him as he weighed this against the destruction of one powerful enemy frigate and the capture of another. He was full of praise too for the repairs carried out in Delagoa Bay and the valuable intelligence gathered on the long voyage home. "Capital stuff Captain, by God sir, you have made the bleaters sit up and take notice!"

"Thank you sir, I hope that we may have an opportunity for a refit, the ship has several defects that need attention."

"So I see from your returns. As it happens there is at present an opportunity for you to have her docked and the underwater repairs done – I will make the order to the dockyard on your behalf. But I warn you that it will necessarily be a short refit, I have great need of every ship I can put into service at present, the *Grand Armeé* is camped, even now, just across the channel and their fleet is likely to attempt an engagement to force the crossing at any time!"

"I understand sir, which must raise another question. I have temporarily promoted one of my Midshipmen to act as Fifth Lieutenant, a position he has fulfilled admirably for six months now. My remaining Midshipman is due for promotion and I have every confidence he will make a fine officer if given the opportunity. Had I been in a position to do so I would have sent him home with the prize, but it was not to be. As you can see I had two more die in action or of wounds resulting from the action against the *le Revolution* and of course, young Mr Heron's disappearance leaves the ship almost devoid of Midshipmen."

"I am of the opinion that I can certainly do something for the two who remain to your complement then. Your voyage seems to have been singularly hard on young men of that position – but I will see what can be done to appoint some to you. I shall have my clerk draft a commission for your Mr Bowles and I will consider appointing Mr Tanner to a suitable commission as well. I am sure we can arrange for him to sit his examination if need be," the Admiral paused and then added, "I expect that your First is also due a reward, I have a sloop about to be recommissioned, the *Kestrel* twenty-four guns, a small ship, but a step towards bigger things I should hope!" He smiled, adding, "But I expect that will remove him from your ship just as you need him most?"

"Indeed sir, but Thomas deserves this appointment and my remaining officers are quite capable of managing until he can be replaced."

"As to that, I think I can provide you with a suitable replacement," smiled the Admiral, "it so happens that I know a young man who is chaffing to have a chance to leave his present appointment on the Port Admiral's staff and would leap at the chance to join your ship. I will arrange it. A great pity about the young Midshipman – Heron was it not – that device is like no other we have record of and must needs be studied by the Royal Society no doubt. You will have written to his parents I take it?" He nodded on receiving the affirmation and the information that the family were acquainted with the Captain. He rose and extended a hand, "Good day Captain Blackwood, your despatches will be well received in the Admiralty and now I must ashore myself – I am due to take a post chaise to London tonight to see the First Sea Lord."

The Captain completed his round of the Dockyard and returned to the ship, already preparing for her docking, the Admiral's clerk having been extremely busy while the Admiral himself prepared to go ashore.

Captain Blackwood found himself greeted by a beaming First Lieutenant, Thomas Bell bursting with pride at his new orders, yet saddened to be leaving *Spartan*. Midshipman Tanner had been summoned to the Flagship with his Journal and certificates and Lieutenant Bowles had received a formal confirmation of his appointment as Fifth Lieutenant. Despite this the ship was already working to prepare to be docked, the Docking Master already aboard and in discussion with the Second and Third Lieutenants to arrange for the stores and guns to be taken out of her in preparation. "Well Thomas," smiled the Captain as they ducked beneath the poop and entered the Captain's quarters, "You will want to be away as soon as possible to take your new command?" He held out his hand, "She may be small, but with twenty-four guns she will be well placed for some exciting work and opportunity for prize money!"

"Indeed sir!" beamed Thomas, "and I thank you for the support and opportunity you have given me sir!"

"Nonsense Thomas, you have earned this and more! I suspect that had we been in home waters instead of the East, you would have made this step long since! Congratulations my friend it is very well earned." He looked up as there was a knock on the door and it swung open to reveal a somewhat flushed Midshipman Tanner. "Yes Mr Tanner?"

"Sir! I am just come from the Flagship." He paused and seemed to be in a state of shock, "and I am made Lieutenant sir, appointed to the *Kestrel* twenty-four!"

"I see, Mr Tanner," said the Captain gravely, "I shall be sorry to loose you, you have served very well in this ship and I consider your appointment well earned." He smiled and winked at Thomas Bell, continuing, "I take it you have knowledge of the *Kestrel's* commander?"

"Why no sir. I am told only that she is fitting out and will be commissioning again in a few days, her Commander is yet to take up his appointment!"

"Well Mr Tanner, it would be well to meet your new Captain would it not?"

"Indeed sir and I should like to apply to you for leave to join my new ship as soon as possible so that I may be there when the Captain arrives!"

"I think I can do better than that Mr Tanner, I can arrange for you to be with him when he does!" he laughed and continued, "Mr Tanner, meet Captain Bell, your new Commander!"

※ ※ ※

Four hundred years and several dozen light years from the Portsmouth of 1805, Midshipman Harry Nelson-Heron stood beside Sersan on the planet Pangaea listening to a mechanical translator as it transferred the Lacertian language into his own tongue. With him stood Sub-Lieutenant Trelawney, Paddy Murphy, Hans Dinsen, Ferghal O'Connor and Danny Gunn. It was his sixteenth birthday, but he neither expected anyone to know, nor to mark it. He listened to the description of their escape from the Johnstone facility and of their freeing of the Lacertian pair – Sersan and his companion named Scisantha – his ears pricking up when he heard them mention his having altered the computers to affect this. He glanced at Dr Williams, Georgina Curry and Dr Maartens as it seemed strange to him that these new people had singled him out as having played some unusual part. Frankly it embarrassed him that they seemed determined to honour him for doing what he considered had been his duty, no matter how unusual the means of doing it and he saw nothing unusual or special about his navigation skills, another matter the Lacertians seemed to think a special gift.

The Lacertians, or Sinoians as the 'official' designation had, until now, recorded them, formed a crescent around the perimeter wall of the domed enclosure, about thirty in all. Harry had time to notice that their skin patterns were as individual as human faces, skin tones and personalities and, having spent so long in their company, no longer noticed their lack of clothing. In fact he realised they did not need any as they had little external indication of their gender in the human sense, but equally, being covered in minute scales and a skin rather less sensitive to the elements than a human one, there was less need to protect it. This made him wonder about their sensitivity to heat and cold – something they had not had much opportunity to explore in their voyage through mainly tropical seas, the wind and temperatures on their voyage having been fairly moderate.

He was feeling distinctly embarrassed as he listened to Sersan explaining his role in their release. He had been surprised to learn from the science teams xeno-anthropologists that the Lacertians had an exceptionally strict code regarding 'honour' when it came to someone who had rendered assistance to anyone not of their immediate family group, which could be quite extensive. They therefore considered themselves to be honour bound to give their lives in the protection of the people they considered had saved and liberated them. From the discussion he gathered that the Minehead Group of Lacertian prisoners regarded the Marine Platoon that had first entered that facility in something like the same light and felt as strongly about their 'liberators' as the group from New Caledonia – with one complication. What none of the humans involved had realised up to now was the fact that Sersan and his mate Scisantha were in fact the acknowledged Clan leadership of the entire group. Harry sensed that his companions were as uneasy about their new status as he was, and he added his voice to theirs as they protested that they had done no more than decency demanded in rendering aid to fellow creatures in distress. The Lacertians would have none of it. They had their honour, and that meant they were bound to the blood bond of defending their human allies. In Harry's case, Sersan hinted, it ran deeper, suggesting that Harry was now bonded to him 'in our blood and in our spirit'. When asked what he meant Sersan explained that Harry had in some way been 'joined in blood', adding that this linked him, in Lacertian belief, to the donor, in spirit. "Wheee haarrrre one in blood, you and me. Aaand yourrrr frrrriend isssssssss wonnne wisss ussss assss well," hissed the Lacertian, the translator unit taking some, at least, of the sibilance out of the statement. Since the Lacertians had no understanding of DNA or genetics this could not be explored further, but it did start the scientists thinking and planning some new tests.

Permission having been given for the party to stay with the Lacertians for a period, with the science team accompanying them, they had come equipped to do so. It was to prove an interesting and very rewarding time for all involved. The bond of shared danger built up on the voyage of the little *Victory* was strengthened as they learned more about the Lacertians and their culture. As the science team had surmised, they were evolved from an amphibian reptile of warm blooded physiology. Their world being a warm and water filled place, they were also a seafaring race and had found Harry's rig and handling of the converted cargo hulk more than just interesting – their own sailing designs were not as efficient and they had revelled in being able to question him on the workings of this and other rigs he was familiar with.

"We were fortunate," Harry told them, "that the *Victory* had been 'ship' built with a long keel, conventional framing and a good solid transom. That enabled us to fit a rudder to the transom and then rig the steering gear and the keel gave her a good grip in the water. The mast was more difficult as we had to cut into the deck and then step the mast on the keelson." He explained how this could be done and the advantage of the fore and aft rig over the greater spread of sail in a square rig. But it was the navigation which surprised him most, since the Lacertians navigated on their own planet by means of a device very like the one he had constructed and were amazed and very excited when he drew a picture for them of a sextant explaining how it gave the navigator greater freedom and accuracy. All too soon however, they had to return to duty on the *Vanguard* and very reluctantly took their leave of these now confirmed friends.

There was one last unnerving moment for Harry before they left, when they were asked to share in the dedication of a plaque recording the voyage they had made. Taken to a new dome in the complex destined to become a new Cadet Academy for the Fleet, they found themselves surprised into speechlessness. Right in the middle of the dome, resting in a pool obviously prepared for the purpose, was the little *Victory*, her sails neatly furled and her oversized ensign now held out to display by some form of stiffening. Even the scars of their encounter with the Pleurodon were still visible and told their own tale when seen from this vantage point, making them sharply aware of just how lucky their escape had been. Closer inspection led them to a large lectern which gave an account of the voyage in International English and in what they realised was Lacertian. To Harry's huge embarrassment there was a picture of him as well and a description of how he had suggested the creation of this small ship and then navigated her from the island of New Caledonia to the capital. He turned to the others and protested, "But Mr Trelawney was in charge, I just suggested this to him!"

"Issss true," hissed Sersan, "busss issss you hasssss maaaade thissss." His gesture indicated the little ship in her isolated lake.

"It's no good arguing Harry," laughed Sub Lieutenant Trelawney, "It's based on my report – I recognise my words there – and the Admiral has authorised the erection of this plaque, so you'll have to live with it I'm afraid!"

\* \* \*

The Royal Marine force, under Captain Bob Wardman of the *Vanguard*, stepped ashore on New Caledonia to be met by Marcus Grover and several of the townsmen. At full company strength the Marine unit made an impressive sight as they unloaded their weaponry and equipment from the landing transports that had delivered them. Captain Wardman acknowledged the greeting he received from Mr Grover, saying, "Ah, yes, I have heard that you helped our people leave here."

"They made it to Pangaea City?" responded the townsman sounding slightly surprised, "we thought they were mad taking the snakeheads with them and the Pleurodons make any trip on the water a gamble. How long did they take?"

"About six days I believe. I am told that you helped them get the ship ready – an interesting exercise I think!" Captain Wardman confirmed. He briefly told of the little ship's final movements and the fact that the Admiral had ordered its preservation. Then he got down to the business in hand. "We're here to secure this island and to search and secure the facility the Foundation was running here. My orders are to secure it and arrest any survivors from it. The Civil Government will have to deal with any collaborators and Sub-Lieutenant Trelawney has given us a list of the people in your community who were in the pay of the Consortium." He paused and continued, "I take it they are all still in good health?"

"Oh yes," smiled Marcus Grover sourly, "Even Stepan Glinka, the idiot. He still doesn't know how lucky he is that kid with the big blade – a cutlass? – didn't kill him outright!"

"I heard about that. I'm afraid that TechRate O'Connor grew up in an age when threatening someone got a very swift and violent response!" He grinned, "I gather this Mr Glinka has a number of serious injuries to recover from as a result?"

"Too right he has!" exclaimed the other, "That kid took his arm off and damned near did the same with his leg! But then stopped when Stepan's wife and child appeared. The other youngster – the same one that came up with the idea to rig out the barge and looked as if he'd been to hell and back – stepped in and did some amazing first aid. The two seemed to be almost in a master and servant relationship."

"That's one way to describe that pair. Midshipman Heron and

TechRate O'Connor come from a very different society to ours," Bob Wardman commented wryly, "I'll get our Surgeon Lieutenant to look at the wounds and see what can be done for him." Changing to business, he said, "Now sir, I need to have all the information you can give me on the facility up the hill if you don't mind. I'd appreciate it if you can tell me where the entrances, exits and any underwater access points are located and which parts are damaged and which still functional."

※ ※ ※

An hour later the scouts of the Marine skirmishing party made their way into the upper and above ground levels of the facility. Scenes of devastation met their advance, evidence of weapons fire was everywhere, some of it obviously targeted with precision, and some seemingly random damage. Decaying bodies littered the corridors, some human and some Lacertian although there were very few of these last in evidence. All with the marks and wounds to show that there had been a desperate battle. It was made all the more strange by the fact that some of the damage seemed to be completely disproportionate to the number of casualties. The second wave entered through the tunnel used by Sub-Lieutenant Trelawney and his party to escape. This brought them in below the main accommodation and general working areas, but here too they encountered signs of a furious fight as they gradually worked their way down to the lowest levels. It was in these that they finally located some survivors, shut away behind heavy blast doors in a part of the facility evidently designed to be accessed only by a very few important people or their guards.

The survivors made no resistance when the Marines cut open the doors and deployed inside, all of the survivors looking as if they were on the edge of sanity and almost all of them suffering severe dehydration and starvation. Among them were MedTech de Vries and Ms Mela Ceausescu.

※ ※ ※

The summons to the Medical Centre aboard *Vanguard*, the party having been shuttled up from the planet the evening the Marines landed on New Caledonia, was delivered with breakfast the following morning. Harry, Ferghal and Danny reported as ordered, speculating on what this was all about. When they were called by a Senior MedTec and directed to the Surgeon Commander, he lost no time in telling them – it had everything to do with the revelation of exactly what had been done to Harry, Ferghal and possibly Danny by the Foundation's geneticists.

Once Len Myers had informed them of the reason for the recall, they found themselves very rapidly undergoing an extremely thorough new series of tests. Len explaining carefully that the information that had just come to hand made it necessary to give them a very thorough check including one on the genetic signature the medical team held from the trio's earlier incarceration in the *Vanguard's* MedCent, with one taken immediately. Recalling the file he had accessed during his captivity in the Foundation computer, Harry quickly told Len what he could recall from this, adding, "It is a section of the RNA I think, and it is taken from Sersan's tissue samples. I think it will be in the data files in the storage units Ferghal brought back from there."

"I wish we'd known that sooner!" exclaimed Len sharply.

"I'm sorry sir," said Harry, abashed, "I forgot all about it until Sersan suggested it and now you have told me this – it didn't seem as bad as some of the other things they did!"

"OK Harry," said Len, relenting slightly, "I think I know what we can expect so let's not worry about it until we see what can be done and what the results are."

As the checks would take some time, Len suggested that the three should spend a little time with the scientists while they tried to work out what had changed in the way he interfaced with the computers around him and how this might be influencing his abilities in other fields as well. "That implant of yours is supposed to work only when you specifically activate it – or when we send you a learning packet activated on a special code. It now seems to be open virtually all the time – and more importantly, you seem to be able to do things in the computer that should not be possible." Len smiled, "And you, Ferghal, are starting to do it as well it seems!"

Later, when they were rejoined by Sub-Lieutenant Trelawney, Paddy Murphy and Hans Dinsen they were still no further forward on that problem, but had at least not found any others. "What's this all about?" demanded the Sub-Lieutenant as soon as he joined them, "Oh, sorry sir, didn't realise that you had us all under the microscope!"

"Mr Trelawney, the day I put you under a microscope, I expect to find a great deal of interest!" smiled Len Myers, "This is all about the fact that your hosts on New Caledonia have done some genetic engineering which may involve you as well as Harry, Ferghal and Danny. I want to run some checks in case it is something we need to counter, although, from what I have learned so far, it appears not. In fact it could possibly even be beneficial in the long term – which will not be the first time good has come out of evil, but it may also be one time to many!" He indicated the waiting Surgeon Lieutenant, and said, "Lieutenant Menzies and her team will have some results for us in a few more hours – and then we will know how to move forward." He reached for a com-link as they left the room and keyed it. "I need to see the, er, Lacertian leader Dr Grüneland, I'd appreciate it if you or Dr Scheffer could arrange for him to see me here."

"Certainly Commander Myers," responded Silke Grüneland, "I will ask Dr Maartens to bring him across to you. Is this in connection with the genetic transfer in the Facility?"

Briefly he confirmed this to her and received her assurance of co-operation from her team. Then he leaned back in his chair to await the arrival of the Lacertian who he hoped, would be willing to allow a check on his DNA and confirm what he prayed would be the answer he suspected.

※ ※ ※

In the event, three days later Surgeon Commander Myers studied the results. As he had suspected the genetic splice had taken a part of the RNA and the DNA sequences from the Lacertian genetic code which was responsible for the regrowth of damaged limbs and organs. Both Harry and Ferghal had been subjected to this but Danny proved to be clear. More interesting to Len was the fact that the RNA seemed to be the crucial link which had enhanced Harry's ability to link himself to the computers, a point not lost on the scientists!

"Poetic justice I think," Len commented to the Commodore as he presented the results, "our friends may well have inadvertently given Harry the power to fight back. From their own records, it seems they may not have realised the import of the fact that the Lacertian language is in part 'intuitive' or, more crudely, telepathic. This gene splice, coupled with the implants we gave these two youngsters seems to have gone a bit further than its architects thought it would." He handed the tablet with the reports to the Commodore, adding, "Long term, and barring any other intervention, these two should outlive us all by quite a margin – God willing!"

# Chapter 22

# Cleaning up the mess

Commodore Heron looked up as Brigadier Kernan entered the office he was using in the government building on Pangaea, "Hello Mike, take a seat will you. I hear your people have cleaned out the facility on New Caledonia and brought back some interesting evidence? Dr Grüneland tells me that she and her team are due to go there as soon as your people have it safe to dig around in it."

"That's right, and there's plenty there to interest them. Quite a bit of evidence already to hand in fact, your young men seem to have taken the place apart – or at least induced someone else to do it," the Brigadier laughed, "but more importantly, as you already know, we found a couple of very interesting survivors. Your deserter spy tried to bluff it out, but gave up once we showed her what we already had on her and is now co-operating. The other is no less than the Consortium's legal mouthpiece – and she is singing like a canary! I have my Adjutant Advocate and a civilian Magistrate taking down her deposition. The names she's spilling and the sources she's quoting for evidence are going to be the equivalent of dropping a very large nuke on Brussels!"

"Good! As you know we have been recovering the records that Sub-Lieutenant Trelawney and his group brought out in the datachips from the computer there – and I just wish we could bring everyone involved out into space and give them all a walk without an EVA suit!" He frowned continuing, "Frankly it makes me ashamed to be part of the same species!"

"I know what you mean. I have seen a bit of it myself." He stared at the Commodore for a moment, "There is also the matter of the two lads at the centre of this, both of them seem to have had some experience with the Foo Fighter crew – we really do need to know more about them, starting with who they are! There is this business with the

Lacertians who seem to think they have some sort of blood debt to pay as well – a bit tricky since they insist they have to serve us." He leaned forward, adding, "And I think you should see this, it's the deposition from your deserter – de Vries – she confirms that the scientists at the New Caledonia facility were using the Mid in a test to see if the Lacertians ability to regenerate parts of their bodies could be transferred to humans using some sort of genetic engineering. It seems that they had run him to collapse and then used a serum as a transfer medium to implant a modified gene. As soon as my people passed that on I sent it to the Surgeon Commander and the scientists we brought out with us to have a good look at him." He gave a grimace of disgust, adding, "She seemed quite disappointed when we told her that the tests had shown up no ill effects. Makes you feel sick, doesn't it?"

"I agree," the Commodore looked angry, "And thanks for acting on it so quickly. Keep that damned Tec out of my sight will you, I'm not sure I can control myself at this stage! Fortunately the tests show that the gene they spliced into him seems to have given him a remarkable ability to recover from bruises and other injuries far more rapidly than normal. And," he frowned, "it seems to have had the unexpected affect of enabling him to interface with a computer far more effectively than anyone else around here, so does young Ferghal." He keyed his link and issued a string of orders when his writer answered, "Now, I expect we had better make sure that Ms Ceausescu is kept under maximum security – we don't want anyone getting at her while she's in our care – you can bet it would be made to look as if we had not taken proper measures to protect her from some vengeful 'victim'."

"I agree – so I've put my Colour Sergeant in charge and he has a hand picked team around her, all of them Special Squadron members. God help anyone who tries to go through them. On a more positive front, the science team have been really busy in Minehead and have turned up some really interesting developmental items our friends were working on. As we suspected, a lot of it is WeapTech stuff that we were told had been 'dead ended' and could not be made to work," the Brigadier continued, "I hope they hang the damned bureaucrats out to dry over the sell off of our weapons development units!"

"So I gather; I have just been going through one of their reports. Someone in Brussels really does have a lot of answers to give on this one!" frowned the Commodore, "and even more answers on the fact that these Lacertian people seem to have been enslaved by the Consortium with the full knowledge of certain interests in the government. You can't tell me that no one in Brussels was aware of them!"

They were interrupted by a link message from the Commodore's senior writer. "Sir, I have the full damage reports from the squadron for you. The reports from the Smit Salvage crews are there as well, they say they now have all the wrecks in stable orbit so the danger of a major planet strike from a wreck is over. One more thing sir, the *Vulkanwerft III* has arrived and has started docking the *Bellerophon* and the *Phoebe*."

"That's good. Bring in the reports please and arrange for all Captain's to attend a conference onboard *Bremerwerft II* at seventeen hundred today." He smiled at the Brigadier, adding, "I'd appreciate it if you could be there as well Mike, although you have probably already had some of the news!"

"Yes, I think I have – the fight in the Seraphis system?"

"The same. Admiral Cochrane and his fleet have managed to surprise another group of Consortium ships and a large body of their land forces. They are still fighting on the planet surface – Sinoia – but our troops seem to have theirs on the run. It seems the Lacertain population have had word from their people here and have decided to join forces with our troops. The news from Brussels is pretty encouraging as well, they have suspended or arrested almost twenty-five thousand senior bureaucrats and politicians who were up to their scrawny necks in the whole thing!" he smiled angrily, "I expect a lot will wriggle out of the noose anyway – but anything which reduces the bureaucrats power has to be good. We've had nearly five hundred years of their slowly strangling everything, its time to chuck them out."

"I agree, but its not going to be easy – especially as we really need to reform the whole government structure – and I for one am not in favour of the military doing it!" frowned Mike Kernan, "There are too many precedents of the military making a complete hash of civil government. We need to do what we do best – keep the peace and facilitate the best interests of the government – but the current political and bureaucratic structure has got to be reformed and made completely accountable."

"Dead right, but one more little gem to emerge from this cesspit is that the Consortium's board was on the ship we blasted straight through hyperspace!" James Heron grinned, "I gather not even their own people shed too many tears over the demise of the Chairman, but," he became serious, "there are indications that a new 'Board' has already taken over. WeapTech's data files on just about everything we have have been wiped and the Coms Techs tell us that the files have evidently been transferred to someone else. That means that we can expect the Consortium to try a comeback at some stage. Apparently three big freighters departed to unknown destinations before anyone thought to arrest everything and anyone at a WeapTech base."

"I thought that might be the case – especially with what we have been turning up in some of their facilities here." The Brigadier frowned, "By the way, I have had to move the officer prisoners from the *Ramillies* to a more secure facility and we've placed them in solitary confinement. We found that they were organising a mass escape attempt – and my Security Chief is tracking down several more 'officers' from the Consortium survivors who seem to be attempting to hide as ordinary rates while they re-establish control over their former crewmen."

"Good idea, I am expecting Bruce Wallace of the *Ramillies* at any moment as it happens. You know his Executive Commander tried to take over the ship en route here? Almost a third of Bruce's crew were Consortium turncoats. I have asked him to bring me all the data files and the logbooks from his ship so the Adjutant Commander the Admiral appointed to us can start preparing the case against them for mutiny and treason. I suspect its going to get very ugly." He made a disgusted gesture and finished, "They had even sabotaged the primary weapon on her the way ours had been – but with a safeguard that allowed them to bypass the sabotage on a code. Had they succeeded she would have jumped in and very probably destroyed us!"

※ ※ ※

Aboard *Vanguard* Ferghal reached into a panel to reconnect the fibre leads he had been helping draw in to replace a harness damaged in the battle. As he did so, his hand began to tingle and he made to draw back in shock, assuming the lead to be charged, even though he was certain it could not be! Fright clutched his stomach as he found himself unable to withdraw; indeed, compelled to do the opposite and place both hands firmly on the terminals he was attempting to connect. Suddenly he could 'see' the whole computer, all its databases, all its many termini and all its damage – and crucially, he could see that the control system for the largest fusion reactor aboard had a vital component about to fail! As soon as he registered this in his mind, he was released and drew back, sweating. Frantically he keyed his comlink and asked for contact with Engineering, to find himself speaking directly to Commander Allison. Quickly he explained the problem, ending, "My apologies Commander, I cannot explain how I know this, but it is about to fail."

"Very well, I will want you down here to assist us when we deal with it." After recent events and some of the unusual things that she had seen in recent months, this hardly seemed the moment to argue, so she ordered, "Contact your team leader and get clearance, then get yourself to Engineering Control pronto." She sighed, given the amount of damage the ship had absorbed in the recent battle; this would be just one more item to add to an already overloaded task list, albeit a decidedly crucial one! She would be glad when the ship could be docked in one of the repair ships and she would have the full resources of the repair staff to help seek out and find all the hidden defects that generally only came to light when they failed!

Snapping off the link, she turned to her control panel and ran a swift diagnostic on the reactor control. She was about to log out of it when she noticed that there was a slight variation in the containment field stability of the reactor, immediately she activated the reactor failure alarm – and began the process of reactor shut down! "Damn," she said to Lieutenant Commander Browne as he reached her side, "I don't know how that kid knew this, but he's right, the field stabiliser is failing! We'll have to shut down Reactor Two while we fix it and then we need to get it started up again – always a pain!"

"Right, we'll get the load shifted to the other reactors and run them up to capacity," said Stuart Browne, signalling several of the other members of the engineering team.

Within minutes the load distribution had been transferred without any serious glitch in any part of the ship. The shut down process in the reactor was a trifle more difficult and took commensurately longer. Unlike the now discontinued fission process, the reactors aboard *Vanguard* relied on magnetic fields and artificially induced gravity in the core to

*Out Of Time*

contain and direct the immense forces involved in a hydrogen/helium chain reaction. This created a miniature sun inside the containment sphere by utilising massive pressure and the constant balancing of the hydrogen/helium core. To stop the reaction required a gradual reduction in pressure and a removal of the fuel – no easy task under normal circumstances and certainly not to be rushed, even in an emergency. In the event, Ferghal arrived, accompanied by Warrant Officer Claude Chin, in time to see the last phase of the operation and the purging of the reactor chamber.

The replacement of the failing unit took less than ten minutes, a point not lost on those who now faced the task of restarting the fusion reaction and bringing the reactor back on line! "Damn," exclaimed WO Chin, "that itty-bitty piece of junk is going to keep us on the hop now for twelve hours or more while we restart this dust bin!" He tossed the enclosed unit to Ferghal, "I don't know how you knew that unit was failing, but I'm glad you did – and annoyed at the damned thing as well! Those things are supposed to be good for ten years service and that piece of junk was only installed a year ago. I bet it's another of WeapTech's recent production units – everything they have made since they were privatised is junk!"

"Warrant, you're right," interrupted Commander Allison. "I wonder how many more of their components we have aboard are under spec?" She turned to Lieutenant Commander Browne and said, "Get Lieutenant Callaghan to run a check on every unit of this type supplied to this ship in the last refit – I think we better make sure we haven't any more about to drop us in the dirty recycle tanks!"

"Ma'am," asked Ferghal as the Lieutenant Commander left to attend to this order, "How do you restart this reactor?"

She gave him a quizzical look, then smiled, "OK, fair question, it's a tricky operation." Over the next half hour she explained carefully and patiently while she monitored her team as they began the process by which a helium liquid core would be created at the centre of the sphere, condensed and contained by a process of magnetic containment, pressure and artificially induced gravitational force. As the ball of helium was compressed under these forces, it would heat up, increasing the pressure until liquid hydrogen jets could be injected into the field and the resulting collisions and mixing began the reaction process. "It's tricky and dangerous – it can go unstable and badly wrong if we try to rush it!" she finished.

"Thank you Ma'am," responded Ferghal looking serious, "Ma'am, I'm not sure what this means, but something in the computer wants me to show you this," and he stepped forward and used the terminal next to hers to bring up on screen a schematic she had never seen before, "It says, Ma'am, that if we do this," he indicated a series of formulae that appeared next to the schematic, "the reaction will start and stabilise within an hour." He looked at her worriedly, "I beg pardon Ma'am, I do not mean to offend you!" he added stepping back as she frowned at the screen.

"No offence – Ferghal isn't it? No offence," she frowned studying the schematic and the formula. "I can't see …" she began, then exclaimed, "Of course! It certainly should work, and the process is less complex than our present system. But, before we try it I want to get one of the scientists to look at this – Dr Scheffer is a specialist in this field – in fact he has been leading a project to find a way to reduce and make easier the start-up for some time – so hold everything while I get him to run through it with me." She made a comlink call to Thomas Scheffer and quickly explained what Ferghal had called out of the computer.

Minutes later a flushed and slightly breathless Dr Scheffer arrived in the Reactor Control room. "Commander," he began, "where is this new schematic? All our efforts in this field have so far been unsuccessful; there is a factor we are not able to identify which seems to be essential!"

"Here Doctor," she replied, indicating the screen in front of Ferghal. She explained again quickly how it had come about and he nodded several times as she spoke, interrupting with several questions as she did so. Turning his attention to the screen and the procedural schematic displayed there, he ran through the protocols alternately calling up other data and cross-checking with other readouts and data files. Occasionally he exclaimed in German and then dived back into data – or used his comlink to demand further data files or information from his team. Little more than an hour later he leaned back and said, "This looks very good. I calculate that it will in fact be more efficient than the existing system and should give almost 15% more output once it is stabilised." He looked at Ferghal and asked, "And you are not a fusion physicist?"

Ferghal blushed and tried to explain what had happened and how he had come to have access to this proposal. Commander Allison and Dr Scheffer laughed at his confusion and then she said, "OK, it's worth a try – I can always hit the SCRAM and override it to shut down if it starts to run away."

Minutes later her reactor team was assembled and watched as the new start-up procedure was programmed into the system. While they were busy Thomas Scheffer hovered in the Control Room, watching every movement and trying to read all the data monitors at the same time. If she hadn't been so busy herself, Mary Allison might have found it amusing and offered him a role in the process – but she was far too engrossed, and yes, excited at this new technique's apparent success, to take much notice of him. They watched the monitors with bated breath as the readouts began to change and just on forty minutes later the reaction fired into life, the readouts leaping up the scale and registering outputs normally only achieved after several more hours! "Eureka!" breathed the Commander, "Reactor Control, bring the turbines online and notify Reactor Rooms One and Three that you are taking over the load share. Ferghal, I'm not sure where you got that from, but that has just been one of those great leaps forward for humanity!"

"Ma'am, I don't know how to explain it, but it was the same as when I knew the field unit was going to fail – its as if something in the computer tells me." He looked at her worriedly, "Do you think I should talk to Surgeon Commander Myers about this?"

She laughed, "Perhaps you should – but don't let him take it away from you! I might need your diagnostic skills again!"

*  *  *

Among the vast clouds of debris drifting between the planets and asteroids, a number of remotely controlled robotic scavenger units collected debris and manoeuvred it towards the larger barges which gathered it into their holds and brought it back to the huge repair ships now orbiting beyond the outermost of Pangaea's moons, Gitchegumee. Among the many pieces of scrap were the remains of men and women killed when strike craft were destroyed, or hulls breached during the fight. Some remained intact, some were partly destroyed, others, still enclosed in their EVA suits had not been lucky enough to be found before life support failed, or had died of injuries sustained and now drifted among the debris like any other piece of junk. These were also recovered by the scavengers and slowly brought back to the ships to be identified and given a decent despatch into the life beyond this. Very occasionally a scavenger would locate a survivor, one lucky enough to have been able to keep the life support in his or her cockpit going longer than normal – or more frequently – someone who had made it to a lifepod capable of sustaining life for up to twenty or more for longer than a week. Most of these last were found to be Consortium troops or shiprates and so, after a spell in a MedCent unit, would be despatched to a prison camp or ship.

Lieutenant Commander Karl Pedersen had resigned himself to the fact that his brother Bjørn was dead several days ago, so he was not prepared for the summons to the Emergency Med Unit onboard the Repair Ship Dock *Vulkanwerft III*. He found his way there with some difficulty and entered a scene of carnage. "Lieutenant Commander Pedersen?" enquired a statuesque woman in the uniform of a Fleet Surgeon Captain.

"Ma'am," he responded, staring at the activity in the unit.

"This way please," she ordered.

He followed, not really knowing what to expect as she pulled aside a curtain. "You may spend a few minutes with him, he is badly dehydrated and seriously malnourished, but he's survived."

"Bjørn!" exclaimed the elder Pedersen, "My God! Where have you been? Why did you not use your emergency tracer beacons?"

"Mainly because they were shot to hell," his brother grinned weakly. "I had to bail out of the survival pod when it ejected." He sighed, "then I got lucky, I found a lifepod that must have ejected from one of their ships. Three of us managed to get inside it – but it had a leak in the life system somewhere, and the food was useless as well." He grinned weakly, "But we figured you'd find us eventually."

"Well, you gave me one hell of a scare little brother," he grasped his brother's hand and felt the chill of collapsed circulation in it, "listen, you just hang in there and pull through! I don't want to have to salute your last journey yet!"

※ ※ ※

Commodore Heron looked across the desk in his newly refitted quarters aboard *Vanguard* as his new Flag Captain entered; he smiled and moved from behind the desk, indicating a chair. "Congratulations Richard, I'm glad the Admiralty agreed with my recommendation and confirmed you as Captain. It's not before time you know, but you're going to have a hell of a problem replacing my Executive Commander – people of his calibre simply don't come along every day!"

"Thanks," grinned Richard Grenville, "actually, I don't think I'm going to have too much trouble with that. You built such a good team on the Command level that I'm able to do a bit of a shuffle round and bring in some new blood lower down where we can train them into our ways rather more effectively."

"OK, so what have you in mind?"

"Well, I thought that Ben Curran could move into the Exec post, his number two is a pretty on the ball officer just in the zone for promotion so why not make him up to Navigation Commander and we can fill in the gap below him again." He paused and then continued, "I looked at all the others, Nick is at present needed on the fighter and strike Command, and we have a lot of casualties to fill in there, Val is keen to stay with her weapons of mass annihilation for now, Mary is reluctant to leave her precious power plants at the moment and Fritz was so wrapped up in his Coms that he just laughed when I asked if he was interested."

"Good, I'll push through the necessary for confirmation with HQ, although I suspect they have their hands full at present."

"Lower down the food chain we have a few considerations as well which I'd like to discuss with you if I may?"

"Certainly, what do you suggest?"

"Well as you know we lost quite a few ratings and officers in the engagement, mostly from the interceptor and strike squadrons, but we have also lost people from damaged compartments. *Sydney* was hard hit, so was *Bellerophon* and the four cruisers also took a lot of punishment. By some miracle the three frigates seem to have come off lightly, perhaps because they got in so close."

"True, I have looked at the casualty lists, taken with the deserters and the traitors we managed to isolate and weed out we obviously need quite a number of new replacements." He glanced at a tablet in his hand,

"I make it three Lieutenant Commanders, five Lieutenants and four Sub-Lieutenants just between our three heavy units before we look at the Flight Officer losses. *Ramillies* is down twice that number thanks to the Consortium's traitors onboard – plus two full Commanders. What do you suggest?"

"Well, if you agree sir, we could promote Sub-Lieutenant Trelawney to full Lieutenant, he is just in the zone for it, and I think you will agree he's demonstrated his abilities rather well, he is also in the Navigation team and can fill the opening we will have there if you agree my recommendation of Lieutenant Case being promoted. Two of our senior Mids are also coming due for examination and promotion, John Jellico and Ute Zimmermann could be made up immediately and so could Jean Hern. Paddy Murphy is already a qualified Atmosphere pilot and could help fill the gaps in Flight if Nick agrees and can get him trained up without having to send him away for training. We have another five or six Sub Lieutenants who could be made up as well and spread to fill gaps. They could help make up the numbers on some of the other ships as well if necessary. Then, as we are short of Technical Officers, I would like to suggest that we could look at offering several of our best young Technical Rates the opportunity to become Officer Cadets and possibly Midshipmen in due course." The new Captain finished.

"That sounds sensible, very well, let me have the list of people you think should be promoted and get similar lists from the other ships, let's see what we've got. Then I can make a decision on how best to deal with this." Changing the subject he asked, "How is the repair coming on? I see *Sydney* will be ready to fire up her reactors again in a week. *Bellerophon* is clearing the repairship today and *Aurora* and *Ariadne* are due to be completed by the end of the week." The discussion now moved on to the various repairs and completion dates, much of what remained to be done on *Vanguard* had to do with the replacement of faulty components supplied by the privatised WeapTech while under the control of the Consortium's front companies – a fact which annoyed both officers immensely.

※ ※ ※

Harry rejoined the ship from a spell on detached duty 'dirtside' assisting in carrying out an exercise in surveys for the creation of accurate maps and ocean charts. He returned to the ship on the day she left the embrace of the huge repairship *Bremerwerft II,* her turn at the repair facility having been delayed by the discovery of a major structural defect in *Bellerophon* which had necessitated her being docked again. It also coincided with Fleet Orders confirming promotions for several people including Sub-Lieutenant Trelawney, Midshipman John Jellico, Ute Zimmermann, Jean Hern and Paddy Murphy all got a step up in rank while three more of their number were moving to new postings to fill gaps left by other promotions and the death of one of *Penelope's* Midshipmen. Two surprises awaited Harry, one was the celebration of the promotion or posting of his fellow Midshipmen, the second was Ferghal's arrival in the Gunroom, with two other former TecRates, complete with new kit and the rather self-consciously displayed patches of a Cadet.

Dieter Weich, George Singh and Colin Hardy were the three posted to new ships, Colin going to *Ramillies,* George to *Aurora* and Dieter to *Tiger* very much to the envy of the others, frigates, as ever, being seen as cocky and independent craft free of the constraints of the battle fleet's bigger ships. Petroc Trelawney, contrary to the original suggestion, would be leaving *Vanguard* to join *Bellerophon,* that ship now desperately short of officers thanks to a serious hit which had damaged one of her Control Stations and started a serious fire. Even among the remaining members of the Gunroom, with Ute Zimmermann now it's Senior, there would be changes as several of the denizens, as they referred to themselves, would be changing departments to fill gaps or to take advantage of opportunities to move to a specialist area they wished to follow. The celebration rapidly became quite a party when the others learned that Harry had just passed his sixteenth birthday, a fact let slip by Ferghal in a somewhat one sided conversation with Sophie Xavier, his sense of social order still reeling under the shock of his being 'promoted' to Cadet!

"Hey everyone," yelled Sophie, rattling a fork against a glass to get their attention, "Harry tried to sneak his birthday past us by being shoreside for it! He owes us all a party!"

Harry's protests to the effect that those being promoted should be the one's to throw the party were swept aside in a boisterous tide of jokes, laughter and teasing. Good naturedly he surrendered, secretly flattered to have been so fully adopted by this group of peers.

"Congratulations Harry," grinned Paddy, "Tell you what, just get Chief Steward Huw Powys on the comlink and ask him nicely for a cake and some party snacks – he'll sort it out for you in a snap! And," he added conspiratorially, "we've already organised with him for some other stuff as well on our own account, so we can all chuck something into the pot!"

With a little help from the Chief and a lot of fun from the celebrating Gunroom, the night sped by. It was a tired but very happy group that turned to in the morning to carry out the days routines – much to the amusement of their superiors. For the first time all three interlopers in the Twenty-third Century felt fully part of their new society and at home. Harry was, for his part, delighted to have Ferghal's company in the Gunroom and for his friend's good fortune and promotion. It seemed a very long way from Scrabo and the homes they had left together to join the war against Napoleon, and here they were, still at war, but against a new enemy, one from within.

※ ※ ※

Late in October 2205, an observer in space above the Earth would have witnessed the activation of the newly repositioned Near Earth Gate; Southern Indian Ocean, and the emergence in rapid succession of the starship *Vanguard* followed by *Bellerophon*, *Sydney*, four cruisers and three frigates. The squadron was home and would remain in orbit above the Earth while their crews cycled on home leave for a period. Already Fleet was planning their next assignment but, for the Commodore and his weary crews, it was time to rest and refresh themselves at home.

For some a happy return, for others, perhaps, a time for sadness and mourning.

## Chapter 23

# Letters from the Admiralty

The road from Belfast climbs out of the Lagan valley and up the shoulders of the hills north of Scrabo, the remnant of a long dead volcano. Skirting south of the village of Dundonald, the messenger allowed his horse to canter gently as the ground levelled out above the village and he was able to make his way between the fields on either side, scattering the occasional straying sheep as he followed the road toward the landmark of the folly which crowned Scrabo. Had it not been raining, he knew he would have been able to look down upon the rolling countryside toward the towns of Comber and Newtownards and the long waters of Strangford Lough, a difficult and dangerous haven for any but the most accomplished seaman. The rain sent rivulets down the gaps in his oilskin coat and, despite his broad brimmed hat and the thick neckerchief he wore for the purpose, trickled down his neck and formed a wet patch between his shoulder blades. Eventually the rain lifted briefly and he caught a glimpse of the low stone house, crouched next to the road, its old fashioned arrangement with the stables and barns forming a compact square behind the house itself spoke of its age as much as the tidy and well kept hedges and enclosing walls spoke of the care and good husbandry of the family who owned it.

From the vantage point of the house, the countryside rolled away behind it to the South, the vista of Strangford unhindered by the low range of stables and barns that formed the southern boundary of the enclosed yard, from the upper floor windows which faced this view. The horseman urged his horse on, anticipating a welcome from the cook and a chance to warm himself before the kitchen fire with a warm drink in his hand before he must continue his ride to Mount Stewart. With luck he would be able to return to Newtownards and thence to Downpatrick where he could expect a bed in the barracks. His leather mail pouch nestled beneath the oilskin coat, safe and dry, its contents no doubt filled with joy for some, despair or anguish for others and orders for the garrison. He cared not which for who, his only concern was that he must deliver all intact and to the correct addressee for that was the work he was paid for and the wage, though small, kept his wife and family in reasonable comfort. It was not dangerous work, but it did require some diligence and it meant he had to ride out in all weather, which was sometimes hard enough and deadly to the unwary.

A typical son of Ireland, the horseman knew almost all those he encountered on the road and greeted them cheerfully despite the weather. He also knew the majority of those for whom he carried mail and so knew the handwriting on several of the letters he carried for the house below Scrabo to be the work of the youngest son of the house, serving at sea on one of the great "wooden walls". Two other letters he did not recognise, although one carried the seal of the Admiralty and he supposed it to be some formal order from their Lordships in distant London. Being himself from Dundonald, he knew the family whose yard he now entered, and greeted the stable boy who dodged out into the rain to greet him cheerfully. "Good day to you Liam, and my greetings to your father. I have letters from young Master Harry today, so perhaps there is news of Ferghal also!" He dismounted and gave the reins to the lad, "I'll away to Mrs Ferson, don't make him too comfortable in the barn, he'll not want to be away again otherwise!" He laughed and stamped across the yard to the kitchen porch.

"Mr Corrigan!" exclaimed the housekeeper warmly, "to be sure, you're a welcome sight, but on such a damp day as this, it must be important mail that brings you out to us!" She bustled about to hang his now dripping coat on a hook near the fireplace and then to pour a mug of small beer for him from the cask she kept in the kitchen for the purpose.

"Aye, it is a packet of letters from Mr Harry, and some more from London for the Major," he told her with a grin as he carefully opened the pouch and drew out the packets with their seals and ribbons, placing them on the table. Just then the door from the house side opened and a tall and well built young man in his early twenties entered, greeting the mail rider with a warm smile.

"Well Seamus," he greeted, "I see Mrs Ferson is taking care of your refreshment, what news do you bring us today?"

"Thank you Master James," he picked up the packets and offered them, "these have come on the mail packet yesterday, some from Master Harry I see, and some from London, I know not from whom – but yon one is from the Admiralty by the looks of yon!"

Accepting them, the newcomer, smiled and said, "Thank you! I wonder what scrapes my brother has to recount to us this time! His last missive from the Great South Sea was full of fantastical beasts and marine marvels," he added with a laugh, then continued, "I will take these to my father, thank you for bringing them out so swiftly. How goes it with your wife and the youngest? I believe he was poorly the last time we spoke?"

"That he was sir, but thanks be to God, he is now recovered! 'Twas kind of your mother to send the apple jelly and the parcel of pickled and preserved fruits for the wife, she was mightily grateful."

"I shall tell my mother, she will be pleased to know," replied James, "she knew your wife from her home in Castlereagh."

"Aye sir, and Bertha was pleased to be so well remembered."

Making his excuses, James withdrew and hurried to his father's office, a cluttered room where the small estate's records and accounts were kept in shelves and chests, the overstuffed drawers on the great desk filled with the Major's correspondence. Word of the mail had already reached his mother and sister and they came bustling into the room almost as he arrived to present the packets to his father. The Major accepted these with a smile and handed the packet of Harry's scrawl to his wife, saying, "Bella my dearest, take you Harry's latest and I shall await the pleasure while I deal with these official looking missives, the one of which I see is from Captain Blackwood." He fished around on the desk seeking the letter knife he kept there, and swiftly lifted the seal to open the letter.

His wife was still exclaiming and enjoying the contents of the first of Harry's letters while her daughter, Mabel, exclaimed over the enclosed carefully executed sketches and ink wash drawings, when Major James Nelson-Heron carefully folded Captain Blackwood's letter and without a word passed it to his son. For a moment longer he stared into the fire burning cheerfully in the grate then said heavily, "My dearest wife," he paused until he was sure he had her attention, "the letter from Captain

Blackwood brings dire news. Harry is dead, killed in an action with the French somewhere near Mauritius on their way home. There is much more in his letter, but our son, our beloved Harry, is gone and so too is Ferghal."

"But he cannot …," gasped his wife, "I have here his own letters," she snatched up the sequentially numbered packets that had been enclosed in the wrapping and quickly found the last, swiftly opening it to find, with a deepening chill in her soul, what she feared – the last letter was unfinished and unsigned. She looked at her husband, happiness draining from her face as the import of the unfinished letter and of her husbands words sank in. Then she covered her face with her hands and swept from the room sobbing, her daughter following.

To his remaining son, Major James said, "James, comfort your mother and sister for a moment, I must go to Sean O'Connor and give him the news myself."

# Chapter 24

# A new start

"Please sit yourselves down," beamed the tall, rather spare and patrician gentleman with the mischievous eyes, "Niamh will be along in a moment, she has been doing a little research and is presently battling with her culinary replicator. She is determined to reproduce something you may have enjoyed as a boy!" He winked and added quietly, "With luck it will be edible!"

"I heard that," exclaimed a striking woman, her grey-white hair still showing traces of its former flame colouration. "Typical!" She smiled broadly as she advanced into the room, "James, you allow Theo to frighten these boys before they even have a chance to introduce themselves! I am shocked, I truly am!"

"Niamh my dear," grinned the man she had addressed as Theo, "you malign me! Allow me to introduce our guests. This is Harry, our correspondent these last months, Ferghal the man behind the models, and Danny whose music you have heard."

"Harry, I think I would have known you anywhere!" she exclaimed glancing from Harry to the tall figure of the Captain. She embraced him, "Thank you so much for the letters you have sent us, it is so refreshing to get something so beautifully descriptive! And your sketches are wonderful, Theo here, has made an album and bores our visitors endlessly with them." She gave him a hug, adding "Your parents must be so very proud of you!" Releasing him she moved to Ferghal and took both his hands in hers, "And you will be Ferghal O'Connor! What a journey you have made! Your models are amazing young man, but I dare say that you have other skills as well! Are you happy in your new life and role?" she asked with quizzical look.

"Aye Ma'am," blushed Ferghal, "we're doing well!"

Giving him a kiss on the cheek, she said, "So I am told – and a friend who takes care of his friends!" Releasing him she looked at Danny and grinned, "Ah yes, the musical one! Well young man, you're in the right house for music! Have you ever played the harp?"

"No ma'am," said Danny seriously, "but Ferghal has taught me the Ceilidh fiddle and the Celtic drum," he finished proudly.

She glanced at Ferghal, and said, "Has he now! Well, later we shall have to hear you both!" she stooped and hugged the slightly disconcerted boy then straightening and said, "Welcome home to you all! Boys this is your home anytime you wish to come!" She looked at Commodore Heron and laughed, "Is that not so James?"

He smiled and said, "Well, I think my lads may want a say in it!"

She gave a tinkling laugh, crying, "Typical! You men are all the same! As if there's anything too say! Well Harry? Well Ferghal? And what about you Daniel? Do you object? I thought not!" She looked at the grinning faces around her and poked her tongue at the Commodore, "There, you great stuffed shirt! There's you answer!" To the trio she said, "Welcome home!" and almost danced out of the room and into her kitchen.

The evening slipped by with the three young men relaxing into the easy ways of a home, something they had not known for some considerable time. It was enlivened by the production of a meal which contained at least three dishes the boys vaguely recognised — at least Harry recognised three, the others having come from more humble backgrounds recognised one and there was a great deal of laughter over the fact that tripe served in an onion sauce had never been a favourite with any of them! Then had come the revelation that Niamh LeStrange was an accomplished player of the Irish harp and her husband a violinist. Within a very short time, a musical entertainment ensued with harp, fiddle, pipe and drum exploring rhythms ancient and more recent. It was very late before the participants found their respective bedrooms, the three young men falling asleep with the ease of youth!

Theo, Niamh and James Heron sat a while longer over a glass of fragrant Irish whiskey, discussing the future for the three. "A remarkable trio," said Theo LeStrange thoughtfully. He peered through the golden amber liquid in his tumbler at James Heron, "I'll consider the fee paid in full!"

James laughed, "Generous of you Chief Justice! Congratulations on your elevation by the way! Harry and Ferghal seem to have fitted into the Fleet routine far more readily than I would have thought possible." He sipped his whiskey appreciatively, adding reflectively, "Remarkable really when you consider how much they have had to learn and endure." He eyed his friends, "And I must thank you for agreeing to receive Harry's letters. You can have no idea how much that has helped him – especially after his abduction."

"That experience of Harry's when those monsters used him in their experiments must have been horrendous!" exclaimed Niamh, "there was something in one of his letters that touched on it – but he seemed almost to brush it aside!" She shuddered, saying, "I feel violated just thinking about it! How can any human being even consider doing anything like that to another?"

"History is full of such monsters my dear", remarked Theo, "one never has to look far into the past to find an example!"

"True," nodded the Commodore, "but I rather think Harry has left a mark on everyone involved in that little episode!" He sipped his drink and asked, "Have you considered my suggestion for young Danny?"

"We most certainly have!" exclaimed Niamh, "and now that we have also met the young man, my mind is made up. If he would like to live with us until he is ready to follow his career choices, we will be delighted to give him a place in our home!" She squeezed her husbands hand as he smiled and nodded, "Harry and Ferghal too should they need one!"

❉ ❉ ❉

Harry stood silently and stared for several emotionally charged minutes at the simple brass plaque on the wall of the small church he vividly recalled having attended as a child in the company of his parents, brother, sister and several servants. Earlier they had managed to find, with considerable difficulty, the weathered grave stones of his parents and he had laid a small bouquet there for his mother, promising to return and restore the stones and the graves. Now, in the old church, the enclosed pew they had occupied was no longer in evidence, replaced by simple chairs arranged informally. The atmosphere of the place felt different too – somehow lighter and more welcoming than he recalled even though the sign at the gate and the service times still showed the familiar name and service pattern. At his elbow, Ferghal shifted easily and whispered, "Seems strange to see this church again, but I never thought your father would have me remembered as well."

"And why would he not?" asked Harry a little defensively, "surely you recall he treated you like one of us when we were small."

"Oh aye, and he did that," responded Ferghal, lapsing into the accent of his youth, "but to have us both on the same plaque – people would have talked in those days, and he would have known it too."

"Aye, he would," grinned Harry, "and damned them for their evil thoughts!" He read the plaque again, "I wonder what he would have said could he have seen the places we have, or the wonders we have seen?"

"To be sure, he'd have wanted to see them for himself!" laughed Ferghal, "and your mother and sister would have had the devil's own job to keep him from it!" He read the little plaque's inscription aloud, "*In loving memory of Henry Nelson Heron, Midshipman serving aboard His Most Britannic Majesties Ship Spartan 74 guns. Lost at sea in a sea-fight with two frigates of the French Fleet the 30th day of November in the year of our Lord 1804. Born 20th May 1789 Died at sea 30th November 1804. Also to the memory of Ferghal O'Connor, Boy Seaman and sometime stable boy in this Parish, friend and companion of the aforesaid Henry, lost in the same sea-fight. Born 11th February 1787 and died at sea 30th November 1804.*" He paused then added softly, "But we are not dead, we are just out of time – but all those who remembered us are long gone."

"That may well be, and I hope that we may join them yet some day, but now we have a new family and a new life and must make the best we can of it," said Harry. He paused thoughtfully, then continued, "You know Ferghal, we have come home at last, later than usual and my father would be stern and my mother scold us, but we are home and with such tales to tell. Come my friend, our Commodore awaits us and we had better not keep him." He turned to face the rather plain altar table at the Eastern end of the church, and grinned, "I can just hear old Mister Paisley breathing fire and brimstone and raving at the Papishness that has befallen this place – but, do you know, I think I like it better like this – and I'm sure my parents would!"

Ferghal grinned, "Careful Harry, I am a Papist as you know well! I'd not want the old man's ghost to come storming in after throwing me out now!"

"Come on then," laughed Harry, "we'll be on our way," he looked again at the plaque and said, "do you know, it would not surprise me if that isn't exactly why father put it here. He always said it was all stuff and nonsense to be so divided – the machinations of bigoted men. 'Beware of politicians, lawyers, clerks, greedy and power hungry men and the insecure men that serve them making up rules to bind others my boy', he used to say to me, 'they will enslave us all and destroy the world if we let them!'"

"Well, if the events we have been part of and the histories we have been studying are the truth, he was very right," laughed Ferghal as the two left the church.

At the door Harry paused, grinning at his friend, and said, "I wonder what the Fleet College holds in store for us? After Pangaea I suspect it will be quite dull."

"After some of our adventures, and the manner of our getting here, sure and most things will be quite dull!" laughed Ferghal.

The weather had changed and a soft rain had begun to fall. The two young men engaged the clasps to close their new weatherproof uniform coats and walked to the wicket gate where the tall figure of their guardian waited, talking to the transformed Danny. He stood as they approached and studied them with an interested expression, "Well, did you find the plate I mentioned?"

"We did sir," smiled Harry as Ferghal nodded, "it seems a bit strange to see your own memorial like that."

"I expect it does, but we have at long last closed the chapter with your return here. That memorial marked a mystery, one which has been the stuff of family legend since no trace could ever be found of either of you – or of young Danny – and there was always a question over what really happened to you. Now we know," he ducked into the waiting ground transport and waited until they had settled into their seats, and then continued, "I doubt that anyone then would have believed the truth had they known it – and we have had enough trouble persuading the bureaucrats today that it is true! I shudder to think what would have happened to anyone trying to tell the authorities back then!"

The transport hummed into life and joined the queue of similar units heading south to the Dublin conurbation and the continental interchange port. Here Danny would leave them to stay with the Theo and Niamh so he could attend the Academy in Dublin. Harry and Ferghal had their orders to report for a spell at the Fleet College for officer Cadets and Midshipmen. Danny's education would now include the development of his musical talents at one of the best private academies Ireland had to offer in the Twenty-third Century. Harry watched the countryside as it sped past and relaxed. He had come home; he had paid his respects to his family and their memory. Now he was going home, to start afresh, new family, new friends and new challenges. He heard his father's voice from afar *"We are citizens of the world and maybe of the wider universe my boy, like the wild geese, we go were the wind and the notion takes us and none shall stop us. Only the great creator God knows who we truly are and what we will eventually become, for now we must all travel the road we have been given – and journey in hope, with honesty, respect and courtesy our constant companions."*

To himself he said quietly, 'I hope so father; and I hope we will fulfil your hopes for us at last.' He grinned at Ferghal and whispered, "And so we begin my friend – and there is so much still to see and to learn! Out of our time we may be, but now it is our time."

# About the Author

Patrick Cox was born in Cape Town in 1946 and grew up in a small city on the East Cape coast called East London. He has long had a fascination with both the sea and ships and the world of science fiction and space travel. Educated at Selborne Primary and College in East London, he worked in commerce and industry before joining the Fire Service in South Africa. In 1988 he and his family moved to the UK where he continued his fire service career finally retiring from the service in 2006. He is a published technical author and has ventured into fiction for his own pleasure as much as anything else. While his career has been focused on dealing with emergencies and in trying to prevent them, his interests have ranged far beyond the technical and include a love of history, especially naval history, science, the exploration of space and some simpler pursuits such as painting and simply reading a good book. Among his favourite authors are such luminaries as Isaac Asimov, Robert Heinlein, Douglas Reeman, C S Forrester and Terry Pratchett, with whom he shares the view that writing is the most fun one can have on one's own.

A Reader in the Church of England, he has a deep faith and is active in the work and life of the Parish he serves. Possessed of a quirky sense of humour, working with and too the civil services of two different countries he has also developed a deep cynicism about the entire process of government, both political and bureaucratic. He subscribes to the view that the more things change, the more they stay the same. Each generation simply has to deal with the mess left by the last and hope they aren't making it any worse.

The characters in this book, while not intended to represent real people, are, in some instances, modelled on friends and family both living and dead. They will know who they are. The hero is named after his Grandfather who ran away to join up and fight in the trenches of the First World War aged fifteen.